CW01636995

PANI

'PANIC O'CLOCK secures for its author a comfortable place among the best catastrophe writers – Verne, Wyndham and Wells.'

TIMES LITERARY SUPPLEMENT

'. . . well told and thrilling and – what is rare in tales of this kind – the end is entirely satisfactory.'

Kingsley Amis – DAILY MAIL

'. . . horrible plausibility.'

PUNCH

'. . . virtually unique of its kind for betraying a sense of humour.'

THE OBSERVER

'. . . millions of us, may some day have reason to thank Christopher Hodder Williams for the vividness of his imagination (or the clarity of his vision).'

SHE MAGAZINE

Also by Christopher Hodder-Williams

THE CUMMINGS REPORT
CHAIN REACTION
FINAL APPROACH
TURBULENCE
THE HIGHER THEY FLY
THE MAIN EXPERIMENT
THE EGG-SHAPED THING
FISTFUL OF DIGITS
NINETY-EIGHT POINT FOUR

Panic O'Clock

Christopher Hodder-Williams

NEW ENGLISH LIBRARY
TIMES MIRROR

First published in Great Britain by United Writers Publications in 1973

*

FIRST NEL PAPERBACK EDITION AUGUST 1974

*

NEL Books are published by
New English Library Limited from Barnard's Inn, Holborn, London E.C.1.
Made and printed in Great Britain by Hunt Barnard Printing Ltd., Aylesbury, Bucks.

45001923 3

ONE

Though it appeared to start abruptly the probabilities are that it did not. Ministry files are incomplete on the initial details and anyway it is distinctly odd that the motorways, especially to the west, were closed down so rapidly. Nor was the research being done at Staines unique; as always, parallel projects were under way in several parts of the world. It has nearly always been the case that, quite spontaneously, the same basic concept has struck several scientists at the same time, with no plagiarism involved.

But certainly, there was nothing wrong with Alec Keeling when he departed for the Institute that Wednesday morning. He did what he always did before leaving his home at the Glenmore Estate; checked the contents of his briefcase very carefully while only going through the bare motions of eating breakfast. While Diana dealt with the idiosyncracies of the toaster – it had been a wedding present way back and had never worked right, alternately hurling burned bread into the air or trapping it, black and smoking, inside the works – the children crawled all over him, then squabbled over the breakfast cereals before arriving at a decision.

Alec never noticed much at breakfast; if the twin boys had come downstairs stark naked, or if Jennifer, aged three, had suddenly addressed him in fluent Japanese he would probably have regarded it as normal. Work at the Institute began at 8.30 – a good half hour before anyone else on Glenmore had to arrive at their office. Once out of bed, his mind was on getting there on time, with the right documents and the right schedules in his briefcase and his mind respectively. And as usual he got away on time in the Triumph 2000, leaving the mini parked near the grass, ready for Diana to take the twins off to school. As he left he said to Diana, 'God, don't let's have any more parties if they turn out like last night's.'

Diana said something appropriate – the whole thing had been hell – then prepared to leave with the twins. Jennifer always came along for the ride, she had to, there was no one to look after her at home, at least not till their latest acquisition – an au pair-cum-nanny – arrived on the scene next week; and Jennifer always slowed things down, last downstairs and last through breakfast. But Diana could handle all this like clockwork; she didn't flap and knew just how to lure the children into the mini at the right time. So she got them off to school, on time as usual; then returned to Glenmore and loaded up the dishwasher.

Though conscious that she and Alec had more money to spare and spend than most of the families on the Estate, Diana Keeling was actually no more ruthless than any of the other wives, though on this particular morning she had cause to think about it. She went over the details of the party in her mind as she added the soap powder, then tried to shrug it all off as she switched on. After all, every now and then you're bound to get a guest who was sheer disaster.

In this case the troublesome partyite had been a discontented writer – at least, he'd struck Diana as being discontented. What other explanation was there? 'All writers,' he propounded, 'must be a disturbing force. We accept nothing as it stands.' – Nothing, apparently, except hospitality. Eating food and drinking drink which he himself couldn't have afforded, the bloody man had torn the whole Glenmore way of life to shreds.

Diana checked her makeup scrupulously in the mirror, retouched an eyeline, gazed thoughtfully out on to the central green where Jennifer was now playing in and around the mini with some of the other Glenmore children, and found herself still brooding about the evening fiasco. In the end she decided to go and unload to June Trent, who lived three doors along. But she had to await the moment; June was generally slower off the mark than she was and it would be tactless to catch her in the middle of the early morning scuffle. So Diana watched the hasty departure of the other men as they shunted noisily off the car park, and made sure that Jennifer wasn't getting too much in their way.

June Trent was in fact running true to form. She had omitted to sterilize the bottles and prepare the baby's milk the night before; Baby Caroline had been bawling for it much too early and June couldn't get into the bathroom to fetch the Milton because Richard was still in there. She yelled 'Oh, hurry up, for God's sake!' – and went downstairs to try and get organized.

Outside the cars were revving up and Richard was going to be late.

Like Richard, few of the men bothered with a cooked breakfast (certainly there wasn't time for one now). Like the other women she found it better to tip out some cornflakes, deal with the toast problem, and try not to burn it when strapping babies, like Caroline, into plastic seats; stay wide awake enough to prevent them strangling themselves in the Hoover wire instead, or falling out of bed because for an instant you'd left the cot side down while searching for nappy pins, only to find plastic baby bowls knocked over, just as the telephone rang over some change in the husband's day . . .

'Is Richard still there, June?'

'He's in the bath. Can I take a message?'

'Yes, tell him – '

'Just a minute, I'll find a piece of paper.' Paper, paper . . . Baby Caroline was sick on the telephone pad yesterday . . . oh golly, the milk's boiling over. At last: 'Yes, go ahead.'

'Just tell Richard not to go straight to the office, he's to pick up some advertising copy from Stilling & Franson first. Okay?'

The pencil wouldn't write so June had to memorize it anyway. Stilling & Franson. 'Yes, I'll tell him.'

June dumped the baby for a second, ran up the stairs, sleepily repeating the words Stilling & Franson – it could have been half a dozen other clients, you had to remember which one, there was no room to manœuvre if things went wrong. Richard was doing well but a lot of people in advertising were losing jobs, Richard's keeping his head above water – just – and if we're ever going to move out of Glenmore to a bigger house – and goddammit we can't go on here much longer – it's got to stay that way.

'Richard! The office have just phoned.'

'Sorry, the bath was running. What's that?'

'The office phoned to say call at Stilling & Franson to pick something up, before you go to the office.'

'Pick what up?'

Pick whatever it was up, Richard opened the bathroom door, nodded with his mouth foaming with toothpaste, said Damn because that threw something else out. June dashed down the stairs, nearly tripping by the pram parked in the hallway, just managed to rescue Baby Caroline from falling off the edge of the couch by the telephone table.

Except for Alec Keeling, the husbands were still leaving,

starting their cars within a few toast-bites of each other. Sun already beating on car roofs, the smell of baking upholstery was unleashed as doors were yanked open and ignition keys inserted in one movement. Ignoring each other by long mutual agreement, the breadwinners reversed off the narrow strip of car park and dodged Jennifer who was leaping unpredictably in and out of Diana's mini.

It was an hour after the male exodus that Diana Keeling came round to see June Trent.

Usually someone did drop in for coffee around ten. It was necessary, it made you feel vaguely civilized; somehow you'd slapped the make-up on by then and the worst of the previous evening's debris was at least stacked in the sink, if not actually washed up.

Diana said. 'But apparently we're *not* civilized – not according to our principal guest at dinner last night, anyway.'

'Oh?' June looked at Diana briefly, noted that as usual Diana managed somehow to look as if her clothes were new that day, which was annoying, but then Diana was so well organized, how did she manage it, with three children? 'Which reminds me,' June said through the serving hatch, as if it followed through from their conversation. 'Is Jennifer's birthday party still set for Friday?'

Diana said, 'I meant to ask Alec.'

'Surely he won't want to get involved?'

'We'd better compare notes, though.' Diana made for the phone. 'Mind if I check? I sometimes get dragged off to see colleagues of his.'

'Help yourself.'

Diana tried the number, found it engaged, tried again one minute later, still engaged, hung up as June came in with the coffee. They settled to talk, Diana smoking, June resisting the urge, she'd almost given it up, not quite, but unless things got unbearable she usually stuck to the rules. 'So how was the evening?'

'Apart from this writer, all right.'

'Did he get drunk?'

'He's one of those people you can never tell if they're drunk. He was terribly tense.'

'So of course he made everyone else feel terribly tense?'

'He was more or less all right while we ate. Then it began, I can't remember quite how. It wasn't that he sneered at us, exactly . . . Oh, I remember, I was telling him how, as neighbours, we had to help each other out a good deal – well, we do, don't we? He said, only to a very limited extent. He said that if anything went seriously wrong with any of us, we put up with it for a few days but if somebody really faltered they'd be out on a limb before long. Well, that's just not true, is it? – Do you remember when the Dawsons were having a really bad time? We all mucked in, didn't we?'

June said, 'I bet he's not married.'

'He's not. He's got some woman – '

' – Did he bring her?'

'She was supposed to come but she didn't turn up.'

June said, 'Then it was probably that. He was upset over her and took it out on you. It's understandable.'

'But maddening, June. Naturally, he hasn't got children – at least, he didn't mention any, illegitimate or otherwise – I think he's been married once. But anyone who's got a family knows, well, there are limits on how far you can go with other people.'

June's mind was only half on the conversation. She had to get up and give the baby a rusk, to buy another ten minutes peace, but she was wondering how long it would take to get her figure down to something like Diana's, thinking it would be even more difficult without smoking – well, *almost* without the smoking – if only she could get out more, too. How did Diana manage so easily, all those baby-sitters, and come to think of it Diana was pretty unhelpful when it came to offering one from *her* list. Anyway, quite frankly with things as they were, Richard couldn't afford to take her out all that often, and anyway he was usually so damn tired. You couldn't blame him as the baby seemed to be awake half the night. The office hadn't expected any less of Richard during her pregnancy; she knew it would have been unreasonable to demand special treatment then, even a company has to keep its head above water and they were beginning to regard Richard as a key man. You have to keep going.

Aloud, June said, 'You have to keep going. Unless you're a nun or something.' She smiled. 'Not that I know anything about nuns. But I should imagine that if one nun goes off sick there's another nun who can do her work.'

'Nuns,' said Diana, thoughtfully turning a bangle on her wrist, 'don't have babies.' And as if it arose somehow from the same point she went on, 'As a matter of fact we're getting a nanny.'

June's eyes glazed over. On Glenmore, you simply couldn't

avoid knowing exactly how well the other wives were doing, it was all very well for writers to sneer at it – if Diana's guest really had, actually Diana was a bit sensitive about being at Glenmore anyway – but it was easy to feel jealous, you needed respite, you never got any, and now Diana was recognizably ahead.

June was skilful at masking her feelings; and though she was never conscious of this trick with her eyes, nor aware whether or not other people noticed how she could shut them off like that, she knew how to cope with her own feelings – especially when talking with someone like Diana who, in June's estimation, never had to – not those sort of feelings anyway. June was once again aware of the mini parked out there on the green. The two-car symbol of the Keelings, though only a mini-irritant, indicated blandly that the Keelings were doing better than anyone else.

June said frivolously, 'But not a nun.'

'No. Alec and nuns don't mix.'

June thought Diana sounded a bit brittle over that. 'Will she live in?'

'There's precious little room; but we're getting a double bunk for James and Stephen; they can share – they did sometimes when we used Stephen's room as a guest room, they got on all right, though they kept each other awake half the night – '

' – And therefore you!'

'And therefore us. But they'll get used to it. I hope. The nanny can sleep in with Jennifer. And if we have any guests they'll just have to put up downstairs. We're getting one of those couches that open out into a double bed.'

June was doing some sums. Estimate: over fifty pounds for the double bunk; more for the couch thing. And God knows how much a week for the nanny. Good for Diana. Only the eyes glazed over a shade more at the thought. She had to get up again, the baby was positing – that's another thing, why are Diana's babies *never* sick? – and then the phone rang, so she wiped the baby's front like lightning with a J-Cloth, doubled round the settee where Diana sat so comfortably announcing the forthcoming nanny, and took the call. 'Oh, it's for you, I think it's your husband.'

Diana said, with automatic facetiousness, 'Tracked me down again. Just think what I couldn't get away with . . . Yes, Alec?'

'You with June?'

'Yes of course.'

'Can she hear me? . . . No, don't answer that. Don't sound surprised, or anything. Just go back to our own house straight away, well, give it five minutes. Don't look rushed. Then sit by the phone. Make sure it's properly on the rest, check it's working when you get in. Okay so far? Answer very casually.'

Diana glanced quickly at June, then said, 'It's probably in your desk, Alec. I'll go and have a look.'

'Fine. If anybody else phones, before I get through, hang up on them the moment you can. And if I don't get through to you by ten-thirty, try and reach me at the Institute number, my private line. Is that all quite clear?'

Diana twisted her bangle. 'I don't suppose it's lost really, darling. Among the insurance things, I expect.'

'Okay. Call you at home.' The line went dead abruptly. There was just a burr.

June said, 'Anything wrong?'

'The usual. They need so many documents up there at the Institute, Alec never has the right ones.' Diana embarked on finishing her coffee, not in one hasty go, but some carefully timed nonchalant sips. 'Alec's getting more vague,' she lied, 'I'm sure of it. It's only a question of time before he goes off to work with my handbag instead of his briefcase.'

The baby started crying again. Very casually, June said. 'You forgot to mention Jennifer's party.'

Diana watched the baby and took another sip. 'And I'm accusing Alec of being absent-minded! I'm sure it'll be on, though.'

June said, 'Fine,' and went over to Baby Caroline, and undid the seat harness. 'The rusk is played out. She'll have to play on the carpet. Then she'll be sick. So more J-Cloths. Same old war, isn't it?'

Diana got up, and stretched. 'It's getting hotter. We all ought to get out of town, somehow. Thanks for the coffee.'

The Glenmore houses, recently built yet already showing signs of poor workmanship and cheap materials, were packed tightly together to form three sides of a square. In the middle was the green, where the children played. The car park, inset so that it flanked the grass, was by now nearly empty. Diana glanced across quickly to check that Jennifer was okay, then entered her own house, trying not to fumble the keys, in case June was looking. Diana thought June's tone had been a bit odd when she'd pointed out the omission on the phone about the party.

Once inside, she lifted the phone off the rest, found the dialling tone normal, and placed the receiver back firmly, confessing to herself that she'd been badly frightened by Alec's voice. He didn't normally flap, except when he'd been getting a lot too close to the non-nuns. Then, he perversely seemed afraid of the male competition around Diana, and was anxious in bed with her . . . a situation which had the peculiar consequence of freeing her from her own inhibition and sense of inadequacy. She liked him nervous, though she hated the reason. But Diana, gullible sometimes about the claims of other wives, hinted at over coffee if only to account for the sluttish state of the kitchen, seldom really let go in coitus, lay too often wondering what it should be like to achieve relaxation.

But guilt was one thing; fear was another. It had been instantly detectable in Alec's voice – the more so because he'd had it so well in check. When Alec was really hiding something, that's when it showed.

The phone went almost immediately. It was the Dawsons, both of them, one on the extension and one downstairs. Bill Dawson never seemed to be at work, and told awful jokes. Now he wanted to talk about Jennifer's birthday party. The wife chipped in occasionally, apologizing as always for the ill-timed jokes, this time a remark about Jennifer being so dishy she'd look like Lolita by the time she was twelve. Diana said, 'Can I call you back? Everything on the cooker is boiling over.'

Mrs Dawson said, 'That doesn't sound like you. Your air of efficiency always makes me feel like a bull in a china shop.'

Bill Dawson chipped in. 'Funny sort of bull, she is.'

Mrs Dawson said, 'You can't very well call me the other thing, darling. As a matter of fact, Diana, he does, frequently.'

Keeping the desperation out of her voice, Diana said, 'You sort that out between you. See you and the children on Friday.'

Diana hung up again and a big jet from Heathrow lumbered through the hot sky overhead and rattled the windows. Planes didn't usually get on Diana's nerves. This one did. But she watched it, wondered about the people in it, wondered how many of the passengers had ever had a phone call from a husband like the one that had just come through at June's. She watched Jennifer again for a minute, then withdrew from the window and started thinking about lunch. To do this she had to walk the length of the living-room, larger, better furnished, better thought out than June's. The trouble with June was she over-fussed about the baby, worried forever about the carpet, didn't realize that carpets could be quite easily shampooed. 'A bit sluttish of her really,' thought Diana, 'because she's too lazy to run the Bex-Bissell over it regularly, waited until the stains had dried solid.' Then Diana felt a bit ashamed; although it was the norm to bitch each other on the estate, it wasn't fair to pick on June. She'd only had her first baby seven months; it takes time to get used to it. With James and Stephen both at school Diana had them out of the way more or less until Alec got back from work, so there was only Jennifer to cope with and she mixed readily with the other children on the estate. When Alec came home he liked to play with the boys anyway; so she herself could take her time bathing Jennifer and getting her off to bed.

And soon there would be the nanny . . . well, more exactly, a girl who was sort of halfway between a nanny and an au pair. She should have explained that to June, come to think of it. She'd certainly been very careful to make it clear to Alec she wouldn't be paying the full nanny price. Alec had rather balked anyway; with the boys at a fee-paying school things were getting . . .

The phone rang and Diana snatched it off the hook.

'Diana? Alec here.'

'Alec, what in God's name is going on?'

'Did June suspect?'

'Suspect what?'

'Skip it. And listen. Get a bag packed and for Pete's sake don't do it as if we're off to the Bahamas. Grab what you really need. Put it in the car and don't be seen. Make sure you haven't got to come back to the house, then load it on the car . . . '

' . . . Alec, will you *please* . . . !'

'You got the telephone pad handy?'

'Yes, all right. I won't interrupt. I can see it won't do any good.'

'Too right, it won't. Write all this down and burn the two sheets of paper underneath the one you're writing on.'

'Nobody's going to come in here and snoop.'

'They . . . might. Later. Right. When you've got away from Glenmore, fill up with petrol – for God's sake don't run out of that. Then go to the Concourse shops. I've phoned up Barnley's and the manager there has a list of where else you have to call. He's no idea why I'm doing it this way; I've implied we've got a sudden chance of a holiday and we're short of time. Tell Jennifer the same thing when you bring her.

'Now. The one thing I couldn't lay on with him is the fact that you and the children and for that matter me too, we've all got to go on to a drug . . .'

'A *drug*? There's nothing wrong with us!'

'For God's sake don't argue. Go to Pease, the chemist on the Concourse. I've managed to give the impression that a doctor he knows at this place has authorized a prescription to be confirmed in writing later. It took some doing, and old Pease may be a bit suspicious. I made the quantities as large as I dared; no one else in the Concourse will wonder about our sudden departure but he just might. Actually, for reasons you'll learn later the quantities won't be anything like enough, but I know where there are some more and with luck I'll manage to get hold of them in time. Don't argue; just tell me if you've got that straight.'

'Yes.'

'Right. As soon as you can, pick up James and Stephen from the school. I've already phoned the headmaster there and told him we think they've been in contact with a mumps case. He'll be quite glad to see them off. All right; having done all that, drive to Sunningdale level crossing – you know it? . . . it used to have gates but they've made it one of those automatic things.'

'Of course I know it! But why there? Surely it's quicker to get on to the motorway via Feltham?'

'The motorway's clogged.'

'Well then, further down. Say, at Maidenhead.'

'Diana, for Pete's sake . . . Don't you think I know the bloody motorway? It's closed to all domestic traffic, and don't ask me why, because I don't know. Fortunately, nor does anyone else – ordinary drivers, I mean.'

Diana digested this and forced herself to listen without all the obvious interruptions. 'All right. Sunningdale. Go on.'

'Wait for me there. You should make it by one-thirty however heavy the traffic and unless anything unforeseen goes wrong I should be there by then myself. I'll be in a Volkswagen Dormobile thing, and not in the Triumph. We meet where there's a turning to the left, immediately after the crossing. Park outside the fruiterers' . . you can't miss it. The turning is bang opposite the big garage that almost adjoins the station.'

'Then what?'

'Then we transfer the kids, and all the stuff you'll be carrying, from the mini to the Dormobile. We head West.'

'To where, for Christ sake?'

Alec paused, then spoke in a lowered voice. 'Diana, I've got to tell you exactly where; but I promise you, if you breathe a word to anyone about our destination it'll be nothing short of catastrophic. You may even be asked by a police patrol. I can't explain that part now, but you might. The point is, we may not succeed in meeting at Sunningdale. Give me till three but not a moment longer. I don't think I'll get delayed but I just can't know for certain. So you may have to go on by yourself. If so, your real destination is the Dorrington Hotel at Jaybury, which is a few miles out of Exeter. Whatever happens, tell no one that. Say you're heading for Taunton, anything, but not there. If we miss each other at Sunningdale, that's where I'll be – somehow.'

'Alec you're terrifying me. Are you expecting an atom bomb, or cholera, or just the end of the world?'

'I'm expecting you, Diana, to stick precisely to what I ask and to this in particular; don't, whatever you do, go through Staines. Take the by-pass where you'd normally join it from the A308. Now just check back and repeat that you'll keep clear of Staines.'

'Alec, I'm not a child.'

'Diana, *please.*'

'I'm not to go into Staines,' she said, blankly.

'The police may try and direct you there, I just don't know. But they might. If they do, find a way of ignoring their instructions. It probably won't happen but we have to think of everything; and everything, Diana, is just what the police don't know. If they did you wouldn't get through at all. Now the other thing is this; and it's every bit as vital. If you see any sign of panic – got it? – any *panic*, in whatever form, take a capsule each of the drug. All of you, immediately. Just dish it out and make sure it's swallowed.'

'Wouldn't it be simpler to take them when we get them?'

'We can't afford to waste a single capsule of that stuff. No, do as I say.'

'But I'm worried about Mr Pease. Supposing – '

' – Pease thinks the drug is needed here at the Institute.'

'Alec, he'll have had time to think, by then. He isn't going to believe the Institute can't get their supplies in bulk.'

'Yes, you may be right . . . Think of a story, a misunderstanding over factory deliveries, anything. The drug is needed in a hurry for experiments on animals – yes, say that. But by tonight there won't be a capsule of this stuff Estofort in any chemist shop from John O'Groats to Lands End.'

'What about the roads? Will they be clear?'

'Well, it's midweek. It shouldn't be too bad. But you may find isolated cases of crazy driving . . . I don't just mean the normal madmen who think their cars are sex symbols; I mean, *crazy*. Hang on a sec.' He broke off. Diana heard him talking urgently with someone else, said something like 'not even 999? . . . What about the trunk lines? No, don't wait. Try it again now.' He came back to Diana, 'Look, I've got to go.'

'Alec . . . you're frightening me terribly.' Diana gripped the receiver hard, found herself trying to swallow. 'Alec, are you sure . . . ' She tried again, swallowed, for some reason it made her feel better. More calmly, gently, she asked, 'Darling, are you sure you're not exaggerating? Everything seems so normal here. Couldn't it just be something at the Institute that . . . '

He cut in. She could hear that he was having to hang on to his self-control like the last rung of a fire escape. 'It won't be normal for long. That I guarantee! We'll be lucky if things are still "normal" by the time we get to Sunningdale.'

'What if June sees me loading up the car? What shall I say?'

'Diana, in a spot you're the most resourceful woman I know. Think up something that fits. If possible load the car out of sight. Move it off the central verge and shove it over by the garages. Load it there.'

'So we get out from whatever terrible thing is afoot and leave everyone else to rot?'

'It may not affect them.'

'You're lying.'

'Diana, *listen.* I may succeed in getting June and Richard down there later – with their baby – but I don't stand a chance if you argue now. *Trust* me. I'm hanging up and utterly relying on you. Now get on with it.'

The line went dead. Diana thought, this can't be real. I'm going to wake up in a minute and find it's all a mad dream.

Then she thought of James and Stephen, and went back to the window to watch Jennifer, who was laughing and giggling and pretending to drive the car. This was no dream. So, trembling a little, she got the larger of the two suitcases down from the cleaning cupboard, and unclicked the catches.

TWO

Inside the mini, with the boys now aboard, there was hardly room to move. Diana, never a relaxed driver, was unable in this thickening traffic to forget her nerves as she usually did by just putting her foot hard down. Now, she had to do the opposite and drive over-cautiously. This in itself was nerve-racking.

James and Stephen, non-identical twins who hardly looked like brothers they were so different, sat in the back with the boxes picked up from the Concourse shops; Jennifer, restive from the rising heat inside the car, sat in the front next to her mother. The excited prattle that had erupted from the boys, from the time they'd been sprung so abruptly from school, had died down to something more thoughtful. Stephen, the more introverted and sensitive of the twins, displayed an intuition Diana found unnerving.

'Well if it's a holiday, Mummy, why didn't we know?'

'I thought you'd like a surprise.'

James gazed ahead at the endless line of traffic. To do this he had to clamber over the boxes, as Jennifer wouldn't keep her head still in front. He said, 'Like them. I expect they're all having a surprise.'

For most of them it was no doubt quite true.

Mass decisions, as in election landslides, are curiously unanimous: and in this case the weather – being British weather and no other – had a lot to do with it. No doubt a proportion of the gleaming cars, packed nose to tail down the Staines by-pass, were those of families who were, for various reasons, able to start their summer holidays mid-week; you could spot these from the boat-trailers and the roof racks piled high with cots and prams. But the majority were domestic malingerers, people who had ruthlessly saved up their regular attendance at factories and offices for the moment when – as now – there seemed nothing more glorious than to wheel the car out of the garage and head for the coast. Naturally, each car-load was surprised, annoyed, and thereafter frustrated to find they were not alone in this conspiracy; the main roads were packed tight and both the police and the motoring organizations were taken by surprise. Midweek roadworks, planned to coincide with minimum traffic demands, now became bottlenecks. None of these had yet seriously held up Diana. But remorselessly the congestion was thickening all the time.

Diana said. 'It's this lovely weather.' But anxiously she was looking at the temperature gauge on the dashboard. The mini was overheating. It was all right so long as the west-bound motorists kept up this fairly steady pace, but a traffic jam could make the water boil . . . the thermostat had been faulty for weeks and the garage had forgotten to replace it. The omission could be crucial if in fact Alec couldn't meet them and she had to drive on. Reluctantly, she used Alec's old trick of turning the car heater full on with the blower going. This drained off some of the engine heat but made the car almost uninhabitable.

Jennifer said, 'Mummy, I'm hot.'

'It'll cool down soon. James, open a bottle of coke, will you?'

James said, 'The coke's hot, too.' Then, timing the accusation with a well-gauged pause, he added, 'Stephen's been sitting on it.'

Stephen, whose mind was on something else, didn't react as James' temperament demanded. 'Everything's hot in here.'

James persisted. 'There's no need to make it hotter. Get off it.'

'I can't move,' said Stephen, but he wasn't looking at James. There was this peculiar zigzagging of one of the cars in front.

James, now furious, said. 'If you don't move right this minute I'll slosh you one.'

Diana checked her own temper and managed, 'Children, keep still. There just isn't room for a fist fight.'

James said, 'But Stephen's sitting on the coke and he won't get off it.'

'I *can't* get off it.'

Jennifer looked cross and said, 'I don't want it anyway. Mummy, can't we stop?'

'Not yet, dear. When we meet Daddy. It won't be long.'

'But I want to do a wee.'

'I told you to do a wee before we left.'

'I did. I want to do another wee.'

'Think about something else, Jennifer. Think about our lovely holiday. You'll be able to paddle in the sea. Won't that be nice?'

Jennifer smiled and said, 'I like paddling.'

Diana smiled back, in calculated determination to draw attention away from what she'd just seen. That car, three ahead, after persistently swerving about, violently lurched broadside across the road. There came a desperate squeal of tyres and the hissing of pneumatic brakes as a truck coming from the opposite direction pulled off a minor miracle and squeezed through the tiny gap. The car leapt over the opposite grass bank, smashed its nose through some railings, and ended up in someone's bed of roses, its occupants screaming and pounding at the jammed-up doors.

Under any other circumstances Diana would have stopped to help. A driver a few cars behind her did, pulling into a lay-by and getting out to investigate. Diana felt a pang of guilt but could not shake off the persistent tone of Alec's voice in her telephone ear.

Panic?

She stole a glance around the car. Fortunately James, unsuccessful in his attempts to goad Stephen, was now bickering with Jennifer, who had turned round in the front seat to do her best – with a somewhat limited vocabulary – to insult James' back.

But Stephen had seen it, all right.

Panic. Okay.

Very casually, she said. 'I've got some pills in the car, special pills which won't make you feel so hot. James, they're in a box on the floor, by your feet. I want you all to take one now.'

James said obstinately. 'I don't feel hot.'

'You soon will. Come on. I'm going to take one too. And Stephen, I'm sure you can shift enough to get one of those coke bottles out. Can't you?'

Stephen said nothing, but got hold of a coke bottle nonetheless. James had the opener and grabbed the coke bottle and said, 'No, *I'll* open it.'

'Come on, boys. One of you open it. We need something to wash down the pills with.'

Jennifer said. 'I'm the hottest. I'll have one first.'

Diana saw they were handed round – one each – and took hers last, without stopping the car. The fear inside her was growing. It was of a type she could not recognize.

In fact, ever since she'd picked up the drugs from Mr Pease, she'd been trying to analyze it – even considered the unlikely possibility of Alec heading for a nervous breakdown. True, he had been abstracted and rather sleepless these last few nights but Diana had a shrewd idea about what – or rather, who – was on his mind. Alec was Alec; you loved him or not, what could you do? Those urges of his came on and there'd be a business trip. Nervous breakdown? – no. To all intents and purposes, the opposite. Damn him.

Mr Pease, the chemist, had been more than a little curious. Diana had asked him what the drug did. Mr Pease, an elderly throwback to the old-time dispensing man who always performed the preparation of medicines very slowly and methodically, as though still using a pestle and mortar, had still been shovelling the enormous quantity of capsules into containers when she'd arrived at his shop. Without either greeting her or even looking up, he remarked, 'Frankly, if this order hadn't come from where it did, I would have refused this quantity.'

Diana lied, 'Well, I have to take it up to the Institute and something came unstuck with their bulk ordering system. What's the pill do, anyway?'

Mr Pease arranged another count of capsules on the measuring tray and said, 'You might generally class it as a tranquilizer; but the word covers a multitude of sins, these days. It doesn't get prescribed very much round here, hasn't long been off test.' He snorted. 'Doctors in the Glenmore area are cautious about the gimmicks. There have been too many clever-clever things for their liking and you never know the side-effects until people start getting ill with something different as a result.'

He finished the counting and, very ponderously, started writing out sticky labels to go on the four large bottles into which he'd poured the capsules. 'You can tell those professors at the Institute they're pretty lucky. If it weren't for the fact that people here mistrust things like Estofort we wouldn't have anything like this quantity in stock.' Handing it across, he added, 'I take it you've got something to lock them in? I wouldn't care to estimate the number of fatal doses you'll be carrying around in your car.'

'I'll lock them in the boot.'

'All right. But I advise you not to leave the car until you've delivered them safely to the Institute. Good day, Mrs Keeling . . .'

From the back of the car Stephen said, 'What's this about mumps, Mummy?'

'Mumps?' For a moment she'd forgotten what the headmaster had been told. 'Oh . . . we think the Dawsons' children are down with it.'

'They were playing in the garden yesterday.'

'Yes, with necks swollen out the size of a football, dear. Didn't you see?'

Jennifer said, 'I thought they were going to come to my birthday party on Friday. Aren't I going to have a birthday party now?'

'We're going to see the seaside instead.'

'Will I have a party there?'

Diana suddenly wanted to scream. She controlled it and said tensely, 'We'll arrange something.'

James said, 'Mummy, I've been thinking. Why haven't we got any of the beach things in the car?'

'Perhaps Daddy will bring them.'

'Oh. Did he go back for them, then? They weren't in the car when he left for the office. He'd just cleaned it out – I helped him last night. Then I saw him off this morning. He'd just got his case with him. Nothing for the beach.'

Diana turned and forced a smile. 'My, my, don't you two want to know everything at once! Don't you like surprises?'

James, his uncomplicated smile dominant, exclaimed, 'Of course we do – when it means getting out of school!'

'Well then.'

Diana looked in the mirror at Stephen. She thought, that intuition of his is working overtime. With James things great and small tended to slide from consciousness like water off a duck's back. Stephen was different.

Once, Diana and Alec had had a dreadful row, in bed, in the middle of the night. Alec, whom she'd refused for the third night in succession, purely because she was going through one of her nervous things, had got jealous and suspicious and finally they'd been screaming at each other. Stephen and James had burst into the room, possibly in the faint hope of discovering burglars. Diana, who was scared of spiders, had pretended that one had been found in the bed. James, who had no particular feelings toward spiders – except sometimes he pulled their legs off – had accepted the explanation with a guffaw and offered to trap the thing in a matchbox, and pursued the imaginary spider under the bed and round the room until he'd satisfied himself that it must have escaped through a crack in the window.

Stephen had just stood there, wrestling quietly with his hands. From then on he had been terrified of spiders and for many weeks had refused to go into his parent's bedroom without knocking.

Now, Diana could see, through the mirror, the same expression on his face.

So of the three children, Stephen was the one who possessed that indefinable instinct for truth which depended neither on facts nor figures. Catching his eye in the mirror, she saw instantly that he could see right through the holiday fable. Whatever was really going on, he was as likely to sense it as she was. The realization instilled the first tangible stab of real terror. Up till now there had been too much to do; but those knowing eyes, watching hers in the mirror, challenged in one glance all the lies and reassurances.

'I don't think we're going to get mumps, Mummy,' he said.

* * *

The Institute at which Alec Keeling worked was divided into two halves.

The largest building included the neurological wing, which was under the watchful eye of the Ministry, though some of the projects were sponsored or at least subsidized by one or two of the principal foundations. The smaller and more up to date building, connected to the other only by one narrow corridor, which served as an umbilical cord between officialdom and industry, housed various wings of commercial concerns with a stake in medical development. The idea, dreamed up by one of the more adventurous ministers of a previous government, was to improve relations between public and private sectors in many matters concerning health.

In a way it worked, though not without a certain farcical evolvement of species of etiquette designed to overcome the problem of Grades. On the commercial side, most of the liaison staff, like Alec, were both senior and highly qualified – otherwise they wouldn't have been there. There wasn't room in the building for matters of conventional routine, which were dealt with by teletype to each of the various interested companies concerned.

But in the Beveridge Building, colloquially known as the 'Hat Rack' in view of its weirdly outdated Festival of Britain architecture, people were almost absurdly conscious of rank and seniority. In there, promotion was abysmally slow. By contrast, the architecture was rapidly growing obsolete. Trendy and exciting in the early fifties, the 'Hat Rack' already looked fit only for very old hats. Those who wore them guarded their rights as dictated by their grading; and tried to impose this acute sense of hierarchy on the commercial wing down the corridor.

Alec, who had now been there over two years, was used to it now. There were certain people who flattened themselves against the wall, on passing within the umbilical corridor, and these always smiled. There were others who tried to force you to do the same thing back. Various methods of doing this were adopted, the simplest being to walk three abreast so that there wasn't room for the individual trying to make headway in the opposite direction. Alec's method of dealing with this was to pretend to be absorbed in some document or other, then steer a last-minute course straight through the middle, so that the central member of the approaching phalanx had to dodge nimbly out of the way. Alec got on pretty well.

Events at the Institute on that hot Wednesday morning, the events which led up to Alec's clandestine phone call to Diana at June's place, began merely with the sluggardly reluctance, on the part of Wednesday Routine, to occur quite as it should; for Nuttall, who shared Alec's office in the commercial wing, greeted him by saying, 'A funny thing happened on the way to the Institute.'

'How funny?' Alec didn't like the easy-going slickness of Nuttall's googlies. His remarks came at you obliquely, invariably from a lolling position of sustained indolence. Compared with Alec's, Nuttall's job was a sinecure though much more could have been made of it by a more conscientious man.

Languidly, Nuttall jiggered the phone rest and said. 'I can't raise anyone over at the Ministry block'

Alec beamed without humour. 'Haven't you been across to find out?'

'I don't need any exercise this morning, thanks. I had plenty last night.'

Alec ignored the tasteless sexual bragging. He just said, 'It's these bloody phones. They're always going wrong. Try and get them via the outside line.'

'I have. No joy there, either.'

'Well, they're late, then.'

'*All* of them? It's conference morning.'

Alec glanced through the window at the Hat Rack car park. 'There are plenty of cars there.'

Nuttall looked up. 'I know. But the Security Gate said most of them have been there all night.'

'They're getting very conscientious, all of a sudden.'

'But uncommunicative,' said Nuttall. 'I'm supposed to be doing an equipment demonstration over there this morning. If I don't set it up beforehand, they'll put me off another week.'

'Which equipment?'

'The auto-encephylograph. It's my favourite toy and they promised to let me play with it.'

Alec said, 'Well, I'll go over and see Dr Crossley, and see what cooks. You coming?'

Nuttall said, 'I'll wait here for the technicians. The machine has to come up from Langley, by truck. If they go to the wrong car park I'll be spending the morning trying to explain the one-way system, and I don't even understand it myself.'

The umbilical corridor was long and straight. Halfway down, a clock stuck out on a single piece of steel tube from one side of the wall. It said ten minutes past nine – not all that late. Technically speaking, work in the main building was supposed to start at eight-thirty, though it seldom did. And of course the shift people would have been on all night. Alec thought the cars on the top car park must belong to them.

Beyond the clock, Alec saw Melhuish approaching from the Hat Rack end. Melhuish, a noted scraper against walls, was short and rather flabby-looking, rounded at the shoulders and large in the head. Normally his rubbery mouth would contrive itself into a polite, Grade Three smile, then mould the thick lips into a mumbled Good Morning. Flattening himself obligingly against the wall, he would then wait for superior beings to indulge their right of way.

Alec dreaded the threatened encounter as soon as he saw him. It wasn't fair that people like Melhuish had been trained to cringe all their lives. The trouble was he had no less than five children. The idea of getting sacked was so awful it haunted him every moment of his working life. As Melhuish saw things, it was a necessary duty to his children to mince, sacrificing all trace of dignity if it meant that superiors in need of lap dogs would continue to employ him. And by now the reflex had long become indiscriminate; if the office cat had wished to pass he would have done the same thing.

Yet Alec knew him to be reliable, honest, and far less devious than this conduct implied. There were those in the Hat Rack building who managed to conduct themselves with far more superficial dignity, yet sunk to almost any depth of intrigue if it ensured their own upgrading at the expense of someone else's.

This time, however, Melhuish remained exactly in the middle of the corridor and did not attempt the plastic smile. 'Don't go through, Mr Keeling,' he said.

The confrontation was so unusual and so out of character that Alec couldn't think of anything to say.

'I beg you, don't go through.'

Alec said lightly, 'What's happened? Are the shift people showing blue films?'

Melhuish narrowed his shoulders and clasped his small white hands together. 'There's sickness there. A dreadful sickness, Mr Keeling.' Melhuish's big eyes conveyed more than the words. They were absolutely still; and gave the impression of being greatly enlarged.

'But this place is full of doctors.'

'It began with the doctors.'

'When?'

'Last night.'

'Have you called an ambulance?'

Melhuish said shakily, 'I don't think you yet appreciate the scale of this problem. I doubt if anyone would.'

Alec said quietly, 'Look, can we just go along to the reception office? We could talk in there, and there's an outside phone I can use if necessary.'

'I doubt if it'll be much use to you. There's nothing we can do here.'

Alec's first thought was that Melhuish himself must have gone round the bend – evidently he'd scraped himself against one wall too many.

Reception was empty; and this in itself was unusual. On the mornings of the Wednesday conference there was usually quite a number of visitors – some of them merely observers, others who would take the platform and voice the slightly eliptical theories the Institute went in for. These days there were so many Ph.Ds in such cut-throat competition to get articles printed or notions quoted that they came to the Hat Rack in droves, just to get a paragraph in *New Scientist* or – rarely indeed – a research project under the wing of one of the Foundations.

The girl who normally supplied coffee, biscuits, and chalk for the blackboard wasn't there either.

Alec said, 'Just tell me what happened. Make it as brief as you can. I may have to get help.'

Melhuish obviously didn't think this suggestion made much sense; but he told what he knew concisely enough. 'I got here early this morning. To be honest I was in a bit of a state myself; Dr Crossley had asked me – told me – to make certain arrangements for Mr Nuttall's demonstration and I confess I was anxious. We never get enough time. Those people come pouring in while we're still installing equipment in the lecture room. Before we can get it working properly someone gets up on his hind legs and . . . Well, anyway; the first person I met was Dr Crossley himself. I could see immediately that he was ill.'

'Where did you see him?'

'Coming out of the neurological wing. As you know, they've been putting that new drug through further tests – '

' – Which one?'

For some reason Melluish seemed reluctant to name it. He looked down at his Oxford shoes, carefully shined as usual but showing their cracks. 'The one your company produces down at Exeter.'

'Estofort?'

'Yes.'

For some reason this monosyllable conveyed a shame-faced admission. Alec couldn't make it out. 'Go on.'

Melhuish cleared his throat, raising a small hand with which punctiliously to cover his mouth. 'Dr Crossley came rushing up to me and at first he couldn't speak properly. Then he said they'd run out of Estofort, but needed some urgently to complete the tests.'

'What tests?'

'He didn't say.' Melhuish looked directly at Alec, steady-eyed but frightened. 'Believe me, Dr Crossley was in no condition to explain.'

Alec frowned. 'But we're already marketing Estofort. It's been fully cleared as a Schedule "A" drug and declared safe.'

'I'm only saying what happened, Mr Keeling. It sounded odd to me, anyway. All a doctor has to do to get some in an emergency is to write himself out a prescription. Besides, a tranquilizer like that shouldn't be necessary for someone like Dr Crossley.'

'It isn't quite a tranquilizer but never mind, go on.'

'Naturally, I rang the nearest chemist but found they were already out of stock.'

'Wait a minute! What time was this?'

'Must have been just half past eight this morning.'

'Half past eight? – What were they doing open at that hour?'

'Apparently the dispenser saw people queuing up outside. They were trying to smash their way in.'

'People from here?'

'Yes! And while I was doing all this telephoning, trying to get hold of a pharmacist who'd got some – '

' – Well, a lot of them don't even stock it yet. It was only released in April.'

'But Mr Keeling, even the ones that did had run out.'

'So by that time it couldn't only have been people from the Institute? – Sorry, you were saying – ?'

'While I was doing all this phoning Dr Crossley just . . . gabbled. Normally he hardly says anything – especially to me.'

'What sort of gabbling?'

'Well, you know Dr Crossley's particular line of research?'

'I know he's got some bee in his bonnet about what he calls Virulent Panic; but I've never believed in it and anyway he's never explained – to my knowledge – exactly what it means. What *does* it mean?'

Melhuish said, 'You'd have to ask another doctor here what that's all about' – He added limply, 'If you can find one who's coherent.'

'You mean there are other people still in the building who are in this kind of condition?'

'I mean,' said Melhuish shakily, 'I can't find anyone who isn't.'

'And where is this chemist shop that was broken into?'

'Staines.'

Alec said nothing but went to the window. From the Hat-Rack building you couldn't see as far east as Staines. The westerly end of Heathrow Airport was visible, though, and so was a stretch of the Staines by-pass, at the point where it re-joined the old road at the roundabout towards Egham.

All you could see really was that traffic on the by-pass itself was flowing normally. There seemed, though, an abnormally thin line of cars coming up from Staines itself.

Melhuish was saying, 'Whatever this thing it, Mr Keeling, it seems instantly contagious – almost like one of those new viruses they've been developing for biological warfare.'

Alec left the window. 'Do you seriously mean a virus?'

Those coat-hanger shoulders shrugged. 'How can I know? I was speaking figuratively. People catch it, just like that; then react almost instantly.'

'Then why haven't you got it, if you've been hobnobbing with all these people that have?'

'You don't believe a word of this, do you?'

'I honestly don't know. I don't understand the purpose of the tests.'

'From what I could gather from Dr Crossley, they wanted to see if Estofort could limit the symptoms of various different kinds of neuroses.'

'Neurosis is one thing: instantaneous mental illness which you can catch from someone else is something totally different. That's the part that foxes me.'

Melhuish fumbled in his pocket. 'I didn't want,' he said, 'to tell anyone this. And to be frank, I was in such a state when Dr Crossley went on with this crazy talk I quite forgot about it.' He opened a small carton and tipped out the half dozen capsules it contained. 'I've been suffering a lot of anxiety lately, Mr Keeling. I won't go into details but there's been trouble at home. My doctor recently prescribed these.'

Alec picked one of the capsules up and held it to the light. It was oblong and red, like hundreds of other preparations; but in small figures there was a number written across it, beneath the maker's name.

'Estofort. So you're on that.'

Melhuish smiled wanly. 'Now you're wondering whether someone who has to take drugs for his own purposes might not be exaggerating on a matter like this. I wouldn't blame you, Mr Keeling. But if you're thinking of taking a look round, to check, I wouldn't advise it. Whatever it is that's happening, you wouldn't be able to do a thing about it if you became a victim.' Melhuish looked sharply at Alec, then snatched back the capsules, replaced them in his pocket, and rapped, 'And you're not having these.'

Alec stared back, realized how frantically Melhuish believed his own story. He said quietly. 'You don't think something could have happened in this place – overnight, possibly – that might have just frightened people for a while?'

Melhuish said, 'They were frightened, all right. But fear

on this scale! – I don't think you appreciate quite what I mean!'

'Can you describe the symptoms?'

'I'm no doctor. But I do know terror when I see it. I also know that if anything – ' he sought a word, ' – anything conventional, however appalling or tragic had happened during the night, there were many people here who could have called outside help. Yet they didn't.'

'Granted. How did Dr Crossley's behaviour strike you?'

'I would describe it as a complete loss of the will to live. He kept on saying things like "What's the use?" '

'Anything specific?'

'Anything that came into his head. I remember he rambled on about pollution – you know there's been a detailed forecast made here about the likely endurance of the human race?'

'I know about it. I think it's grossly exaggerated. Even hysterical.'

Melhuish said, 'It came out of a computer.'

'So what? What counts is not what comes out, but what they put in. What else was there?'

'Overcrowding . . . You know, stuff about the population explosion. He said, "Melhuish, you know as well as I do we can do nothing about the real tragedy of the Far East." He went on about immigration here; with some pretty wild estimates of the statistics on racial invasion from overcrowded countries. He quoted – or rather misquoted – from a programme on television last night, concerning the possible effects on – what was it? – the ozone barrier in the upper stratosphere, or something, if the supersonic jets began operating regularly. He got on to food control, the dangers of fungus-grown artificial meat substitutes . . .what else? . . . oh yes, radiation levels in the atmosphere, which he said had been thought to be well within safety limits but were now known to be grossly harmful to future generations and had noticeably increased the incidence of cancer and leucæmia. He went on like that.'

Alec said, 'Sounds as if he's had an overdose of television. It'll probably pass.'

Melhuish said, 'I think not, Mr Keeling, Dr Crossley then rushed along the corridor, forced open the lift doors with the fire axe, and threw himself down the shaft.'

A jet took off from Heathrow, travelling east-west, then climbed steeply out toward Colnbrook. Alec, incredulous over this last horrific piece of information, waited for the plane to bank out of earshot before he went on.

Crossley – of all people! The man who had worked out this so-called Virulent Panic in the first place, and now – if Melhuish was to be believed – its first know fatality.

Alec said quietly, 'Melhuish, don't think I'm criticising but the answer to this question is quite vital.'

'I don't mind being criticized. I'm used to it.'

'You say that when you saw Crossley in this shape, you forgot you were on Estofort yourself. Then you told me you found other people in a similar state – '

'I know what your going to say, Mr Keeling. And of course, when I'd been phoning up these chemists I saw the connection. Shortly after Dr Crossley . . . well, you know . . . I saw other people who were, I promise you, indescribably worse. I must admit I was reluctant to try it – I've only got these few tablets here – but I gave the man in question one of my capsules. It had no effect.'

'So Estofort is a preventative; not a cure. Just as well we found that out. We can hardly afford to waste what there is. All right. There's a sample bottle of Estofort over in my section. I'm going to take one, then come back here and take a look round. This thing may not be as bad as it looks, Crossley may be an extreme case. He may even have had a personal reason to take his own life . . . Okay, I can see you don't think so. Only don't for God's sake let's jump to conclusions. You wait here.'

Alec left the reception room with the instinct to run. He controlled it. If panic was in the air, then he had to watch it in himself. So he kept to a measured pace back to the commercial wing. Nuttall, quite a big man but with rather a round, small head, peered up with a sort of sceptical curiosity and said, 'Any joy, through there?'

Something stopped Alec from telling him about Melhuish. Instead, keeping his back to Nuttall, he went to the filing cabinet where the small sample products were kept. As he searched among the little bottles he asked, 'Your van turned up yet, with the equipment?'

'No. They rang up to say they got delayed. For some reason they came through Staines – or tried to – instead of taking the by-pass. There's a big traffic snarl-up.'

'I see.' Alec found the bottle. Still keeping his back to Nuttall, he swallowed one of the capsules, crunching it in his mouth first, knowing this would speed up the action of the drug. It tasted foul. He fumbled in his pocket, found a coin, went quickly out into the corridor where the coffee dispensing machine stood, selected the necessary buttons, and sipped some of the bitter liquid from the carton. Then he went back into the office, with the drug bottle in his pocket.

Nuttall was leaning back, smoking. His eyes were fixed on the open filing cabinet. 'You're acting oddly.'

Alec forced a smile and said, 'I've got a hell of a hang-over. Can you stay here and take my calls? If my people do come on the line, just say I'm over in the other wing.'

'Okay, will do. And bugger the truck driver for going through Staines.'

Alec said calmly, 'It won't matter too much, things are evidently delayed in the Hat-Rack.'

'Evidently,' said Nuttall. And watched Alec go.

During the short walk back along the corridor, Alec found himself having some unpleasant thoughts. They were ruthless in the extreme, because suddenly he found himself calculating what to do about people like Jimmy Nuttall, should the things Melhuish had reported turn out to be as black as stated.

Nuttall was hopeless in a crisis. Unlike Melhuish he wasn't a worrier, he was the opposite. Or at least his worry showed in a very lethargic, inactive way, producing nil preventive action until it was far too late. If demonstration equipment sent up from his parent factory was delayed, as now, as far as Nuttall was concerned that was that. He made no alternative arrangements, just shrugged it off, better luck next time.

But in a crisis, like this! People were going to be needed. People would have to be *chosen*. For if this thing spread, if other normally responsible people lost – as Melhuish put it – 'the will to live' . . .

Alec checked these thoughts instantly. They were absurd. Melhuish was a worried little man with problems at home. Now he was attributing his own feelings of anxiety to others.

Yet, as Alec turned the final corner back toward the reception room, he couldn't stop a voice inside him which said, 'But Jimmy Nuttall isn't worth it . . . '

Melhuish was still waiting patiently. 'Melhuish. Do something for me. Get on to the Staines police. Find out what the traffic situation is like. Tell them you've got to go there in a hurry or something. Just see what happens. I've taken an Estofort and I'm taking a look round.'

'You'll have to give it time to act.'

'I crunched the capsule. Once in the blood stream, the effect is immediate.'

'Be careful.'

'I will.'

Alec left the room as Melhuish reached for the phone, the green one that didn't go through the switchboard.

The Hat-Rack was a large, high building with protrusions going out from it, cantilevered at intervals, each excrescence arming-outward in a different direction. With inborn logic, Alec decided to start at the top of the building and work his way down, taking a brief look at each department on the way.

As a precaution, he did not take the passenger lift – in whose shaft Dr Crossley was reported to have thrown himself. There was a remote chance of Crossley's survival, even after such a fall. So he took the goods lift – the one Nuttall would have had to load his gear in. It was maddeningly slow.

There were steel gates at each level, not sliding doors like the other one. At each floor Alec took a look along the service corridor. At each, he saw nothing – no people, no activity, no sign of the trolleys which would normally be in place every morning. laden with fresh materials; new experimentation 'broths'; sterile, stainless steel lab equipment sent up from the steam pressure room.

Melhuish's vague reference to viruses hadn't impressed Alec and in any case Melhuish had admitted he was only speaking figuratively. Yet in the Hat Rack, up there in the top two prongs, a lot of work was done on micro-organisms. Both viruses and bacteria adapt, mutate, multiply. Germs seek to defy antibiotics, finding a way round and even contaminating the preventive cultures with the very antibody which immunises the evolved bacterium against the serum.

The species of live organism nurtured at the Institute were harmless – in their original form. But, one chance in a million? . . .

Alec got out of the service lift and went direct to the preparation room. Indeed, you could not enter the wing without doing so. In here, the appropriate gowns, masks, gloves and polythene bags were stored ready for the laboratory staff. Alec equipped himself correctly, then went through the double swing doors into the isolation wing. Here, the atmospheric pressure was kept at a slightly different level from the rest of the place, so that any possible leak would go inward, instead of out. He checked the barometer and found the pressure-differential correct.

Back in 1970, all these labs had been converted to automatic control. The place could run unattended – if necessary for days – and a complex arrangement of alarm systems was built in for various purposes should anything go wrong. These alarms included – apart from the obvious bell systems – direct reporting to positions outside the building complex (there was even a reporting line to Exeter) whereby recorded voice warnings might be transmitted automatically to people many miles from the establishment.

In practice, such precautions were unnecessary except as a 'dead-man's handle'. The purpose of an experiment is to observe it; and normally those who were on the premises to observe were fully trained to take care of the snags, any of which could be detected instantly on the local display consoles.

Alec glanced at the appropriate display for Lab Number One as he entered. All seemed normal; except there was not a soul around. The complicated, globbing array of glass tubes, within which heated fluids were slowly precipitating into purified substances, pursued their chemical course in secret.

In Number Two, where the bacteria broths, all carefully labelled and maintained at precision temperatures, occupied neat benches all the way down, exactly the same applied. A quick check showed that no one had negligently taken off protective clothing and even the coffee cartons were properly stowed under the Perspex cover of the incinerator chute.

Number Three was the same, but here confirmation of Melhuish's most portentous suspicions was finally provided.

For it was in here that a central control booth for all three labs was provided, so that, when short-staffed, the wing could still be run and supervised.

It was seldom used. The last time they had been down to one man in here had been during a 'flu epidemic, when there had been such a shortage of theatre staff at the local hospitals that trained personnel from the Institute had been sent to lend a hand.

The control booth was deserted.

Alec had never felt an odder sensation in his life. To anyone connected with laboratory practices involving micro-organisms it was as weird as going on to the bridge of an ocean liner and finding nobody there.

He was in a small cubicle, three of whose sides displayed the instrumentation for those laboratories connected to the system. And though Alec was not a scientist he could read-off most of the principal gauges . . . you do not spend years as an executive with a drug company without knowing the meaning of *p*H.

At first, all seemed normal and the readings steady. Then, on the panel relating to Lab Number One, tiny jiggers of an ultra-sensitive heat gauge caught his eye.

There were eight of these gauges, lined up in a row which corresponded to the actual positions, in sequence, of the relevant apparata.

And as he watched, so each meter jiggered in turn, as if someone was groping his way along the benches, steadying himself by clutching each cannister in turn, and therefore momentarily sending up the temperature with his hand.

An eerie feeling crept up Alec's spine. He'd just been in Number One and had seen no one.

Had someone been crouching in some dark corner, hiding from him? – irrationally petrified by the presence of a fellow human being?

Alec was just about to leave the cubicle to find out when an abrupt change in air pressure showed for Number One Lab. Someone had let the wind out, as it were, and the barometric level was rapidly reverting to normal atmosphere.

At the same time a red light started flashing over the panel.

This was not the time to dawdle about what to do next. Alec dashed out of Number Three and back along the corridor to the lift end of the hat-prong.

Even at the doorway, it was obvious the room temperature had risen. The reason was immediately obvious. Outside, it was already a hot June morning. And one of the thick, double paned windows had been smashed.

Outwards.

First, Alec ran to the master switch, which would automatically run-down the experiment and bring it to a safe and inert state. Then he went to the window, and looked giddily down to street level.

He could see where he'd parked his own car: he could see the sparse array of vehicles – some of them at odd, random angles – where by now each marked position should have been occupied by the vehicle for which it was reserved. He could see, in the distance, a thick, nose to tail clog of trucks and cars, solidly sealed east of the by-pass.

Then, directly below, he saw.

On the concrete, the flattened, splayed out body of the man who had just thrown himself out of the window lay impacted. The smashed arms and legs were spreadeagled in a crushed cruciform. Splattered blood, some of which had spewed over the car nearest the building, had gushed, jettisoned from the corpse.

For a moment Alec just stood and stared, feeling numb. And it must have been the shock of this spectacle that caused him to omit from this survey the notorious Lab Number Four – Crossley's own particular nursery from which outside visitors were debarred.

It had been two floors down, in the Neurology Wing, where Melhuish had last seen Crossley alive. So Alec took the stairs two at a time: then stopped dead at what he saw.

The image of the dead man lying far below on the concrete was immediately erased from his mind.

Death through violence is appalling enough to behold; living death stimulates a mental holocaust.

The Neurology Wing was a groaning, writhing melée of human agony. Why these people – if you could still call them people – had chosen to take refuge there wasn't apparent, unless, too late, they had somehow reasoned there might be a supply of Estofort with which to calm their minds. Alec now knew that in any case the drug could not have worked, once the victims had reached this hideously derelict stage.

Living death . . . Not one of these souls could respond to his presence. They were paralysed with terror. Some of them uttered little stammered fragments of incoherent speech. Their eyes were unfocused and some even out of alignment. There was the smell of fæces and urine and vomit.

Alec had had enough. He took the fire stairs at a rush down to ground level and arrived panting at the reception room.

Melhuish, still on the phone, reacted to Alec's cadaverous, drained expression with a dead calm. On the phone he said, very politely, 'Thank you,' to someone at the police station and hung up.

The two men stared at each other for a few seconds. Alec sank into one of the armchairs. There was nothing to say about what they both knew.

Drably, Melhuish reported his phone call. 'It took a long time to get through. When I did they were impatient and irritable, so I lied and said I urgently had to get a patient to hospital. I must have convinced them because they put me on to . . . I think it was a station sergeant. He said that normally they'd help out with a police escort, had I tried the ambulance service?'

Alec said, 'Awkward question.'

'Fortunately,' said Melhuish with that same dulled tone, 'he didn't give me a chance to answer. He said that in any case it was impossible. He said there had been a very large number of accidents in Staines, and that without exception all the roads in and out of the town were blocked. He suggested that I tried a hospital further West.'

'West.'

'Were you thinking something?'

'Melhuish, did the police mention anything *outside* Staines?'

'I don't quite see what you mean.'

Alec took him to the window. 'Look. Out there on the by-pass. The traffic is flowing quite normally. See?'

'Yes, that's why they thought I should head that way.'

'So if the traffic is travelling normally, it's for normal reasons?'

Melhuish tipped his head slightly to one side. Loose, rather ill-kept hair fell across his brow. 'I'm not used to thinking out this kind of problem, Mr Keeling.'

'You're going to have to start right now. I have a very strong reason indeed for telling you that.'

'All right. Let's say the accidents were all caused by people trying to get away from here in a hurry. If this . . . thing . . . spreads there, as it did here, they'll contaminate other people, in Staines. Therefore, any traffic actually leaving Staines and heading West – or any other way for that matter – may include people with this Virulent Panic. Well, you can't possibly tell the police that. Is that the kind of thing you're driving at?'

'Melhuish, how many capsules of Estofort have you got left? at home? . . . No don't worry, I'm not asking for them.'

Melhuish said, 'More than I have here.'

'You live out towards Camberley. Is that right?'

'Yes.'

'How many outside phones are there in the Hat-Rack?'

'There's a direct line in the Personnel Office. Among others.'

'Use it. Phone your family and tell them to be ready to leave for Exeter.'

'I can't. Three are at school.'

'Are they at school in Camberly? – or near it?'

'Yes but – '

'Then get them out. Phone your wife and warn her to be ready.'

Melhuish looked suddenly doubtful, tipping his head in that peculiar upward angle which went with the wall-scraping. 'Look, you'd better leave me out of this. My wife could never get things ready in time.' Clearly he was trying to cover for an inadequate woman, as if tact and loyalty counted more than actual survival.

Alec said, 'Look, if things are as bad as I think they are, we're going to have to ignore human suffering on a vast scale and keep just a few intact. You – and your family – could be among them. Or not.'

Melhuish looked down at those cracked shoes. 'I see. Put that way, it sounds pretty ruthless. You're thinking in epidemic terms?'

'You've seen what's happened here. Some of the victims have got as far as Staines – probably farther, by now. How can it be anything other than an epidemic?'

'But we'd be thinking only of ourselves.'

'No. There must be a Cadre, a set of Cadres, which can manage and run things and find a cure. Estofort is a new drug. There's very little of it, though we can step production up in Exeter – *provided* contamination doesn't spread to that area before we get there. We must recruit specialists – especially doctors – to see how this is happening, how it is spread, how treated, and how stopped. To do that, we have to *choose people.*'

'Mr Keeling, that is a terrible responsibility. I couldn't possibly involve myself.'

'How long do your pills last you?'

'About six hours.'

'Do a simple sum, Melhuish. All you have to do is to multiply the population of the British Isles by the number of pills there are. That will give you – assuming the pills could be equally distributed, which of course they can't – the net endurance of possibly the entire population as a sane species . . . unless and until we can contain the situation.'

Melhuish fidgeted with his fingers and looked blankly out of the window at those cars. 'You and I are standing here, making decisions for literally millions of people, because of something that neither of us even begin to understand.'

'That is precisely it.'

'Then I suggest you at least talk to Mr Nuttall. He's a lot

brighter than me and much more used to decisions.'

'We can't have him. He wouldn't contribute enough.'

'Then why me?'

'Because you care about people. Because you will carry out orders. And because, through your long experience here, you may ultimately help me throw some light on what happened last night. Now. Before I start my own telephoning, here's a job for you – which you do *after* you have made arrangements for your family.'

'I'll do my best, Mr Keeling.' – The old Melhuish still.

But Alec had a hunch such fawning phrases would soon dry off those rubbery lips. So he said, 'Get on to my people in Exeter. Pretend I'm not accessible. Speak to Administration and find out the name of the hotel – it's a brand new place screaming for business – where my company were considering holding their annual conference. I think you'll find they've booked the place piecemeal for next week. Probably, in view of this, the place is still empty.'

'Where is it?'

'Somewhere on the outskirts of Exeter. Find out exactly where. Then phone the hotel. Tell them the company have changed plans and will need it from tonight. The moment you've got that fixed, come back to me here, where I'll be using this phone. I want the address, phone number and capacity of the hotel.'

'What if I don't succeed?'

'I know you will.'

And still Melhuish dithered. It was infuriating, time-wasting . . . and yet it had to be tolerated and understood. Time spent now in rejuvenating a beaten man would show huge dividends later. Now he wanted to know, 'How will we pay?'

'By subterfuge. Either this dreadful disease catches, or it does not. If it doesn't, then somehow I'll square the hotel. If it does, who will know?'

'You're talking about death as if it could become commonplace.'

'I'm talking about survival for those that can make it.'

Melhuish said, 'There may be other drugs that'll work in the same way.'

'We can only discover that by experiment. We can only conduct such experiments in an atmosphere of order, not chaos.'

'I don't know. Mr Keeling. I just don't know.'

'What choice have you?'

'I can go home and exist until the pills run out. Or I can tell the medical authorities at the Ministry.'

'Melhuish! The medical authorities of your Ministry are *here!* This is their establishment for studying this kind of problem! And this is where the trouble has broken out! Can't you see what will happen if the news breaks?'

'But supposing this condition is only temporary?'

'The condition of the man who just threw himself out of the window can hardly be described as temporary.'

Melhuish stood quite still, folded his arms and said flatly, 'You're really saying it's every man for himself. Otherwise known as "Fuck you, Jack, I'm all right." '

That sounds more like it. The man was coming to life; challenging someone, within the authoritarian precincts of the Hat-Rack, in a way he probably hadn't considered in fifteen years.

Alec said quietly, 'Can't you imagine what it will be like if the entire country goes the same way as Staines?'

'We don't know how bad it really is in Staines.'

'Don't we? Look out of the widow and tell me what you see!'

Melhuish turned and looked. Beyond the airport, thick columns of smoke hung where before there had been only the baking sunlight.

'Well?'

'There do seem to be . . . several fires.'

'I'll say! And that's just the beginning.'

'You've made your point, Mr Keeling.'

'Good. Which is Dr Crossley's car?'

'The Dormobile.'

'I'm taking that. I shall need a lot of equipment from here. Did Dr Crossley's keys go down the lift shaft with him?'

'My God, you're a cool customer!'

'Did they?'

'No. He always keeps them in his desk.'

'I'll find them. Is your car big enough to take your whole family to the West?'

'No.'

'Steal one from the car park. If it's a matter of ignition keys, you may find one on the victim who threw himself out of the window.'

'Are you giving Mr Nuttall any chance at all?'

'Yes. I'll give him two of these capsules. That's long enough to allow him to get out of the area.'

'And will he believe you?'

'Only if he thinks of coming across to this building and taking a look . . . Oh, Melhuish. If you can, choose a car with a fitted radio.'

'What will I hear?'

Alec said, 'Pray God, just pop music. If this leaks out, no one gets a dog's chance. And the roads will be blocked from here to Kingdom Come . . . literally.' He saw that Melhuish still seemed irresolute. Alec was just about to give vent to pent-up impatience when Melhuish came out with it.

'There's something you'd better know. Mr Keeling.'

'Well? Go on!'

'I was hoping it might not be necessary to tell you. It makes things sound so . . . hopeless, I mean, getting down to the West.'

'Look, for God's sake man!'

' – One of the things the police said was that many of the sections of motorway have been closed.'

'But . . . why?'

'They didn't say.'

'But I can guess. Already there must have been multiple collisions.'

'They happen,' said Melhuish. 'It may just be coincidence.'

'Coincidence my third foot!' Alec treated him to a grim little smile. 'Knowing officialdom as I do, it wouldn't surprise me of those stretches have been closed for other reasons – an exclusive getaway for frightened ministers of the Crown . . . and their mighty friends.'

'Could they know, yet?'

'That's something we'll never know.'

THREE

In the blasting heat fortified by merciless, roasting tarmac, Diana pulled off the main road at Sunningdale. The radiator was boiling and she'd made it only just in time.

Diana switched off and opened the doors wide and told the children on no account to leave the car – promise? They did. Diana produced a ration of Jellytots and said to James, 'I'm putting you in charge. I'm going into the station.'

'Why?'

'To get some chocolate.' Actually she wanted to see if there was any sign of the abnormal there. Trains coming from London should contain evidence, if evidence there was.

Jennifer protested, 'I want to be in charge.'

Stephen said, 'Mummy, can't I go with you?'

'No, you help James.'

Stephen: 'Mummy, I must talk to you. I *must*.'

She hesitated. Those looks they'd exchanged in the driving mirror decided the issue. 'All right, you can come.'

James instantly: 'Why can't I? I'm the eldest, aren't I?'

Diana said, 'By about fifteen minutes. And it's because you're eldest that I'm asking you to look after Jennifer.'

Jennifer said, 'It's hot in the car. I want to get out.'

James said, 'Well, you can't.'

'Who says so?'

'I say so.'

They'd got through the barriers just before the red lights started flashing and a train came in. Now an impatient line of drivers stood, outside their cars, doors open, staring at the train as if it just had no right to be there.

Diana searched desperately among the leading cars to see if Alec was among them.

There was no Dormobile visible. So she took Stephen by the hand and walked into the station.

'Mummy?'

'Yes dear?'

'I don't know how long I can keep from frightening James.'

'We don't know that there's anything to be frightened of. Look at those cars. Obviously they're just people going on their holidays. Why do you think there's anything to be frightened of?'

'You.'

'I'm always nervous in heavy traffic. You know that.'

'But it isn't that. Besides, I saw lots of things happen on the road. Funny things. There was that car that suddenly swerved across the road and crashed into the railings. You saw it too, and you didn't stop. And I know you, Mummy. I know you would have stopped . . . If there wasn't something very big to be frightened of.'

Diana bit her lip hard and tried not to yell at him to shut up. And relentlessly he went on, 'And then there was that car with the people screaming in the back. You got past and you thought I didn't notice, but I did.'

Diana went to the barrier and bought a platform ticket. She turned to Stephen and saw that terrible, half-understanding in his face and she said, 'All right, Stephen. You and I have a secret. Now. We've got to keep it to ourselves. We mustn't be heard talking about it, or anything else. When Daddy gets here he'll be able to tell us what it's all about . . . ' (I sincerely hope.) ' . . . You wait here for a minute. If you overhear anything . . . funny . . . tell me later, when you can. But not here, not in the station.'

'Suppose Daddy *doesn't* get here?'

'He will.'

'But if he doesn't?'

'Then we'll be meeting him in Devon.'

'But – '

'*Stephen! For Christ's sake shut-up!*' Then immediately. 'Darling, I'm sorry. Mummy's worried.'

Stephen felt her hand for a second, just said, 'I know.'

Diana went through the gate on to the platform. It was the down-train side – the trains from London – and the stopping train which was holding up the traffic was still standing there.

Diana walked along the train casually. Peering into each compartment in turn, she tried to gauge whether there seemed anything odd about the passengers.

As far as she could see, there was nothing wrong. Pallid people, short of exercise and fresh air, read their papers and wiped their perspiring brows – it had been getting hotter all day and there was that strong thrumming heat-smell you get from electric trains – hot insulation and brakes, and slightly unfresh humanity.

A mother was fanning herself with a cheap woman's weekly, her two children squabbling over a doll which suddenly ripped in half and made them yelp with laughter. Farther along, a grim-looking man in a bowler hat, sitting opposite another grim-looking man, who probably had a bowler hat on the rack, but showed his balding, sweating forehead instead, looked as if he possessed some ghastly secret and Diana stopped for a second outside his compartment.

Then the grim one with the hat yelled, 'Got it! Three down, four across!'

The other man beamed and said, 'Aha! So have I.'

Diana went on until she was nearly at the rear of the train. Apparently the driver had walked all the way down from the front. He was talking to a uniformed man who could have been the station manager. Diana could only hear bits of the conversation.

At first it sounded merely calm and technical, something about the signals on a section of track between Sunningdale and London. Diana stood there, watching their expressions, almost certain by now that as far as the railway was concerned all was normal except for a signal fault. Only some instinct made her stay there a few moments longer.

'Diana!'

She turned round. The voice came from along the platform toward the station exit. Then she recognized him – an admirer from way back. Well dressed and all too hail and hearty, he strode up to her and grinned. 'How marvellous! Where did you spring from? Do you live here now, or something?'

'No. As a matter of fact – '

' – My God, but you look gorgeous!'

'You must be joking.'

'Joking! Good Lord. Wow, what a figure . . . I remember that bangle, by the way.'

She glanced down at it, suddenly remembered this man had given it to her. Now, he evidently thought it must be one of her most treasured possessions and threw her a ghastly conspiratorial look.

One of the railwaymen was pointing down the line where another train was waiting to enter the section. Diana decided to let the awful conversation continue, until she could glean a bit more about the signals. Was it the signals?

The admirer's caddish grin had changed into a nostalgic smirk. 'You're married with kids by now, I suppose?'

'Yes, we've got three.'

'Three! It's hard to imagine. You're ahead of us, then. We've got one, with another on the way. I married Lorna, you know.'

Diana couldn't remember who on earth Lorna was, but thought, poor Lorna.

He wasn't content, though, with swapping marital information. 'Must tell you, all these years later. Remember those parties in Sydney Street? – You know, Roger Lemmon's place? We had a secret ballot, one night, and voted yours the best bottom in Chelsea. If I may say so, it's certainly the best in Sunningdale! You don't mind? Well, Lorna is pregnant. Can't be perfect all the time . . . '

Out of the corner of her eye, Diana noticed that a third railwayman had joined the other two. He was holding a written message in his hand.

By now, the cars on the road, impatient a the long delay at the level crossing, were sounding their horns in chorus.

Lorna's oggling husband enthused. 'And the way you carry yourself! You really should play golf. You'd win every match because the fellas wouldn't be able to keep their eye on the ball, as they say.'

With an awful vulgarity, he was openly staring down at her crotch, noting the perfect fit of her slacks. Diana thought him unbelievable; as if those eyes – laughing, idiot's eyes – which now travelled up her body till they fixed upon her bust, would suddenly jump out of their sockets and alight greedily on her nipples.

However outrageous and dreadful he was, she told herself she mustn't give vent to offence, or the conversation would go on longer than was necessary. But the eyes remained in their sockets after all, and he looked at his watch, which was just visible in its setting of long black hairs growing around it on the wrist. 'My God, I must fly. Took the afternoon off for golf, then this terrible train. You were on it?'

'No. I'm meeting someone here.'

'Hasn't turned up, eh? Must be mad. I was saying. Line terribly delayed. There's been some derailment or some such, back towards London . . . Made us all frightfully late. Foursome, too. Always very irritable, foursomes.' He kissed her on the cheek like a train buffer overrunning the station. 'Gorgeous girl. Look me up soon. Phone me at the club. I'll give you lessons.' He grinned at the prospect, then walked away at an immense speed.

But he'd caused the necessary delay. The station official said, 'I can't get a word from Box 31. So we're not accepting any further trains coming East. Take it slowly. You'll get two reds at the junction if they can't get you through.' Then something Diana couldn't hear, because the cars all started hooting again.

Finally the driver said, 'Well, the whole thing scares me. Never known a driver take that stretch flat out. No wonder he came off. Bloody madman.'

The station official said, 'You'll be a witness.'

'And I'm not looking forward to that.' The driver turned, walked back past Diana to the front of the train. He seemed thoughtful and uneasy, shaking his head once or twice, as if he couldn't quite believe what he'd seen.

Diana got back to Stephen just as the train moved off. He clung to her, held on tightly, burying his head in her body for a moment, then recovered. They walked hand in hand toward the car. Clearly he must have seen something. For a little boy, thought Diana, he was amazingly calm.

Discreetly he told her. 'There was a man. Struggling. They brought him off the train, trying to stop him screaming. But he wouldn't. So they put a handkerchief round his face.'

'How many were escorting him?'

'There were three, at first. Then one of them ran away. For no reason at all, he ran away. The other two got the screaming man out of the station. Mummy, do you know hardly anyone noticed? They seem sort of blind, as if it isn't – I don't know – respectable. Somebody shouted about getting an ambulance. Then they went.'

Cars, so long held up at the crossing, were now pouring past. In the mini, Jennifer was crying. She said, 'James hit me.'

'I didn't.'

'He's fibbing, he's always hitting me, when you're not looking.'

Diana, watching each car and desperately looking out for Alec, managed to say something maternal which calmed things down. She was now worried about the traffic ahead. It had started off all right; but you could see, just beyond the village itself, that there was a long line of lorries, nose to tail, climbing the hill at inchworm speed. They weren't going to get past that in a hurry.

In her mind, she began a sort of desperate hate on Alec. How *could* he be so late? Surely he must know how she felt, how terrified she was for the children, how hard she was hanging on to her control?

Alec had said to wait until three. But how could she wait that long? What if things got really bad and spread as far as here before they could get away?

She was now quite convinced they were going to. There was too much circumstantial evidence – still under the surface, still being carefully suppressed, still on the whole ignored by the vast majority of the drivers, whose only anxiety seemed the normal one of getting to the coast as fast as possible, before the combination of traffic jams and a heatwave turned a holiday trip into a nightmare. Well, *they* hadn't any pills . . .

But no nightmare could possibly measure up to Diana's dream of Alec not turning up at all. The problems of the journey were clocking up in her mind. She'd got enough food and drink aboard; but if the mini had been overheating even when travelling at sufficient speed to ensure ventilation at the radiator, what would it be like in the crawl ahead? She thought of crossing to the garage with the idea of getting a new thermostat fitted. She ruled it out at once; the heat had caused similar breakdowns; cars were being pushed or towed into the garage forecourt and mechanics were shaking their heads and turning people away.

Small domestic matters arose in her mind as if they were major hazards too. Should she let the kids wet their pants rather than risk stopping, thus losing her place in the queue? And Jennifer wouldn't sleep in this filthy heat – suddenly Diana was hating her favourite weather – and would start carrying on, getting on her nerves, making the driving still more dangerous. Damn and hell to that garage that forgot to replace the thermostat!

But it was *not knowing* that really haunted her. They were running away, but what *from*? They were taking drugs, but against what? Suppose the drugs stopped working, or ran out? Would Jennifer or James or Stephen suddenly throw themselves, screaming, from the car? Would they spend a few days in Exeter, depending on a dwindling drug supply, awaiting instantaneous insanity, such as had overtaken that man being escorted from the station? How many people were those drugs intended for? How many days would they last?

Again, she caught Stephen's eye. She was certain he was, in his own way, thinking along the same sort of lines. Both of them glanced down at the box of drugs, then back at each other.

Oh my God.

Her fears were so pent up she wanted to rush into the fruiterers, right by the car, and tell that fat, self-possessed smiling woman weighing vegetables all about it. She wanted to say, how can you be so calm and normal? Don't you know what's really happening?

The woman looked up, for a second, and saw Jennifer, and smiled through the window, and Jennifer waved back, and Diana felt in that brief second that really nothing was seriously wrong, it was only a few people, some incident at the Institute had alarmed Alec out of all proportion. Was he overtired? Had she been neglecting him, thinking about the children too much, or just herself, and missed it? A crack-up, in Alec? It seemed unlikely. He was doing so well. There had been no sign at home, only her own sporadic fears about sex. And were they anything much? She'd talked to June about it once.

June's eyes had characteristically glazed over. 'Probably something to do with your cycle.'

'Are you ever like that?'

June had then suddenly remembered the kettle was on for the coffee. She'd gone out to fix it, then when she came back with the tray she had somehow forgotten the question.

Now, as Diana opened the bonnet, then gingerely turned the radiator cap, she thought of June standing so close to the phone and looking puzzled. And what of June now? And Richard? And Baby Caroline? Had Alec got through to them – or was June still frantically running out of the cigarettes she'd given up, plugging Caroline with rusks and panicking?

With a slight hiss the cap came off. Diana managed to get some water from a shop, replenished the radiator and slammed the bonnet shut.

So more waiting, more guessing, more fighting among the children. With the train out of the way and the barriers raised, traffic was pouring past. How long . . . ?

Then, just as she was steeling herself to go on in the mini, totally convinced that Alec was never going to arrive, he swung round the corner in the Dormobile and pulled up with a squawk from the tyres.

The relief overwhelmed her. She wanted to say something appropriate to the exhausted man at the wheel, whom in her stiff, suburban way she knew she loved.

She snapped, 'Where the hell have you been?'

'Things are a bit rough, back there. I thought I wasn't going to make it.'

'I wouldn't say I'd had a ball, either.'

'Let's not waste time, we'll get everything transferred.'

'You seem to have no end of junk in there already.'

'We're going to need this "junk".'

'Is that filthy old car reliable? Any more than this one?'

'Yes; I took twenty minutes having it checked. It's in good shape. Just dirty.'

Then, suddenly, Diana held on to him very tight. 'Sorry . . . sorry, darling. Don't take any notice.'

'I understand. You and the children. My God, what a responsibility. I was terrified myself. I thought we might miss each other, and then I remembered about the thermostat on the mini, after I'd phoned. I didn't think you'd make it even to here. And look how the traffic's piling up ahead.'

Diana watched, while a whole string of heavy lorries belched diesel fumes and revved furiously past them. 'We'd better just fling everything in the Dormobile and get away.'

'No. We'll do this properly. We don't know what problems we might meet further ahead.'

'Then we'll get caught forever in that traffic jam.'

'I'll break every law there is and get through. There's hardly anything coming back towards London, so I'll overtake the whole of this lot by using the eastbound lane.'

'They'll hate you all the way to Exeter, after that.'

'They won't catch up, once we've blasted our way through.'

'Alec? Are we just utterly ruthless and uncaring?'

'We'll leave the philosophy till later. But I can set your mind at rest about one thing. I got through to Richard. I didn't dare tell June. She's helpless there with a baby and no car. It's too late for Richard and June to come by road; and anyway there aren't any supplies of Estofort left in the south of London. We weren't the only ones to get on to that.'

'What the hell will they do?'

'Richard is trying to hire a minicab or something to get June and the baby up to Elstree. He's got a pilot friend at the airfield. If they can get a plane, they'll fly down to Exeter and meet us there.'

'Thank God. I felt terrible about that.'

'Let's get weaving.'

There were unforeseen problems to do with loading.

Because Dr Crossley had adapted the Dormobile as a kind of mobile surgery, there was a solid partition between the front seats and the rest of the interior, with only a small sliding hatch between. This was big enough for Jennifer to climb through but certainly not the boys. This meant you had to decide where people and gear had to be stowed to last the whole trip – or risk stopping every time somebody wanted to move.

Alec snapped, 'We'll need the roof rack off the mini.'

'Will it fit?'

'It's expandable.'

Diana looked at the big packing cases of electro-diagnostic equipment Alec had brought from the Institute. 'It'll never take those.'

'All right. The biggest case will have to go in the front. You'll have to squeeze next to it and we'll put all the kids in the back.'

'Wouldn't it be easier to have one of the children in front?'

'Diana, for God's sake! I've got to drive a gollumphing-great Dormobile flat out. I can't have children jumping up and down demanding ice-creams every five minutes!'

Diana was struggling at the bolts of the mini's roof rack, using the wrench. 'It won't shift. The bolts are rusted solid. We'll have to leave it.'

'We can't.'

Diana's face was contorted. 'Can't you *see*? The cars are packed almost solid right back to here already.'

'I'm not going to be rushed. I intend to get there. *We've* got pills – *they* haven't. Now, calm down and let's do things properly . . . ' So he had to go across to the garage for some easing oil and proper tools. There, harassed mechanics were already trying to cope with innumerable breakdowns which had cursed the improperly maintained cars of spontaneous holiday-makers. A large tip did it; but when he got back to the Dormobile, he found Jennifer subjecting Diana to a tantrum because she wanted to travel in front. That had to be solved with ice-cream – melting all over the seats. And it went on and on like this; the boys were over-helpful, trying to organize everything to show their metal and then having to be told, as tactfully as Alec's frayed temper permitted, that 'perhaps it would be better if we did it my way . . . ' which soon became, in desperation, 'You'll bloody well do what you're told.' Tears and rows ensuing.

Diana kept darting looks at the big clock over the garage. It was one of those gimmick things which rotate on their axes like a slowly-spinning coin. Visually quavering in the air convecting off the scalding concrete below, the hands seemed to jigger like elastic. But the mesage was clear enough. Time was racing as remorselessly as the traffic got choked. An ambulance, its bell jangling frantically, tore from a side turning and stopped with a screech of brakes when its driver found himself completely blocked off. A furious row developed between an idiot motorist, who wouldn't shift the necessary ten inches, and a truck driver who was trying to make room. In the back of the ambulance someone was flailing at the doors, hammering frantically. A face appeared at the ambulance window. Diana couldn't look. She knew. So did Stephen, who confided quietly, 'Sorry, Mummy, I've wet my pants.'

In Diana, sympathy triumphed over irritation – she whispered, 'You're being wonderful. Don't worry. We'll fix it in a minute. Just sit in the mini.'

Diana murmured something to Alec who had freed the bolts and was fumbling with adjustable tubes on the top of the Dormobile. He nodded and said, 'In a minute, in a minute. Fuck this bloody thing . . . ' And every time Diana drew attention to the clock, Alec kept saying 'Don't flap Diana!' And she kept retorting 'It's you that's flapping, don't blame me all the time' and then Alec had the idea of improving the ventilation in the back by getting a battery operated electric fan. Putting this in took a further twenty minutes but the results were well worth it.

Stephen was looking imploringly at his mother from within the mini, so Diana said to the others, 'Right. Lavatory for everybody. No arguments. Me included.' With the co-operation of the puzzled but sympathetic woman serving vegetables in the nearby shop, Diana shielded Stephen from further embarrassment. Then in relays they all followed. The woman, who saw the underlying urgency which so tautened Diana's face, couldn't understand all the elaborate arrangements she'd been watching through the window, but was well rewarded in the amount of fruit Diana bought, which she stuffed all over the wagon wherever it could be jammed in between children and boxes and spares and – a sudden afterthought of Alec's – pair of walkie-talkie radios he managed to track down at a local radio store. It was nearly half-past two when Alec said, 'Right, grit your teeth, Diana. I'm going to drive this thing like a madman.'

'You'll get stopped by the police.'

'I don't think so. You may not have noticed, but whole squadrons of police cars have been passing us coming from the west. Obviously, something's been happening behind us. Haven't you noticed how little traffic has been coming from London lately?' It was true; movement had practically dried up. And although the barriers at the level crossing behind them had gone down again – and apparently stayed down even longer than before, only half a dozen cars, of which three were merely local delivery vans, were waiting on the far side.

Diana said under her breath, 'We were only just in time.' She slid the hatch open and, with an effort, smiled brightly into the crammed rear of the wagon. 'You all comfy in there?'

With a certain degree of resignation – as well as exhaustion – they said they felt cooler and the fan was working well and there was enough seating to allow any two of them to loll back and doze at any one time.

Only Stephen remained alert. He gazed at his father thoughtfully through the hatch for a moment as if about to say something. Then Diana looked at him imploringly and he changed it and smiled and said, 'How fast will this thing go, Daddy?'

Alec said jovially, 'Let's see!' – and slid back the hatch. To Diana he said, 'Squeeze over a bit.'

'I can't.'

'Okay. We'll manage.' He started the engine and reversed on to the main road. 'Stephen knows.'

Diana said, 'Yes. As much as I do, anyway.'

He said, 'You'll soon know a lot more.'

Alec revved the engine and was away. Swinging immediately outside the congealed line of lorries and cars, he raced for Bagshot and – with a ruthlessness which shocked both himself and Diana – steered head-on for any cars coming from the opposite direction, forcing them to veer with flashing lights and blaring horns on to the opposite grass verge.

In half an hour they were well beyond Camberley, where the traffic, at last, had thinned. Momentarily Alec wondered if Melhuish had succeeded in leaving Camberley himself, by then.

Only one exchange passed between Alec and Diana prior to arriving opposite the old Blackbushe Airport. Alec, who had left the fiddling with the car radio to Diana, and was concentrating much too hard on race-track driving to listen for himself, had asked her, 'Anything been said?'

She shook her head. 'Not a word. I got both news summaries on Radio One. The biggest sensation to date has been a Wimbledon upset.'

'Oh? Who beat who?'

'God knows.' She put up a hand. 'Wait a minute. There's a road report . . . ' She turned up the volume, but Alec couldn't listen. For just then a police Jaguar, coming straight for them in the wrong lane, zagged crazily at a flat-out hundred then whipped across broadside. Digging in tyres till they exploded, the Jag rolled obliquely across toward the air terminal, crimping itself into a shapeless white ingot that cut a deep crevice in the road.

Alec had no time to think, just instinctively held the steering wheel firm and kept his foot down. Either they would hit or they wouldn't. Diana covered her mouth but her stifled scream was for the children. Without seat belts they had a chance of nil.

The Jaguar fireballed off the road on to the grass. What remained of the disembowelled rear end passed so close to Alec's window he could see the smashed wristwatch on a dangling arm.

It was gone. There was a minute's silence between Alec and Diana, with just the radio blaring as if nothing had happened.

Alec chose not to refer to what they'd just seen. He managed, 'What about the roads?'

Diana measured his tone. 'They've re-opened the Basingstoke section of the M3. All other motorways to the West will remain closed.'

He tried to smile. 'You managed to concentrate?'

'I had to,' she said, 'if you understand what I mean . . . '

FOUR

The creeping paralysis that had started at the Hat Rack, and then filtered with repressed menace first into Staines and then, more rapidly, farther East into outer London itself, brought an abrupt end to tennis just after Diana heard the score summary at three. The pretext for this, as announced flatly over the loudspeakers, was the threat of a freak thunderstorm, fictitiously forecast by a baffled met office, who were suddenly instructed to tell unheard-of lies upon an authority even weathermen couldn't ignore.

Although the instantaneous brain fever had not yet reached the crowded grass city of the Lawn Tennis Association, certain vague rumours had reached the BBC camera teams on the spot, via the line circuits back to the Television Centre in Shepherds Bush.

The notification of trouble – such as it was – still took a very indirect form. Power failures were occurring at various points along the grid line; an aborted take-off, with slight damage (no fire; no casualties) to a jumbo jet, had blocked one of the runways at Heathrow; and the television relay circuits, through which the tennis tournament had to be channelled to master control, were faltering. So far, only colour quality was failing. But since no one could raise the engineers concerned, either on intercom or by public telephone, the problem was perplexing, and most hurtful to the pride of the cameraman.

Much more significantly, the telephone system over a wide area was heavily overloaded and much of it apparently dead, as if multitudes of people, in the middle of their conversations, had broken off without either party hanging up. Thus even the automatic lines couldn't clear; and operator calls were becoming impossible.

Whitehall, slow to respond to anything – especially during lunch – had at last conceded that *something*, however little it actually concerned officialdom, was bunging up the works. The debate in the House of Commons was not, of course, interrupted – it concerned the introduction of a bill on restrictive practices in the resale of deep freezers – but a discreet message brought into the Home Secretary, who was bored stiff, caused him to leave the Chamber hurriedly and go to the nearest telephone.

What he learned, though more interesting than the intricacies of refrigeration, did not greatly enlighten him. He gathered that all was not well in Staines; and that all was not *entirely* well in Slough, though apparently most of the factories there were in normal operation. Since the Home Secretary had been educated at Eton – two miles out of Slough and to him a good deal more significant – he was eager to know if this whatever-it-is had affected the boys there? The voice on the other end, which did not belong to an enthusiast for practice-eights on the Thames, nor even the long drawn-out cricket games on – what's that? – Agar's Plough, could not supply the Home Secretary with this vital information. The caller had just begun a fresh sentence, however, when the voice suddenly rose to a scream. The line went dead and the Home Secretary, who didn't approve of people who for some reason couldn't keep their heads in a crisis, informed an Under Secretary curtly that somebody was either being a Damn Neurotic or playing Silly Buggers and would the Under Secretary kindly find out what was going on? The Under Secretary said yes, he would; and his superior went back to the Chamber to hear more about frozen chicken.

Since, by now, Staines Police Station had closed down, the Fire Brigade at Langley failed to turn out for a factory explosion; and all trains between Paddington and the West had come to a permanent halt, the Under Secretary was white as a sheet by the time he re-united with the Home Secretary in a frantic little confab held in one of those curious little gothic office places beneath Big Ben.

Oddly, the penetrations of this disease into the metropolis was on the one hand frighteningly fast and on the other peculiarly selective. A casual observer in Westminster Square would have been unlikely to notice anything amiss at all. All the year round people are taken ill; the urgent alarm bell of an ambulance careening through London streets is far from unique. The fact that there were slightly more of them than usual was not – as yet – particularly obvious.

The disease was picking off its easiest victims first.

By half-past three the neurological hospital in Russell Square had got its switchboard jammed. In the Information Room at New Scotland Yard high-ranking officers were exchanging long, hard stares. The markings on their wall map, relating to totally inexplicable events which were all so different it was impossible to find a common factor, had spread in larger and larger concentric rings from the trouble centre at Staines. As one superintendent put it, 'How do you relate a burned out power station to a barge collision in the Thames? – or a railway accident near Sunningdale to the ceasing all play, in bright sunlight, in the middle of a set, on the Centre Court at Wimbledon?'

As he spoke, a sergeant drew yet a further ring, much larger than the others. The circle he had drawn exactly intersected the county town of Andover.

* * *

Had they known it, Alec and his family were only just ahead of the symptoms' vanguard. Doing nearly ninety along the Andover by-pass they were still only ten minutes ahead of a multiple collision that had taken place on the section of motorway behind.

But however gruesomely unjust, the trail of bottlenecks spaced along the roads behind them was paying a dividend. It meant that the spread of plague to the south-west was being greatly slowed down. Traffic was thinning – you could see this clearly from the sparseness of cars on the by-pass – and therefore contamination in the general direction of Exeter was retarded.

'Diana, how are the children?'

She turned and quietly slid back the hatch. Then she closed it again. 'Miraculously, all three are asleep,' she said.

'But there isn't room.'

'Jennifer's lying half across Stephen's lap.'

Alec said, 'Bless him.'

'Better not do any sudden turns, Alec. She'll fall off.'

'There aren't any, till the roundabout the far end of this stretch.'

'I'm amazed,' she said, 'that they managed to sleep – I mean, all of them.'

'They're tired, and – to them – the worst of the crisis must seem over. Also, inevitably there must be some sedative element in Estofort.'

'But not,' she said, 'in you. Will this thing hold ninety without blowing up?'

'It's a Dormobile. It'll hold anything . . . Diana?'
'Yes?'
'Diana, we must. We must.'
'Must what?'
'It's . . . I don't understand it.'
'You concentrate on your driving.'
'Diana, for God's sake!'
'Alec, have you gone mad?'
'I don't know. It must be the instinct for survival, or something. Christ, don't you see how I feel?'
'Darling Alec, please use your head. Here? In broad daylight? . . . It's because I'm pressed hard up against you.'
'Well I'm sorry, but it's too late to wonder about why. There's a wood there.'
'Alec, we can't. We just can't.'
'To go on like this would be dangerous. My driving – '
'Oh, yeah?'
'I can feel how you feel, Diana.'
She said, 'It's reaction. It'll pass.' But her lips were parted in the most wonderful way. She felt half-breathless, detached from the pace of the journey, the meaning of the journey, the subtle and unnerving unknowns from which they were fleeing.
He looked at her and could only adore. He said frankly. 'You don't often feel like that. You know why?' He slowed the wagon. 'Cardboard houses. Thin walls and inquisitive people. Not quite the formula for hot pants.'
She said in his ear, 'There'd be quite a few inquisitive people if we stopped for that where we are now.'
'But you don't really care? – Do you?'
Her hand, not stiff and unsure as it so often was in bed, but soft and caressing and calamitously sensitive and intimate, rested now on his flies and that marvellous, lineless expression, that he'd hardly ever seen on her face since their honeymoon and a memorable holiday in Cyprus, erased all thoughts of any self-consciousness or suburban-acquired inhibition. Her back was hollowed, now, and she was undoing his flies and kissing him and there was frantic, unison breathing between them as, with almost superhuman control, he drew the truck to a crawl, then turned under some trees, as nearly as possible out of sight of the highway, and as bumpless as possible for fear of waking the children.
Before he'd stopped the engine they were convulsing like teenagers in some Chelsea bed-sitter, with the same sense of

bawdy abandon that went with the pop music faintly playing on the radio, the same mutual demands made upon each other to frankly exhibit such geometric displays as would excite as only the uninhibited may excite. In such frenetic committal they felt emotionally united in some unique way. Afterward they didn't even remember whether or not they'd got out of the truck – probably must have done because there simply wasn't room inside – but found themselves lying half-stripped on warm grass, conscious eventually of the sound of crickets and the indefinable hum of living creatures around them, and feeling, in their souls, a strange peace and an unbelievable release, so that anything seemed possible, and anything *was* possible, even survival.

Frownlessly, without a muscle visible in her face, she turned her head to his and said, 'I shall never understand, Alec.'

'I know. Don't try.'

'It must be something . . . '

He covered her lips with his hand, adoring but not wanting the intrusion of mere words . . . So just her hands, soft yet contradictorily alert and entwined and responsive in his, conversed about their survival so far, conversed about the safety – so far – of Jennifer and James and the ultra-astute little face of Stephen, and how he must be guessing something of this, even in sleep, and how it would help him somehow, because, in his awareness, he was more deeply affected than the others by the underlying terrors which were so hidden in the hot sunlight of the approach to Salisbury Plain.

Diana and Alec got back into the wagon without a word. No quivering in his hands now; no quickened heartbeat and excessive pressure, no more actual pain across his chest. Assuaged and massaged into some other dimension which for a time would remain unseen and unfelt, he drove fast and drove relaxed.

Diana felt a warmth of confidence in his driving where before her heart had been in her mouth at the risks he had been taking, passing other cars with minimal margin of safety, taking bends on brakes and tortured tyres, over-revving a protesting engine and sending up even the Dormobile's lethargic temperature gauge into the red segment.

The heat outside too was diminishing; it came up from the road still, but the sun, getting lower and almost due west, no longer blistered the rubber fittings into that acrid stink, nor heated the upholstery so that your clothes stuck to each other in an itching, saline sweat-seal. Yet driving west half-blinded you . . .

Alec said, 'The sunglasses. Did we bring them?'

Diana groped for them in the glove-box, handed Alec's across. She said, 'Have you noticed anything?'

He nodded. 'Fewer cars. That snarl-up has given us time in hand. Sunningdale, Bagshot, Camberley – that accounts for a hell of a lot of cars.'

'They'll find another way round,' she said. 'We'll meet them crossing the Plain from Devizes.'

'Not if I keep my foot down, we won't.'

There came a rap on the sliding panel behind them. It was Stephen. He was still a little sleepy, more in repose. 'Did we stop, Mummy?'

Diana touched his head lightly and smiled. 'Yes for a while.'

'Why?'

Diana said, 'Daddy wanted a rest.'

'Oh. Was he very tired?'

'Well you see, there's quite a long way to go, yet.'

Stephen nodded thoughtfully. 'Yes. Things seem better now. I think we'll get there all right.' Having satisfied himself on this point, he withdrew his head and slid the hatch tight shut.

Diana kept the mood light for a while by describing her absurd encounter, on the platform of Sunningdale station, with the golfing roué. Alec asked inscrutably, 'How many more of those did you discover, in your Chelsea era?'

'Nobody quite like him. He was an invader from Kensington, anyway.'

'Is that different?'

'A different race altogether. I don't think I ever received attentions quite like that in my sweater and jeans stage . . . much later on there was a rival for sheer vulgarity, though.'

He glanced at her. 'That must have been after we were married.'

'It was. One of your more gruesome office parties.'

'Oh? Who?'

'A man called Jimmy Nuttall . . . Why does that make you flinch?'

'Nothing personal. Go on about him.'

'I've annoyed you, now.'

'No.' He took the roundabout – gently, so as not to jog the children. 'There's quite another reason. You never mentioned this before. Why didn't you tell me?'

'You had to go on working with him. He's a slob and I think you would have got in a temper if you'd known. If you remember, things were a little . . . taut . . . between us, just then. Why?'

Alec said, 'He was there this morning – intact. I could have brought him down to Exeter. But I don't trust the man.' He gave her a look. 'Not just the kind of thing you've just mentioned.'

Diana said, 'A man who was more trustworthy in the sense you mean would probably have been better at it.'

'Making a pass?'

'Well, he struck me as singularly unloved. He probably "gets them" – as he would put it – but the performance hardly appealed to me. If Jimmy Nuttall found out about what you're going to try and do – this plan of yours, the cadre centre and so on – what would he do?'

'I don't see how he can know. Melhuish certainly didn't say anything and we made sure no calls went through the switchboard.'

'I wouldn't underestimate a stoat like him. Was he the only one sane, this morning? – apart from Melhuish?'

'Yes. And I'm afraid he still is.'

'You gave him pills?' She saw him nod, and she went on slowly, 'It's an awful thing to say, but I wish you hadn't.'

'I couldn't just leave him there to rot.'

'Nobody decent would.'

He said. 'You must have learned quite a lot about him in a short time.'

She shuddered. 'He treated me to a view of his boring prick.'

'What!' He changed down savagely for the next bend. 'What did you do?'

'Told him to trade it in for a better one.'

* * *

At the time when Nuttall put his call through to Alec's head office in Exeter – and it took him an hour of patient waiting to get through – there was no hint of crisis beyond the precinct of Staines and the surrounding area.

Nuttall, never unruffled by telephones, felt quite certain that if he tried long enough he was bound to get through. The line to Exeter was on STD; long distance lines to the south west were heavily overloaded but functioning. All Nuttall had to do was sit back, slouched as usual, and continually dial and re-dial until he got results. He could do this like an automaton; it required no thought and no effort. Eventually his patience was rewarded.

When he'd got the right man he said. 'You may know that Alec Keeling is off ill today.'

'We did wonder. We got a rather garbled message from a Mr Melhuish, asking us to confirm the annual conference. It seemed a bit odd.'

This was a break Nuttall hadn't expected. 'I share the liaison office with him here at the Institute. He phoned me up from home . . . Could I know who I'm speaking to, please?'

'Maynard.'

Maynard . . . Nuttall had heard the name mentioned by Alec often enough, not always in very flattering terms. And in Nuttall's judgement the voice sounded *marleesh* . . . there was a couldn't-care-less note in it, as if Maynard was one of those who had been passed-over for promotion.

Nuttall's tactic was therefore to proffer a minor carrot, re-alerting, if not ambition, at least a shortcut to opportunity. 'Alec thinks that the latest craze over at the Hat-Rack might improve relations between your company and the Ministry.' – This assertion was based on solid ground; it had always been a bitter bone of contention that Alec's company had taken all credit for the development of Estofort – when in fact a Ministry man – Dr Crossley, no less – had done the basic research.

Maynard replied cynically, 'That wouldn't do us any harm.'

Nuttall said, 'Apparently there are some matters coming up this morning at the weekly conference which concern the export distribution of your drug Estofort.'

Mildly enough, the voice at the far end audibly raised a pair of puzzled eyebrows. 'Export? I don't see how that concerns the pundits over at the Hat-Rack.'

Nuttall fiddled with the second capsule Alec had given him, rolling it this way and that, then spinning it round, till it jumped into the paperclip tray. He said, 'I can only pass on what he told me. The experts in the Hat-Rack want to do a detailed survey of the effects of Estofort throughout the world. What they intend to do is to identify actual consignments going out from ports in Britain, then get back reports from each foreign buyer with numerically associated details, assessing consumption of the drug in various areas by locating the destination of each of your consignments. This will be fed into a computer, so that –'

' – Look! Take it easy! I don't want to know all that stuff. Just tell me what you want and we'll try to do it.'

Nuttall smiled faintly to himself, having got precisely the answer he wanted. To a man like Maynard, with his dulled thwarted mind and flat, unimaginative personality, opportunism was one thing: meticulous detail was quite another, Nuttall said, 'I agree it's very involved. What the Ministry wants is a list – now – of the present consignments waiting to be exported, together with a note of where the various crates actually are . . . You know, which wharf, and if possible, the actual shed.'

'They're not asking much, are they?'

'Alec Keeling says they can't do the survey unless they place special tags on the crates themselves. The Ministry will liaise with the appropriate port authorities.' – Nuttall knew in any case that Alec's company always used the same shipping company and what he was now hoping for was an instruction from Exeter to the shippers, to provide him with the schedules. It was a long shot but a paying proposition if it worked.

The voice at the far end sounded tired at the thought. 'We can't arrange it direct from here in any case. The factory output at Exeter is all handled by the contract shippers, once it reaches their depot in London.'

Yes, but *which* shippers? . . . Nuttall feigned impatience. 'Look, I've got my own problems. My own company's involved in the project and at the same conference I've got to – '

' – What time does this conference start?'

'In half an hour.'

'And does Alec honestly expect – '

Nuttall lowered his voice. 'What Alec thinks is that this might be a bit of a leg-up for you personally. The Ministry are hot on this idea; my company are providing computer aids and it's not doing me any harm, either. How about it, Mr Maynard?'

'Alec mentioned my name? – personally to you?'

Nuttall detected the faint note of surprise and dealt with it. 'He wanted this to go through you for reasons you probably appreciate.' – This guess actually had no meaning for Nuttall himself. Would it for Maynard?

Apparently it did. 'I think I understand,' said Maynard. 'Tell you what I'll do. I'll call Rotoport immediately and see if they have the information to hand. If they have, they can phone those crazy professors in the Hat-Rack, who can then arrange to stick on any beastly tags they like. But some of the stuff may have already gone through Customs, so the Ministry will have to square them too.'

Rotoport! Thanks very much, whoever you may be . . .

Aloud, Nuttall said, 'Okay. I'll be over at the Hat-Rack myself by then. Why don't you get Rotoport to call me there?' He gave the number of the direct line in Reception. 'It's my computer we have to program; we can save time.'

'Yes but . . . ' Maynard now reverted to the buck-passing caution of the second-rate executive hanging on by his false teeth. 'This really should be referred,' he said, 'to a higher authority.'

'There's hardly time for that, is there?' Nuttall kept all trace of concern out of his voice. 'None of my business, of course, but will your people in Exeter exactly thank you for questioning the requirements of the Ministry? – I would have thought the whole point of this liaison office is to see that they get what they want when they want it.'

'I just don't see why they want the actual *schedules*, Mr Nuttall.'

Nuttall replied immediately, 'If the consignment numbers aren't registered from the beginning they can't identify the consignments with the read-outs they hope to get at the end of the survey . . . Look, if you can't manage it, I'll just have to tell the Director it can't be done. But he won't like it.'

The voice contrived sweet repose. 'You may assure him that we'll do everything we can. And thanks for your help. Tell Alec to ring us when he's in better shape.' And a tart postscript: 'Then perhaps he can explain why this wasn't anticipated and arranged in reasonable time.'

FIVE

Melhuish concluded that never in his life had he been anywhere as normal as Exeter.

It was Thursday and it was cheerful and still warm, though not with that drumming, almost audible heat that had made stretches of highway feel yesterday like Colorado desert plains.

Complying with a message received from Alec, Melhuish rode the five sets of escalators all the way to the top of Bobby's – Exeter's largest department store – through lingerie (Melhuish was always a bit embarrassed by lingerie) and through carpets, then summer dresses, children's wear, finally washing machines and television. The argy-bargy of busy shoppers, all so casual and chatty and complacent, seemed unreal. He couldn't feel part of it; feeling, rather, that if he suddenly addressed one of these people they wouldn't notice him, as if he were somehow invisible.

By ten o'clock exactly he was sitting comfortably in the top floor restaurant, choosing a table by one of the big windows through which you could see a quarter of a mile down the High Street toward the cathedral.

The restaurant was nearly empty – the main coffee insurgence would begin at ten-thirty. So he just sat there waiting; and marvelled that he had in fact managed to arrive there at all.

He very nearly hadn't. Melhuish and his unkempt family had finally fled from Camberley like refugees from a volcanic disaster area – but not before interminable delays.

Initially trapped for two hours in the traffic hold-up which Alec had roared past on the wrong side of the road, Melhuish could do no such thing, even if his timid nature permitted it. For the westbound cars were crammed in four broadside lines reaching hedge to hedge all the way to Bagshot. Once through this, Melhuish found his wife so unresponsive that she just shuffled about making cups of tea and telling him everything would be all right, dear.

Not until the crawling procession through Camberley abruptly became a panic-stricken orgy of hysteria could she be made to react. News from back east – distorted and obscured but nonetheless terrifying – had become a force from the rear which at times led to cars ahead being physically rammed onward by those behind. The chorus of horns became a death wail.

On the phone, Melhuish managed, through patience and pleading, to retrieve his school-age children from school. They arrived home panting but emotionally inert, like their mother. Only then could the crucially last-ditch departure be attempted.

Melhuish had to join the main road at a T-junction in the town. It was clear that no one in this solid phalanx would give way, even if it were possible without being rammed from behind.

Melhuish switched off the engine; and without indulging idiot hero-worship, tried to imagine what Alec would have done. At the junction there was a building site; and stacked near one of the cranes was a pile of steel girders. With the help of two of the older children, he managed to slide the top girder away, then thrust it across the nearest traffic lane. Livid with rage the drivers trapped behind the girder tried to bulldoze it aside; but it jammed under the front suspension of the leading car; and during the time it took for the infuriated occupants to free the mechanism and swing the girder back off the road, Melhuish had taken the corner and was safely in the line of traffic.

Then, sandwiched between overheating trucks which clonked in short surges along the A30, Melhuish issued capsules of Estofort and tried not to count the number left in the bottle.

Cases of sudden disorientation were occurring – even this distance from Staines – and they were the more conspicuous for the compactness of the traffic. Unlike Diana, Melhuish could not distract his children's attention from such episodes, though at least there was no intuitive Stephen among his five offspring to see the significance of these episodes. His wife thought the drivers were simply drunk.

The tension was at explosion point by the time he had crawled on only a few miles to Blackbushe Airport – that humbled and forlorn refuge for light aeroplanes and propeller-driven ruffians now superannuated and only occasionally loaded with cargo for short hops on the cheap.

But the flashpoint did not come from the drivers on the road.

From the sky a crazily ill-controlled airliner suddenly descended to zero feet and attempted a wheels-up landing at terrifying speed.

The result was predictable. With a series of stupefying explosions the landing became a convulsive series of cart-wheels, while huge pieces of torching magnesium-alloy erupted like vivid pyrotechnics, rocketing upward, then down on to the road. A tanker lorry, punctured by burning debris, split like a frail meringue and blew up. Ahead and behind, the flames spread both ways along the highway, blow-torching from car to car with increasing velocity, till a huge line of burning cars and carcasses formed a flarepath nearly a mile long.

With inspiration Melhuish didn't know he even possessed he swung off the highway in the wake of the airport's fire engines. If he succeeded in passing the blazing wreck of the airliner he thought he might just manage to run the length of the airfield and still rejoin the highway at the far end, while shock of the appalling spectacle still paralysed the cars up front, so they didn't at once close the gap.

It worked; and behind him now stretched a white-hot fuse which had been motor cars and holiday people but was now a mile-long funeral pyre for screaming families.

Melhuish found himself overpowered with a sickened sense of guilt and injustice. The experience consolidated on his determination to somehow repay what survived of humanity.

With his wife complaining about the discomfort, he hadn't made the journey in one day but spent the night by the roadside a few miles outside Sparkford. From there he phoned the Dorrington Hotel in Jaybury, found that Alec Keeling had safely arrived. Melhuish got off in Exeter, sending the rest of the family on to Jaybury, driven by his eldest son – who didn't possess a licence . . .

So, in the men's room of Bobby's Store he got a shave, straightened his tie, combed the strands of hair with which he still managed to conceal most of his baldness, and reversed the handkerchief in his breast pocket to show the cleanest side.

Before him, now, was a modest order of coffee ('I like it very weak, please') and toast. He couldn't manage the toast – could still smell burning flesh, still see Crossley's tormented, warped features as he ran from the neurology wing, still recall the gut-exploding thrump of the body on the concrete which had crashed through the lab window up top. Sipping prissily from the coffee cup, he waited there for Alec.

Alec, a paper under his arm, not a London paper but the local one, came without a word to Melhuish's table and poured himself a coffee. Then he indicated the short paragraph at the foot of the front page. It referred briefly to traffic congestion at Staines – with some note about a new one-way scheme proposed by a Ministry spokesman. On the back page, in the Stop-Press column, there was a guarded report of an air disaster at Blackbushe . . . 'Flow of holiday traffic was affected for several hours. There were some casualties. Names will not be released until next of kin have been informed.'

Melhuish nodded and handed back the paper. 'What about radio and television?'

Alec sharply flicked the newspaper to warn Melhuish. Three fat female shoppers were hovering nearby. Weighed down by bulging parcels, they hesitated as if about to squeeze themselves in at the next table. But evidently they considered Alec's T-shirt ill-chosen and they waddled off to the far side of the restaurant, rustling their parcels petulantly, then snapping at a thin but firm-busted waitress on the urgent subject of gateaux. The waitress, who may well have been to bed overnight but certainly hadn't slept, had love bruises clearly visible to anyone qualified to recognize them. The ladies were not. But they knew a cake-trolley when they saw one; and grabbed at the sickliest with predatory impatience, talking through mouthfuls of synthetic cream.

Alec tried to visualize them suddenly overtaken by Virulent Panic but his imagination failed him. He said, 'I got here too late last night to see any television but I gather the national network broke down during the afternoon. Television here then resorted to local programmes – mostly repeats and old films but one or two interviews and some horsey scenes, from some agricultural show. As a further check on communications I tried a few experimental phone calls. You can't get anything east of Sparkford or north of Bristol.'

Melhuish described the terrible scene at Blackbushe. 'We were among the last to get through.'

'Did any other drivers sleep overnight by the roadside?'

Melhuish said, 'Only people who'd been hauling caravans. It's normal for them to leave London and places at the crack of dawn and take two days for the journey.'

Alec nodded. 'I saw some of them kipping down on my way through. Most of them were nearer here, just before the Exeter by-pass.'

'But some of them stayed over longer than they normally would. There were a lot of tents up, by the roadside.'

'Why?'

'Waiting for friends who didn't get there,' said Melhuish. 'I talked to an AA patrolman. He said it's common practice for groups to join up near Exeter, then go on in convoy to Cornwall. But the police were trying to move people on, because the expected friends just hadn't turned up.'

'Most of them never will.' Alec glanced at the cake addicts. One woman, with blue hair rinse, suddenly burst out laughing. Visible cake crumbs were jettisoned from her mouth as she did so. They landed on the trolley. The shagged-looking waitress hastily wheeled it out of range. 'So for the moment these people down here are immune?'

Melhuish said soberly, 'But it won't last long.'

'It's got to last long enough for us to get organized. I have an appointment at Sindham Hospital in a few minutes, where I'm trying to gather a specialist research group. It's not easy. Most of them critically underestimate the problem and ironically I have to be careful how much I say for fear of starting a public scare. I'm getting treated as a kind of crank.'

Melhuish said flatly, 'Ever known that not happen when something new develops?'

'Some of them have little excuse for it. For instance, the factory research people. I talked to our chief scientist, Dr Blessing, he always wants everything both ways: now sees an opportunity for recognition of the drug by the sceptics – yet won't accept why it's needed. My plan is to see him at the factory after I've got some backing from Sindham Hospital . . . I've got certain evidence – '

' – What evidence?'

'I'm coming to that. The point is that even at the Sindham there are opponents to Crossley's work. But Crossley had friends there. If my "evidence" is enough to carry weight with the Sindham they may back me up in my proposals at the factory.'

'Which are?'

'To freeze all supplies of Estofort and hold up outgoing consignments. The trucks normally go out today and will be loading now. Then I want export orders – lying about Britain in various ports – to be impounded and placed under guard.'

'How long will those supplies hold out? – Even if you persuade them to go that far?'

'Not long. But the factory could almost double its output

if they drop the bloody aspirins and things. Yet if I can't convince people in time, the plague will penetrate to here – factory and all – before protective drugs can be issued to key personnel.'

Melhuish said, 'What about the County Council? – Couldn't they cordon off this whole area? Close all roads?'

Alec said, 'Even if it isn't too late for that already, we can't convince the Council in time. They may suspect something is wrong but they wouldn't swallow what we know.'

Melhuish's large, sad blue eyes assumed again that unswerving stare. 'And, of course, the need for selection? – Are you still sticking to that?'

'To the limit, Melhuish. Qualms of conscience may tempt you to deviate from them.'

Melhuish seemed a far cry from the sycophant who flattened himself against walls. 'You can't very well stop me if my conscience dictates a need to disregard that understanding.'

'I'm hoping,' said Alec, 'that trust in me might. I got you here – that's no justification in itself. Except it does mean my judgement has so far been expedient if not actually virtuous.'

Melhuish said, 'I shan't act against you without consultation.'

Alec choked back a furious urge to remind Melhuish of how things might have been had he not taken him into his confidence in the first place. And yet he knew that the resuscitation of Melhuish's self-respect – whether due to him or not – was as vital a tool in this affair as any. So he just said, 'I appreciate that.'

'What is this evidence you have for the Sindham Hospital?'

'An actual victim, Melhuish.'

'But – '

'I know what you're thinking – the danger of contamination. But I don't believe this virus idea . . . nor do you, really . . . and one of my reasons for getting you down here is to tell me all you can remember of Dr Crossley's work.'

'He never let any of us into Number Four Lab.'

'Then I shall have to get back there and take a look.'

'You'll never make it.'

'The Sindham people will need any data they can get. Estofort isn't an antibiotic; nor is it a vaccine. It's doing something to people that protects them from something quite different. We have to find out what.' Alec lowered his voice again as the waitress approached. 'So I found a sufferer, gave him intravenous sodium-amytal, and – this will horrify you, I'm afraid – strapped him to the roof rack under a tarpaulin. He's only slightly more comfortable now; but don't look at me like that, he's been unconscious all the time.'

Melhuish didn't betray his feelings. 'Who is he?'

'He's a superintendent of police from the Windsor area. For some reason people seem to think that policemen don't usually go mad – I'm banking on it. But this one did. When we picked him up he'd smashed his car into something like a ham sandwich and killed his passengers outright . . . Look out! – the waitress.'

'Cakes, Sir? – She had a kinky, under-nourished sex-appeal in direct conflict with the sticky cakes. Melhuish, undisturbed by women for some years, because he knew he couldn't disturb them, noticed how acutely aware was Alec to the female, even at such a time.

The observation twanged a vague memory of Crossley – one of the few tangible clues to the man's work. Melhuish couldn't tie it down. But it seemed to belong . . .

The girl's knees brushed Alec's. It wasn't deliberate. But a tiny smile passed. The girl shook her head a fraction, you're nice, but I'm booked . . .

'Cakes,' she said firmly.

Alec remembered the spittle spouting from Blue Hair Rinse across the way and decided against the cakes. The girl wheeled the trolley away.

Melhuish tactfully prompted Alec. 'You put this policeman under sedation. What happens when he comes round?'

'We know. Don't we? He'll be as insane as before. Even if I'd given him Estofort he'd be as insane as before. It's a one-way trip.'

'Where is he now? – If not still on the roof rack?'

'Lying asleep in the back of the Dormobile – strapped down to the floor; the car's on the top storey of the car park.'

'My holy God.'

'I've covered him with a blanket, no one will see. From earlier experimentation, he should stay under – from that enormous dose – for a further two hours. But we can't feed him. He can't drink. And even if they manage to force-feed or drip him at the hospital he won't be any different, once conscious, to your own Dr Crossley. He's just organic evidence. I'm hoping it may be enough to convince . . . Listen, stay with your coffee, I have to phone Sindham. There's a phone in the restaurant foyer. I'll be right back.'

Alec went out there and dialled. The number came through normally but his contact at the hospital said, 'Can we delay this thing till after lunch? I can't seem to get hold of all these people you want and no one can quite understand why it's so urgent. They've got their jobs to do.'

Alec damned them all. 'They've got a bigger one on now.'

'You haven't yet said why.'

'Am I coming through your hospital switchboard?'

'Of course.'

'Have you a direct line to the Registrar?'

'Not,' said the voice curtly, 'for you. Only top emergencies from the other hospitals and you're not having *that* number.'

Alec forced control on himself – he knew that if he showed alarm it would detract from credulity. 'What's the earliest time they can manage?'

'Two p.m.'

Alec said, 'Get them to make that a promise. I have a feeling that by that time they'll be only too glad to get there!' He slammed the phone back, and the girl at the desk looked at him sympathetically. Alec wondered for an instant what she thought his fury was about. Her deductions must have been wildly out, for she just went on filing her fingernails and said, 'You won't have any luck with the waitress, either. I notice everything.'

Back with Melhuish, Alec reported the result.

Melhuish nodded. 'It's what you feared. What will you do?'

'Reverse the order. I'll go to the factory first and locate those export consignments and see about a production step-up. The trouble is, this way round it won't work nearly so easily. Without the Sindham Hospital having a chance to examine the patient first I may meet a blank wall. Dr Blessing is hardly my favourite man and has always been pathologically jealous of Crossley. But I've no option; I just can't turn up at the Sindham with that victim without the Crossleyites being there.'

Melhuish said, 'Don't forget your policeman will need another shot.'

'Good point. Now, Melhuish. Do some shopping . . . some plain ordinary shopping, around this store – carrier bag and all.'

'Why the shopping?'

'Because there are bound to be rumours and people will be watching for anything unusual. If they spot us they'll track us and when they know what's needed they'll fight for Estofort like madmen. Keep a sharp look-out for two things; latent symptoms and on snoopers. Any idea what developing symptoms of Virulent Panic may look like?'

Melhuish paused a bit. 'It all happens so fast.'

'But something must come first. Think.'

'No honestly . . . '

'Melhuish, you dreamy old Grade-Three layabout! I said, *think*!'

He did. 'All right; one thing. Not very conclusive. One or two of the Hat Rack people had been complaining, for several days, of insomnia. They did look a bit red eyed but as they never get any fresh air they often do. I didn't take much notice at the time. They stay up and worry; they watch television until close-down; they eat badly and try alcohol and turn up with hangovers; they fumble their work a bit and then seem to go through a short period when they're perfectly normal . . . Until.'

'You never said this before.'

'You asked me to think. I'm not used to it yet. Also, I may be being wise after the event. We're an indoor-loving society at the Institute. Only the golfers get the sun. I may be imagining it.'

'But if you're not – '

'If I'm not, this thing may not be always as sudden as we thought at first.'

'Always?'

'Well,' said Melhuish, 'suppose the ones with the more gradual symptoms are carriers?'

'Carriers.' Alec stared at him. 'You *are* thinking. My God, they could be among us and no one would know until somebody flipped . . . So we may have two types to cope with; two manifestations of the same disease. Analogue to Typhoid.'

'It's only an idea, Mr Keeling.'

Alec grinned across at him. 'Man of ideas – what about man of action, too?'

Melhuish's expression remained precisely the same – correct, inscrutable, unhumorous. 'Have you something in particular in mind?'

'I want you to beg, borrow or steal a short-wave radio transmitter. A receiver as well. Combined – as they often are – the two are known as a transceiver.'

'Won't you need two? – You're thinking of your plan to go back east? – communications between us and you?'

'I am. But I'll pick one up for the car on my way. If things get . . . as we think they're going to get, that won't be difficult. But you'll need a set for this end.'

'Those walkie-talkies you brought with you won't do?'

'Not for this. They're short-range gadgets which may come in useful. But I've got to be able to talk with Jaybury from Staines.'

Melhuish said, 'A list of radio-hams from the post office might help me. I'll try. How do we get the set to the Dorrington Hotel without being seen?'

'Have it boxed – try and use a refrigerator box . . . washing machine . . . anything that will disguise it. Then leave it for me to collect. Use a taxi to get it as far as the car park behind this store, leave it with the car park attendant for me to load on to the Dormobile later. Give my name.'

Melhuish, who held his coffee cup in that way which would have so maddened the inhabitants of the Glenmore Estate, took one more prissy little sip and replaced the cup exactly in the centre of the saucer. 'I admire your foresight, Mr Keeling. At least we have a few hours grace. Look outside. All those shoppers. Suppose they knew?'

* * *

But where radio-telephone had been in routine use, as at Exeter Airport, the story was different. There, ever since the tennis stopped the previous afternoon, a security blackout had been imposed and with it some very strict embargoes on landings made, or rather attempted, by aircraft arriving from the East. For instance, the light plane in which June and Richard and Baby Caroline had made their exodus, on Alec's tip-off, was denied clearance to land. So the pilot tried to ignore the tower's instructions and throttled back for an approach.

Promptly, fuel bowsers, jeeps and fire tenders were driven out at high speed and parked at tactical positions on the airport, making an illicit landing impossible.

'My God,' said the pilot, 'they must have the wind up.'

June held more tightly to her baby. The baby started to cry.

The pilot said, 'Shall I radio that we've all taken the drug?'

Richard said, 'For Christ sake don't.'

The pilot shrugged. 'Okay. So we find a field somewhere and land in that. We might as well make it near your hotel. What's the place? – Jaybury?' He banked away to the south-west and studied the map on his knee.

* * *

Since the moment at Glenmore when Diana Keeling had finished her coffee, after Alec's clandestine phone call, events had soon begun to seem unreal to June. In this she differed fundamentally from Diana. June didn't have the same sort of awareness anyway. Tense by nature, she had learned ever since childhood to conceal internal pressure by a sort of slowed-down casualness; often, when her voice sounded at its most relaxed, her body was at its most taut. At those times when her eyes took on their characteristic opaque-looking glaze, her thoughts ran counter to the words she used to express what she *ought* to have been thinking.

Since pregnancy and subsequently since Caroline's birth, June's whole metabolism had tightened a notch or two – a process hard to spot, in her, both because of the elaborate precautions she took against other people's observation, and through the more mundane fact that she had not yet slimmed down to the vital statistics she would have preferred. She still looked predominantly maternal.

Only Richard really knew how different she was underneath that contrived repose. In his endlessly competitive world of advertising, with its succession of anxieties, disappointments and rumours, he was in an excellent position, in the condensed married state imposed by the tyranny of Glenmore, to know the conflicts everlastingly arguing with each other in her mind.

The moment Diana had cupped her hands around the receiver, June knew there was something up. Very much on her mind were the remarks, reported by Diana only a few minutes before, made by the awful author about the true extent to which neighbours at Glenmore would care about each other in a crisis. And here was the crisis; and what did Diana do but finish her coffee – oh, so casually! – then sneak off to her own front door to get the details. Then the loading of the mini – done secretively, while reversed supposedly out of view – and the grabbing of Jennifer and the abrupt exodus and then just nothing.

June tried to call Richard, missed him at Stilling & Franson – where he had to call to pick up that advertising copy – and subsequently couldn't raise him at his own office.

There followed a three hour wait, with Baby Caroline refusing to sleep, and being sick on the carpet, and no cigarettes, and no prospect of going out to get some because Richard might phone in the meanwhile and she might miss him again.

And then turning on the radio, and hearing nothing abnormal, and so trying to shrug off Diana's astonishing departure, despite the car full of luggage and some more stuff on the roof rack and Diana looking tense and drawn and anxious and suddenly very uncalm and uncasual about Jennifer playing on the green.

Richard phoned just before noon. He sounded loving and over-gentle, and began with a few domestic banalities before he went on, 'Listen, darling. Can you do something a bit sort of off the cuff?'

'Do what, darling?' – God, was this it?

If so, June knew she would act it out Richard's way. She dare not ask the obvious direct question but listened instead to the lilting-smooth reassurance in Richard's voice and decided to take it face-value. In a crisis, this was the way they led each other through, one playing parent to the other, and the other not questioning it. When the bottom had dropped out of Richards' last advertising job and she'd heard what was going to happen before he'd been told – because she was a close friend of an executive's wife – she'd played the mother and she'd done the double-talk and he'd pretended it was all going to be all right because June had said so . . . which had made it possible for him to say, 'June, I think after all we won't change the car, let's stick to the old one for a while, it's a buyers' market just now, things will change of course – ' Finally they'd had to sell the car altogether, and redeem some insurance just as Baby Caroline was on the way . . .

Now he said smilingly, 'The thing is, I want you to bring Baby Caroline up to North London, well, Elstree as a matter of fact. Just an idea of mine but, well, it is a bit important and I want you to get here as fast as you can. The point is, I don't want you to bother about tidying up the house or anything. I'll explain it all later – there's nothing to worry about – and I've got a minicab to collect you, as a matter of fact he should be there quite quickly.'

She caught her breath and the lips tightened and the eyes withdrew just as they always did when the precise facts had to be evaded and the fantasy believed. 'Yes, go on.' Baby Caroline started crying, and it was difficult to hear properly, and she grabbed Caroline unceremoniously and somehow held her and rocked her with one arm while she wrestled to hold the receiver tight to her ear with the other. And thought, my God, giving up smoking is one thing, but *running out of them* is another.

'Now darling, I know this sounds a bit silly, but there are three things to remember. They're important. First, don't let the driver take you anywhere near Staines.'

'But we wouldn't go towards Staines to get to Elstree.'

The gentle, patient voice agreed. 'I know, but just in case. Anyway, second: tell no one at Glenmore you're doing this. No one. And third, don't let anyone talk to you or go near you or Caroline on the way. Keep the windows wound up tight – I know it's hot, but I mean it – and just sit quietly, understand?'

'What about money?' she asked realistically.

'Bring what cash you have and bring your cheque book and bankers' card. Bring some baby food – '

'I'll worry about things like that,' she snapped.

'Good. Fine. Well, I should see you in about an hour, perhaps a bit more. Don't keep the minicab waiting . . . '

Thereafter it had been a sort of dream, and June had the gift of making it so. A pilot called Stan Something, a nice, calm man who shared with her husband the same reassuring manner, obviously by mutual agreement, but she didn't allow herself to notice why. Stan had an unusually boyish complexion for a man who must have been in his late thirties, a sort of glow, well soaped and very clean shaven. There was a certain urgency with which superficially languid arrangements were carried through – there was all the time in the world and every moment counted.

The tower people were behaving oddly, you couldn't put your finger on it, they were listening for things. Then, just as June was boarding the tiny aeroplane, so frail and vulnerable, there had been some news about Blackbushe, and people had looked very drawn suddenly, and then a few men had come out of what seemed to be a club-room, and were trying to wheel out aeroplanes from the hangar, and getting in each other's way, and it was looking ugly, with everyone trying to get airborne at once, and there was this engine trouble to put right on their plane, and the mechanics were getting what seemed to be huge bribes from everybody at once.

The capsules – Richard had been waiting for them, had sent somebody off to get them, and it took a long time, two chemists locally had, for some reason, a run on them in the last hour, most extraordinary, but at last a car raced up to the airfield just as Stan Something said well they'd better give up waiting, and just taxi out, the engine was okay now, but anyway the man brought them, and they all took one and gave half a capsule to Baby Caroline, and hoped that was the right dose.

Then, just after Stan had got them all in and started the engine, a group of men who had been standing nearby all looked at each other, and evidently came to some decision, and started running toward the aeroplane. Richard, whose mouth had been getting very small and thin and his face very aquiline and stern and his movements sudden and precise, suddenly yelled, 'Stan, get her off! Those people are going to charge us . . . !' Those people, despairing human beings who suddenly realized at least a little of what the Blackbushe event had signified.

Stan didn't wait to take off properly upwind, but opened the throttle wide, and they were bumping over long grass, with these men still running after the aircraft, trying to grab the tailplane. And the machine was rocking very dangerously, almost scraping a wingtip on a concrete post as they roared around the signal square in front of the tower, gaining speed but having to fight long grass catching the nosewheel. But the pursuing men fell back; and Stan, seeing this, throttled back just enough to curve around and get on the concrete proper and June's breath was coming in little snatches, as she clutched Caroline so hard she feared she'd crack the baby's ribs, yet found to her horror that she couldn't release the pressure with which she was clawing the baby, almost as if the baby were protecting her instead of vice versa.

Then they were airborne, and the bumping stopped, and below them was the M1 motorway.

Stan, who had already learned from air traffic control that the motorways leading to the south and the southwest had been closed, registered rapidly despite the panic departure that although hardly anything was moving toward London, except what appeared to be armoured cars, the northbound lanes were choked. For a moment he hesitated in choosing course; if exodus was considered safe to the north, why go west, where it obviously wasn't?

But it was only a fleeting moment of indecision; a trained pilot, he stuck, if only through sheer habit, to his flight plan and continued as instructed. And all the time they were climbing into the sun, which drew starform patterns on the plastic windscreen; and all the time the tension in the aircraft was unclicking, until it was actually possible to generate enough saliva to speak. And Stan said, 'I didn't think we were going to make it.'

June was whimpering quietly to herself, sitting behind the other two – Richard and the pilot – and for a while nothing was said. The baby had suddenly gone to sleep.

Twenty minutes later, Richard, who had been gathering himself for the task, at last turned to June and said, 'Now I'd better explain a few things. Not easy things. But we're safe for the moment so I won't try to disguise what I know . . . ' So the dream had to be abandoned, the let's-pretend was over, the glazing of the eyes wouldn't work. So June forced herself to come fully alive again, and nodded capably at all the right places, and tried not to think of other Glenmore families the awful author was so right about.

* * *

At Jaybury there was an agricultural show in full swing. As Stan banked the machine and started to look for a suitable field, bulls were parading into the ring, and crowds of people, not very attentive about the bulls but very active around the stalls and the icecream vans and the various drink tents, wandered in heat-wave sunshine. Neatly parked cars flashed sunlight back into the sky. Picnickers straddled the grassland between the cars and the showground, total families islanded on rugs, with their hampers and Thermos flasks and wasps getting at the sandwiches.

Idly, Richard read-off the exhibitors' names on the showcase set-pieces containing milking machines and tractors, irrigation equipment and crop-spraying gear . . . phoney trees displayed by the Forestry Commission in a sort of film set where buzz saws kept halving the same old bit of polystyrene timber.

As an advertising man he could discern the exhibitors by the general shape and style of the company logos, without yet being able to read the actual print. That ingenious type-face belonged to the Milk Marketing Board and just said 'milk'; nearby, that was Massey-Ferguson, then BP and Lister Engines and Kodak and Lloyds Bank and the AA. It was a reassuring sight, contrasting almost ludicrously with Elstree, where decent people had been ramming each other's aeroplanes, crumpling wings and rendering flying machines so much scrap metal, shearing off wingtips, cutting off elevators and consequently their only means of escape.

Stan said quietly. 'There's a dip behind those fields, a slight valley, with a field that doesn't look bad. If we land there we won't attract too much attention.'

Richard was looking over his shoulder at the map. 'It could hardly be better, if you can make it,' he said. 'That ground there, right beyond it, must belong to the Dorrington Hotel. Look, there's the line of pylons that cross the garden; and that patch of water must be the new reservoir.'

Stan, his hands looking misleadingly relaxed on the controls, like a concert pianist playing a difficult piece practised over the months, certainly didn't relax his concentration. 'Maybe,' he said. 'And high-tension wires are all we need! This is a short field.' He throttled back. 'Straps tight, please. It's bumpy ground. If I hit something and turn her over, I've told you what to do, so do it. There won't be time to argue if we catch fire.'

They had to glide down between a narrow approach hemmed in by trees and somehow dodge the high-tension wires. Worse, the valley narrowed suddenly into a tight neck, and too late, Stan realized they were committed without choice – there wasn't a hope of aborting the landing and climbing away out of it, because though obscured from aloft the actual shape of the field was triangular. Its far apex was wedged either side by sharply rising hills.

Telephone poles, appearing catastrophically from nowhere as if they'd been erected instantaneously by some fiend dedicated to the destruction of flying machines, menaced them abruptly beneath. With precious little speed in hand Stan banked left sharply, and heard the gasp of June's unleased breath as she, too, saw the proximity of the starboard wingtip to the nearest pole. The plane seemed to hover for a moment, taken by surprise, terribly close to stalling at this speed when suddenly turned. Stan pressed hard forward on the controls and there came a shudder. The plane almost ceased to fly, then made for the ground like a tea trolley flying out of a hotel window. All three wheels struck the ground together, grinding hard mud and trying to twist the frail frame while the wings juddered at their roots.

Stan snatched at the fuel cock and rammed back the hatch. Dust hurricaned into the cabin and through it Stan glimpsed a barn dead ahead. They were closing on it crabwise as Stan kicked the rudder as hard as he dared. A wingtip dug a mound, miraculously slewing the aircraft right, missing the barn by mere inches, then stopped with a jolt on a stoney patch by a brook.

There was silence, except for the gentle ripple of cool water diverting itself around rocks in the stream.

Then from a distance an amplified voice, rather fruity and hearty and Young Conservative Member-of-Foxhounds, echoed down the valley: 'Ladies and gentlemen, the next event will be Junior Jumping. Will all competitors now assemble in the preparation ring. And we have an announcement: Will the owner of car number . . . '

Stan pointed past the barn and said, 'Your Hotel. Not quite door-to-door service but we can walk it in ten minutes. Only, can we manhandle this aircraft into that barn? It may come in handy later.'

SIX

Alec parked the Dormobile as inconspicuously as possible just inside the back gates of the factory. This entrance was seldom used; so the vehicle and its sinister occupant would probably remain unnoticed for long enough.

The factory lay behind the town proper, occupying a stretch of land tangental to that hectic highway for plodding caravans and hurtling cars, skimming the city itself; the Ring Road. Alec checked that traffic-flow along it – throughway for the A38 – seemed normal. He then walked the length of the factory, doubling round the far end to make it look as if he'd arrived via the main entrance.

ESTO was, ever since the early sixties, the prefix for all products of the company. The original title which made up the initials had been *Exeter Sedatives, Tranquilizers & Orthopeadic Services Ltd* – a formidable mouthful condensed long ago to Esto-Druggists Ltd, dealers in a wide range of clinical products, both consumer and surgical.

Alec, before being transferred to the Staines Institute as liaison representative, had spent three years here and knew the Thursday routine by heart. And as expected, the long line of articulated transporters were at the parking lot, waiting to enter – one at a time – the automatic loading bay. There, apart from bulky products like disposable nappies, incontinence pads, sterilization equipment, throw-away syringes – such things were trolleyed to the trucks where they now stood – the major products like Estofort would roll down the conveyor belt direct from the drug production line.

Counting the trucks, Alec saw only a few missing. No doubt the loading foreman would shrug these absentees as victims of nothing more ominous than the usual bank holiday cram on the A38.

But Maynard, the gangling, anæmic-looking executive Alec most frequently dealt with by phone from the Institute, was peering anxiously at the gaps on the lorry park. And when he saw Alec approaching he seemed visibly shaken.

Alec only had a few seconds to theorize upon Maynard's evident alarm; for Maynard was not the man to get caught up with if you were in a hurry. The drill was to wave your brief-case cheerfully at him, grin about the weather (or grimace if more appropriate) and think up some quick piece of tele-graphese which could be exchanged without actually stopping.

Alec did not vary this procedure, though he wondered momentarily why Maynard looked so shattered. It was quite normal for Alec to appear unannounced at the factory if matters took him there.

Tanya was at the reception desk; Tanya who liked other people's husbands, and who liked Diana's husband the best. She, too, was startled to see him, only the reaction was different.

During a wet night on the road to Torquay, Alec and she had been kissing so hard that his foot slipped from brake to accelerator. That particular evening had turned out innocent, by the technical definition, because a police patrol car had been following. There had been anxious moments and breathilizer tests and the threat of a Dangerous Driving charge . . . all this while Diana was uneasily shifting about at a cocktail party in Glenmore, knowing about the girl and wondering about the indulgent way in which Alec was uncharacteristically bringing back presents from Exeter after each frequent visit.

Thus it was not an entirely uncharged greeting that was exchanged between Alec and the girl Tanya; and with Alec's expression as it was set now – hard and grim and determined – Tanya found herself practically melting on the spot.

So much so, and so obviously so, that Alec for a few moments allowed himself to be distracted from the terrors that had pursued him. He therefore did not see Maynard, who had clearly been about to go out to his car, had darted back into the building toward his office in the Consignment Wing.

Tanya said, 'You again.'

'Me again.'

She said, 'If I didn't know you better I'd say you were tired.'

'But as you know me better, what's your verdict?'

'Very much on the job.' She lowered her voice. 'You are a bastard.'

'Why?'

6

'You know why.' She indicated the array of phones in front of her. 'That's why.'

'That's the whole trouble. Once I start calling you – '

' – Your foot starts slipping off the brake pedal?'

He nodded. 'And usually into my mouth.'

Tanya asked, 'Did your wife ever suspect?'

'Wives always suspect.'

'And husbands?' She was watching his face carefully. 'Do they suspect the suspicious wives . . . ?' She nodded omnisciently, as if he'd somehow answered her. You'd hate it if her foot slipped too.'

'I never denied I loved her.'

Tanya smiled ruefully. 'That's what's perverse about me, I suppose. I don't want the ones that love me.'

'Not yet,' he said. 'Have you been behaving?'

'Have you the right to ask?'

'No.'

'Well, I have.'

'Any particular reason?'

'Yes. You're the one man I've ever been with who thinks I'm intelligent.'

' "Potentially intelligent" was what I said, Tanya.'

'Meaning what?'

'Meaning that you try not to be.'

'Spoil my fun?'

'Might do.'

'Not with you though. Are we going to . . . Meet?'

'Tanya, Diana and I are getting along a lot better.'

'That's no answer. I'm not the same thing. Am I? Admit it?'

'I admit it.'

She said, 'And it's my proud boast that I've never broken up a single home.'

'Judgement? – or luck?'

'Fate,' she said. 'The universe has a use for me. I'm a solitary planet that orbits and occasionally comes within range of one of the regular ones – '

' – Whereupon the forces of gravity prevail until the next time round? Mind you don't have a head-on collision.'

She said, 'That's what I'm afraid of.'

He said, 'What else are you afraid of?'

'Diana's down here with you, isn't she? . . . Or are my spies telling me lies?'

'She's here.'

'So there *is* a flap on.' She looked at him frankly. 'That's a big measure for you to take. Normally you keep your women two hundred miles apart.'

'Exactly what do you know, Tanya?'

'There's a rumour about your Dr Crossley. The Hat Rack king.'

'To what effect?'

'He rang up here, apparently, in the middle of the night.'

'Which night?'

'Tuesday night . . . Well, actually Wednesday morning.'

'Were you on the switchboard?'

'Don't be daft. You won't catch me doing night duty.'

'Tanya, *please*!'

'Okay . . . I don't know much. He was incoherent, terrified. In the end, the night operator – a fella, not a girl – plugged the call into Security and they taped a bit of it.'

'How many people know this?'

She said, 'You're privileged. I tell you things I don't even tell the other husbands. The night man knew, and he told me. We were both hauled up in front of Dr Blessing – no less – and sworn to deep secrecy. Mit threats. But I know it was taped.' She was talking in a low voice now – not the special one modulated specifically for closed cars on rainy nights, but quiet and cautious. 'Then Blessing started trying to talk to various people at the Institute. No answer from anyone. Very curious. We're not allowed – now – to attempt calls to London at all.'

'Why?'

'Because they don't get through, and for some reason Blessing doesn't want that known, either. So a thin story has been put out that the Post Office are changing over the lines . . . switching to underground cable instead of overhead wires. I'm instructed to tell this fable every time.'

'You sure it's a fable? – It may even be true. You know what telephone engineers are.'

She said, 'I don't. But I know what people like Alec Keeling are. And I can see you're lying your hat off. Where did you leave it? – on a Hat Rack?' She saw she'd scored a hit, so she went on, 'I see. May I ask when you were last in the Hat Rack building?'

He stonewalled her. 'It's Dr Blessing I've come to see.'

Then it came.

A part of Alec's mind, cold and detached, observed Tanya, as a specimen, noted how fear showed itself in such widely differing ways. Now he could see Tanya's way.

And it was purely animal. She was the female in the jungle, vying with rivals to gain the protection of the strongest beast. Using every gift that God and hormones had provided, she fought for protection, below and above the belt, a mixture of tenderness and grit . . . teeth that could part for a penis or sink deep into flesh. Now, they were the focus of a question.

Alec tensed himself against it. To shelter her because she was a perfect specimen would be like norturing a master race.

She said, 'If I'm right to be so scared, will you look after me? Will you?'

The conflict must have been in his eyes.

Fumbling for her dialling pencil Tanya said, 'We owe each other nothing.' She spoke into the phone and hung up and said, 'Dr Blessing will see you now.'

Alec didn't move. He thought. You'd be good to breed from. That seems almost like Hitlerism . . . 'Tanya, I don't know. P'raps you do have some special place in this universe.'

'Meaning . . . what?' But she knew what he meant: somehow it was up to her.

Alec thought, God, how many decisions do I have to make? And do they all have to be for the wrong reasons?

* * *

Dr Blessing, head of the research department of Esto-Druggists Ltd, was an unlikeable man with a face like a crimped relief map. Over-educated, addicted to formal dinners at which he made eloquent speeches, he was conscious that he had much better men under him at the company yet conversely felt wasted on Exeter.

His thinking behind this was paradoxical – but he was forever trapped by paradox. Roughly his argument went that though brilliant researchers might reasonably be kept functioning in West Country greenhouses, intelligent humanity was a thing apart, best stimulated within the exclusive confines of the ancient universities, where he, as a kind of permanent guest of the Oxford Union, would be the ideal shoulder-rubbing raconteur for putting renowned professors at their ease. They then might stand the best possible chance of instant inspiration, moving technological mountains with one well-aimed kick, while lesser scientists required years of patient research – all because they didn't know which way round the table you had to pass the port.

But Blessing slid on his very own banana skin. He had no mind for the improbable or the daring, until time had proved its originator a genius and him a nonentity. Strident spokesman for the virtues of common sense, Blessing crunched subtle concepts underfoot like a blind man driving a steamroller. Obscure notions were irrelevant, neurotic, and damaging to the interests of the shareholders.

He greeted Alec by saying, 'Of course, all these stories we've been hearing are grossly exaggerated. Obviously we must take precautions; but what kind?' The question was clearly rhetorical. 'We seem to be faced with some kind of mutated virus. Some kind of miolitis or meningitis has struck which happens to be unusually contagious.'

'But if it's a virus – '

Alec's objection was waved aside.

'Two things stick out a mile,' said Blessing, illustrating the statement with an arm more used to raising glasses at university dinners than telegraphing the wisdom of his clinical views. 'One is that Estofort only suppresses the symptoms, rather than curing the disease; the other is that Estofort has properties we never knew about when we developed it. Clearly it arrests the progressive effect of the virus on the nervous system; so that if the drug is taken in time, the virus remains in the body – possibly in its inert, crystalline form – but does no further harm. The patient under such drug protection nevertheless becomes a carrier; and the virus seeks a new host body in which to thrive.'

There were so many holes in this eloquently stated theory that Alec had to do a good deal of throat-clearing before he could manage a reply.

Blessing, mistaking Alec's stupefaction for tacit applause, sat back and folded his mind tight shut, as if it were an encyclopædia fully consulted and therefore replaced on the shelf in which it belonged.

Alec said, 'I still think you are thinking too – ' he nearly said 'conventionally', but that would have been a damaging choice of words with a man like Blessing. ' – thinking too much in terms of actual organism in the accepted sense.'

Expressionlessly, Blessing said, 'At the Hat Rack, several floors were devoted to the process of brothing supposedly harmless organisms and immediately below these departments were the experimental wings equipped for the detection of neuro-psychological symptoms. Dr Crossley may – I say *may* – have got over-excited about some discovery of his and done something careless. Some kind of bug penetrated the very elaborate isolation barriers provided for personal de-contamination and initially carried this bug down from the organic labs to the psychological wing – where of course no such measures were either necessary or in operation.' Before Alec could stop him posthumously accusing a colleague of criminal negligence without a shred of evidence Blessing continued, 'Actually I am not greatly concerned with the causes or the nature of the disease. Things have gone too far for any such research undertaking.'

Alec said, 'I think such a project is the first essential.'

Blessing smiled. 'You've been mixing too long with too many purely theoretical men. We are faced with a pragmatic situation in which we know our drug can control the condition.'

'Then if your drug only controls it, you haven't solved the problem of dealing with the virus itself.'

'We will have to leave that to the antibodies we all possess.'

'And if society breaks down in the meanwhile?'

'To some degree, society always breaks down in the face of an epidemic. Even 'flu. Factories sometimes close, hospitals become understaffed; schools have to break up early. You're exaggerating all this, Alec. Nevertheless, I have imposed the strictest rationing of the drug – even here, on the factory premises. No one gets so much as a milligram without my signature.'

'And you're stepping up production?'

'Do you need to ask?'

'What about the transporters outside?'

'They'll be loaded and sent out as usual.'

'Even though you have my word that by the time they reach their destinations – if they ever do – the cases in the areas the trucks are heading for will be too advanced for the drug to operate?'

'What's the alternative?'

'I want you to hold those truckloads, keep them locked up and out of sight, until at least I have a report from the Sindham Hospital – where I have a meeting scheduled for two o'clock.'

'Thus delaying vital supplies to areas where they are urgently needed?'

'Yes. I realize how it looks to you, Dr Blessing. But at least let the Sindham express an opinion before you make up your mind.'

'I see no earthly reason to delay or conceal those trucks.

There is no sign whatsoever of the disease having reached Exeter. Before we go much further I think I should inform you that we received a request from the Hat Rack to aid the authorities in a world-wide study of the effects of Estofort. The consignments are to be specially tagged and that is taking place outside at this time. Because of that, you will, purely by chance, achieve a degree of delay; and if the Sindham are able to convince me that they have a positive diagnosis differing from what seems almost certainly the case, I might feel entitled to hold the transporters at the factory until I have re-checked with the department concerned.'

'You mean Staines?'

'Of course.'

'You have no idea what the situation is, at Staines?'

'I understand the lines are down. Presumably they will be restored by the time you have visited the Sindham Hospital.'

'Dr Blessing, what time did you get this message about the export analysis?'

'Sometime yesterday morning.'

Wednesday!

'You know, of course, that the initiative for this could not have come from Dr Crossley?'

Blessing smiled urbanely. 'It's hardly his sort of project, is it? He doesn't like working with a team. He doesn't even permit visitors to enter his key laboratory. He's hardly likely to mount a collective project like this one.'

'You didn't know that by office hours yesterday morning Dr Crossley had thrown himself down the lift shaft, and that not one researcher in the whole of the Hat Rack was coherent enough to explain what had occurred – let alone phone through to you the details of a major research scheme?'

There came a long silence.

Blessing rose from his seat. He was, despite the wisely shaped head – wise in the sense that in conveyed through ponderousness an impression of wisdom – a smallish man. The strong shoulders, when visible over the top of a desk, coned down into a body that failed to sustain the illusion of power. 'That really is tragic,' he said. 'No, I didn't know. How did you? I had at least two quite independent reports by telephone that you weren't there. We were told you were off sick. So naturally we were all rather surprised when you turned up here this morning. I suggest that you really are sick – in which case a visit to the Sindham would be beneficial to you personally.

You weren't anywhere near the Hat Rack and it's clear that you have been subjected to highly hysterical exaggeration and hearsay.' Blessing smiled unpleasantly. 'Or are you going to change your story, now that it doesn't quite fit?'

'Who did you get these reports from?'

Blessing sat down again and went on smoothly, 'One came from an underling at the Hat Rack itself, who simply wanted to check – apparently for your benefit – upon the date and location of the annual conference so that your indiposition wouldn't cause you to miss it.'

'And the other?'

'Oh, come off it, Alec. You're trying to be a one man band, jumping to one conclusion after another, without even a pretence of getting the details. As soon as the lines are through to Staines I'll check back . . . ' He shot Alec a grim look – ' . . . And find out, among other things, just what your own participation in all this has amounted to. But I am not going to act hysterically just because you are.'

'Dr Blessing, did the other report of my alleged absenteeism come from a Ministry man?'

'No.'

'Did it come direct to you?'

'As it happens, it didn't. I do delegate some of the work here, even if Dr Crossley can't part with minutiæ of detail up there.'

'So you didn't get the details of this . . . tagging scheme either in writing, or by word of mouth from anyone in authority?'

'Alec, there are limits to the degree to which you can be insubordinate with me. I think you've gone far enough.'

'My point is that *you* haven't gone far enough. What was to stop you convening a meeting yourself, with those experts at the Sindham who have done work on this?'

Blessing said icily, 'Because they would merely be echoing at second hand the views of Crossley, with which I am only too aware. I am, incidentally, also aware of your own attempts to restrict your afternoon meeting solely to the Crossleyites. Do you think that very objective?'

'You've phoned them?'

'Certainly. I am in constant touch.'

'So it was through you – in fact – that I was cold-shouldered in such a way that I was forced to see you before seeing them?'

'I can't allow your personal fright to become public property,

Alec. Naturally I hoped to . . . tranquilize your views before you started a scare.'

'Isn't it you who's scared, Dr Blessing? Aren't you so scared, in fact, that you are fighting your instinct and clinging to glib theories which wouldn't stand up for five seconds in a class of first-year medical students?'

Blessing had gone white, but he controlled his voice as he said, 'Alec, valuable though you are to this company, I may yet be forced to fire you if you go on like this.'

'Would firing me help the double-think, for just a little bit longer? – so you can go on disregarding plain fact? . . . No, hear me out. You know as well as I do the Post Office wouldn't whip out every single line out of Exeter. Yet by half-past ten this morning everything east of Ilchester, Langport, Sparkford, was dead. You can't check with Staines either about my absence from work yesterday or about the validity of this peculiarly sudden research project, not one word of which had been mentioned the day before. You're peed out of your mind, Blessing; you've been wrong about Crossley from square one – though you pinched all his patents – and you've probably stuffed your car full of Estofort, ready to bolt when the time comes. Does that give you the right to throw away the survival of this city?'

For a moment, Alec thought Blessing would attempt physical violence. Shaking uncontrollably, he had walked halfway across the room in a blind rage.

Then, abruptly, the other half of the paradox took over and seemed to root him to the floor. It should have been pitiful; it succeeded only in looking ludicrous. Perhaps Alec's shot in the dark about a secret supply of Estofort in Blessing's car had done it. Whatever had, Blessing was beaten. Slumping back to his sumptuous office chair, he said, 'My God, my God.'

Alec, totally merciless, went on flatly, 'Will you have those trucks held here and placed out of sight?'

Blessing replied almost inaudibly, 'I'll hold them until you get word from the Sindham. I'm not shifting them; it'll immediately draw attention to the crisis.'

Alec thought there was an element of Blessing's famous common sense in this and didn't press it.

'Then will you mount a guard on them until you get word from the Sindham Hospital?'

Blessing had his head in his hands. 'Yes . . . yes.'

'And you're fit to do so? – A great deal depends on it.'

'I'll issue instruction to that effect immediately.'

'And you'll personally see them carried out?'

'Damn you, yes.'

'And will you immediately interview the individual who received the alleged research instructions from the Ministry people?'

'Leave it to me.' Blessing seemed partially to recover. 'Now go. Please. Just go!'

The name of the man being Tannoyed all over the building, as Alec strode back down the corridor to the entrance hall, was Maynard.

And Alec suddenly found himself wondering about Maynard's inexplicable conduct, on the steps of the building, only half an hour ago.

Who, then, had phoned Maynard from that stricken building in which demented men slithered on laboratory floors and hurled themselves out of windows?

Upon leaving, Alec found himself being studied by Tanya, from the desk. She looked, to Alec, as if she were close on praying.

SEVEN

Once a worrier, always a worrier, thought Melhuish. Estofort or not, he could not get the image of Nuttall off his mind. And he thought he was alone in this until, checking the baggage in the corridor of the Dorrington Hotel, he came face to face with Diana Keeling, who had stooped down to shift one of the packing cases Alec had brought from the Institute.

'It's in the way of my own things,' she explained.

'Let me help you.'

They both observed the stencilled markings on the offending crate. Containing electronic equipment it clearly originated from Nuttall's firm. A label stuck on the side was inscribed with his name. 'Odd character,' said Diana.

'I'm afraid your husband had a low opinion of him.' They both stood up together. Melhuish carrying Diana's suitcase into her room – virgin new and fitted out with everything from radio to razor point.

Diana thanked him, then caught his eye for a moment as she glanced in the mirror. 'Was Mr Nuttall the only person there, except for you and my husband?'

Melhuish, always accurate to the hilt, replied, 'The only one there who was sane.'

'Has my husband said anything about him since we arrived here?'

'Not to me, Mrs Keeling.'

She smiled slightly, reassuring the man – or trying to – about their future relationship. It seemed absurd to be addressed as Mrs Keeling when, probably without realizing it, Melhuish had placed himself in charge of administration at the hotel and was already thought of by Alec as a key man. 'The name's Diana.'

He shook his head, that rubbery smile of his indicating a measure of self-deprecation. 'If you don't mind I'd prefer to behave the way I'm used to. Somehow it makes things seem more normal. Besides . . . ' What he had on his mind was, supposing things did get back to normal? 'I'm not going to step out of my Grade now, only to have to get used to it again later.'

'I understand.' Somehow she felt a bit snubbed. She'd thought it was up to her to decide how she should be addressed.

Melhuish said, 'You don't trust Mr Nuttall either?'

Melhuish, who had tactfully got together with the retired major who owned the hotel, despite the verbose digressions of the major's twittering wife, had quietly decided who should sleep where and then stuck labels on the doors.

The major, though mystified by the nature of the invasion, especially concerning the presence in the hotel of Melhuish's unprepossessing family, was for the moment able to quench his own curiosity. No doubt Mr Maynard would very soon explain it all. Eccentric or not, the clientele supplied by Esto-Druggists meant solid business when the hotel brochure had remained lamentably ignored by the tourist agencies. To his print-dressed fusspot of a wife he'd remarked. 'At least our hotel is properly finished. Why do they all go to Spain and put up with the concrete mixers still churning muck in their rooms?'

She'd replied, 'These people aren't doing much for the tone of the Dorrington, dear.'

He snorted, 'Nor would a series of empty rooms.'

'Does that man Melhuish know what he's doing?'

It seemed so. People were settling down despite their exhaustion. Melhuish worked methodically and had a calming effect, particularly on June Trent – the most anxious of the guests. She was asleep and so was the baby. She was allotted a double room – plus a cot – next door to Diana's. Jennifer, Stephen and James had a room arranged for three on the opposite side of the same corridor. Later, if the Dorrington 'cadre' grew and accommodation became tighter, families might well all have to sleep in one room. But for the moment there was a spaciousness amounting almost to luxury.

Melhuish left Diana to it and went out to see about the generator. The hotel, erected on the site of an old sawmill, was connected to the main supply but the old engine was still there. Built to last forever, and so covered in grease that there was scarcely any rust, the equipment was still basically serviceable and only needed a few hours' attention to be restored as a source of emergency current. Melhuish had added a two-way knife-switch so that the change-over from mains to emergency could be made easily. The problem now was to acquire diesel fuel in quantity. So he was planning additional tankage and making hectic arrangements for the bulk delivery of oil. He'd already been on to the makers' agents about spares.

June awoke to the sound of the old generator being started on test. She couldn't think for a moment where she was. Then she saw her own bottle of Estofort on the bedside table and it all came back in a rush. Baby Caroline was still asleep.

June crept out of the room, and knocked on Diana's door.

June said, 'Isn't Richard back from town?'

Diana said, 'He's already made several trips with various supplies. He's gone off again.'

They talked in hushed voices because Edna Melhuish – the bumbling wife for whose protection Melhuish had spent half his life cringing – was just outside in the corridor, clumsily sorting her belongings.

Melhuish had, with a dreadfully embarrassed washing-action of his white hands, tried to explain to the other women that Mrs Melhuish was 'ever such a nervous and sensitive lady, you know; she's suffered from a lot of illness and I haven't yet taken her into my confidence'.

In their different ways, Diana and June were both snobs: Diana showed it by an unconsciously dictatorial manner she couldn't help – even her insistence on being addressed by Melhuish as 'Diana' was a kind of warped expression of this difficulty; June was elaborately over-polite and solicitous, offering Edna Melhuish all sorts of things that people like Edna Melhuish simply didn't have a use for. So both were more than relieved that the Melhuish's were accommodated in the 'T' of the building . . . the passage that led off at right angles to theirs. Naturally, this was Melhuish's own idea. Faced for years with the problem of hiding his wife away, without being unkind about it, he expended a great deal of energy in dealing with this, his greatest personal problem . . . especially when it had come to the upbringing of his large family of highly assorted children – some of whom had taken markedly after Edna.

Diana said, 'What about baby food? – Is Richard getting you plenty of that?'

June said, 'I hope you don't mind, but I asked him to put that at the top of his list.'

'Of course I don't mind! What about the hotel management? – Won't they be . . . curious? – The major paces up and down like a lion in a cage.'

June said, 'Mr Melhuish has told them some of it – I don't know how much.' Her eyes misted into their secret expression. 'They'll have to have pills eventually, of course.'

'Of course. And your pilot? – Stan? What about him?'

'Him too.'

They looked at each other, then away. Each was wondering about some terrible moment in the future when they might all be competing for a dwindling and irreplaceable supply.

Then Jennifer ran in and said to Diana, 'Mummy, they've got gooses.'

'Geese, dear.'

'Geeses, then. Aren't they funny? Just like the Ugly Duckling in Danny Kaye, you know.' – Diana thought, poor Hans Anderson has lost his identity forever.

Jennifer ran out again and June, who had managed at last to get some cigarettes, lit one with rather histrionic surreptitiousness and said, 'I wonder if this thing will show in the animals?'

* * *

Alec, motionless at the wheel of the Dormobile, caught by the lights on the corner by Bobby's Store, surveyed the scene in the shopping centre, alert for any possible changes. Narrowing his eyes against the glare, he watched with the acute perception of a species under threat.

One reason for this was the Sindham. He couldn't prove it, but it had looked very much as if something had gone wrong over in Casualty, the obvious department in which to deposit his incarcerated patient.

Referred to a detached block in the hospital grounds containing the E.E.G. Room, Alec was briefly interviewed by a young doctor who was clearly in an awkward position – trapped between the Registrar's official attitude and the beliefs of the late Dr Crossley, with whom he secretly identified.

The two were not allowed to talk alone. All the time a grim-faced deputy from the Registrar's office remained with them; and the conversation descended to the absurd – a discussion not directly about the diagnosis at all, but rather concerning which division of the hospital the unconscious man should be treated by.

By this time, the critically dehydrated victim was on a theatre trolley; and as Alec talked he watched, through the window, the fantastic spectacle of the trolley being pushed alternately from one end of the hospital to the other – Isolation, then Neurology then Isolation again.

While this *grand guignol* shunting operation went on, there were urgently whispered dialogues taking place between groups of housemen, outside on the lawn. Their eyes kept darting across toward Casualty.

The third party in the E.E.G. Room kept trying to conclude Alec's discussion with the young doctor, interpolating sharply whenever the official line – the virus theory – was in any way infringed. Alec could do nothing except filibuster, hoping that something might happen to call the medical gestapo off the premises.

It did. Abruptly the third party was called away for an urgent phone call. He said pointedly, 'I shan't be away long, Mr Keeling. Let us please agree to maintain a responsible attitude. This is a medical matter and I would remind you you're not a doctor.'

During his absence the younger man proved himself a convinced Crossleyite, if also something of a moral coward. Sheepish over his obvious fear of the deputy's authority, he confided, 'Several of us are with you. A few doctors – me included – have immunized themselves with Estofort. I phoned two neurologists this morning, after I got to hear of the rebuttal you received when you proposed the meeting.'

'Thank God for that.'

'I'm not so sure. Give me a phone number and if they can cooperate we'll call you.'

Alec told him briefly about the Dorrington set-up and gave the number. He was just in time. The Deputy-Registrar, clearly enraged, told Alec curtly. 'Dr Blessing has phoned. Very much against my own convictions, he has persuaded the Registrar to allow your meeting. It will take place here at eleven o'clock tomorrow morning.' He then called his junior off for an 'urgent discussion' in the Admin. Wing.

Tomorrow morning!

Judging from the hectic activities outside, it seemed to Alec that Blessing had only compounded pig-headedness with irony: the move had been made far too late.

Now under no delusions concerning the likely timing of the epidemic threatening Exeter, Alec had returned to the Store's racked-up car park, collected and loaded the boxed radio equipment faithfully left there by Melhuish, and was now waiting at the traffic lights which marked the T-junction with the main street.

Differences? . . .

Wasn't the traffic getting thinner? – Weren't there fewer shoppers around?

The lights changed to green, just as Alec spotted June's husband entering the supermarket over the far side. Had the crowds been as thick as they ought to have been, on this sunny weekday, Alec would never have seen him.

Alec parked the Dormobile on a double yellow line and followed Richard into the supermarket. There were some three dozen people in there, all loading trolleys with huge supplies. the shoppers as usual were mostly women. Some of them were wheeling two trolleys at once, with an infant stuck in the front one among the amassed cans of preserved meat and other long-term supplies designed for storing – a scare pattern which certainly hadn't been apparent at coffee time that morning at Bobby's Store.

Alec waited quite a while before attempting to speak to Richard. He didn't want to be seen doing it; the layout of the supermarket, with its long parallel rows of high shelves, would provide the opportunity sooner or later. In the meanwhile Alec just wheeled a trolley like the others, chucked a few immediate requirements into it, like butter and other short-term consumables. For a while he steered his trolley clear of Richard, who, aware of the interest being taken in the quantities of tins being wheeled about, was at great pains to keep these out of sight at the bottom of the trolley, piling on top such items as fresh vegetables, lavatory paper and kitchen towel rolls.

Alec and Richard didn't know each other nearly as well as did Diana and June. Female neighbours, there at Glenmore all day, depended on each other for daily companionship, sharing the shopping, minding each others' children, taking each other's phone calls – and thereby often snooping on the various intrigues, large and small, that kept them stimulated and informed.

The men, only at home weekends, conformed to their own pattern; and though authors might sneer at the predictability of their preoccupations, the fact was that in business it was necessary to wash the car and maintain it; it was obligatory to take some of the pressure off the wives by bathing the babies and vacuuming the carpet, and essential to do the bulk of the local shopping so that the wives could prepare for their evening guests with some hope of keeping the children in order and comparatively undamaged in sudden outbreaks of war between various Glenmore child-gangs; when bicycles became military tanks and space guns ceased to fire their death-rays and became instead instruments for giving hostile forces a slightly over-realistic swipe on the leg.

Alec quite liked the wiry, bantam-weight Richard Trent though their worlds were poles apart. Richard wore the trendy long hair and peacock shirts, used the latest Carnaby-Street cum American jargon, like getting-it-together and all-hanging-out, even though this didn't at all suit the essentially bourgeois existence at Glenmore and was even less suited to the diffident, socially-indeterminate June. Whereas Diana blandly measured her class status against ambition potential success and ultimate riches as gained by her mate, June often reflected on Richard's past rather than his future. A railwayman's son among a large family, Richard had, as a boy, played cops and robbers in a noisy side street, taken his pennies to the paraffin-smelling sweet shop on the corner, and done the paper round. At home, his father came home exhausted, put his feet up in the kitchen where his slippers were always ready for him, and drank large mugs of very strong tea. Until his death in a railway accident the father had remained a determined and virile head of the house, with that unquestioned authority which, in those days and in those streets, was the accepted role of the man of the house.

So now, Richard was a fast-moving, up-and-coming, always very nervy but seldom actually panicked advertising executive; not yet earning big money but on the way up; not yet as sure of his ability and qualifications as Alec but somehow knowing he soon would be. And, since he had June as a wife, he'd cultivated a convenient dual-personality, dropping all the Wardour Street argot and mannerism while chumming and pubbing with the other Glenmore residents over the weekend. On these occasions he compromised with the roll-neck sweaters and accepted canvas slacks of the junior executive off duty.

He wore this rig now.

Alec waited until he and Richard were ambling down opposite sides of the same row – Alec on the household goods, Richard at the canned meats and vegetables. Richard took three cans of potatoes from a rickety tower of tins at the top. Through the gap he'd made he murmured, 'Alec, it's closing in.'

Alec took a packet of detergent. 'Have you seen any actual cases?'

'It's not that.' Richard darted a look straight to his right, toward the deep freeze cabinets, then peered back at Alec through the slit. 'A man's been following me from store to store.'

'Is he in here now?'

Richard shook his head slightly, moved on to the Spam, took some of that. 'I thought that was him down by the freezers. Not though.'

Alec grabbed a couple of soap bars. 'How many stores have you been to?'

'This is the sixth. I've already taken two car-loads back to Jaybury. We dare not shop too much in the village there. But when I got back to Exeter this time someone who had seen me shopping earlier got the idea. I dodged around the back of Cathedral Square, moved the car on to another car park, then came out through the alleyways.'

'Who is he? What does he want?'

They moved on to the next shelf, getting nearer to the steady hum from the freezers, each of whose gauges indicated precisely the correct temperature for the concrete-hard edibles preserved in the bins. Richard said' My own guess is he's after our pills.'

Alec said, 'I don't understand how or why so many people know.'

'Sheer bush telegraph.'

'Yes; well that's about the only system of communications that's working.'

Richard said, 'Not quite. Ever heard of a man called Nuttall?'

Alec knocked a display over. 'Why?'

'Apparently he did a broadcast from somewhere up North.'

'About what?'

'I didn't hear it. I can't find anyone who actually did. But whatever he said, it's caused an under-current of worry here. They don't say much.'

Alec looked toward the cash registers. 'But they buy plenty.'

'Or stay at home trying to tune in for more. I gather reception's getting bad, though. I discussed this broadcast with your man Melhuish. He went all quiet and thoughtful, a bit weird. Anyway he said he'll raise it with you when you get back to Jaybury.'

Alec was at the washing-up fluid. 'How are things there?'

'Okay. Melhuish is busy supervising the installation of a large tank for storing diesel fuel. He's got a tanker lorry coming over with bulk supply.'

'I take it that he is thinking of that ancient generator?'

'Yes.'

'Does it run?'

'Melhuish says it does, yes.'

'We'd better get a spare generator too.' Alec fumbled in the freezer, thought better of it. If they found themselves down to emergency power there'd be no spare electricity for running freezers. He began on packets of sugar instead.

Richard said, 'Melhuish has thought of that too.'

'In time?'

Richard nodded. 'I know what you mean. There's bound to be a run on them, too.' He snapped his fingers. 'Got it!' Several faces turned. Nerves were hypersensitive. Richard dropped his voice. 'The Agricultural Show at Jaybury. They'll be packing up the stands by now; but Lister Engines had some exhibits. I noticed them when we flew in. If we're lucky we'll pick up a plant on the spot.'

'Good. If any research is to be done at the Dorrington, reliable electricity is a must.'

'Are the Sindham people going to cooperate?'

Alec didn't give details but said tersely, 'If they don't, no one else will.'

'I gather things weren't too good at the factory?'

'It looks all right on the surface; but the man in charge on the spot is paralytic with terror. Won't face any one set of facts – then wonders why he can't make sense of the situation.'

'Is he on the Board?'

'No. Ever known a board be around when you need a decision? They're based on London, anyway.'

'So what happens?'

'We may lose all the stocks of Estofort still at the factory. It's as simple as that.'

'What about guards?'

'He promised to organize something. But Dr Blessing . . . he's something special. When trouble brews, he freezes. What is it, Richard?'

Richard moved back behind the stacks of tins, murmured softly, 'My shadow again.' How the hell did he find me?'

Alec said calmly, 'More important, how the hell do we shake him off?'

'Well, he can't follow us both.'

'And he mustn't know where either car is.'

'But isn't that your Dormobile right outside?'

'He won't know it's mine. And he mustn't. Richard, you take all this shopping – both lots – and put it in a taxi. Shake him off and don't go anywhere near your car until you're certain you have.'

Richard said, 'It may not be easy.'

'No . . . Look, in a sec we'll make sure he's in earshot. We'll arrange a phoney meeting place for his benefit.'

'Okay. Where?'

'The entrance to the University. There's a reason – '

'He's watching us, Alec. Better make this fast.'

'No, just keep on shopping. He can't do anything till we leave. Then he'll have to decide who to follow. We've got to make sure it's you. When you leave, keep going towards the University until you reach the road works this side. There's a one-way system now in operation and some temporary lights. But you can dodge round at the far end and cross the earth-works where you'll see all the bulldozers. They'll let one car through because they won't be on to it; but if I know the angered British workman he'll stop the very next car to try it.'

They reached the girls on the cash desks. Richard glanced behind. The shadower was standing some way back, waiting. Richard started piling the goods on the counter. 'Will a taxi driver do that?'

'He's got to do a lot more that that. Hand him a fiver and tell him to go the way the buses go. In this town the buses go against the one-way system. If the police see what's happening, they're most likely to stop the rear car first. But if there's trouble your driver will probably know some side street that'll do the trick.' He glanced back. 'Your friend is coming up to the desk. Are you clear on all that? . . . Then I'll see you at the Dorrington Hotel when you've picked up your car. Now for the Charades!'

Richard said soberly, 'I hope I can pull it off. I was never much good at cops and robbers.'

'I have a feeling we're both going to have to get used to it, Richard. Today's charades are just the curtain-raiser.'

* * *

The smell of old sawdust still haunted the old generator room at the Dorrington. In there, an hour later, Richard joined

Alec and Melhuish. Outside, a firm of contractors were noisily clanging a large storage tank into position.

Richard realized Alec and Melhuish were on to some new crisis. Both men broke off to make sure who it was entering.

Richard's mouth tightened into a small, determined slit. 'What's been going on?'

'It started with the local television.'

Alec said, 'But they're not getting any real news through, surely?'

'That's not the point, Mr Keeling. It suddenly closed down. In the middle of some horse show . . . ' He jerked his head sideways, 'Probably the one that's still going on near here, across the valley.'

'Any warning?'

'None. Just went off the air gradually, as if the power was failing . . . ' Melhuish nerved himself for the next bit. 'But not, unfortunately, the radio. Apparently one announcer decided that the news blockade contravened the principle of free speech, and described some of the scenes in London.' Melhuish's thick lips had turned nearly white. 'Even from the guarded things he said about it, the situation sounds quite fearful – far worse than we expected at this early stage.'

Richard said, 'Can we have details?'

Melhuish said. 'Your wife took it down in shorthand.'

'My God. She heard it.'

Melhuish said, 'She was too engrossed in taking down shorthand to lose her head.' He added, looking down, 'I wish I could say the same for dear Edna.'

Alec said quickly, 'She'll rally.'

Melhuish said nothing in reply, but recovered his composure and went on, 'They're making an effort to get the television – the whole network – going for about an hour tonight because there's to be a speech by the Prime Minister.'

Alec said, 'That should be . . . memorable.'

'Yes.'

'Was this what Richard told me you wanted to discuss?'

'No, it's only just happened. But there's something I should have mentioned when we talked this morning. Somehow it slipped my mind.'

'Judging from what you've managed here it must be the only thing that has.'

Melhuish acknowledged the compliment with a humble nod.

'It was up in Staines. Before I left the Institute – which was, of course, after you'd gone – I went back along the umbilical corridor to check all switches off in your own section. Mr Nuttall was still in the complex, but I could see he'd gone out to put some things in his car. So I took a look round . . . It was on his telephone pad: Do you have a man, here at the Exeter factory, called Maynard?'

Alec's pulse quickened. He remembered some of the things Blessing had been saying about some Ministry research scheme – even though the message concerning this had, nonsensically, been phoned through from the Hat-Rack long after there was anyone there sane enough to phone it. Could it have been Nuttall who called the Exeter factory? And if so, why? . . . Maynard's name, called over the Tannoy system, pursuing Alec down the corridor, rasping urgently from Blessing's office . . . Alec's mind then was more on Tanya's desperate look. He knew he should have been on to it, by now. Melhuish wasn't the only mind to slip on this issue. Both men were over-loaded; neither realized that the indolent Nuttall had flair or initiative. In normal times he clearly lacked any such quality. He should have gone downhill like Blessing.

Alec urged Melhuish to continue.

Melhuish went on maddeningly slowly, trying to get the details as correct as he could. 'I didn't dare tear off the top sheet, but he'd been using a Biro and I got the sheet immediately underneath. I can't make it all out; but there's a reference to a company called Rotoport, then a lot of figures and things which all cross over each other, because the top sheet had been loose and had shifted while he'd been writing. I've copied out as much as I can read; but you might know of someone here who could process the under-sheet so that you can read it clearly. It's probably nothing, but – '

But. Why Maynard's rabbit-like reaction when Alec had turned up at the factory? And why should Nuttall, who had nothing whatever to do with company matters concerning Estofort – let alone its export distribution – be getting on to first Maynard, then Rotoport?

Melhuish said, 'Where are you going?'

'Straight back to the factory.'

Richard said, 'Couldn't you get Maynard on the phone?'

'He's evasive and cowardly. If he thinks he's put the cat among the pigeons he'll have a cover story by now. I want him face to face.'

He broke off as the tanker lorry arrived with the fuel. Melhuish excused himself with an almost comically elaborate politeness, but Alec said quietly to Richard, 'Don't be put off by his apparent unctuousness . . . Did you shake off your pursuer okay?'

'Yes. But I have a feeling – I think there was some kind of organized collaboration between him and some other people. He picked up the trail, when you saw me in that supermarket, when single-handed he just couldn't. Then later, at the roadworks you mentioned, I used your dodge; but another car took over the chase. Fortunately, he bought it when I went along the bus route; the police couldn't catch me but they did stop him.' Richard paused for a moment. The facial tissues had gone taut, pulling in the mouth; and the eyes met Alec's hard on. 'Alec, sooner or later they're bound to find this place. And then . . . Well, who do we think we're trying to kid?'

Alec said nothing, just walked away. In the garden he passed Melhuish, who stopped a moment, turned, and came back to speak to him. 'You're angry, Mr Keeling?'

'It'll pass. I've just realized something, though. In a situation like this, it can be damaging for people to say what they really feel.'

Melhuish said quietly, 'Some people have to, Mr Keeling. You don't, so you may not understand. But with all you're taking on – even considering going to the length of returning to Staines to look over that lab – you may find that even your stiff upper lip needs to relent, just a fraction.'

Alec said, 'You're a curious mixture, aren't you?'

'From the standpoint of Grade Three, Mr Keeling you learn a very great deal about human beings. May I say this? – Don't worry about Richard Trent. He's moody, nervous . . . and very sound. But if I were you, next time he wants to sound-off; let him.'

'Have you thought any more about that lab?'

'I never set foot in it.'

'But people must have talked, surely?'

'Yes, they talked about Crossley as an eccentric. After all, he had so many conflicting interests. He never seemed to concentrate on any one thing.'

Alec said, 'What can seem quite unconnected to other people might well have a connection in the mind of the man concerned. For Crossley, everything added up to one thing.'

Melhuish nodded. 'Like cooking. You may have raw eggs at

one end of the kitchen table, and some baking powder the other. Only the cook knows that the result of mixing them will be a cake. But I don't know which ingredient Dr Crossley kept in Lab Number Four.' Melhuish smiled nervously. 'What's getting on your nerves, if I may say so, is not the personal shortcomings of anybody here.'

'You don't miss a trick, do you.' Alec looked at his watch. 'Well, if the Sindham won't call me, I'd better ring them . . . '

When he'd done so he went straight to Richard. 'How's your nerve?'

Richard said cheerfully, 'I've just had a cup of very strong tea. I can stand anything.' Quietly he said, 'I gather you've just spoken to the Sindham.'

Alec said, 'Of course, it was inevitable. Casualty got some cases from some very nasty road accidents on the A38. Need I say more?'

'My God, we should have thought of that.'

'We had no say in it. Blessing deliberately blocked the meeting I tried to fix for the morning. They would have been forewarned. Luckily one or two Crossleyites got the hunch in time and took the drug. But Sindham Hospital, as such, isn't a hospital any more.'

Richard's lips broke apart and he snapped as if internal elastic had stretched too tight. 'For God's sake, Alec! Why don't you face facts? The hospital's a gonner, the drug supplies won't last, organized gangs are on the streets, people like Nuttall are making broadcasts and getting into power – '

' – Nuttall hasn't made Prime Minister yet, Richard.'

'And just what use is the man who is? We've got to stomach *his* broadcast next. I expect he'll look most impressive on colour TV. Just what will that commercial do for people shrivelling into nothing but village idiots? – We don't have a hope in hell, and you know it!'

Alec checked his instinct to hit back. He had to grip the back of a chair to do so. But he had deep respect for Melhuish's compassionate wisdom. So he said very quietly, 'Don't you get the point yet? In a sense it's even more horrific than yours, only not in the way you mean. Richard, if we, with our organized cadre, can only hold out long enough . . . '

The two men stared at each other. Alec's thoughts were starkly clear, but they were truly dreadful by implication.

Richard finished the sentence, not looking at Alec, but at

the men getting the hose down from the top of the tanker. 'If we hold out long enough here, there won't be anyone sane enough left to attack us.'

Alec went on calmly, 'Except, of course, for people who've got small supplies of the capsules already and are desperate for more. They're the ones we'll have to help if we can.'

'What with? – Our own supplies? And how long would that last? And, for that matter, how long have we got, even if we don't give a single capsule away?'

'I'm telling no one that – not even you.'

Richard took the point in silence. The men outside had screwed up the nozzle of the hose, started pumping in the oil. Melhuish was signing for it, going about the job with careful precision, so as not to dirty the delivery note. 'I take it,' said Richard, 'you have some plan to get some more supplies?'

'Yes.'

'From the factory?'

Alec wasn't yet ready to confide his full plan – not, at any rate, until he was sure he could leave Richard and Melhuish to carry on here without him. 'That's one possible source, but I don't have any say in how their stocks are to be distributed. If it's left to officialdom – if there's any officialdom left – my guess is they'll spread it out thin – one or two each, to a great many people. You know what that would mean.'

Richard said thoughfully, 'It somehow sounds far less ruthless than our way.'

'It is. The only trouble is, it can't work. Our way just might. Sindham are sending their research team – what's left of it – over to us and we'll be equipping a makeshift laboratory here. The surviving experts will mount a research programme as soon as they can get their stuff over. It's the only chance: we *must* find out what this Virulent Panic really is. Only then can we know the final outcome.'

Richard said soberly, 'it's that word "final" which I find discouraging. A species kept alive by a drug – for as long as supplies last – is like a man in an iron lung waiting for the battery to go dead.'

'Then we have to find him a new battery.'

'Is that what you're planning, Alec?'

'What do you mean?'

'It's no use trying to kid me along! And you might at least take me into your confidence! – Everything you do reeks of some kind of safari. And I can tell you flat; it's crazy.'

'Are you setting yourself up as a mind-reader? – Or are you going to give me a chance to explain what I have to do, and why?'

'Alec, you found out how things were going to be, up at your Institute place, and you thought up this cadre idea so you could play for time. I think you're hoping the real answers lie in Crossley's work. According to Melhuish – '

Alec grinned. 'Oh, so you tried to pump him?'

'Wouldn't you? – All he said was that Crossley was a secretive old bugger – or words to that effect – and something about "Lab Number Four".' Richard gave Alec an unwavering look. 'You're going to Staines. And you're raving mad to try it.'

So Alec decided. Richard was intelligent enough to guess that much. Why not tell him the rest? 'There are at least three reasons why I must go: One, to get more supplies of Estofort; Two, start other Cadres – how can we justify the survival of one tiny community or hope to restore order on a national scale from here? – and Three, you're perfectly right, get Crossley's data. His work took years; he had ideal conditions and all the facilities he wanted. That data is somewhere in Staines – probably at the Institute itself. It must be brought here.'

'Christ! What a proposition.'

'You're not to tell Diana yet. She thinks I'm staying on. You and June will have to give her some moral support but she'll be okay after a while.'

'But if things are as you say they are all over the country – '

' – Then it's going to be a tough assignment. Agreed. Any suggestions?'

'Yes. Let me come.'

'Sorry. You've got to run things here. Melhuish can manage administration problems but you're going to have to raise a defence force. You've go to recruit unaffected people in the town and choose them extremely carefully. They, too, will have to be supplied. It's a hell of a job – possibly a bigger and dirtier one than mine, Richard. But my justification for calling you up was not the matiness of Glenmore, though I admit I may have been looking for an excuse to make it you and June and Baby Caroline. My justification was that there had to be someone I knew and could trust, who could do what I'm asking you to do now.'

Richard said petulantly, 'I suppose I should sound grateful. I mean, in spite of the secrecy of your phone call to Diana, with

June only a few feet away from the phone, you still managed to think of a reason why we shouldn't just be left there to rot.'

Alec said calmly, 'And then you found yourself doing the same thing, Richard. How many people did *you* save?'

'I kept my word. You swore me to secrecy and you didn't tell me what the issues really were.'

'And you now know what the issues really are.' Alec's voice was shaking. 'So why don't you go and hire a loudspeaker van, Richard, and tell the whole of Exeter? I'm sure that both June and Baby Caroline will be better people for it. And of course, you'll be a Better Person. So what the hell are you waiting for?'

'Damn you!'

'Accepted. I feel very damned indeed. The feeling will grow as I see the rotting bodies of the suicides on the pavement and in the road, while I try and retrieve what I can of the drug we addicts need for our miserable survival.'

There was an ugly silence. Melhuish or no, there were limits to what Alec could stand. He said carelessly, 'Oh just one more thing. Melhuish has a list of frequencies and check times for our two-way radio. Please help him maintain contact with me. You'd better make sure one of your recruits is a radio engineer with spares at his disposal – so there's one more for you to save.'

Richard tried to resume his calmer tone. 'But what will you do for a set?'

Alec said, 'You don't realize. The pickings for the sane will be wide open. I can go anywhere I like and just take one. I shall also replace the Dormobile with something more suitable, whatever comes to hand. In that, I'll install a radio and call you at the times and on the frequencies specified.'

'Alec.'

'Yes.'

'I'm sorry.'

Alec said bitterly, 'There's no way of saying how either of us feel, Richard. Nobody's yet invented a language to cover it.' Then, remembering what Melhuish had said about Richard, he managed a weary grin. 'Anyway. I know why you're suddenly making such an issue of that hush-hush phone call to Diana.'

'Why?' Richard was grinning back.

Alec clapped an arm on Richard's shoulder. 'I'm beginning to understand you; you're furious that you can't come on this trip!'

EIGHT

It wasn't yet dark, not what you could call night, when Alec left the Dorrington on Thursday evening in the Dormobile.

In the west, there is often a kind of illusion that the day lasts longer; tractors with trailer-loads of cereal and chaff, manure and root crops, are still chugging irritatingly along main roads, no lights showing; cattle are still being driven in a way best calculated to choke the roads and infuriate the motorists behind them, no lanterns. Bicycles never show any lights.

But if it wasn't technically dark – even allowing for the west country definition – it was possible for Alec to see a deep red glow in the sky that didn't conform with the regulations even of the most exotic sunset. It illuminated the sky directly ahead.

His farewells with the family had been understated. There was too much going on for a properly managed departure. Diana, who held the major stocks of the drug, had a whispered discussion with Alec about distribution. Melhuish was brought in on this later and then Stan burst in on them and said wasn't Melhuish the expert on getting fuel? – and hadn't they better have a supply of aviation spirit, in case the aeroplane was needed? So Stan and Melhuish went off, then Jennifer hung around and helped everybody, and wanted to know why she couldn't play with the Melhuish children, and of course there wasn't a real reason except Diana's obsolete snobbery, and anyway it was a means of getting Jennifer out of the way for a few minutes, so snobbery gave way to convenience.

James, so unlike his twin both in looks and temperament, had turned the whole matter of evacuation into one huge adventure. With the instinct of an embyonic soldier, he adapted unquestioningly to whatever life had to offer. Like a boy playing cowboys and Indians and then coming across a genuine wigwam he had romped into the role demanded by the situation. Now he lingered outside, watching the installation of the new generator – which by inspired thought and action Richard had got hold of direct from the local agricultural show, where they had been dismantling the exhibition stands and suddenly found themselves making a last-minute sale.

Stephen, ignoring his brother's almost frolicsome activities, was too wise for his own good. He wasn't in terror – he had enormous trust in Diana – but would have been had she not seemed so self-possessed. So he watched her, from time to time, for signs of weakness. She was very conscious of this; and although it was a strain it was also a control on her nerve. Stephen knew more and believed less than the perplexed owners of the hotel, the major and his print-dressed wife, who were aware of some state of emergency but were too stolidly middle-class to grasp anything unorthodox. A major with war service in India, and a wife who looked as if a scratch on the dining table was the greatest threat to the hotel, were scarcely geared for all this. Marching ants and deposed Viceroys, yes; Virulent Panic, no. Secretly, the ex-major and she were also worried about payment; already there was no possibility of confirming with London banks the validity of Alec's cheques.

During the reloading of the Dormobile the major argued against packing the pair of walkie-talkies . . . 'Short-range things, you know. Who will you want to talk to with those? Frankly, during the war we found them pretty useless. They wouldn't work farther than you could shout.'

'They've improved them a bit since then, major. I'll take them. I may find people who are normal and mobile. If so, intercom between vehicles will help.'

The major nodded wisely. 'You'd be safer, certainly, in convoy. Where will you find a long-range set for communicating with us?'

Alec tried not to sound impatient. He didn't want to leave the hotel in the hands of a resentful and hostile management. 'I honestly don't know. Any ideas?'

'Try a military headquarters, in exceptional circumstances they might allow you to make a transmission, if something really urgent came up.'

Alec nodded gravely. 'Thank you major. If I may, I'll mention your name and rank.'

With all this rushing about going on, Alec found himself talking to Diana as if she weren't so much a wife as a company commander. Diana said, 'You're so tense you'll explode.'

He managed a softer voice. 'Yesterday you found the most sensational cure for that.'

She murmured, 'With Stephen asleep on our bed I'm afraid that's hardly on the menu.'

Alec looked thoughtfully at the curled-up figure of Stephen, then at Diana.

She said, 'I know exactly what you're thinking.'

His voice felt thick at the throat. 'I've just got to succeed.'

'You've done it so far.'

He asked, 'What about June? She's terribly dependent on Richard. He's having to humour her along an awful lot. Will her nerves last it out?'

'As much as anyone's. June and Richard always do that to each other anyway – taking it in turns to play parent. It works. Besides, June's got Baby Caroline to worry about. If ever there was an unmanageable baby – '

Alec grinned. 'Good. You're still bitching. You must be all right.'

'I happen to wish to hell you weren't going away, Alec.'

'We'll talk on the radio. You'll feel safer when things settle down . . . '

* * *

Nearer to his destination and driving in ominously thin traffic, Alec now saw that the factory was ablaze. Appalled, he watched – much as Melhuish had done at Blackbushe – as great tongues of flame leapt out from the main building and set fire to the transporters. Men, pillaging at the trucks, ran screaming, their clothes in flames, as they stampeded from the vehicles. A solitary fire engine hosed ineffectually at one end of the building, making no impression of the conflagration and then having to beat a retreat as an exploding laboratory sent a shower of combustible metal and a stench of poison gas bursting through a split in the wall, right opposite the fire ladder.

The ladder melted with the firemen still on top of it, then collapsed surrealistically in a warping, twisted hybrid of human gut and blistering metal.

So much for the official guard detail – confusion was erupting from the building with the same all-consuming ferocity as the fire; and and outsurge of frantically colliding vehicles all zeroed on to the same narrow exit when the gap the other end went unnoticed.

Alec, vomiting over the steering wheel and on to his lap at the spectacle of men literally running like ignited torches, swerved the Dormobile toward the gap and made straight for the automatic bay. It was just barely possible that a transporter, with the only remaining supply of Estofort aboard, might still be at the end of the conveyor.

The loading bay was housed in a tower just round the corner from the factory's back entrance, and only yards from where, on his visit that morning, Alec had parked the Dormobile and its inert human cargo. Now, the contrast was stark. Already the blaze was licking at the loading bay itself. The rollers of the conveyor were still turning. But the tail-board of the truck, shunted-in for loading, was already smouldering. Parts of the tarpaulin were alight.

Choking, Alec dashed into the bay.

Down the conveyor, boxes of priceless drugs inexorably followed each other. From them poured thick, acrid smoke. Where the loading gang should have been there was now a hot ooze of molten chemical and charred, curling cardboard, stacked up high.

Desperately grappling with those crates on the conveyor which seemed only singed, Alec fought for breath till his lungs felt like bursting. He hurled as many unburned boxes into the truck as he could, whamming them up to the front end of the lorry, where it was coolest.

He staggered outside again, gasping for air, then went back for more – knowing that if he judged it wrong the fire on the tarpaulin would spread to the fuel tanks.

By now, pungent fumes caused by the fusion of chemicals with hot rubber made breathing an agonized process of near-asphyxiation.

Liquid fire, a continuous lava of molten drugs exploding within their capsules, now flared down the conveyor belt, igniting the boxes still remaining on the floor.

Then the belt suddenly burned through and parted, meshing itself into the machinery and finally wrapping itself round its own roller – the loose, incandescent thong of the blistered rubber slapping against the top of the conveyor tunnel and each time showering debris and sparks. Solid blobs of sludge, stuck to walls and cealing in burning patches, sent forth such a malignant stench that breathing ceased to be possible at all.

Alec rushed, coughing his guts out, to the cab of the transporter and got the engine going. He drove furiously out of there, just in time to see the whole tower falter, split down the middle, and crumble like sponge cake into the oven below.

He now had to put out the fire that had caught around the tarpaulin and tail board.

Checking that the panicked drivers had still overlooked the loading bay exit, and finding himself miraculously still on his own, he drove the transporter with squealing tyres around to the chemical wing, where tanks containing basic chemicals, including – thank Christ! – Carbon-tetrachloride, stood like floodlit gantries in the backglow of a building that had now become a furnace.

He'd just quashed the spreading flames when he heard screaming coming from somewhere overhead.

Up there, in the western end of the office block, and immediately above the chemical storage tanks, the general office windows were still only venting white smoke.

Framed in one of these windows, three storeys up, Alec saw Maynard. He had one leg over the side of the wall, Instantly, on seeing him, Alec understood the significance of the bit of paper in his pocket – the undersheet from Nuttall's memo pad retrieved at the Institute by Melhuish.

The vivid shock of Maynard's contorted face ripped through Alec's mind with the speed of a computer. 'Jump!'

'I can't.'

'Jump. On to the tarpaulin. *Jump, you fool!*'

Suddenly the smoke changed colour and started pouring thickly from Maynard's window. An inner wall had collapsed, releasing a violent draught of super-heated air and toxic gas.

Still Maynard hung back. But literally vaulting over him someone else took a header out of the window and landed on the tarpaulin at the only point where the impact couldn't be fatal – halfway between two of the steel frames that supported it.

It was Tanya.

Her clothes were scorched off almost down to her pants. She was not badly hurt, managed to climb down via the steel ladder of the chemical tank nearby. 'Alec! Alec! Take me with you!'

'I can't. I'm sorry. No favourites. There'll be thousands.'

'I've something to sell.'

'I've never in my life had to pay for what you have to sell.'

'Alec, I *know* things. Things that will help you. Things you can't succeed without.'

'Such as?'

'Alec, for God's sake, why *not* me? It's true, what I'm saying . . . I can trade. I'll help you, take any risks. But I want to live, I'm made for living, try to deny that!'

Alec said through his teeth, 'I know all about Maynard. I know all about Nuttall.'

'You don't. You don't know which places he's already raided, how he's organized his group, how he's marketing the stuff and who to – ' The words came through in a rush. 'Nuttall and Maynard managed to get a line through. Maynard wanted to join up with Nuttall. It's all on tape – here!'

'How did you get this?'

'Alec, we can't wait here any longer. The fire. Those people – '

' – I'll decide when to move. Let's see if you do have something to trade for Estofort.'

'Stop feeling so damn guilty! You may be an adulterer but your wife is a hell of a lot safer than you're likely to be, once you drive out this truck!'

He said calmly, 'How did you know about the call?'

'I was on the switchboard, suddenly saw the indicator for the Staines tie-line. It hadn't showed for hours. The call wasn't for Dr Blessing, but Maynard! I paralleled it through to the Security room, and ran the tape. If you don't have a bloody machine to play it on, that's not my fault. I still have a vital tape to trade for my life. Oh God, Alec, you need me anyway! Be honest and a man and admit it!'

Alec surveyed the scene rapidly as it now was beyond them. The burned out hulk of the main body of the building cringed on its girders and shook. Even at this end all three storeys were alight at the windows.

The screams had ceased. There was just the primus stove of fire burning in high pressure gas. It roared increasingly, till the eardrums deadened against it, and Alec had to shout. 'Get in, you bitch. Get in the cab. Where we're going you may well be mobbed and torn apart by maddened animals. I've nothing to offer but terror. If you want that, be my guest!'

He handed her a little box from his coat pocket.

With a tremendous effort of will, Tanya avoided fumbling, for fear of scattering them over the cab floor. But very slowly, very carefully, she took one of the capsules and swallowed it. Alec stuffed the box back into his pocket, then reversed the truck rapidly back to where he'd left his own car.

He shouted to Tanya, 'Wait there!' – then dashed across

to retrieve the main items of gear. He nearly left the walkie-talkie sets, then changed his mind and brought them too; slinging all these items into the back of the transporter.

Checking the instruments he found the fuel gauge read low. That meant they'd have to find a garage that could serve a diesel truck. Which might not be easy.

'Okay. You asked for it. Let's go.'

They drove east, along the A38, many times having to veer off the road and on to the grass and manœuvre their way around pile-ups of mangled cars whose passengers had either fled or simply screamed themselves into oblivion while still trapped inside. Sometimes they had to use the transporter like a bulldozer, shifting small cars out of the way by scooping them brutally sideways over some bank, until they fell down the ravine.

It was a sickening process which consumed Alec with self-revulsion. Once or twice Tanya let out little whimpering cries as she saw ahead some human remnant or observed through the side window actual living beings who were writhing like horse-flies after being sprayed with insecticide. She shot out a restraining arm when Alec swerved to dodge a group who seemed locked together as if in a Rugby scrum.

'Can't we stop?'

He said nothing, just watched her vomiting through the window and put his foot down all the harder. Minutes ago he'd thought of saving Maynard's life. Now he found himself savagely neglecting human relics by the hundred – yet compounding the guilt by lusting for Tanya and knowing he couldn't wait long. How could this be? – Am I a monster?

If he was, he found a ready mate. Once Tanya had thrown her bile over the side, she responded there beside him with profound appetite.

Survival of the luckiest? – or what? It was no good choking at the thought – it was fact . . . They wanted each other as never before.

Physically erect and thinking himself mad, Alec raced on. Once they narrowly dodged a police car, travelling towards them very fast but with quickwitted normalcy, light flashing, siren wailing. It ripped past and was gone.

Clear now of the Ring Road and taking the less cluttered routes, they spent the last of their fuel in search of a garage that could dispense diesel fuel. They found one just as the tanks went dry.

'Lucky,' said Alec.

'Too lucky.' Tanya was right. Here the power had failed, which meant they would have to pull up steel covers on the concrete, open the cocks, and manually pump oil into the tanks . . . a long and complicated business without power.

Alec thought it out for a minute and said, 'We can't go any further in this thing anyway. It's got *ESTO* written all over it and even if we paint all that out, we're too slow and too unmanœuvrable – sitting ducks for trouble when it comes. Do you agree?'

She knew that the question really being asked was a different one altogether. Such decisions as the one he was voicing aloud were not hers to make. But the mutual one had already been made.

The back glow of the headlights, reflected off the spruce, smartly painted exterior of the fillling station, lit the interior of the cab dimly and showed Tanya's eyes as they shot to their corners and watched him for a second. In that moment she thought, we've been a twosome often enough, just us and the steering wheel, never like this.

Her silent message was caught by Alec and he replied, also wordlessly, I need you there, you're keeping me in the fight, I couldn't bear it alone.

Tanya, always a paradoxical mixture of the soft and the hard – both in the physical and emotional sense – looked then just as she claimed to be; made to live. All subtlety was stripped from these instants just as she was stripped down to charred remnants of a dress and improperly expensive bra . . . much too Parisian for decent Exeter, much too provocative for daily office use. Though Tanya felt herself often a whore, she was amoral rather than immoral; she loved having money spent on her by men but she loved the men a lot more.

Verging on the petite, she contradicted that definition almost bursting out of it – as it were – because sensually there was so much to her and to look at and to hold she presented a fullness that couldn't be explained by her economical vital statistics. Her erotic impact at the touch defied the slim, neat body seen demurely at the reception desk inside a factory . . . there was a yielding extravagance there; yet what fleshiness she had could instantly shift into lithe, sinewy strengths, once her metabolism transmuted in response to the man, and the invitation to the dance had been played and was accepted. She was one of the few women Alec knew whom it was essential to kiss and to whom sex would have been nothing short of rape without it.

Alec's hand was on her bared thigh, where the crinkled burn-line had undressed and so nearly damaged her. Nothing except those outrageously expensive pants interceded between his hand and the nerve centre that, for Tanya, was the essence of life and, by her own judgement, her passport. Existentially, love was what she was for.

The hunger arose in one spasm, at once and together, and he had the frail pants stripped down her legs through a more enlivened impulse than any factory fire. Her nipples were paired peaks throwing sharp shadows across the truck, then these shadows were darkened as he consumed them, and turned her into position as if the cramped dimensions of the cab, far from restricting movement, defined its course; so that his hands shifted fiercely to her frenetic rump and they were in seizure. No turtle-doves these, but desperate people replenishing each other to the accompaniment of helpless cries; till the stored pain could fall away. They were children frightened in the dark.

Tanya said, as she started pulling on those pants, 'You know what? If you didn't have an irresponsible streak, you couldn't take on all this responsibility.'

He said, 'Let me help you with that,' – and he dressed her, in the limited attire now at her disposal, with a sensualness that revealed so much to Tanya about Alec as a man.

She knew that with Alec the cure was never complete. It had never struck her so much as now . . . how even immediately after intercourse he caressed her body as if every nerve end in her thighs was a spring of life, and as if he were already in readiness for such a spring to overflow again.

He said, 'I don't think of it as responsibility.'

'I know. You can't help it. You're a born survivor.'

'Am I just selfish, at heart?'

'No, you're just healthy.'

So he patted her bottom while it was still in a position accessible to the possessive act, you're a bad girl – thank God, you're a bad girl. Then they were sitting up and thinking.

She said, 'What now?'

'We bury a proportion of these cartons here – in those woods will do – as a reserve supply of Estofort for the Dorrington Hotel. If we come unstuck ourselves we must radio in time, to

Richard Trent or to Diana at Jaybury, and tell them where to find it.'

'Why not tell them ahead of time?'

Alec fiddled with the clicker of the brake lever. Obliquely, he remarked, 'Desperation does funny things to people. We can't tell anyone yet.'

'Where do we take the rest of the stuff?'

He opened the door his side. 'I'll tell you as we go.'

'You haven't said where we're going.'

'The Institute.'

She'd been wrestling with the door catch her side now she froze in the act. 'That's near Staines?'

'Correct.'

'I think I'll call a taxi,' she said.

He slammed the driver's door. 'That's the hell of it,' he said. 'They're never around when you want one.'

* * *

As it turned out there wasn't room in any one vehicle for the quantity of boxes that they had to take on to the East; so in the end Alec chose from the show room two used estate cars – a Ford and a Vauxhall – and planned to drive in close convoy.

Tanya said, 'But then you won't be able to tell me what you plan to do.' She clung with just the touch of a hand. 'Alec, I don't think I could stand it if we can't talk to each other.' She looked beyond the garage into the blackness. It's . . . unearthly out there.'

Alec said, 'We can talk.' He showed her the two walkie-talkie sets. 'With these.'

'Is there anything you haven't thought of?'

He said briskly, 'They're very simple to work. Make sure the aerial sticks well out of the window. As long as the rod doesn't get too close to anything metallic it'll operate – in an emergency – up to about five miles. In practice though, don't drop back more than a hundred yards from me. I'll watch your lights all the time.' As a second-string plan they contrived a simple code of headlight flashes.

As they prepared to leave, with the two cars loaded up, she said, 'Alec, a dress shop. We must find one and smash our way in.'

He nodded. 'I've been thinking about that – not that I don't prefer you as a slightly toasted Cinderella – '

'Kinky.'

'Sure! – But we'll have to be desperately careful where we stop, and when. And at *night* . . . '

'Okay. I can always turn the heater on, if I get cold. But if we find a place . . . a cafe or something . . . that hasn't been affected, I wouldn't mind a hot meal. And in this garb it might turn out hotter than I bargained for.'

He replied, 'Obviously you don't yet know what you did bargain for. The juke boxes have been slightly switched off. V.P. has left a trail as thick and as wide as a swarm of locusts.'

She covered her sense of idiocy with a crack. 'Cut the lecture on migration and tell me what V.P. is.'

'Crossley's lingo . . . Virulent Panic.'

She did a sort of pout, then climbed into the Ford. Winding down the window, she went on, 'Not that that makes me any the wiser. What is it?'

'You've seen it.'

'I mean, what causes it?'

'That's what we've got to find out.'

She said, 'You're not going to try and tell me it's simply a disease?'

'What made you say that? Do you know you're the first person other than pure Crossleyites to draw the distinction?'

She tried to shrug it off. 'I don't know. I don't arrive at things by thinking.'

'Don't you?' He watched her thoughtfully as she started the engine. 'You're being taken in by your own image. It's always suited you to act dumb.'

As he led off in the Vauxhall he had the strong impression that, dumb or not, Tanya possessed a brand of intuition that was pure animal. He couldn't think, for the moment, exactly why the thought struck him. Was it some word or phrase she'd used?

On the radio they kept up the patter, never allowing silence to reign for long. Lose verbal contact for even a few seconds; allow the intimate companionship to diminish even a fraction, and the whole nightmare flooded over you until your brain was swamped with horror.

Tanya thought, as she doggedly kept Alec's tail lights at a fixed interval, that there must be some kind of a parallel in the way some women coped with birth pains – though the whole essence of the experience belonged in a different world and even the pain of labour was a creative one. But all those breathing exercises, the idiot things you were trained to say – even singing nursery rhymes as some women did – were calculated to keep your mind off the agony and concentrate on a focal point. Afterwards Tanya wondered what on earth made her draw the comparison. But it seemed to make sense at the time.

Mercifully there was a kind of numbing effect, too, in witnessing the same kind of scene over and over again. However appalling the spectacle, you couldn't go on being shocked by the same thing. Indeed, what you saw wasn't nearly as bad as what you conjectured; for the odd thing was that despite the number of car wrecks, which sometimes made the going almost impossible, there was so little sign of human life. Even where the accidents had clearly been trivial in impact – certainly not severe enough to cause serious injury – the survivors were not to hand. Except for a few scattered groups of bewildered, sickened human creatures who clung together at village corners, most people had simply disappeared. But where?

Only on those sites where high-speed, multiple collisions had occurred could you sense – and horrifically sometimes see – that human beings were trapped, still whimpering, inside their cars. At such moments an overpowering feeling of guilt and remorse overcame you . . . You were driving on, doing nothing about them, obeying the law of the jungle and letting the suffering of less fortunate animals take its course. You didn't say it aloud – what was the point? . . . It would only be paying lip service to the concept of humaneness. So you stayed cheerful, objective, and on the job . . .

Alec said, 'I want to catch the Prime Minister's television broadcast somewhere. But so far the power has been dead all the way.'

She said, 'You'd stop for that but not for my clothes!'

'A remote cottage with a TV would be safe. That's the kind of place I'm looking for. A shop in a high street would be sheer lunacy.'

'Well, you'll be lucky. I haven't seen a light yet, apart from a few flickers that were probably candles. What time is he speaking?'

'Eleven . . . That's just over half an hour.'

Tanya said nothing. She couldn't see what the hell difference it could make to anybody whether the Great Man spoke or not.

Alec broke the longest silence so far and explained, 'I want to see if there still is a government.'

She said, 'Yes, that's a point.'

But the power failure seemed to be universal. Even the roadsigns were in darkness; and at the roundabouts those isolated arrows, normally displayed on bollards, failed to provide the now entirely spurious advice that it was better to go around this way instead of that – During this whole section they'd only met three cars, all of them going full pelt, without dipping their headlights. Alec radioed soberly 'I somehow never imagined it could *all* be as bad as this. What I thought must have happened – I mean back nearer Exeter – was that whenever the traffic jams piled up, as they do in summer, people got out of their cars to commiserate with each other over the delays, and spread the thing that way.'

'But you saw what was happening – didn't you? – on your way down?'

'I know: I've been kidding myself. You try to forget.' He dropped the subject and went on about his plans . . . 'So Crossley is going to tell us posthumously what his research results were.'

She said, 'That part I can see as being . . . faintly possible. But this idea of other cadres – '

'We've got to try, Tanya.'

'There are two of us,' she said, succinctly. 'And as for beating Nuttall to all those wharfs and places, you'd better listen to that tape first.'

Abruptly Alec said, 'Lights ahead!'

The glow came from over on the left, a military headquarters evidently, with an unblemished bullshit drive-in, where a boom barrier had been lowered, painted black and white. You could now see that there were lights all over the place, right on to the far horizon. Here, at least, the promised power supply had been restored.

Alec pulled up on the grass verge and signalled with his arm for Tanya to do the same. She drew up behind him and switched off. Stealthily, silently, Alec got out of the Vauxhall. Keeping to the grass, he went back to Tanya's car and spoke softly through the window. 'This place may be intact. If it is we can get help. I'm going in to find out.'

'What if it isn't . . . Intact?'

'If I'm not back here within an hour, or haven't called you by radio, drive across to the M3 by the new Horster Tower Building, where the sign is. Even if you can't actually get on to the motorway you'll reach the roundabout. There's a copse on the far side – you'll see it easily in the headlights if the power's off – and there's a rough stone road leading up. I used to work at Horster Tower and I know you can get up to that wood. wait there, where you'll be out of sight. If I don't manage to make it by two a.m., something's come unstuck. I may get taken prisoner or any damn thing. Turn back if that happens and head for the Dorrington at Jaybury. You know where the reserve stuff is buried so tell them at your discretion. Keep trying the walkie-talkie all the way back. I've put spare batteries in your glove compartment.'

She'd never felt less like joking at this particular prospect but managed, 'You see? – I told you. You do think of everything!'

He simply said, 'We have to. If this place is contaminated but still has survivors it's going to be dangerous. But in any event I'm going to try to pick up arms and ammunition for each car.'

'I've never used a gun in my life.'

'I know. But sooner or later you may have to – '

'But Alec! – '

' – *Keep your voice down*! . . . I'll also try to beg or swipe a long-range radio so we can talk to the Dorrington Cadre. We have a check call due in just over an hour. Okay? Show no lights and stay in the car. Don't for God's sake make a sound. Don't use the radio unless it's essential and wind the windows up if you do . . . You simply mustn't be heard outside the car.'

'But talking to you on it is the only thing that – '

' – Tanya, if you must, you must. But they'll have sets in the headquarters and you're at point-blank radio range. That's why you won't have to stick the aerial through the window. And move the car under those trees. Now.'

'Alec?'

'Yes?'

'For God's sake don't get trapped, in there. It's you who make me feel that I even exist.'

'Same applies. So be careful.'

'But I'm so useless . . . just hiding.'

'There'll be plenty to do. later. Stay off the air and be a bad girl. That way I'll feel confident and come out alive.'

* * *

At first, Alec thought the place really was normal. The overwhelming relief at the prospect made him light-headed. He thought the major at the Dorrington, who hadn't moved a muscle when Alec had asked, Can I use your name and rank? –

Well, they were moving in convoy all right, but hardly the sort the major had envisaged . . .

There was the usual guardroom just inside and a boom-barrier straddling the approach road, lowered as you would expect. All seemed spick and span under the brilliant perimeter lights. There were no personnel visible; but no doubt the guard detail was touring the headquarters. In the guardroom itself Alec would surely discover the sergeant, sitting before one of those huge tin mugs of cocoa. There would be a duty officer alert in the Mess. Through military channels he would know much about the situation farther East. With luck there would be a meal – Tanya might after all get her steak and chips. First aid kit, radio, all the gear they needed. Tanya could get a rest while he –

The truth hit him the moment he entered the guardroom. The scene inside presented a grotesque conflict between order and chaos. It was as if the sovereign priority of Bullshit could almost – but not quite – rule supreme over any human aberration that might exist.

Alec could imagine the initial episode there. No doubt the first cases among the Other Ranks had been marched before a commanding officer with the usual deafening 'quick MARCH left-rightleftrightleft' from a poker-backed warrant officer who would regard instant schizophrenia as being in direct contravention of Section 40, conduct prejudicial to good order and military discipline.

Thus, the huddle of victims in the guardroom had managed their disorientation in an orderly manner. In ghastly mockery of superdrilled minds, the men who lay victim had made some attempt to arrange themselves in a row on the floor. The vomiting had been done into the fire bucket and not over each other; the writhings, slight and only intermittently visible by now, were convulsions by numbers. The bodies shook but after each spasm the limbs returned to a semblance of straightness, as if lying to attention. The effect was that of tin soldiers which had tumbled; and had its grim absurdities – all the more grotesque for the razor-edge distinction from comedy – as if some mock-military command would restore them to their feet.

A glance at the guard report showed that the sergeant must have been going gradually berserk as he attempted to make the final entries:

Unable to raise duty officer.

Corporal Cresswell sick as well as Private Relton
Still unable to call duty officer
Rang fire triangle, no answer feeling ill myself now
Must get a copy of Playboy Magazine
Phone now dead and closed barrier
What is wrong with the sky is coming down right on top of the spirit level and I can't wind my watch
Playboy gosh Playboy what about that double page nude – Christ I could fuck her stupid
My head's coming off and I . . .

It ended in an illegible squiggle.

Alec left the guard room and crunched the gravel drive along to where it said 'Officers' Mess'. Only one man lay there – presumably the duty officer. He had shot himself with a service revolver which lay a few feet away. It shared a lake of blood with its willing victim. The phone nearby was hanging from the hook; and a tap was running in the bartender's washing-up sink, as if the duty officer had first tried flushing his face with cold water to revive his senses before finally obliterating them with a gun.

Seeking out the signal office, Alec found a suitable short-wave transmitter and a receiver to go with it. The voltages appeared to suit car batteries and though the equipment was rather bulky he found room for it in the front passenger seat.

Next to the signal office was the weapon store.

An NCO, lying at the entrance, his mouth omitting froth, was mumbling, 'Immediate Action . . . Fires a few rounds and stops again.' Alec dimly remembered what this meant: training procedure on the Bren Gun.

Alec hesitated.

Up till now, action on his part had been confined to the protection of life against an unknown force – not against humanity. Was neglect now to be transmitted into hostility? – by stealing lethal weapons over the prone figure of a plague-stricken soldier? Come to that, what inner force had guided him through this fearful crisis anyway? Was it some unnatural superselfishness, not far removed – in its way – from insanity itself? Tanya didn't think so. But she herself might be a symptom. Was he adding to the score of his own brutality of adultery by reinforcing it with guns?

But then there was Nuttall. And the gangs. The thought was enough. He raided the armoury, snatching up boxes of ammo; a crate of six new service revolvers, and – Oh God – a sub-machine-gun with its magazines of lethal steel capable of mowing down an entire street.

Why? How could you justify the perpetuation of life by using the currency of other lives in payment? Oh God, Oh God; if I do live, what memories will I be living with?

And he took the guns and he took the ammunition and he stacked them high in the back of the estate car.

In his agony, he wanted to call Tanya on the walkie-talkie, as if a few crisp words of reassurance and commonsense with her might summarily dismiss all the disquiet in his mind. Put some of the blame on her, make her share it and condone it; use her own urge for survival against her, so that when and if they started killing people he could weakly declare, 'You were in on it too, you hypocrite.'

No, thanks. At least keep adultery as clean as adultery can ever be. Be a coward and shoot if you must. But don't be that kind. Besides . . .

And he knew what he meant, in his thoughts, by 'besides'. In a way that frightened him too . . . Tanya, Tanya, please just be sexy. You're unlocking a secret door to my emotions and I never realized it was even there. I have to talk to Diana on the radio. Tanya, hands off, and let me indulge my selfish needs at your expense.

Troubled by a two-threat situation, Alec doggedly continued his reconnaissance, now following the neat signposts round the camp in search of the M.I. Room. Surely there'd be survivors queuing-up there? For via jungle telegraph, the immunizing effect of the drug had become known from the earliest hours. Would the M.O. have had Estofort among the time-honoured 'Number Nines?'

Alec cursed himself for that brand of idleness which caused him, week by week, to leaf through the medical journals in five minutes flat. The arrogantly uncommunicative Dr Crossley had not often been a contributor to the *Lancet*; but when he did write it was because he had something to say . . . Unknown properties of current tranquilizers and their harmful side-effects, yes. Scathing correspondence comprising a running battle with the Dunlop Committee, over the dangers of handing out Largactil without insistence upon prior psychoanalysis – certainly. Quoth the Committee, 'What's that got to do with us?' – What indeed? Often Crossley was merely a crosspatch.

But there was something else . . . statistical findings painstakingly gathered and published very recently.

But on what, and for what?

Alec had some vague idea that Crossley had been doing some research in Norway. What goes on in Norway, except for the plodding perpetuation of the Grieg Concerto?

Fjords. Norway was dripping with fjords. Why should such idyllic landscape attract the interest of a grumpy genius whose lifework lay solely with brains? Animal brains, perhaps? Fish? Somehow the spectacle of Crossley solemnly swimming about in flippers and underwater snorkels observing their mating habits didn't ring true. What other animals, then, were to be found in fjords?

Certainly there seemed nothing wrong with the animals in Britain. The lethargic sheep in Jaybury fields had shown less sign of Virulent Panic than chronic boredom. At the Dorrington the children had quiescently watched the cattle in the fields. Cows champed at the grass is if the world were unchanged; later, show-jumping horses, suddenly turned loose when the plague reached the warm grass and the beer tents and the exhibition stands, then being dismantled, had cantered contentedly away from the agricultural show and grazed indolently in the paddock adjoining the hotel, only a few hundred yards from the point where June and Richard and Baby Caroline had been so skilfully landed in a tiny field by the inscrutable, pink-faced Stan. The geese, squawking irritably around the hotel, had ushered their young protectively without a frayed nerve; there wasn't even the usual warning about foot-and-mouth disease. The only disquieting element, audible occasionally on the night drive to here, was the baying of lonely dogs, seeking in vain the companionship of their masters. In them there existed a certain canine sadness, but no disease.

Disease . . . a new thought struck him as he turned that last corner for the Medical Inspection Room. For whatever the nature of the present epidemic, inevitably it would lead to another.

Neglected drains and sewage; radioactive contamination from nuclear power stations no longer supervised; festering food and untreated water supplies; rotting bodies of the suicides picked at by predatory animals and washed over by new rain . . . all these could add up to the spread of disease much better known and – if not treated and contained – just as catastrophic to what was left of humanity than V.P. itself . . . Typhoid and other scourges, almost invincible because so much unprotected food would be totally impossible to test and select . . . and no chance of organized vaccination against smallpox and other fast-spreading diseases that went with collapsed social hygiene and a breakdown in the will to survive.

How long would it be before such added terrors threatened?

Ominously, the M.I. Room was in darkness. Even in the glow from the camp's street lighting it was all too obvious what had happened. Bullet holes pocked the door; the lights had been shot out; broken bottles and phials and the smashed glass panes of medicine cupboards told their own story.

To make a final check, Alec searched for the drug book – easiest to find than any other evidence of the availability – or otherwise – of the vital drug needed by those who had shot their way in.

Estofort, new as it was, simply was not carried by the M.O. But from the wreck that had once been a spotless M.I. Room, one grim element of truth was strongly suggested, if only negatively.

For those stocks of conventional tranquilizer, the amytals, barbiturates, even the powerful chlorpromazines, had clearly been tried and discarded, as useless as the sugared hundreds and thousands they resembled where they lay crunched on the floor. Littered there, cartons emptied of sedatives and sleeping tablets, syringes with the needles broken and glass smashed and trampled by the stampede underfoot, suggested that at some time the M.O. himself or at least the Orderlies had attempted to treat what – according to the guardroom log – must have been a very sudden outbreak. No doubt a staff car or a truck-load of blokes returning to a perfectly sane camp after a welfare ride to the cinema, had brought unwittingly the carrier or the struggling madman who had spread the plague, at tempest speed, from hut to hut.

This time, there were no bodies and no suffering men, clinging to radiators or table tops or grotesquely – as in the guard room – lined up like organic dominoes on the floor. They had fled, and Alec didn't want to know where.

Reconnoitering completed, he went to the car and called up Tanya on the walkie-talkie. For half a minute – terrifyingly long – there came no reply; then her voice, so cool it irrationally angered him, said, 'I'm here, sorry, couldn't find the button. Have we struck lucky?'

'Hardly that.' He spoke coldly, walking back to the officers' quarters holding the radio. 'There's a television in the Officers' Mess. Just follow the signs round. Park your car next to mine.'

'Okay,' she said cheerfully. 'Can't wait to hear all those words of wisdom from Whitehall.'

Alec switched off. He entered the Mess and stooped over the duty officer's body. He couldn't understand his own peevishness at Tanya's cheerful calm, suddenly wanted cruelly to leave the body in view.

But didn't he depend on her calm? – Stop looking for someone to ease your conscience, you shit. It was you who took the guns.

So he dragged the officer's body into the kitchen quarters and returned to switch on the television.

Tanya drove in five minutes later, made Alec accept a whisky, which some ridiculous and irrational scruple had prevented him from stealing, and tossed one back herself.

Alec, waiting for the screen to light up, was almost relieved – however perversely – to see how white and shaken she looked in a properly lighted room. She was a woman and was suffering for the understated and the unseen; and her imagination filled the gaps which the sheer absence of people explained for those who still cared enough about people even to notice. Aloud, Alec said, 'Tanya, I've been trying to make you take the blame for everything I feel.'

'At this moment,' she said, looking away, 'you would prefer to be with Diana.' – He said nothing, but they both knew it wasn't true. She held out a hand to him. For once, the touch wasn't in any way sensual. Then they looked at each other frankly.

It was an unbearable moment for reasons they couldn't define.

Quietly, Alec said, 'With some things, there is no way back.'

She said, 'It's the situation.' Then, brightly, with her usual practical streak, she pointed across the Mess. 'Over there, Alec! A tape recorder.' – She conveyed, but did not state, that her need for a passport now was emotionally rendered redundant. Neither of them had forgotten one nuance of her frantic transaction at the fire.

Alec absorbed her stare, then turned away and crossed to fetch the machine. 'Good. We'll take it along with us.' His hand was trembling as he picked it up, avoiding Tanya's eyes by glancing at the television.

The screen came bright and a blurred image appeared, then came into focus.

The Prime Minister, urbane, suitably jacketed, shaven to the last facial hair, straightened the handkerchief showing in his breast pocket, and opened his mouth to speak.

NINE

The tortuous route whereby Nuttall's racketeering enabled pills to reach the Prime Minister's briefcase, involved and convolute though the processes of delivery thereto had been, did not delude the country's leader about their actual source. He was, as he would have put it, one of the privileged beneficiaries of good fortune and careful planning in the interests of his country. In other words, he knew he was alive and kicking because of dirty work.

Prime Minister do not always have time for investigating too thoroughly the intricate matters described by lesser persons as moral integrity. Presumably, had there been time for luxuries of this kind, Nuttall could have been indicted and the capsules impounded. Their significance realized, measures might then have instantly been taken to cordon off the Exeter factory – exactly as Melhuish had envisaged – and override the ditherings of Dr Blessing. But Whitehall was as slow off the mark as it was frightened for its own; and Nuttall had banked unfalteringly on an attitude of personal expediency on the part of those he offered his wares. Five pounds sterling per capsule of Estofort was, of course, well within the bounds of the P.M.'s pocket; and in view of his overwhelming responsibilities to the Nation, could no doubt, in due course, come out of Expenses. Who could possibly blame him? – Like everyone else he wanted to live, thank you very much, and fortunately he had the income, influence and quick-wittedness to do so.

Corruption, in Whitehall, is not common. The desire to survive is universal; and the information that suddenly came to hand, concerning the limited availability of supplies from one particular quarter – and, by now, no other – sent innumerable officials rushing to their bank managers for hasty applications concerning increase in their overdrafts. Ingenuity knew no bounds; suddenly Whitehall, seldom the incubator for creative thinking, acquired a lively sense of imagination. Bankers who became daily bored by the dreary and predictable excuses of the majority among their customers for yet another loan, leaned forward on their desks with a freshened fascination for inventive ingenuity and many of them gave ground almost solely on the merit of the originality of each man's case. Naturally, supplies being down to the frightful ebb at which they stood, the bankers did not benefit from their customers' secret knowledge. Desperation is desperation; and unless the government machinery of the time can bring about emergency controls, chaos will not only make possible the high-priced favours, but indulge them, nurture them, and create the optimum opportunity for the chap that can come up with the goods.

The chap was Nuttall; and his unique advantage was the close cooperation with the Post Office enjoyed by the company he represented. Through the personal contacts liaison work at the Institute had engendered, he was able, through trading Estofort for facilities as well as cash, to take control of those telephone circuits which, by careful selection, he wished to keep open for his operations. No longer selling only to the high and the mighty in government circles as his exclusive contribution to smooth government, he spread himself to include every scrap-metal millionaire in the game and doubled the price of the pills. And unable to grasp that the large sums of money he was acquiring would be meaningless in a jumbled, decimated society, he was a miser in a hatter's castle, involuntarily preparing to ignite his stronghold with paper currency.

He handled the potentially disastrous tinder with characteristic lethargy, as careless of the terror he caused those who couldn't pay the price as he was blind to the fact that for every capsule he sold off, there would be one less for himself and his enlisted staff of thugs. Slouched back in a swivel chair, comfortable in the evacuated Manchester office of his firm, he dialled unhurriedly the chosen few who waited so hungrily by their telephones. Those black eyebrows, inscrutable crescents signifying lifelong discontent, seldom rose in surprise or crimped in annoyance if his price couldn't be met. One more phone was simply cut off; and he glanced lazily at the next name on the list. He felt no excitement; only a vague sense of gloating at the reprisal he was taking against a society which had ignored his significance hitherto. The loose-fingered, detached manner of dialling was the same as always. Only the price was different.

Telecommunications being so vital, he ensured early on that moguls in electronics were among his customers. For these there was a reduced price, set off against certain circuits provided in return. For instance, he'd got the tie-line re-opened to the Exeter factory, as a priority step; and it was over this link that, having gauged the anæmic personality of Maynard, he attempted to increase the range of a system which – if Maynard hadn't unexpectedly caught fire – would have made operations even more efficient and profitable. But the magic facilities didn't stop there. So the P.M. wanted to ensure that his television broadcast was made available to a network which had, by now, gone as dead as the telephones? . . . Very well; the UHF links would be re-activated by selected technicians who would be provided, in time, with sufficient supply of the drug to last out the transmission. What happened to them thereafter was an unfortunate matter of fate and the unknown; and Nuttall could be held responsible for neither.

The price was fixed and the men were helicoptered down to the various points along the TV relay routes to keep the system open. Similarly, key personnel who could maintain the power stations in operation – without the need to anticipate tomorrow's continuity or the routine continuation of normal maintenance, were provisioned likewise and established along the National Grid.They didn't all get there, but current was available in fifty per cent of the cities by the time the P.M. sat before the cameras in Downing Street – though tragically there were far more television sets accessible and able to function than there were people to view the Prime Minister's message of hope.

Although the speech, carefully typed on small sheets of paper, was basically fatuous and banal, there was an underlying reason why such a speech was politically necessary. The need concerned not so much the domestic viewers in England but the maintaining of sympathy and confidence abroad.

By now, interest and alarm and then sheer incredulity had struck capital cities from Washington to Paris and Rome. Moscow had nothing to say but plenty of guesses – there, and only there outside Britain – a drug very like Estofort had been developed because of scientific suspicion over some strange and alarming symptoms among cosmonauts. The United States did harbour a few specialists who not only knew of Crossley's work but had an inkling of a possible crisis – which, however, they anticipated as lying years ahead – but no such drug existed there and prospects of sending help to Britain were inhibited by the obvious dangers to any relief personnel sent. Diplomatic excuses for delays were very voluble, via satellite, while scientists in America quite justifiably wondered what on earth they could do. The only blessing – which worked back-to-front – was that so many air disasters, cancellations and aborted take-offs from England had occurred that few passengers were actually arriving in foreign lands. Those who did arrive in America were placed in isolation at least as efficiently organized as had been the precautions taken over the first astronauts to return from the moon. All aircraft from Britain were diverted to a desert field and supplies dropped them by parachute. Meanwhile a grim array of military vehicles encircled the unhappy passengers and crew, who scorched-out their sweat in fuselages that had become boilers. The army vehicles didn't venture closer to the contacts than three miles. So as an added luxury the Air Force laid an inner circle of barbed wire from helicopters.

With such rigorous and somewhat inhumane precautions being taken there and elsewhere against the British, the Prime Minister had further telephoned Nuttall – who was by now not far short of a celebrity – to acquire the use of the satellite relay system. Addressing the world by this means, the P.M. hoped to improve the exchange rate (which had slumped, rather naturally, upon the closing of the London stock market in such circumstances), emphasize Britain's 'unique powers of recovery in times of crisis', and try and give the impression that matters were under control.

The technicians abroad were prepared to accept this whimsical demand on their television relay system. They felt that Virulent Panic, whatever it might be, was nice and remote when the pictures had to go all the way to outer space and back again before reaching foreign audiences. Thus Britain was never more an island since Cæsar first found out.

However, nobody's perfect; and Nuttall was no exception. He'd remembered the basic electronic details for resuming the networking of television so far as *vision* was concerned. What he'd forgotten was the *sound*. The Prime Minister was seen by those who cared to look – or who cared for anything – to talk to them wordlessly for nearly twenty minutes. Those few who might possibly have been capable of lip-reading might have learned of all the Stones that wouldn't be left Unturned; but for the majority throughout the world, including Alec and

Tanya at the military base, an element of black comedy had crept into an otherwise profoundly unfunny situation – the jaw moved, the gestured arms waved, the determined fists clenched and occasionally hammered down resolutely on a nice clean table. Otherwise the audience were left none the wiser . . . for all the difference the oratory would have made in any case to a situation which was as surely out of control as was the sound channel. There could, in fact, have been no more articulate comment on the extent of the crisis than so farcical an anticlimax to such a terrific effort. The mask was off – and the Prime Minister didn't even know.

Tanya, after a lucidly meaningful look at Alec when the calamitous omission had become clear, fell asleep in his arms for a time. She was still Cinderella, but a dependent and inviolable one. Alec thought, we're taking it in turns, borrowing strength from each other, then giving it back next time around . . .

Gently he carried Tanya across to a settee, then crept out of the Officer's Mess to his car. There, he set about connecting the radio equipment first to the car battery, then to the domestic radio aerial with which the estate car was already fitted. Tested, working, and tuned to the agreed frequency, the radio was now ready to exchange the first scheduled check call with the Dorrington, due in twenty minutes time.

Alec switched off, made sure his watch was wound and ticking, and crossed the smart parade ground back to the mess, where Tanya had now woken and was brewing up coffee and frying bacon and eggs. 'I feel domestic,' she said.

'Oh.'

She spoke with her back to him. 'Am I stepping out of line?'

He tried to toss it away. 'It's an innocent enough act,' he said, 'and we're both hungry.'

Yes. And we both know I may never see Diana or the children again.

As if conceding the same thought, Tanya said, 'Have you fixed up the radio telephone to Jaybury?'

'Yes. I'm all set up.' He didn't add that he was puzzled by the amount of static that seemed to afflict reception. Europe seemed to be fading out; the test signals from Jaybury, considering the relatively short range, were inexplicably faint. It came in spasms; one moment it was all as clear as a bell; the next, a mush of hissing and crackling nearly obliterated reception from all parts of the world. It worried him. If conditions were like this from here, what would they be like from Staines? Aloud, he said, 'Our first call is due in exactly twelve minutes.'

'I don't envy them.' Tanya found the milk and handed Alec the coffee. 'Being pinned, I mean. Hemmed in like Red Indians about to be charged by Custer.'

'Tanya, for God's sake!'

She said quietly, 'You do see what you're trying to do, don't you?' she passed him a plate. 'Knives and forks over there.'

'Tanya, I've got to speak to Diana in a few minutes.'

She looked away. 'And your little Stephen? . . . If anything happened to them you'd probably end up hating me.'

'So you are capable of ordinary jealousy?'

'I seem to be now. Tight corners mean different things.'

'I shall go back to Diana and she'll survive all this and then there will be family life again.'

'In a very different world,' said Tanya, 'almost unrecognizable socially. Many of the things Diana stands for will have simply gone.'

'She'll adapt. I don't see what you're trying to say.'

'You do. You and Diana will be strangers.'

'And you want that?'

'Alec, don't be dishonest. I can see why you think you've got to be. Those radio calls you have to make are vital to Diana's morale. But I'm not blind, and I'm facing facts. You and I are not just playthings to each other now. How can we be? Admit you love me, Alec. Go on caring for Diana and the children for the rest of your life – which for all we know might be ten minutes or forty years – but for God's sake . . . ' and she ran to him and clutched him, ' . . . admit to me now that you are in love with me.'

'Diana will sense it. Even admitting it to you is in a way admitting it to her.'

'I see what you mean but you've got to weigh the odds.'

'I am. Look at the other side of the coin. If Diana feels a rift between herself and me – at these distances, with nothing she can do about it, and all the torment of not knowing – will she have the strength to go on, taking the responsibilities with the kids – especially the penetrating mind of young Stephen – and competing with the on-the-spot unity of Richard and June?'

'Alec darling, of course I see. But you can't manipulate these things by wishful thinking. It's either true or it is not.

You just have to hope things will work out.' She caressed with fingertip tenderness. 'I just want . . . fair treatment.'

He said reasonably, 'We didn't make terms when I rescued you.'

'Is that fair? Your rescuing me was your salvation. And you know it.'

He said, 'That's true.' He stared out of the window at the camp lights. 'So you've chosen to become a woman – fully-fledged – now, of all times. Ironic, isn't it? All these terrible things happening around us – happening to millions. And yet a domestic matter between three people can still seem more important.'

Tanya said, 'When it stops being important, that's the end of life . . . What are you going to tell Diana?'

'Certainly not that you're with me. In the age-old way of all sinners, I shall bluff my way through and lie at every opportunity. He added bitterly, 'Just one more notch in the butt of the gun. Anyway, one thing's certain. She can't know you're with me.'

* * *

He was wrong about that. Through an unkind fluke she already knew.

Earlier, when news of the factory fire had been handed grimly to Melhuish, by one of the runners recruited by Richard as part of his assigned duties concerning defence of the cadre, Diana's one thought had been the ordinary one of trying to satisfy herself that Alec had survived it. She knew, from the timing (just before dinner . . . ?) that he must have got there at the optimum time. Later Richard, who had, among his recruits, enlisted probably the last sane police patrol in the Exeter area, had revealed in conversation that in the cab of the one transporter that somehow got away there had been not one individual but two.

'Two men,' said Melhuish thoughtfully. 'Well, the other couldn't have been Dr Blessing.' – Melhuish left out the details in front of Diana but Blessing's body had been found by the police officers impaled on the vent pipe of the tank containing carbon tetrachloride. It had gone clean through the chest and out through his back.

Richard said, 'The other man must have been one of the regular drivers who had the sense to get the hell out of it.'

The patrolman said, 'I know most of those drivers by sight.

I'm sure it wasn't. This driver was someone quite unused to handling a vehicle of that size.'

By now, Diana was quite sure who the driver was and felt reassured. Alec would have got away. He'd been expecting trouble and so had the edge on those who were still under the late Dr Blessing's spell. 'Two men?' she asked. 'Are you sure it was two *men*?'

The patrolman hadn't been sure. He'd seen the truck, heading East along the Ring Road, going very fast. 'I suppose the other occupant could have been a woman.' It didn't seem important to the patrolman; and Richard, who hadn't realized yet that the driver of the truck must have been Alec, had with inadvertant tactlessness allowed the conversation to go on in front of Diana.

So the cat – hardly out of the bag, thought Diana – was well and truly snuggled inside it.

'Whoever it was,' deduced the police officer, 'must have jumped from one of the west windows. The office block. I raced to the scene. No one could have got out any other way.'

And no one, Diana had immediately concluded, would have been so acceptable as an extra soul to replenish with rare pills as the one woman who could so sumptuously meet Alec's needs.

So the radio call from Alec comprised an exercise in double-deception: Diana knew that Tanya was there and Alec was pretending she wasn't. Like a guilty telegram from a husband on one of those business trips, Alec sounded clipped and stilted 'It must be the reception, Diana,' he diagnosed hopefully. 'We can talk properly later, when it improves.'

Privately, Diana thought that reception from Alec's prevaricating transmitter was a sight more revealing than the dumb-show from Downing Street she had just switched off. She said, 'I can hear you well enough,' And bringing a little healthy bitchiness into play she added, 'You must be awfully lonely.'

'I'll make out.'

You bet you'll make out, you two-timing bastard.

Yet, after the radio call Diana was unable to resist the still small voice inside her which couldn't help saying, thank God he isn't alone . . . Not the first time she had been grateful for the spin-off from a highly undesirable missile.

Diana, wrechedly sleepless and doing some hard thinking that night, philosophized on the fact that it was situations, rather than personalities, which decided so many things in life. Diana had always dismissed Tanya as a fantasy pin-up, a retouched Playboy nude come to life. She conceded Tanya was an excellent sample but too much of an archetype for a man to love. Alec, though, would believe what he needed to believe, and retool the model into the custom-built speciality demanded by events. He would then return to his wife, neither greatly impassioned nor excessively remorseful, and persist – or not persist – with Tanya as his mistress. It was a sane and sober deduction. The only thing wrong with it was it made her utterly miserable.

She lit a cigarette and lay on her back and thought how characteristic of Alec this was. And although being wise after the event, she realized now that she'd had an inkling of Alec's virtual resumption of his affair with Tanya, on his return from the factory after lunch.

After lunch. Diana smiled at herself ironically for thinking still in those terms – Glenmore terms. No doubt Alec would have been the first to point out, certainly in his present mood and present company, how obsolescent this kind of habit now was. He had always thought her inflexible, a snob, dependent on certain things she had used to shore up her personality.

Diana stubbed out the cigarette, and reflected on the irony of Alec's sudden, wild love-making on the Andover by-pass. For she knew that in some odd way it had made matters worse. It was like eating; the more you ate the more you wanted. The matter of who prepared the meal, as long as it suited the palate, was secondary to the existence of appetite . . .

Stephen, evidently unable to sleep next door with the other children, now that Daddy had suddenly gone away, sneaked into her bed and curled himself up in a dependent little huddle beneath the sheets. What if he should find out?

Diana suddenly wished there was someone she could talk to, tell real things, express pain and cry. She knew it could never be June, who would respond with the kind of reassurance that she would have needed herself, half fact and half fiction and leaving everything in a state of confusion and internal suspense. There was nobody: Richard had never been able to talk to her, in some way struck her as being slightly afraid of her, like a boy who, picking up another child's over-realistic doll, feared that it might suddenly come alive in his hands and do something unpredictable.

'What's the matter, Mummy?'

So Stephen knew there was something wrong beyond all that was wrong already. And he was still afraid of those spiders . . .

'Go to sleep, Stephen.'

'Did you talk to Daddy on the radio?'

'Yes.'

'Is he all right?'

'Perfectly all right.'

Stephen thought this out a moment, then said, 'That's what I thought.'

Diana frowned into the darkness. Stephen's deadly intuition was working with its usual accuracy. For what he meant really was that Daddy was *too* perfectly all right.

Now, Diana lay on her back, her eyes wide open, listening to Stephen's regular breathing and thankful that at last he'd got to sleep. She found herself wondering eventually if the one person in whom she might eventually confide would be Melhuish.

Melhuish had annexed an office for himself from what had been designed as the American Bar. He was still sitting in there planning while Diana was lying sleepless. The surviving doctors and specialists from Sindham were due to arrive with their equipment within an hour. They would have an armed escort. provided by the 'troops' sorted and equipped by Richard Trent. The escort would include the police patrol car which had started the unfortunate snowball concerning Alec and the girl.

Once at the Dorrington, laboratory equipment would have to be installed and working as quickly as possible and the main lounge had been cleared out – much to the Major's dismay – for use as the main base. Additionally, a bus had been driven in and stripped of its seats, so that mobile work would be possible. For this, arrangements had had to be made for systematic battery-charging and all the rest of it, with both generators ready to run at a moment's notice.

After he had finished lying to his wife, Alec had explained on the radio to Melhuish that he thought he would reach the Hat-Rack by early morning, where his first objective would be to turn up as much as possible of the late Dr Crossley's secretly documented work and transmit it back to the Dorrington 'laboratory'. By this means; the imported Sindham experts would have data which they could immediately work on. But Melhuish, who knew Crossley's jealous caution in guarding the secrets of his research, wondered how on earth Alec could hope to find the records. It was he who filed everything Dr Crossley chose to make available to the Institute. The material consisted solely of confidential reports on his colleagues, few of which were flattering.

Just before the Sindham convoy was due in, all the lights in Exeter failed simultaneously. Melhuish, nodding to himself as if this were merely a part of some perfectly normal chain of events – instead of one more sign of the bedlam to follow – got up without hurrying and walked by torchlight out to the generator room. He started the more elderly engine and left the other ready in reserve. The key lights came on, though it was unnerving to look out over the meadows and see utter blackness where before there had been the ten mile span of distant lights that had lit the sky. Now there wasn't even a star to relieve the isolation. Still, the generator chugged consolingly and marked the difference between Order at the cadre and Chaos for hundreds of square miles beyond.

* * *

In one unanimous series of loud twangs, every master switch in Britain cut out the main supply, and power station after power station ran down the scale and became motionless. Huge pylons latticing the British Isles in one gigantic mesh, became dead totems to an entire technology. The fruitless clicking of dead switches by people who could not grasp the extraordinary changes of the last few hours was, for some, the trigger of final despair.

* * *

Alec and Tanya were just about to leave the military headquarters when the whole place went black.

'Tanya, got the torch?'

'No, I left it in the car.'

'We're both damn fools – I did too. It doesn't matter this time; next time it might mean the difference between life and death.' He led the way out to the cars by striking matches. Then they drove both estate cars round to the Transport Section, where hand-operated petrol pumps were available. 'In future,' said Alec, 'the easiest way to fill up will be to syphon petrol out of abandoned cars.'

They left the main gates of the headquarters for the last time, and with headlights blazing and the usual prattle on the walkie-talkie they headed for the A30 which would ultimately take them back through Sunningdale – Alec felt odd when he thought about Sunningdale – and finally to the Institute outside Staines.

Resolutely they ignored the hideous shambles that lined and often blocked the main roads, sometimes having to take detours through tiny villages which – again – showed a strange lack of overt symptoms of trouble, until smashed windows diffracting the beams of the headlights, and abandoned toys – pathetic kiddy cars and crushed go-carts – were visible beneath the front suspension of the car wrecks. Children had died in these; but the eerie lack of human life, demented or otherwise, seemed even more terrifying.

On the main roads – like the Andover by-pass and the M3 – you were spared the worst spectacles through sheer speed. Only at Blackbushe, where the amorphous line of gutted vehicles still smoked, blocking the road, did they have to veer completely off the highway and use the runway of the airfield instead.

Occasionally a car, careering in the opposite direction, shot past at high speed, as if one or two of the sane were still managing to get away from one sort of hell in search of another. There was no attempt on either part to stop and compare notes. The danger of leaning out of a window and talking to a possible carrier must have been uppermost in the minds of those still sparsely using the east-west lane of the highway. Somehow, these drivers must have escaped contamination so far but their very determination not to stop Alec's two-car convoy implied they were unprotected by the drug. Just what they thought they would do when they ran out of petrol or places to go – and not go – was a matter they couldn't have considered. They just blindly hoped. Alec said on the walkie-talkie, 'Poor buggers, little do they know.'

Tanya didn't reply. There was nothing to say.

At five o'clock in the morning, when they reached the Institute, it was beginning to get light and there was no urgent need to start up the emergency power, although Alec knew there was a small plant there to keep experiments running in the event of a power cut.

It was an eerie experience to pull up, once again, on the car park he had quit at such breakneck speed, still less than forty-eight hours before . . . the more so when he saw his own car parked exactly as he had left it. Tanya pulled up and said, 'What do we do now?'

'We sleep.'

'Hadn't we better take turns?'

'It's not necessary. I'll set the burglar alarms.'

'Will they work?'

'They run off batteries. Anyway, there's very little chance of any survivors getting as far as here. This is the worst area in the country – we're only two miles from Staines.'

She said, 'Sort of like Hiroshima. God.'

Alec refused to take up this line of talk. 'The only faint possibility is if Nuttall finds any reason to return. But I'm going to chance it. We will have to work together, you and I. We can't do that if one of us is asleep and the other one trying to manage single handed.'

They went to his own liaison office. The sample drug cupboard door hung open, as if some desperate character had searched the place for any remnant of Estofort.

They made up bunks on the floor, taking cushions from the smart waiting office used for entertaining visitors from industry. When they bedded down Tanya said ruefully, 'You did promise that we'd break into a store and get me some clothes.'

'I didn't dare waste the time.'

'But we will tomorrow?'

'Yes, I promise. But until we do . . .'

'Alec! You said *sleep!*'

'Can you think of a nicer way of going bye-byes?'

'No.'

TEN

The unnatural silince to which Alec awoke had no peace in it. The uncanny absence of the underlying thrum of traffic; the failure of aircraft engines, at nearby Heathrow, to run up the scale in anticipation of take-off; the dead silence prevailing even from the irrepressible BBC on domestic radio . . . these were symptoms not of tranquillity but of a deadly inertia. Alec, the more used to audible evidence of the habitual rat-race of outer-London rush hour, found the silence a positive entity, an unnerving stimulus which made his pulse throb deafeningly.

He had awoken first, started the Institute's immaculate electric generator – a far more sophisticated affair than either installation at Jaybury –and boiled a kettle for coffee, on the ring in the back office. By now there was only canned milk, which he normally loathed, but the degree of normalcy even this sickly fluid suggested gave him strength. He watched Tanya's regular breathing, calm upon the couch contrived from those V.I.P. cushions, and left her there while he went out to the Vauxhall for the morning check call.

Reception had got worse. Alec wondered why and asked Melhuish, who was on duty at the far end, what it was like from there. He had to ask the question three times before he got the answer.

'I've asked the radio engineer to come across to the shack,' Melhuish replied. He had to shout this message. Alec never remembered ever having heard the man shout before. It seemed oddly uncharacteristic. Melhuish continued, 'The Sindham people are urging me to ask you for technical data, however trivial it may seem. I pointed out that – ' The voice was obliterated by static . . . and what weird static, too; a sort of zinging noise, going right down the scale and up again.

Alec shouted. 'Heard it up to "I pointed out that". Go on from there.'

'I pointed out that it couldn't be done in five minutes. And,

Mr Keeling, the stuff may well be at Dr Crossley's house. Do you know the address?'

'No. Give it.'

Melhuish did. He added, diffidently, 'Only half a mile out of Staines. And another matter. The doctors here request you stand by on radio all the time – not just for check calls . . . Just a minute, here's the radio engineer. He wants a word with you.' An unfamiliar voice came on. Incongruously he had a broad Glasgow accent, difficult to hear in these conditions.

Alec finally got the gist of it. To improve transmission, Alec was to run a long aerial right to the top of the Hat-Rack tower, slinging it to the flagpole. He was given instructions concerning the design of the feeder-line down to the car. Alec acknowledged this, then got back to Melhuish and asked, 'How the hell do I get to Crossley's house if I have to stay by the radio twenty-four hours a day? I've now got to sling up a permanent aerial. To take the car out I have to disconnect and so lose contact.'

Melhuish replied with what sounded like guarded tact. 'We hoped by now that you might have a helper with you.'

Alec said nothing to this. But his jaw set hard. He did not relish the idea of sending Tanya alone into Staines or anywhere nearer the place than they were already, with only the airport between. Additionally he couldn't leave the Institute himself without risking unopposed invasion, the possible theft of all Estofort – by now unloaded from the cars – and even a personal attack on Tanya whether he left her behind with the radio or not.

Obviously it was a cleft stick; if he moved the car with the radio in it, the permanent aerial would have to be disconnected – and even as they talked reception was worsening. If he stayed where he was he couldn't get to Crossley's house.

He said, 'I'll try Lab Number Four first.'

Melhuish said something which came over garbled.

'Say again please.'

'I said, I don't think you will get in there. It's kept locked.'

Alec checked his temper. 'Put the engineer on again, will you?'

A pause.

By this time Tanya, sleepy eyed, had wandered out to the car park. Alec motioned her to silence. She nodded, but listened. The engineer, in his broad Clydeside dialect, was jabbering away but Alec couldn't catch a word of it.

Tanya said softly. 'It sounds like a girl's name.

'What name?'

'Don't panic. Not mine. Sounds like Aurora.'

Alec on radio: 'Did you say Aurora?'

At last the phrase came through clearly. 'Aurora Borealis.'

Alec was none the wiser. He'd heard of such sky-lighting but had never seen it. It was in any case seldom seen in this hemisphere. Spectacular though it was as a nocturnal spectacle, it seemed unconnected with the threatened breakdown of communications.

Alec turned to Tanya. 'Mean anything to you?'

'Fuck-all,' she said, non-Dianawise. 'But I tried getting some foreign stations on the transistor in your office. Nothing coming through. Surely there isn't V.P. in Luxemburg?'

The engineer was still talking. Bits of his transmission came through amid the violent interference. 'Get that aerial up . . . Aurora means . . . ' The voice blanked out yet again.

'Means what?'

'Sunspot activity. We may lose radio contact for days . . . ' After that, nothing.

* * *

Access to Lab Number Four was gained via a corridor running the length of the second hat-prong from the top. Then there was a green baize door with Crossley's name on it, together with a terse plaque inscribed KEEP OUT.

Evidently people did. Up till now, even Melhuish hadn't mentioned that the inner door to the Lab was code-locked. 'Secretive old bugger,' said Alec. 'Now what do we do?'

'Blow it,' said Tanya with enthusiasm. 'A loud bang would break this unholy silence.'

'And risk destroying whatever's inside?' He examined the locking mechanism, a sturdy affair, built evidently to order by Chubb. He'd never seen anything quite like it before. 'And I doubt,' he said, 'whether Messrs Chubb are going to be all that active at present. We'll have to leave this for the moment and see if we can find other clues. I'll get tools later – we'll need oxy-acetylene equipment – there must be some around this place but it'll take time. Let's search the building, particularly the Neurological Wing where Crossley spent so much time.' He saw her expression and said, 'I'll clear the place of bodies first. For God's sake let's find some alcohol. Even Estofort isn't potent enough for this spectacle.'

They found some Scotch in the reception place. Evidently the more V.I.P.-ish customers got a dram or two before lecturing, as a distinct improvement on the usual flask of water at the lectern.

While Tanya concentrated on the more obvious sources of information, like documents or physical models, Alec lashed up the generator to the Hat-Rack's large computer and went through every program for which software could be found. This was an immensely long, finicky business. Not knowing the basis on which Crossley had worked, nor by which of the many methods he had adopted – if any – for sorting information and working out their routine, he had to start from scratch using his very limited knowledge of computer practice and learning as he went along.

Apart from a rather obscure thesis on what Crossley had termed 'eye-to-eye communication' they had found nothing by noon. By then, radio reception had got a good deal worse. There was loud hissing that sometimes obliterated everything else; and occasionally the weirdest sound like somebody rattling a piece of tin across a corrugated iron roof.

Faintly, Alec could hear bits of the conversation – but it soon blotted out, until suddenly and very distinctly he heard Diana, saying something about Norway.

Norway again!

She said, 'Don't you remember? You said Crossley was being incredibly mysterious about it . . . Darling, do you love me?'

Tanya got up, feeling wretched, and left the car.

'You know I do,' he said.

'What? What? I can't hear you . . . I can't . . .'

It blanked out, this time for keeps.

Alec and Tanya ate out of some cans in silence. Then over coffee she said, 'Look, you can't leave here – at any rate not yet. I'm going to Dr Crossley's flat to see if I can find any stuff on his researches. With his secretive nature, as Melhuish says, he was more likely to keep it there than anywhere else.'

'You can't possibly. It's too dangerous.'

She said brightly, 'There can't be much danger because you know as well as I do there's hardly anyone around. Besides, much as you lust over my singed pants, it's time I looked a bit more respectable. You never know who you might meet.' She kissed him lightly. 'There are lots of nice things in the shops, darling, and it'll make a change.' She added softly, 'I can't remember you ever complaining about me in a dress.'

'You are not going out there alone, Tanya.'

'I'm entitled to earn my Estofort.'

'You're earning it here.'

'Alec, you can't give me orders. I want some clothes. You want the data. Staines is a morgue but I can stand the spooks if I know you're here.'

'I tell you it's too dangerous.'

'Would you mind telling me what isn't? I may be a cinch for your own randy advances but you'd be surprised what I'm like when someone I don't like tries to dial my number. And you know as well as I do I can't talk on the radio . . . Even if Melhuish suspects, Diana doesn't. Melhuish isn't going to add to his problems trying to explain an extra voice. So you're the only one who can stay on the job here, and you know it.' Lively eyes regarded him across the table. 'Alec, one briefcase of your Dr Crossley's scribble, if we get it before the radio conks out completely, might give those doctors down at Jaybury a chance to get going. A long, pregnant silence won't. Now. How about it?'

He was forced to concede. 'For God's sake take care.'

'You'd be surprised how forcibly I can cross my legs.'

* * *

Tanya couldn't grasp the change – the enormous difference in not having company, the right company, Alec's. Driving out there on to the sunlit road that looked, on the face of it, so normal, gave her the feeling that she had a hole in the back of her head.

The street leading from the Institute teed on to the north-south boundary road of Heathrow Airport, normally one of the busiest places in the world – 'and I should know,' she said aloud. With a certain Frenchman – a husband, naturally – she had more than once left for Paris from here; and the one thing airports didn't suggest was silence.

Now, only the birds sang. Stationary aircraft, parked in odd positions (one was rammed up against the wire-netting adjacent to the road itself) looked as if they were toys which had been kicked haphazardly by a child in a tantrum, all over the nursery floor.

But it wasn't this kind of disorder that was upsetting her. Alec and she had grown, if not used to it, at least to the point where it came as no surprise. The feeling she had was intangible, an extraordinary sense of dissociation. LSD, she thought, must make you feel something like this. How can people possibly *want* it? . . . For suddenly she couldn't altogether believe that Alec still existed, that the Hat-Rack was still there, or that way down in Devon a small group of people, including the ordinary, pleasant, attractive but nevertheless bourgeois wife of her lover, were struggling to get through on the radio for the purpose of acquiring the essential information she herself was attempting to find.

Am I real? Do I exist? Or am I dead, too?

She remembered, suddenly, the walkie-talkie that lay on the seat beside her, and wondered whether the man who didn't exist might have considered switching on. She said fearfully. 'Alec?'

Immediately he came back. 'Here! Sorry, I should have told you to switch on.'

She felt a fool, now. 'I was feeling a bit lonely.'

'You'd better come back, Tanya. This isn't a very good idea.'

'No, I'm all right now.'

He said, 'The trouble is, you probably won't hear me as far as Staines.'

'No. I'm all right. I really am.'

'All right. Keep in touch until just before we're out of range and note where that point occurs. If you're in trouble, get back to that point and call me. Clear?'

It turned out that communication stretched as far as a cross-roads only one mile out of Staines, which didn't seem too bad. They were able to chat for most of her journey and that terrible feeling of not existing receded. By the time she reached the town itself she made a point of doing everything so fast and so systematically that there was little time for brooding.

Apart from an unpleasant smell of what seemed to be escaping gas there was no more disorder here than in a dozen other towns she and Alec had been through. Shop windows were smashed, buses had collided, fires had burned down whole blocks and then petered out. It was bad. But it was now the norm.

The norm! My God, it's normal to expect this, now!

She ran into a department store, still somehow expecting to find people. There must, for God's sake, be *some* people . . . !'

But the total desertion by humans was the one inexplicable thing, above all others, that now so frightened her. Apart from victims of motor accidents, lying pulped beneath lorries and cars; apart from those few who had, like Crossley, hurled themselves into oblivion – a few lay in the street – there was no sign of life. However demented or panicked; however rushed in their terror to get away, *where had the people gone*?

Summer dresses, third floor.

Ladies' Underwear . . . Not Tanya's favourite phrase. It should be lingerie or bras and pants. Please not ladies' underwear. Alec wouldn't be at all amused by products aimed at such ladylike customers.

Well, it wasn't too bad, the stuff. She chose quickly, and accurately; and was just about to change on the spot when her animal alertness to danger frightened her into a motionless waxwork.

Far in the distance there came a sound; and sound, in the ghost-town of Staines, was as alien as seeing two suns in the sky.

Motorbikes! Approaching from the bridge!

For a few fatal seconds she panicked. She thought of her car, parked in the middle of the road, engine still warm, symptoms of surviving life.

And the walkie-talkie radio, lying on the seat, her only link with Alec, her only chance of survival if attacked.

She didn't wait to dress. Still in the scraggy remnants of torn dress and scorched underwear, she dashed across to the window.

A procession of sparkling-new motorcycles, ridden by a gang of youths, roared past the far side of the store.

Inevitably, the traffic system would take them around the three remaining corners of the building, until they came upon her car. Her everything.

She decided to run for it, get there first, drive away before the gang had rounded the building. They would meet obstacles. She already knew where the obstacles were . . .

She grabbed up the pile of new clothes and bolted across the department and knocked a display of swimwear flying. It crashed against the door of the emergency stairs and jammed it.

Now, the bikes were audibly turning the next corner of the block.

Desperately, she clawed at the collapsed rubble of hardboard and clothing, wrenched it clear, banged open the release mechanism of the exit door and raced down concrete steps two at a time.

At street level the doors were designed to open outwards, by means of a pushbar. Panicked by the increasing noise of approaching engines she was frenetically pulling at a pushbar. The echo of clanging steel reverbed up the stairs and and came back at her, amplified percussively by the concrete hollow.

The door flew open to garish sunlight.

The motorcycle thugs – five of them – were waiting for her as she came out.

The nearest of them, evidently their leader, grinned broadly, signalled to the others to switch off their engines, and gazed.

Slowly he raised his goggles, looking at her up and down in the charged silence, lasciviously inspecting her inch by inch. 'That's quite an outfit you've got there.' He had a strong, insolent-looking face which should have been handsome but was tarnished by a twitch around the mouth and the cruel lines beneath the eyes. He repeated appreciatively, 'Quite an outfit.'

Tanya held up the bundle of new clothes. Assuming a busy, secretarial voice she said, 'Yes. Well as you see, I'm about to improve on it. So if you wouldn't mind – '

' – So you're on the Kick.'

'The what?'

The leader grinned around at his companions. Then he turned back to her without the smile. 'Oh, come on! Who do you think you're fooling? The Kick. Esty and Meth., we've been on it ever since May.' He licked his lips and contemplated her nipples. 'The merry month of May.'

With a frantic effort Tanya hung on to her control. 'I honestly . . . What "Kick"? Will you please let me get to my car?'

The leader made no move.

One of the others, an emaciatedly thin intellectual, elaborated on the details. 'Estofort and Methedrine,' he said. 'And it's no use pretending you don't know.'

The leader nodded. 'Of course she knows. Or how would she be around to . . . inspire us? It has pot beaten at the starting gate, wouldn't you say?'

Tanya edged round the front of the leader's motorbike but he inched it forward and jammed the wheel against a wrecked car. 'Not so fast, bird without feathers!' He chuckled at his own wit. 'Bird with no feathers . . . How about that, fellas? I think she needs company, don't you? I think she ought to kind of join up with us.'

One of them said, 'She does seem a bit lonely.'

Tanya said, 'When you've finished with the jokes would you mind letting me get to my car?'

The leader said, 'Who's joking?'

The intellectual said, 'We could make a deal with her.'

The leader said, 'Who needs deals?'

'Because we're nearly out of Esty and you know it.'

'That's a point. You tell us where your Esty is, pretty bird, and we might just let you go.'

Tanya looked at the gloating, suggestive smirk on the leader's face with its twitch of drug-addiction and recovered her sense of cunning. 'Okay,' she admitted, 'I've been on the Kick. But I've got exactly two capsules left. If you don't believe me, search my car.'

The leader made to move. 'Then what were you thinking of doing?'

'Obviously – getting some more. And you can too. All I have to do is to use that radio.'

'This bird,' grinned the leader, 'has things really organized!'

'There's a condition,' said Tanya.

'You think you can make conditions? – I told you,' he lilted, 'I wasn't joking, baby-love.'

She said evenly, 'I'm going to tell my contact that if you so much as touch me, you don't get one single capsule. And I hope you believe me, because you won't get a second chance.'

There was a long silence. The grin on the leader's face suddenly looked haggard, as if the truth was beginning to dawn. However far-out he was from the effect of mixing a thing like Estofort with amphetamines, he evidently did realize his certain fate if he ran out of the first.

Tanya's heart raced.

A muttered conference, held in a huddle around the motorbikes, reduced Tanya to a state of heart-burning tension. She knew that whatever they were planning would be a one-sided bargain, that no promise they made could be believed. Rape terrified her. Moreover, if these hopped-up cookies became obsessed with her sex, then all other considerations – including the acquisition of Estofort – would be neglected . . . hers too.

They still talked and her heart still pumped and a clock in the far distance struck the half hour. It was a solitary sound indeed.

At last, the leader turned to Tanya. 'Okay.' He gestured toward the radio on the car seat. 'Call them up.'

She said. 'But not from here.'

'Why?'

'It won't work from here. We have to go out of town.'

The leader turned to his gang. 'The bitch is setting a trap. Let's – '

The white-faced little intellectual interrupted. ' – She's telling the truth. The metal in these high buildings here would screen VHF. We need open country . . . nearer Heathrow.'

'You sure? I don't trust her.'

'I don't trust her,' said the underling. 'But I'm sure.'

'Okay.' The leader snapped his goggles back into place. 'There'd better be some Esty at the end of this ride. Or this bird, well, she won't feel like flying, not anywhere! Let's go!'

Five bikes were kick-started and revved. Tanya was motioned into her car. And in procession, with Tanya leading, they roared out of the town toward the crossroads. There, she signalled and stopped. The bikes pulled up, surrounding her.

With an obscene intimateness, the leader put his head through the car window and said, very softly, 'I hope it works, darling.'

She said nothing, but steadied her hand by holding the walkie-talkie against the steering wheel. 'Tanya calling. Tanya calling . . . ' And then the big gamble. Would Alec catch on? 'Tanya calling Jimmy Nuttall. Jimmy, are you there? Over.'

She was watching the leader's face. The expression had changed and she knew she'd struck lucky so far. Evidently they'd already heard of Nuttall as a source of supply.

There came a long pause. Tanya could imagine Alec's mind racing as hers had done. He would know there was trouble, would be wondering what she expected of him, wondering what traps there were waiting for her should he make a mistake. He played for caution. 'Go on Tanya,' he said harshly, 'what is it this time?'

'I need some more supplies, Jimmy. Me and five fellas.'

Again a pause. But this time Alec struck an attitude, trying to be the sort of Nuttall a gang of thugs might expect. 'Tanya you're not coming here again. You've given trouble. Big trouble.'

'Jimmy, I won't do it again. I swear.'

The gang-leader hissed in her ear, 'Tell him we have money.'

Alec's voice came back. 'They may have the lolly but they also have you, and you mean trouble.'

'But you're not going to let me run out of Esty?'

'What do your new friends think their money will buy? If

they want Esty they can work for it. How many of 'em did you say there were – five?'

'Yes. Five.'

Alec was careful not to sound too keen. 'I don't know. That's quite a lot of Esty. How much have they got left? Ask them.'

Tanya did so. The educated thug, three bikes along, said, 'We'd better tell him.'

The leader nodded, and the fear suddenly showed in his voice. 'We're down to almost zero.'

Tanya repeated this, and the voice came back reluctantly, 'They can have a few . . . a week's supply each, for the moment. And they can return to you and bring yours. Only don't you come near this place.'

Tanya said, 'Jimmy darling, I know how you feel about me, what I did. But please let me come back.'

'Too late. Thanks and all that but I'm fixed up.'

'Well, at least let me tell these fellas that they mustn't lay a hand on me.'

There was a pause, as if Alec was having to hold on to himself to stay calm. But he sounded convincing enough when he came back on the air and said, 'Can they hear this thing?'

'Yes.' Tanya held the instrument closer to the leader's ear.

'Anyone,' crackled the radio, 'who touches my property, new or soiled, gets their drug supply cut off – forever. And you know what that means . . . Tanya? Keep the set switched on, stay where you are now and keep talking. Send your . . . friends . . . to the Kingston Town Hall, where my set-up is, and they can collect. They can then take back your share. But you damn well stay out of it. That clear?'

'Jimmy . . . thank you. My God, thank you!'

'Cut that out. Just do as you're told.'

The leader shoved his head inside her car. 'Just for security,' he said, 'I'll take what capsules you've got left.'

She held up the emergency bottle she carried. 'But I only have two.'

'You won't need them. We'll be back.'

The leader snatched the bottle and took a capsule. He was as desperate – then – as that. Grinning again, he gave the signal once more for the start-up. And the five bikes roared away – in the wrong direction.

Tanya watched the dust churned up as they departed at such speed. Then she wept.

'Tanya?'

She couldn't for a while answer.

'Tanya!'

'I'm all right, Alec.'

'Have they gone?'

'Yes.'

'What made them swallow that story?'

'They're addicts. They mix Estofort with some other thing, been doing it for some time, that's why they're still going strong. But they're out on a trip, don't really know what's happening, except they wanted to rape me.'

'My God. Come back here. Straight back. Promise?'

'No. I'm doing what I have to do. I got some clothes. I'm only a short distance from Crossley's house. There's time to have a quick look there before there's any chance of . . . reprisals.'

Alec shouted harshly, 'Do as I damn well say! I'll come out and search Crossley's place.'

'And leave our remaining supplies unguarded? No, I'm doing it. And we're wasting time. I'll be back. Over and out.'

* * *

Alec left the radio car for a moment and thought, who the hell do you pray to? But. No crying over milk so nearly spilled forever. Tanya wouldn't benefit from that.

But a warning was a warning. The Staines area, apparently so dead, still contained nooks and crannies from which emerged the monsters, and there could be more. He should never have allowed Tanya to leave the place – let alone without a gun. So he loaded the Thompson and two of the service revolvers, then worked out angles from which he could cover the entrance to the Institute Complex.

His precautions were rewarded by the arrival of a strange deputation indeed. Ill-matched and almost comically unsuited to a crisis, a carload of visitors cautiously turned the corner and drove on to the car park.

Alec, grim and alone, feeling Tanya's absence like the loss of an arm and still scared for her life, welcomed the visitors with the Thompson ready cocked, and made them line up on the car park.

'All of you,' he commanded, 'hold up your tablets of Estofort, high above your heads. If any of you have guns, don't try anything. This Thompson has a full magazine.'

There were injured looks. Then the five haggard intruders

felt in their pockets, watching each other as if to assess the quantities each possessed, and complied. But they all had supplies of the stuff and Alec took a very careful look at each container to make sure none had depleted to desperation level. It bore directly on their motives for the visit.

Still keeping the sub-machine-gun trained, he said, 'Who are you?'

A pot-bellied, rather elderly man in city clothes was their spokesman. 'My name's Stoddart,' he said. The voice, though strained and tired, had the unmistakable ring of the board room.

'In full, please.'

The man added the handle without pomp. 'Sir Ralph Stoddart, Chairman of Unilectric.'

Telecommunications! Unpromising though this Dad's Army appeared to be, telecoms was premium tender indeed.

Stoddart hardly looked like a desperado, and his motley followers seemed more bewildered than unified into a purposeful or cohesive team.

Stoddart said, 'Look, put that gun down and let's talk.'

– Not on your life! Talk, yes; undefended, no. What if there was a back-up section hanging around outside the perimeter?

Alec said, 'We'll talk. You and I. Inside. I shall cover the rest of you – *and* the exit – with this Thompson. Sorry I can't be more friendly.' Alec gestured to Stoddart, indicating the office entrance with the barrel of the gun. Actually he felt not only slightly ridiculous in these precautions, but really rather sorry for Stoddart, who looked ill and ageing and out of his depth. But however outrageous the handling of this interview seemed to Alec, he had a bitterly fresh memory of unknown perils. Tanya was refusing – he hoped it amounted only to refusing – to answer him on the walkie-talkie. Though unlikely, she might for all he knew be this new intruder's prisoner, somewhere out back. There was no leeway for errors of judgement.

Once inside the liaison office, Alec immediately went to the window and positioned himself where he could fire either at the car park or at Stoddart. He began. 'I take it you people got your supplies from Nuttall?'

'Frankly, yes. Most of the people I know did. It was the only way. If you had to, you'd have done the same.'

'Where is Nuttall now?'

'Somewhere up north. Manchester or Liverpool. I think. He's got something of a private army organized by now, and wants a fortune for each capsule. The price has gone up twice since Thursday.'

'Have you any idea what it's like, up North?'

Stoddart cleared his throat. 'I have access to certain sources of information, yes. Whether I tell you depends on your own conduct.'

'In other words,' said Alec harshly, 'you have connections with people in high places who keep you informed? – and presumably bought their sanity from Nuttall regardless of the consequences to others?'

'You sound very sententious, young man. We are all, just as you are, trying to survive. Nuttall is an underling in a rival firm. I knew him – or thought I did – through my own executives. He offered me survival, at a price. I accepted. Who wouldn't?'

'Did his terms include the use of your telecoms facilities?'

'I am not proud of my dealings with him. Yes they did, in part. Now let's hear about you. Your name is – ?'

'Keeling, of the Esto Corporation.'

'Quite so.' Ralph shot him an appreciative look. 'A useful club to belong to at present, Mr Keeling.'

Alec took the point but persisted, 'Surely the first obligation on your friends in high places was to bring Nuttall to justice and take control of the drug supplies he is selling on the black market?' Stoddart's face sagged. Alec said tonelessly, 'So Nuttall controls all the communications links which might otherwise have been available to us?'

'Only in part. In a way I'm driven to double-dealing; I have ways of using those links he just doesn't know about.'

'What about the West? We're losing radio contact because – I'm told – of sunspot activity.'

Stoddart shook his head. 'When teams were sent to various relay points for the Prime Minister's broadcast, they eventually ran out of Estofort.'

'As you knew they would.'

'No!' Anger showed for the first time on the chairman's face. 'That was Nuttall's work – not mine. But when they went berserk, these men destroyed the equipment – including the restored tie-line through to the Estofort factory.'

Alec nodded. 'And of course you came here because you realized the connection between this Institute and the use and production of Estofort? You know that the factory burned down?'

'I do. I also know you tried to save it.'

'How many are there of you, Sir Ralph? – apart from those people outside?'

'We aren't properly organized and I can't tell you for certain. There are scattered groups trying to keep in touch. I had an inkling you might be here. We came to try and make ourselves useful.'

'And is it now too late to take Nuttall in hand?'

'If you mean by normal processes of law, of course it is. In a sense, Nuttall became the law. Certain officials – acting well ahead of me, Mr Keeling – condoned Nuttall's trading and thereby handed him power. Some civil servants – and I don't blame them however weak they may seem to you – became his blackmailed informers and by now it's impossible to know who to trust. Confide in the wrong person and the drugs are witheld. It functions virtually like the gestapo.' He added flatly, 'A few brave men took that risk. I have seen the results. I do not therefore consider I am here to be judged. If you knew and witnessed their fate, nor would you.'

Alec felt less hostile but ruthlessly avoided being swayed by pity. What he had to judge was the odds. 'What about the people you do trust?' He gestured through the window. 'Them, for instance? Do you trust them?'

Stoddart gave a portly shrug. 'You know the form as well as I do. The only people you can trust are those who have a reasonable supply of Estofort and a chance to hang on to it. When supplies get short, trust diminishes in direct ratio. It's as simple as that.'

Alec said, 'Yes, but the solution is not just to hang on and wait for the inevitable, but to find out the whys and wherefores of this condition.'

'Which is why we came here. How much do you know?'

Alec said with honesty, 'Probably very little more than you and your Whitehall friends. But we are mounting a certain scheme.'

'That's what I heard.'

'How?'

'Must I say? . . . We know about your establishment at Exeter.' The tired eyes rolled upward. 'Jaybury, to be exact. We knew that Sindham is involved. And we know that you mean what you say – that you are trying to come up with some sort of solution.'

At that moment a car entered the complex from the road.

Alec swung the Thompson in an instant. But it was Tanya, returning at high speed in the Ford estate. Alec desperately wanted to run to her, to hold her and console her, to absorb some of the shock.

But he had learned. In this pitiless new world you did nothing without prior precaution. No situation however humanly compelling, must for an instant take you off your guard.

Stoddart watched without visible surprise as a singed nymph stepped from the estate car. He just waited for Alec to decide his actions.

While the disorderly troop on the car park watched Tanya cross toward the building, Alec did make up his mind on one particular issue. Though he no longer wished to insult this half-crucified, obese refugee from some stricken board room, he wasn't going to relent until Tanya had been consulted first. Between Alec and Tanya there was a tacitly sworn unanimity. Their interdependence was absolute. Privately, he would discuss the issue with her and until then Stoddart must remain a suspect. In the meanwhile there was one important factor to assess. 'Sir Ralph, is there any danger of your lot having been followed here?'

'There's always that danger.' There came a tycoon shrug. 'However, there aren't all that many people to follow, are there? – especially round here.'

'But we'd better not take any chances. Can you move your people over to the right? – about a hundred yards down the car park toward the Hat Rack . . . the Ministry end? That gives me a free arc of fire without hurting your friends. I want to talk to . . . my assistant . . . ' there was a mutual glare at the word ' . . . before we agree to any arrangements.'

Stoddart said, 'I quite understand. We'll wait.'

It was a charged moment . . . the slouched, elderly man walking rather slowly out to his strange bedfellows; Tanya watched them, cautiously crossing the gravel with her bundles, waiting for a signal from Alec, then seing the sub-machine gun in his hand.

Stoddart reached his people. They all moved as directed.

Alec found Tanya shivering and yet triumphant, as if trying to counter shock with her achievement. 'I've got the stuff. At least, I think so.' She slapped a briefcase on to Alec's desk.

'Tanya, aren't you even human? I love you; I thought you were done for. And I let you go.'

'Want me to cry a bit?'

'Yes, please . . . '

They kissed and both found themselves tearful. Alec smiled through them. Gently he said, 'Still Cinderella?'

She indicated the heap of clothes and responded in kind. 'I couldn't find a fairy godmother but I did raid a department store.' She described the addicted hoodlums and he clutched her tight. He asked her if they could have guessed her true destination.

'Not a chance. And by the time they start searching in earnest – '

' – They'll be clean out of Estofort.'

She nodded, almost gleefully. 'I can rejoice in that without sobbing. She thumbed out toward the new group, and said, 'What's that? The Crazy Gang?'

'The rather beaten-down fellow with the Savile Rowe suit is Sir Ralph Stoddart. God knows who the others are.'

'Any use?'

'That's what I'm trying to discover. They're badly organized but in with government survivors. Not to mention Nuttall. But he says everybody he knows initially got their drugs on the black market. We can't be holy about that.'

'And has Nuttall also got a knighthood too?'

'Not yet. He's formed a sort of Party a command force with teeth. Putting up the price of Estofort every two days and protected like a dictator. He's established somewhere up North. Probably very hard to get at. He's stuck to the letter of your bugged phone conversation as per your tape recording.'

She said 'Watch it! You're talking Whitehallese already!' She handed him the briefcase. 'So Nuttall is on schedule. Manchester I'll bet. Rotoport's warehouse.'

'Must be.' He took the briefcase found it locked. 'We'll have to beat Nuttall to Glasgow; that's where the really big stocks are.'

'But how?' Then she nodded, glancing out to the car park. 'I see. Your influential company director. Why should we trust him? – Even if he's not a Nuttallist he's probably just after our pills.'

Alec said, 'I think he's too old to care. Melhuish thinks that it's people with sex-drive who hunger most for Estofort.'

'That,' said Tanya unkindly, 'would seem to rule him out. But he must have done it once. Has he got a family?'

'We didn't discuss his domestic life.'

'I mean he'll protect them – using our supplies.'

'We'll check.'

'How?'

'He'll be in *Who's Who.* There's a copy in the Hat Rack reference library . . . Tanya, can we afford to turn him down? – with his connections?'

'Connections who with? – That dumb-waiter of a Prime Minister? Alec, be sensible. Stoddart's handle has gone to your head. What good are connections now?'

'Telephone connections would be distinctly useful. Tanya, are you going to let me play my hunch? We've got nothing to lose; he knows about Jaybury anyway. Stoddart says he can't help with communications to the West; but he does know what's going on up North. That could lead us to Nuttall.'

'How did he find out about Jaybury, then, when nothing to the West is working?' She added caustically, 'Or do the right people have an exclusive on the bush telegraph?'

'Maynard might have guessed something and told Nuttall when they got the tie-line through.'

She said, 'It's not on the tape.'

'The tape doesn't start at the beginning of the conversation.'

'Nuttall better not know,' she said. 'I prefer to believe in those jungle drums. Okay, let's go and talk to your hunch-back.'

'I shall only issue him with Estofort,' Alec said, as they crossed toward the cars, 'if he undertakes to bring a load back here.'

'Tell him to find a gas man, too. The whole of Staines stinks of it.'

'Gas?'

ELEVEN

Erupting from the radio in Alec's car, frantic phrases, in the distorted voice of Richard Trent, shrilled in spasms throughout the car park. Despite the chaotic din caused by solar eruption, snatches of what he said were clear. The medical men at the Dorrington could get nowhere unless the data from Crossley's research could be transmitted back to Jaybury.

To Alec, this was the height of irony. Tanya had just risked her life getting the information they so desperately needed, yet total radio blackout was now threatening, and Crossley's notes, once Alec had forced the lock of the briefcase, proved a nightmarishly illegible hotchpotch of loose sheets, unnumbered and not in consecutive order. They contained a mass of unfamiliar technical words and concepts, scrawled mostly on the backs of old Ministry circulars. Since it sometimes took minutes to get one simple word back to Jaybury – where reception was worst – it was clear to Alec at once that he would have to summarize Crossley's findings in short, sharp sentences. This meant understanding the material himself first; and a quick check in the Hat Rack library proved there was nothing on the premises to help him. Crossley's approach to what people like Dr Blessing assumed to be a conventionally clinical problem included none of the jargon of anyone's surgery.

The only minor harvest reaped from the reference library was the marital information on Stoddart demanded by Tanya. Rejoining her in his own office section, while Sir Ralph was still running through Tanya's tape next door, he told her cynically, 'According to *Who's Who*, he's no more doddery than anyone else described in *Who's Who*.'

The volume confirmed Stoddart was a bachelor; also revealed by inference that even if not one of the world's self-sacrificing idealists, he had flair as an organizer, however disorganized he appeared at the moment. Obedient to the accepted qualifications for knighthood, he had founded appropriate

Foundations – presumably it was through this hobby that he knew something of Dr Crossley's work – and had diverted a few profits into charity. Clubs: *Directors'*, *Atheneum.*

'Satisfied?'

Tanya didn't look up from her efforts at collating the notes. 'Thrilled. I've always wanted to meet a real live member of the Atheneum . . . Alec, this is going to take hours. Are you sure Crossley was English?'

'If we can't make enough sense of it by dawn, I'll go into Staines tomorrow morning and heave a few volumes down from the reference section of the public library.'

'It means you'll have to leave the radio.'

'We'll work something out . . . Okay, Tanya. I know you don't want me to go there. But I'm more difficult to rape. I'll join you in a few minutes . . . '

Stoddart had entered, carrying the tape recorder. 'I think I've got the details,' he said, to Alec. 'Can we talk?'

Alec said, 'Let's talk outside, so I can be near the radio car.'

Stoddart dumped the tape recorder on the desk, grunting something to Tanya. Evidently he was having a delayed reaction to the strip show. He had no reason now to disapprove. Tanya was dressed as pertly and appropriately as anyone else who might have just stepped out of a department store.

Despite Stoddart's tardy prejudices concerning non-Atheneum displays of scorched nylon and expressively sensual thigh, he took Alec seriously. He'd recovered some of his composure; the old board room phrases began to come churning out, but with ponderous authority. He thought he could 'bring certain influences to bear' and 'plug certain holes' in the Whitehall panic; and 'restore a degree of law and order' in the North, convinced as he was that he could 'mobilize a skeleton army force being held under Estofort at a London barracks' – which he took pains to emphasize was 'less than a squadron so don't expect the Norman Conquest'. He would attempt, however, to impound illegally acquired Estofort and place it in an emergency pool.

Alec interrupted to attempt an answer to a further call from Richard Trent. It didn't get through. Richard just resumed the remorseless, 'Are you receiving me? Are you receiving me? . . . '

On the way to Sir Ralph's car, Alec said, 'Presumably you gathered from the tape that the main stocks of Estofort earmarked for export are in Glasgow?'

Stoddart heaved himself into the driver's seat and replied enigmatically, 'There's more than one way into the Clyde.'

None of Stoddart's followers had said a word to Alec, who secretly hoped, as they got back in their car, were not materially involved in the operations planned. But then, Stoddart himself had looked singularly unpromising when he'd first arrived. Alec withheld judgement and was glad he did: among the assorted group was an electronics expert from Brunel University. He took note of Alec's frequencies and promised to attempt the relaying of signals via a powerful transmitter in London. This gave Alec some hope. Clearly there was no chance of sorting Crossley's notes in a hurry and reception was worsening all the time.

The Brunel man also explained to Alec how he could run a pair of cables from the radio car to the office, so that he could maintain radio watch without having to rush out to the car every time. By now it was obvious to Alec that each of the characters in that car had been hand-picked by Sir Ralph as specialists in particular fields. Alec had under-estimated the chairman of the board once again.

Gravely, as of right, Stoddart accepted a generous issue of Estofort, for himself and his team. He pledged, while starting the car, 'We'll see what we can do about Nuttall's private army. I don't much care for that fellow.' He said it rather as if he intended blackballing him from his club. Then he was gone.

Tanya had brought back some fresh cigarette packs from Staines. Alec ripped one open gratefully and started poring over Crossley's notes. His frown deepened as he did so; and he said eventually, 'What's he referring to? . . . all this stuff about 'regular trails through grasslands, worn routes made efficient by regular cycles of exodus?'

Tanya read another bit: ' "Abnormal periods of excitement prior to emigration . . . sudden surges which relate directly to variations in climate" . . . and "the psychosis of evacuation, stimulated by instability in homeostatic environment" – what the heck does it mean?'

Alec said, 'That we're none the wiser. Homeostatic means – virtually – the preservation of normally controlled conditions. But normal to what?' He thought a bit, remembered all the holiday cars that had suddenly saturated the main roads to the West on a midweek day. 'That Wednesday, when so many people absenteed from their places of work and suddenly decided to take a sunny holiday . . . '

'Well, that's normal enough.'

'Normal because they weren't people from Staines?'

'Normal because they often do it,' she said, and stared at him.

'Still,' said Alec, 'it was due to "variations in climate" – it was a particularly hot day. They took the main roads – "worn routes made efficient by regular cycles of exodus". That could certainly refer to the holiday roads like the A38 to Exeter.'

Tanya said, 'You notice there's not one word about *people*. Even amongst all these bits of Latin – it is Latin, isn't it? – the only Latin word I know just doesn't come up. No mention of homo sapiens.'

Alec leafed through more of the pages rapidly. 'Right: Nor is it here in plain English. And yet so many things apply . . . Look at this bit: "The competitive strain within such communities contributes, eventually, first to individual breakdowns, then to group anxiety. Instinctively each adult member of the species grows aware of the narrow margins within which they must provide for their young . . . " What could be more apt? Psychologists have been warning us for years about the stresses imposed by such "competitive strain". It's dog eat dog – especially in the towns.'

She said blankly, 'He's not discussing dogs, very obviously.'

Alec snapped his fingers. 'You! You said something. Back at the garage where we left the transporter. It's been nagging at me ever since.'

'Me? – uttering words of wisdom?'

'A reprimand . . . What was it? Yes! You said, "Cut out the lecture on migration"!'

She pouted. 'A figure of speech.'

'Yet that's what we're reading about here. Mass surges of panicked migration . . . Well, it was homo sapiens, all right, which was crowding the A38 with holiday-makers, that day.'

'Who wouldn't take a holiday, given the opportunity?'

'Yes, but when is an opportunity really an urge?'

'I don't see the difference.'

'Well, there are references to "response to overcrowding". At least the "abnormal periods of excitement prior to emigration" could cover the frantic phone calls I was making to Diana and later to Richard. Also the "psychosis of evacuation" fits pretty well the frantic attempts by people here to get away, even though most of them only got as far as Staines and then contaminated people there.'

Tanya said, 'But they *did* get further than Staines . . . if not in their cars, they must have got out *somewhere*. The place is practically deserted.'

'Millions of people can't just disappear.'

'Except they have.' Tanya was shuffling the pages. 'Here's more about overcrowding . . . but it talks about warrens and forests. Whatever Staines is, it's no forest.'

Alec said, 'Overcrowding, coupled with hysteria – which Crossley also mentions here – could imply an acute fear of population explosion.' He looked up. 'Yet the so-called population explosion is supposed to reach its peak around the year 2000. Why should stampede break out so prematurely, in the form of mass mental disease? The sudden outbreak suggests a peak; yet neither the rate of population increase nor the drop per head in food supply has gone anywhere near saturation – certainly not in this country. What other peaks have there been, lately?'

She said, 'Well, don't look at me. I'm no sociologist.'

'Tanya, stop posing. Your brain is as good as anyone's and you don't have to go on pretending it doesn't work.'

She said slowly, 'I can think of one peak.' She added softly. 'And so can you.'

'Sorry, I'm not quite with you.'

'Darling, you know what I mean! There's been a certain peak around you, all right! – in the urge to – '

' – Tanya, be serious. Let's keep our minds off our bodies and on our minds.'

'I am serious. Tell me frankly – I'll try not to be jealous. What about you and Diana. Did anything . . . ?'

He said stolidly, 'On the way down we did stop the Dormobile on the Andover by-pass.'

'Even though you were in such a hell of a hurry to get away? With three kids in the back and all that?'

'Why not? I was tense.'

'Frightened, in fact?'

'Yes . . . I do see what you're getting at, though. Isn't it what this note here refers to? – cycles of irruption?'

She frowned. 'Ir-ruption? Never heard of it.'

'It means, roughly speaking, the compulsion to copulate.'

'And today,' she said flatly, 'I nearly got raped.'

Alec confessed, 'Sitting in a restaurant with Melhuish, I found myself wanting to have it off with a little waitress. And she looked so shagged she must have been at it all night.'

'I prefer not to know. Anyway, you're plain randy.'

'Which is what Crossley is writing about here.' Alec skipped a lot of technical stuff. 'I really will have to go to that library. But look how he goes on: "Such a species continues for some time in its normal pattern, though unconsciously its members are storing fear. Exposed to identical stimuli, and observing the rapid utilization of their environment – in terms of food, space, and pollution" – get that! Pollution!'

'Go on.'

' . . . "the group, becomes, prior to the outbreak of panic, usually blind to dangers and unnaturally callous toward each other. They take in the information, though they appear not to. Then suddenly it seems to erupt into total awareness . . . " Tanya, what "identical stimuli" are we all exposed to? – simultaneously?'

'Well, I suppose you mean television. But – '

' – How do you react when you watch? Take those news bulletins, or *Panorama, This Week*; when you see pictures of millions of people starving to death in Pakistan or India, or fleeing from earthquakes in Lima, or killing off the Israelis at the Olympics, what did you do? – Honestly?'

'I got taken to expensive restaurants, or gave my hair a rinse, or spent the night kissing in cars with you. I'm no do-gooder, Alec. Everyone has to carry on.'

'Yes, that's what we kept telling ourselves.'

A pause.

'Alec, oughtn't we to just take these notes as they are down to Devon? – Let them analyse them?'

'I thought of that but there's almost everything against it. We've got Stoddart on the hook and must await results as well as supplies of Estofort. I'm committed to opening new cadres if I can; and anyway these notes are so incomplete they'll be shrugged off as mere notions. We need what's in Lab Number Four; we need to add two and two and arrive at a conclusion strong enough to disprove the virus theory. Finally, we don't know the state of the main roads, by now. They may be sealed off like the motorways were. Anything can happen and we might not even get there.' He stared at the scrappy bits of paper littering the desk. 'There *has* to be some central theme in all this. Crossley may have been a dyspeptic old bore, but he wasn't a fool. These notes were written for his own use; so naturally he didn't have to write down what he was sure of already.'

Tanya held up one of the sheets to the light. 'What's this number scratched with a pencil in the margin?'

He looked over her shoulder 'Some statistic? Crossley was balmy about statistics . . . ' His mind wasn't on that. 'Crossley had ideas about eye-to-eye communication. What's that mean to you?'

Tanya said, 'Isn't it just a grand phrase for looking at someone and talking with your eyes? We do it all the time.'

'What are we communicating when we do it?'

'Almost anything. Especially fear.'

'But it's essentially an animal thing, isn't it?'

Tanya said, 'I hate to labour the point, darling, but sex is essentially an animal thing, and that's when we use our eyes the most.'

He cut her off. ' – Here's something! Fjords.'

She just said, 'What about Fjords?'

'Crossley did a lot of his research in Norway. People keep reminding me, and now it's here . . . bottom of the page: 'Some of the evidence gathered in Norwegian fjords, indicates that after the initial surge, the . . . '

'Well? Go on.'

'Where's the next bloody page? It doesn't run on.'

They shuffled frantically through the scatter of sheets.

Till Alec's movements began to slow down.

Finally he laid a hand over the paperwork and gazed into space. 'That number.' Then, staring hard at her, 'That number! In pencil. Find it!'

'Wait a *minute*! You'll have this stuff all over the floor. What about the number anyway . . . Yes, here it is.'

He snatched the document out of her hand, read the pencilled digits off once again. 'Don't you know what this could be?'

She didn't. 'Not his girl friend's telephone number?'

'You're on the right track.'

'Sorry. It was a silly joke. I'm not on any track.'

'A phone number is a code number. *A code number*.'

She got it. 'The combination of the Lab door! What are we waiting for?'

Halfway down the umbilical corridor, the clock – now registering a crazy hour – stuck out on its single prong from one wall. At the end, the swing doors, through which Melhuish had led him that first terrible morning, then the reception room, where pushy Ph.Ds with ambition achieving eruption-point should have been waiting for interviews, but were not. The passenger lift, in which Crossley's rotting body must still have been jammed somewhere down the shaft. But they ignored both lifts and raced up the stairs. Reaching the decontamination area, they still took full precaution against organism infection, donning rapidly the plastic coats and masks.

Alec, breathless, led on toward Lab Number Four . . . along the narrow corridor of the hat-prong, onward to the green baize door with its rude message – finally up to the sealed entrance.

Alec said, 'You *are* up-to-date on Estofort?'

'Catch me missing out on that.'

'Scared?'

'A little.'

'Of course we don't know whether that number will work on this combination thing anyway.'

They waited in absolute silence. Till it did.

Tanya said, in a hushed voice. 'Let's just open the door a fraction. See what happens . . . sight, sound, smell, anything.'

'Right. Stand back and be ready to run. God only knows what's in that place!'

She held his hand. Her's was trembling. He squeezed it; then, very slowly, eased the sealed door forward on its hinges.

They stared at each other. Nothing had happened. Apparently.

Then Alec happened to look down.

There, near the floor, out poked the whiskered nose of a little animal. It paused there, this exotic little rodent, looking quite interested and friendly, and gazing up briefly at their faces.

The animal was about five inches long, with a short little tail and a rather fat, cuddly little body covered in soft hair.

It seemed grateful for a new friend. Tanya bent down and picked it up, stroked it. It squeaked at her, a sort of tiny little bark.

Alec and Tanya laughed together. The anticlimax was absurd – the first funny experience they'd witnessed since the whole crisis began. 'What is it?' she asked. 'A guinea-pig with a hair-do?'

'I'm trying to think.'

'It's not a hybrid? – Crossley didn't invent it?'

'No. I've seen pictures of them somewhere . . . Norway.'

'What?'

'Norway! That's right! You know what this is?'

The animal gave its absurd little bark once more, as if to inform them. Tanya said, 'You obviously do. What is it?'

'Tanya, don't you know about the lemmings?'

TWELVE

Leaving the little lemming to his friends, they rushed down the stairs, two at a time, then raced for the Vauxhall, whose transmitter aerial, glistening in the sunlight, sloped up to the top of the Hat-Rack tower. The operative length of the aerial, carefully measured, was defined by porcelain insulators. These swayed, very gently, in the light breeze.

Tanya climbed into the back and Alec sat in front, slamming the door and switching on the radio in one reflexive snap.

Faintly, half-throttled by the weird noises associated with disturbance by solar activity of the Earth's radiation belts, the patient, repetitive monotone of Richard's voice came through: 'This is Dorrington Cadre calling Hat-Rack, Dorrington Cadre to Hat-Rack. Do you hear us? Do you hear us?'

Tanya, scarcely breathing the words, said, 'They've got to hear us this time!'

Alec pressed the transmit switch and held the microphone up to his mouth: 'Hat-Rack calling Dorrington Cadre. Hat-Rack calling Dorrington Cadre. We hear you, we hear you. Over.'

No voice came back for a few seconds – only the squelching noises that lately had been the continual feature of radio communication. Then: 'This is Dorrington Cadre calling Hat-Rack. Can you hear us, please? Can you hear us?'

Alec and Tanya exchanged all the eye-to-eye communication just then that Crossley would have expected of them. Alec said wretchedly, 'Same as before. We can hear them, but they can't hear us!'

Tanya said, 'It's *got* to work!'

'If only it was the other way round.' He tried again. He went on trying, non-stop, for twenty minutes. The radio at the far end was taken over by Melhuish; then the radio engineer. But the same. It worked one way, and not the other.

By the time they left the car for Alec's own office quarters, he and Tanya felt the awful futility of being so near and yet so far. They sat at the two desks – Alec at his own, Tanya at Nuttal's. There was a long, miserable silence, till Tanya said, 'Now what do we do?'

'We try all night to make contact and in the meanwhile go on sorting these notes. Tomorrow you can thoroughly investigate the lab – I can't see there's any danger – while I go to Staines library and sort out some reference books.'

'I don't see how that'll help when half this stuff is illegible.'

Alec cracked, 'As the other half is in Latin, which I've long since forgotten, we're not left with very much. Seriously, what Crossley has done is mix several technologies. To understand him, to make sense of his analogy, I need data on each . . . Books on crowd behaviour, eye-to-eye communication, behaviour, patterns of remote African tribes with nomadic and unpredictable habits. I want psychological comment by the planners . . . effects of pollution, sonic bangs, schizophrenia, stress. Then I have to put it in a form that we can transmit.'

'That's a long menu. And supposing, after all that, we don't get through?'

'There's a chance of a relay station. One of Stoddart's men is trying to set something up in London.'

Tanya got up to make coffee. 'I wouldn't bank on it.'

'I'm not too hopeful. Sunspot activity as bad as this removes the ion layers that reflect short-wave altogether. Use of higher power may make no difference at all. But sooner or later we've got to know just exactly what Crossley was driving at.'

She opened a can of Nestlé's milk and said, 'If you sit in the library for that long there's one thing you're going to need for certain – a gas mask.'

* * *

The next major shock came exclusively to Stoddart's notice.

Sir Ralph Stoddart's relationship with communications systems originally designed and equipped by his own company and now partially sold-out to Nuttall was peculiarly inbred. Stoddart, raw though ageing recruit of the cadres, was faced with the unnerving paradox that use of what was now virtually a Nuttall network could backfire in either direction. Either Nuttall could get to hear of aggressive measures being taken against him by Stoddart, or Stoddart might learn of Nuttall's own plan against him. If calls were kept short they might not be intercepted. Nuttall didn't know – at any rate just yet – that his private telephone system was less private than he supposed. It became so because Stoddart had friends in high places. A few of these were still sane and alive. They included the Managing Director of Telecommunications.

The stand-by telephone system to the northern sectors of England consisted of a relay arrangement of UHF links, built by the Post Office in normal times primarily for television networking. The relay stations themselves, high towers on which were mounted dish aerials facing fore and aft, formed, like the ancient beacon fires lighted on successive hilltops, a point-to-point hook up, each tower up to fifty miles from the next one along, which could carry hundreds of telephone conversations along their path. The signals were then, at either end, linked into normal exchanges – those still operating – finally to energize domestic telephones.

Though the Telecomns Chief was unable to reopen ordinary landlines in a hurry – indeed he couldn't see how such a thing could be done at all – he was able to kit Stoddart with a mobile UHF translator which, if lined up with the dishes on the hills, could tie in with the system.

Leaving at night with his tiny military force, Stoddart was therefore equipped to talk south as far as London and north as far as Glasgow. UHF being unaffected by sunspot activity, there was no problem there.

The snag was that he could neither talk to Alec at the Hat-Rack – because the Staines phones were dead – nor to the West, where no channels of any kind existed.

* * *

Stoddart, not an unimaginative man despite Tanya's prejudices, wondered, as he prepared to leave London that night, in what terms he could possibly describe the experience, should he survive to do so, and should others exist to listen.

With great difficulty, the army captain who was nominally in charge of the convoy had dissuaded Stoddart from travelling right in the van. Stoddart had only an open jeep. In it was the technologist from Brunel, with the UHF telephone translater in his charge. The thing had a massive bowl on a swivel; and the accompanying accumulators, generator-set and black box made the jeep heavy and slow . . . a vulnerable target indeed.

So the order of battle was thus; in the lead, a six-wheeler armoured car, crewed by the commander and two gunners, then the jeep, followed by two Dodge trucks, each containing eight soldiers, and commanded respectively by a sergeant and a lieutenant.

Bizarre though it was to line up under a silenced Big Ben with the whole city in pitch darkness, the true eeriness came from the sudden realization that London was such a vast place. Stoddart had spent a lifetime there; he'd never noticed its size, never computed the millions of eggs consumed in a day, the number of matches struck, the multi-millions of words exchanged in the street as a matter of course.

But this metamorphosis was so weird, Stoddart couldn't think of a metaphor. The nearest he could get was the concept of an entire fairground, with its roundabouts and dodgems, big wheel and roller coaster and octopus, raucous screeches from steam organ and brilliant lights from everywhere . . . all running flat out, yet without a human soul in sight. It wouldn't do. The metaphor was back-to-front and understated. But it did suggest the kind of crazy desolation that prevailed.

Noises normally unheard were to the fore. The fluttering feathers of restless starlings seemed louder than someone turning the page of a magazine, right next to your ear, in the stilled reading room of the club. The incessant whining of forgotten dogs, lost and helpless and hungry, provided a background of whimpered misery that somehow infuriated, as if their solitude was the result of your own neglect, blaming you for it.

But the cats. Their vicious tumult gave the game away. Pets? . . . They were jaguars prowling a jungle, released suddenly from human influence as if they'd never licked so ingratiatingly at anyone's saucer of milk. They didn't care and never had; their eyes, suddenly illuminated as the driver of the armoured car switched on his headlights, stared with alien distaste at that species which had supposed it had tamed them. They had been actors, purring to save themselves the trouble of foraging; nudging the fleshy legs of doting owners who had never owned anything but feline appetites; even vampiring heat from the bodies of lonely spinsters asleep, rather than waste effort by generating sufficient warmth for themselves.

Now they yowled in sour chorus; and for some reason they had gathered in great numbers over by the Thames. Those caught in the headlights paused for a second, then dashed to join the mass meeting on the river bank. Stoddart paid little attention to their whim. Probably they were hungry and some barge had capsized, tipping edible matter into the water. He hated the damn things, anyway, and dreaded the thought of some flea-bitten tabby leaping on to his lap. Insects seemed on the upsurge in any case. He didn't want theirs as well.

The convoy proceeded, then, through streets still inexplicably devoid of human beings. There was no easy explanation for this. Millions of people do not leave a city without trace, without reappearing somewhere else to balance the equation.

Some were there. In upper windows, candles flickered, hidden faces parted curtains and gazed at the column of vehicles passing deafeningly below. Once Stoddart saw an elderly woman clinging to the outside of the railings, high on an apartment building near Stanmore. Deliberately, she let go her hands. He was a business man, accustomed to the orderly routines of production lines and the stifling ennui of the board room. Once a fellow director had committed suicide, on the day before the annual audit. He'd done it privately, aboard his houseboat, after unhitching the painter and allowing the craft to drift until swirled down the rapids at Teddington, disintegrating into matchwood.

It had been nothing like this. There had been a logical motive, a sequence of foolish events, an outcome. And the River Board had had to dredge the Thames in search of the body, just to tidy up the case . . .

Stoddart abandoned this line of thought. It made him think of those predatory cats again and now there was work to do.

It was thirty miles out of London that the real snarl-up of impacted vehicles came into view and halted the convoy's progress. The problem imposed seemed insuperable, till one of the drivers thought of swiping a bulldozer from where some roadworks had been in hand. From then on, the bulldozer led the convoy, reducing motor cars to shattered lumps of scrap and then dumping them systematically by the roadside as Alec had done before.

But by now, refugees from outer London, drivers from Stanmore and Watford and Harrow, Barnet, Rickmansworth, had joined the choked motorway in an endless crawling line, letting the bulldozer and its charges pass ahead, then following in its wake. Every few seconds, one less car stayed in the game, blocking the way for those that still did.

Stoddart consulted the map and noted he would soon be in

line with the UHF paths where they intersected the motorway. His expert confirmed it. 'We could line up nicely one mile ahead, Sir Ralph. Have you any particular message to pass back to London?'

Stoddart was grim. 'Plenty. We're not going to make it to Glasgow this way. We're going to have to think again.'

It took nearly half an hour to cover that vital mile. Then the Brunel man got to work, accurately working out azimuth and traversing the parabolic bowl until it faced exactly along the radio path. Switching on, he clicked through the channels to find the circuit for Whitehall. In so doing he caught a transmission already in progress. Stoddart put out an arm. 'Hold that one,' he said, and listened.

He blanched as he did so. The voice at one end was Nuttall's. The content was horrific. Sir Ralph heard it out, and sat slumped for a few seconds. The army captain, thinking him ill, asked what had happened. Stoddart told him about Nuttall's next move. Ironically, Nuttall had clearly planned it because through an earlier interception he'd got to know of Stoddart's bid to go north. Stoddart now even considered a withdrawl, with the idea of leaking his intentions deliberately in the hope that Nuttall might change his mind.

But if movement forward was difficult, retreat was well-nigh impossible. What traffic movement there still was behind the convoy was all travelling in the same direction and occupying the entire width of the motorway – both north-bound and southbound lanes. Where the bulldozer had thrust a way through the crushed and gutted casualties in the slow-motion stampede, the gaps had been first penetrated and then jammed by motorists who had despairingly tried to follow. Nothing seemed more important to Stoddart than that Alec should be informed of Nuttall's new twist; and nothing seemed more impossible.

Forlornly, he still made a try. Enlisting the lieutenant as a motorcycle courier, he write an urgent message to Alec and commanded the young officer to convey it back to Staines.

Nothing was ever seen of the lieutenant again. And Stoddart, aware of the slim chances of getting such a message through, felt both anxious for the young man and appalled at the likely outcome of a total breakdown of communications. Stoddart was sixty miles from the nearest serviceable airfield at the moment when Nuttall's message was intercepted on UHF. And all Stoddart could do was press painfully on. He knew he couldn't reach Manchester in time without the solicitous aid of a miracle.

He didn't believe in miracles.

* * *

Jimmy Nuttall would have seemed to many a changed man. Though he still had the same slouch, he had acquired a Farouk-like authority; and even though he lacked the fatty-degeneration to complete the image there was plenty of degeneracy of other kinds to make up for it.

Ignorance on the subject of sophisticated decadence rendered him a bit amateurish. For instance, when he decided to have an orgy he actually had to ask one of his scrap-metal kings how to have one; for his dreams of erotica lacked a proper imagination.

It happened to be Saturday night when his electronic flunkies, retained in his power simply through the threat of withdrawing Estofort if they didn't cooperate, intercepted a message from London confirming Stoddart's proposed armed attack northward, on Nuttall's present headquarters at Ringway Airport, Manchester.

Nuttall had, in fact, been about to set out for Glasgow when the intercept came through. His helicopter scout reported by radio, however, that the roads north of Manchester were choked solid. Moreover, though Nuttall's private war-machine had now swelled so as to include an air force of assorted transport planes lying around Ringway, whose air crews were blackmailed – as were all Nuttall's staff – on the same drug-withdrawal basis, it was now known that Prestwick Airport was a burned-out scrap-heap. It was therefore impossible to penetrate to Scotland even by air. The heavy machines available to him were not suited to the shorter runways of smaller airfields.

Nuttall's strategic weaknesses stemmed from two main origins; the first being his greed. Having sold-off vast quantities of Estofort he now had very limited supplies. Money was already quite meaningless and the drug was the only currency with which to buy the services of reliable men, and to maintain his harem of stupid girls . . . he only liked the stupid ones. The other problem was physical cowardice; the last thing he wanted was a clash with armed militia. He might get hurt.

Saturday night had always been Nuttall's cue for permissiveness and he'd never been able to throw off the adolescent compulsion which, ever since his teenage era, had got built into his personality as a reflex.

In the old days it had meant backing some giggling teenage girl against a truck on the car park behind the cinema, screwing her peremptorily by lifting her dress briefly as she stood there, then rejoining the rest of the boys in a bawdy hymn of ribaldry along a Croydon street. As a youngster he had been good-looking; the ill-tempered, thwarted look had appeared a bit later, when the girls on the car parks showed a preference for more up-to-date methods of copulation, stimulated by something more original than his hands crawling inside their underwear in the back row of a flea-pit cinema. By then such methods were considered rather square. He'd never caught up with later trends; and a brief marriage flopped after a few weeks when his wife got cheesed off on finding out that Nuttall could only copulate on a car park.

But this orgy thing seemed to work. It covered all sorts of indulgencies Nuttall had never thought of; and as well as keeping him amused it kept his mind off the gaping chasms of dangers now threatening, against which he had taken no measures when he'd had every opportunity, from the earliest hours of the crisis, to do so.

He had power, and very few people called him Jimmy. He had communications, and knew about the Dorrington. He had scouts, using helicopters and light aircraft, and soon got to know of Alec Keeling's emergency cache of Estofort at the lone garage. Nuttall had been looking for the very sort of careless mistake he might have made himself; Alec's biggest slip so far had been leaving that transporter so near the buried treasure. Nuttall got a double kick from the prospect of arranging for the digging up of these supplies. Hadn't Alec left him to rot, at the Institute? – when he, Jimmy Nuttall, had since proved his supremacy as an organizer? Whatever the horrors lurking in the darkness of the future, Nuttall could at least get his own back for the past.

Accordingly he took steps in preparation for an organized invasion of the Dorrington Cadre; and those who clung to Nuttall as a source of Estofort took care of the details. Nuttall was presented with a one-page brief; and all he had to do was phone his own authority through to various outposts, including the corrupted element of the civil service based on London. Their function was to jam all radio transmissions between Alec and his cadre should sunspot activity lift. Nuttall already knew the frequencies being used; for the expert adviser to Stoddart, in a futile effort to relay transmissions from the cadre, had discussed the details on the phone, with the engineers at the radio station chosen for the attempt. A calculated risk had catastrophically misfired.

The remainder of Nuttall's UHF call to London was the fragment overheard by Sir Ralph Stoddart from his jeep on the motorway.

At the instant the Brunel man clicked on to the live channel it was the voice at the London end talking . . . 'But what about the supplies of the drug now held by Keeling and the girl at the Staines Institute? Isn't there a chance of taking them as an additional reserve?'

Nuttall thought a bit. 'There is. But the drain on them will be small with only Alec and the girl there. I'd like them to stay alive long enough to learn the results of our enterprise in the West. When they've digested the full implications of that, we'll send a truck to collect the crates and leave them to their thoughts. We'll be sending an advance party in the helicopter, as soon as plans are ready here, to clear the Exeter runways for the main force.'

The London voice said, 'But those supplies in the ports North of you, Glasgow particularly: Don't you want to stop Stoddart's people getting at them?'

'Yes; I shall attempt to clear those depots as soon as I can, by sea. The roads to the North are so badly choked already – from here at least – that I doubt whether Stoddart will reach them. We'll send a boat up from Liverpool and beat him to it. The old fool will probably drop dead anyway before he can keep going long enough to find out.'

It was this last remark that planted in Sir Ralph the seed of an idea. Undisturbed by being referred to in such terms by the likes of Nuttall, and pressing painfully forward once again on the hopeless trek north, he was recovering from the initial shock of the intercepted phone call and thinking ahead, board-room style, as he did so. By this time the convoy had progressed a further fifteen miles and it was quite impossible to return to the point where the radio beam traversed the motorway.

Turning to the Brunel man, Stoddart asked, 'When can we next reach a position where your UHF translater will work?'

'It's quite a way, Sir Ralph. And we have to take the slip-road off to the left.'

'How far to the slip-road?'

'Some eight miles.'

Stoddart nodded. The convoy had been forced to stop once

again at a seemingly impenetrable car smash. 'Would you mind telling the officer commanding?'

The Brunel man climbed out of the jeep to do so. 'We can't do worse than we are now anyway, Sir Ralph.'

'I agree. But eight more miles of this could take eight days. Is there some way we could leave the convoy and make for our interception point cross-country? – You've got four-wheel drive?'

'Yes. But we're so damned heavy with all this equipment.'

'Try and work something out with the captain.'

'Will do.'

THIRTEEN

Alec said, 'The smell you thought was escaping gas.'

Tanya saw his face. It was shell-like, the flesh sunken and white. 'My God, what's the matter?'

Alec had taken the Vauxhall into Staines, where he'd broken into the public library. Once he'd got the hang of the reference system used there, he'd found no difficulty in turning up material, not only on the lemmings themselves, but on the massive technological breadth of Crossley's thinking. From cybernetics to claustrophobia, it was all there.

The notes were now properly collated – a nightmare task which appropriately Tanya and he had worked at throughout the night. Pages of it were clearly missing; Alec hoped he might somehow fill in the gaps.

Despite the nauseous smell he spent a long time in there, using several tables on which he had the various volumes spread out. Fortunately the windows of the library building had been shut. Even so, the gaseous stench had permeated the place. He had to keep chain smoking as a deterrent.

Slowly, a coherent picture began to form in his mind. Dr Crossley had approached the problem he foresaw historically, and this gave it a lucid form which had been lacking when you read it in scraps. From discussions on the Crusades to the dynamic exposition on unnecessary wars, Crossley followed through, paralleling the rise and fall of sequential civilizations with the equivalent tussle among animal species – the latter, of course, covering a period of millions of years.

Then he came to the lemmings . . .

Of course, if you took the parallel literally, it made little sense. The connection was there, but it applied more in the abstract than in substance. For instance, animals with eruptive migratory tendencies took to the escape routes because overcrowding had already reached an intolerable level. Food would be scarce, breeding, having initially been at saturation level, would be inhibited by impoverished local conditions and this, combined with starvation diet, would cause mass surges toward fresh ground. In V.P. the processes overlapped.

In the human case, imagination would be playing the major part; the ability to foresee what *would* threaten living conditions, if certain trends *did* persist, could – if Crossley's thinking made sense – lead to the known psychosis prevalent in animals faced with the pragmatic fact of extreme cramping. In such conditions lemmings in particular deteriorated into beasts incapable of protecting themselves against ordinary hazards, including alien species like the human race.

Stampeding into rivers and there drowning; or overrunning the edge of the land and consequently overspilling en masse into the ocean were not, in the lemmings, so much deliberated acts of suicide as the by-products of panic, whereby those behind forced those in front onward, regardless of the limits in the terrain.

To Alec, this appeared to correspond exactly with the way in which traffic on the roads had bumpered and then pummelled the leading cars into telescoping.

Further clues existed in other volumes specifically concerned with Crowd Behaviour. These corresponded with Crossley's reasoning on the origins – rather than the symptoms – of V.P. For instance, an apparently stable but tightly-packed crowd in Trafalgar Square on election night could be transformed into a panicked mob through psychological interaction for – as it were – no reason at all.

The stir would begin because the disruption could be imagined – even if only in the mind of one individual. Thus an orderly congregation could be stimulated into a screaming head in terror of mutual crushing and suffocation merely through the hypothetical reasoning that *if* they all panicked then there *would* be a stampede.

There were on record episodes where such events had occurred, notably at the funeral of King George V. A man and his son had suddenly got frightened by the possibility of stampede and had leapt on to the roof of a taxi. People nearby, heedless of the reassurances offered by the police, had caught the feeling of hysteria and done similar things. The crowd had started swaying, this way and that, until women were screaming and holding their children high above their heads. The situation had been brought under control before widespread disaster took a hand; but the lesson was there; and, for a time at least, crowds were kept thinner and more rigidly under surveillance. More recently elements of this had applied in the tragedy of Ibrox Park.

Crossley analysed the numbing effect on human minds of the constant outpourings of news and comment on television – drawing here a point-by-point analogue with subconsciously stored anxiety shared unwittingly by an overtly contented settlement of lemmings. But Crossley referenced this against what he called 'the final trigger' – an indefinable but nevertheless specific feature of eye-to-eye communication – some entirely new form of contact between human minds, probably via the eyes, which cross-confirmed that the individuals in mutual contact had reached saturation, leading to instant mutual terror. 'Not forgetting,' Crossley had written in the margin, 'that network television provides, visually, totally identical stimuli, throughout the nations, with only small local variations which, by comparison, are insignificant.' By these he meant local news and regional commentary that was usually only of a 'sporting, agricultural, or humorous nature'. These did not alter the steady weight of anxiety being 'pumped into the universal subconscious', just as the lemmings were simultaneously and continuously exposed to environmental threats that were not immediately digested.

In his painfully studious longhand, Crossley had written: 'The apparent selfishness which is growing among human beings, their alarming disregard for each other's well-being, their blindness to real suffering in others, and their refusal to see the future wished on their young – despite the cries of the anti-pollutionists – is symtomatic of a loss of consciousness which is only superficial. It enables people to "carry on" – even if carrying on implies making the environment yet more poisonous. Unable to face the need to review and change its whole social structure, society accumulates a sense of guilt and consequent repression because the price ultimately to be paid is subconsciously known all the time . . . ' And: ' . . . The hysteria of Powellism with its statistical implications of overcrowding; the endless use of slogans such as "population explosion"; the daily intake of discussion material about which the viewer may only take a passive attitude; the growing fear of super-control by computer – all these concepts and others like them – true or false – lead to a form of psychological claustrophobia from which there is only a panic cure, as with the lemmings: the compulsive decimation of the population whether through fight, flight, or suicide . . . ' And, ' . . . In short, the difference between the animal psychosis and the threatened human psychosis is one of differing intelligence and consequent modifications to the pattern. The human mind fears loss of identity; the animal is not aware of its individual identity. But once the human *realises that he might just as well not possess* the self-awareness unique to his species, and is therefore heading for the collective, instinct-suggested conduct of the lemmings, then he will react even more wildly than the animal upon which this parallel has been based. For he has so much more to lose . . . '

The smell of gas became so intolerable in the library that Alec had at this point broken off. He picked up an armful of reference books, made sure Crossley's notes were leafed into the top one, and left the building.

The stench outside was appalling. And because the wind had changed – it was now blowing from across the river – it seemed to be concentrated in the stifling confines of the built-up area immediately in and around the library.

Alec made a quick check, making sure no one was around, then walked briskly toward the car. To do this he kept in the shade of the buildings on the side of the road opposite from the river, since out of the direct heat of the sun the smell wasn't quite so suffocating.

The car was parked on the hump-backed bridge over the river. He stood there for a moment, a handkerchief held over his face, trying to locate the source of the stench. He didn't think it was domestic gas or anything like it; certainly there was no gas-works in sight. He remembered vaguely that there had been a lino factory somewhere near Staines – the smell used to hit you at exactly the same spot on the by-pass every trip – but it had been nothing like this.

It was then that something made him glance down into the river . . .

*   *   *

Tanya was stooping over him, gently damping his forehead with a wet towel. Softly she said, 'Tell me.'

'Not even you. I couldn't.'

'You saw something?'

'Oh, yes! I saw something!'

'Where?'

'In the Thames. In the river. Just heaped there, Tanya. Heaped!'

She turned away, couldn't look at him. 'I think I see,' she whispered.

Tonelessly, Alec went on, 'The river is so solid with bodies that despite the drought the level has risen close to flood point. They are packed together, these bodies, in one cohesive, rotting, inseparable mass.' He found himself laughing – a horrible, brittle sound that was unnatural. Convulsing with choking self-mockery he tried to go on, feeling bitterly cruel against himself. 'The thought of one doctor stuck in a lift shaft once shocked me. I felt for him. When I looked in that river I felt nothing but disgust. Am I even human?'

She went on stroking his brow. 'Stop hating yourself, Alec.'

'We simply have no right to survive.'

'We must and we will.'

'If it goes on like this, how can we? And why should we? And how will we be able to bear it even if we do?'

Tanya said, 'Did Crossley comment on what happens to the population once it *has* been decimated?'

'I didn't wait to look.'

'Let me see the notes.'

'How can you want to?'

'I can't explain that, Alec. Perhaps it's something to do with being a woman. You may as well know: I'm pregnant.'

'I . . . I can't react.'

'Don't try. Let me see the notes.'

He opened the top volume, then leafed more frantically through the book, then started chucking each book off the stack, searching desperately.

After a while, his movements decelerated, till he just lay there, quite still. He said, almost inaudibly, 'Gone. I must have dropped them in the river.'

'So we don't know,' she said expressionlessly. 'All we know is that the lemmings, once they've got down to manageable numbers, revert to their normal behaviour.'

'And can you imagine this country returning to its "normal behaviour"? – When according at least to Crossley, it wasn't normal in the first place? Can you imagine those crazed people in the streets, or the struggling Things on the floor of the lab I saw that Wednesday – Christ, *last* Wednesday! – ever returning to their so-called sanity, or any other kind of sanity? – even if they aren't killed off by typhoid in the meanwhile?'

'To answer that,' said Tanya, 'we'd have to know what Estofort actually does; how it acts; what instinct it controls.'

'Yes.'

There was a long silence. Tanya brewed some tea, using canned milk. She served it in the tin mugs they'd brought with them; she felt too demoralized even to wash the cups they'd used before.

Alec said, 'You realize what I've got to do? Don't you?'

She stared at him over the top of her mug. 'Alec, you can't! You mustn't!'

'One of our main purposes in coming here was to get that data. Didn't you insist on that yourself?'

'We've got enough. You've done enough.'

He shook his head. 'I've got to go back there. To the bridge. To the river . . . down into that human slime –'

'– The papers will have floated away.'

'Nothing is floating, Tanya.'

She knew what he meant by this and his expression was so terrible, just then, that she thought for an instant that she could see in his eyes all that he had seen.

She said, 'Then we must both go.'

'No.'

'I'm not your little piece now, Alec. I'm going to have your baby. You can't tell me what to do.'

His voice was a dead monotone. 'I can tell you what is common sense. One of us has to survive. One of us has to wait till the radio works again and then tell them what they need to know.'

She said helplessly, 'Perhaps we know enough. The Sindham people may be able to work out the rest.'

'In the time? We can't all be Crossleys; he had a unique subject and spent his working life living with it. Look. If you're afraid I might die of typhoid, there must be jabs, available either here or at one of the hospitals. I can take the lot, if you like – Tetanus and all the rest of it. But vital information can't just be left to rot, along with those . . . '

'You're going to be sick.'

'I told you, I can't react any more.'

'Oh yes, you can. For the sake of my baby, you can. Alec, you're not going to stop yourself feeling! Because of my own stake in this I'm going to see that you do feel! Vomit, damn you, vomit! Until you do, you're no more alive than those festering bodies in the river!'

He looked at her and she was the same rather exotic Tanya and he wasn't in all truth thinking about her baby but was feeling that she was a woman, that Diana – forgive me, Tanya – was a woman, that they both depended on him, on his being able to think and feel and act.

A few minutes later Tanya said, with a cloth in her hand, 'I'll say this for you, Alec. When you are sick, you're very sick – '

He choked and swallowed and attempted a smile, 'And when I'm not?'

'You're healthy.'

* * *

But on his return to the bridge, Alec found himself no longer merely horrified, but moved.

All the sadness he had ever felt seemed to well up inside him in chorus. Humanity, just at that moment, had failed: and universal love, the force that was capable of creating beauty even out of so appalling a spectacle of such mass slaughter, there in the slow ooze of that plagued river, overwhelmed him, and so he could only stand and gaze in tears. Each family that had fled, suddenly struck down with so insurmountable impulse of terror that even at the river's edge they could not halt themselves in their flight, had a whole intimate history of trying to thrive against odds that had suddenly and unanimously struck them as too great. In one short period, a passage of time no longer than it takes to behold and appreciate and then come to love a newborn infant, and to dream of the child's future hopes and strivings, people with shared feelings of which they could no longer speak or think, all of them different and – for them – special and unique, had plunged, helpless and screaming and emotionally dismembered, universally into this ancient river, as the only solution to what fearful pain God only knew.

Even as he stood there crying, some lone survivor, up high in some window of a neighbouring building, must have been seeking solace with which to express his last despairing message of human love; for a transistorized record player, rather distorted and imperfect, began to throb a theme of music through those stilled, deserted streets. The music was Sibelius's *Finlandia*; and of course it must have been pure coincidence, but the lemming is native to Finland, too.

And despite the music's national significance, as a hymn to hope amidst despair in Finland, it could not have been more apt here. One man's timeless love of life, Sibelius's superb un-histrionic authority over emotion, expressing against infinite sadness an irrepressible love of a land – not this particular land, but any where life could thrust on forward – rang through the empty streets and across the river, pouring out undiluted faith. And on Alec it had its effect. For his spirit, almost destroyed by the spectacle below the bridge, responded so that he remembered the living, too.

Convulsed with aching tears and unconscious of the stench, he listened as the hymn theme rose to its climax. Then there came, upon the last statement of this glorious theme, the smash of splintering glass in place of the composer's thunderous finale. And one more tortured victim was added to the many.

Then, silence.

Of what he had gone there to find there was no sign. But what he had regained was his strength. The conflict between Tanya and Diana would not, just by wishing it, resolve itself. That, in the end, he must work out for them and with them. Important though it was, as were all the human relationships which had abruptly gone to waste; and vital as it was never again to use people as he'd used them, careless of the consequences and immune from wondering about what others concealed beneath all the fun-loving, the overwhelming thought was to help rebuild a society that could never end like this.

* * *

Tanya and he were very quiet together for the rest of that day.

FOURTEEN

Stan's little aeroplane was not quite the same as before. The modifications weren't quite finished; but basically it was now a single seater. Beneath both wings, welded angle-brackets secured within each wing back to the main spar, projected from the leading edges, unexplained.

But at present he was flying quite low over Exeter, watching. Those angle-brackets had nothing to do with this flight.

The previous day he had conducted a similar sortie, only that time he stuck to the coast, flying all the way along to the Lizard, that worn-out heel of Cornwall's boot, the toe-cap of which was Land's End.

So he already knew what Alec knew.

Ascetic that he was, he'd kept his reactions within practical bounds, without telling anybody. Knowing nothing of lemmings or Crossley, sceptical though he was of the conventional laboratory methods being pursued by forlorn specialists at the Dorrington, he had observed all around the coast the balance of an unexplained equation. He alone among those at Exeter knew where the people had gone. The effect on him was simply to accelerate the work he had been doing on the aircraft, for he thought he knew what to expect next.

But now he concentrated on the streets of Exeter, flying low – sometimes actually between buildings – but taking no risks. He knew his aeroplane, and now he knew the city. It harboured no unforeseen obstructions. He could buzz the shopping centre and know just when to pull back on the control column.

The town was just a model. It even looked clean, though its streets were unswept. But then, who was there to deposit unseemly litter? Only the cars were askew.

Banking to the east and following the A38, he included in this reconnaissance a quick look at the airport.

When he saw what he saw, he instantly went full throttle and climbed into cloud. Skimming just inside it, yet still able to see without being seen, he watched a helicopter land near the tower.

Evidently this was not the first aircraft to arrive. A few men were already on the airport, clearing the runways of debris. There were no large aircraft, apart from the wrecks being dragged clear of the operations areas.

Stan did not react, except by carefully using his instruments while flying semi-blind. Merely making sure he would recognize the helicopter again, he resumed the climb till he was above cloud, then headed at altitude back for the tiny field by the barn.

With the telephone poles sawn down and the powerlines cut through at the pylons – his first undertaking after that hazardous arrival with the Trents – the field presented no problem, except you had to land one way and take off the other, disregarding the direction of the wind.

After touchdown, he strolled back to the hotel for a quiet word with Richard.

* * *

If Diana sensed the increasing danger to the cadre it wasn't because of what Stan knew. What was evident to her was the effects of isolation on the community. An emotional weightlessness existed there; it had developed, intangibly but with ugly menace, ever since radio contact with Alec had broken down. Among the children, Edna Melhuish's lot seemed the least affected. Her own Stephen was the one who felt it the most.

He'd been having nightmares, waking from them violently as if afflicted by a spasm. He never said what they were about. That he'd guessed something about Tanya was more than probable, he'd caught Diana crying to herself in the bathroom and, shortly thereafter, she had caught him doing the same. The reversal stopped him crying and they both laughed, hugging each other. But the silence that followed was no comedy. She'd wiped his eyes, expecting him, at last, to ask about Daddy. He didn't. He said, 'I'm frightened about June.'

'Why?' – But she knew why. Soon after that, she found an opportunity for talking in private with Melhuish. He nodded as he listened to her, as if knowing what would come. 'Whatever you do,' she whispered, 'don't give her an inkling of how low supplies of Estofort really are.'

Melhuish asked her, 'You'll forgive my asking; but does June Trent know where you keep your own bottle?'

'Yes. Why? You're not suggesting – '

' – I wouldn't blame anybody.'

'Not people who have so much to gain by living.'

Diana searched his eyes at this. 'Haven't you?'

'Never mind about me, Mrs Keeling. But about survival I'm a realist. Women and children first – yes. But which women? – and which children?'

Diana said, 'I trust June completely.'

'So do I. I trust her to protect her baby and if possible her husband.'

'I see.' Diana looked furious at this imputation and briskly walked away.

But Melhuish had other things on his mind. He'd just been on radio watch in the shack. A new development there had baffled him and he wanted Richard's opinion.

Now, he hovered in the central lounge, careful not to seem disturbed in the company of the doctors and scientists who, forlornly and without enough equipment, were trying with undiminished dedication to spectograph the elaborate molecular structure of one of the most complex preparations ever to be assembled in one tiny capsule.

On a blackboard near the garden end, two of them were arguing quietly about conflicting possibilities of molecular bond. One said, 'Even if you're right, even if I'm right, in either case such balance could only be achieved under very exact conditions. To synthesize such a preparation here is just plain impossible. We might just as well face that now.'

In searching around for Richard, Melhuish suddenly realized that June was there in the room and had overheard this statement. She was constantly hanging around the doctors, irritating them in her anxiety to assess progress. Her face now quite expressionless, she walked quietly out of the lounge but in an unnatural way, as if her thoughts were linked to the motor nerves of her legs.

Melhuish spotted Richard crossing the other end of the lounge toward the accommodation area. There, conditions were much more cramped than before. Apart from housing, feeding, supplying with drugs and generally administering the compact defence force recruited by Richard, there were the new-comers – Crossleyites who had somehow got to hear of the cadre and managed to reach it from other cities. Acting on Alec's plan, Richard anticipated by training these envoys with a view to their establishing cadres elsewhere, should adequate quantities of Estofort become available. For the moment, though, these people were merely stuck there, feeling their uselessness and aware that some people deeply resented the additional drain on Estofort their presence imposed. They radiated unease, scared that if supplies depleted much more they might be the first to be abandoned to the plague. All these, along with the crew of the police patrol car, had to be catered for. Families were often eight to a room; June and Baby Caroline had moved in with Diana and her three; and men who were either single or separated from their wives by the crisis as the sole survivors of the household from which they had escaped were all billeted in one dormitory converted, much to the Major's consternation, from an embryonic but nonetheless cherished greenhouse.

In a low voice, Melhuish said, 'I want you to come over to the radio.'

'Did you get through, then?' But Richard could see from Melhuish's face that this wasn't quite the point.

Not until they were out in the garden, on the way to the radio shed, did Melhuish describe what he'd been hearing. 'I thought I heard Alec Keeling's voice. Then there was just this jumble. Listen.'

Richard did so. 'Can that still be some effect of the sunspot peak your engineer friend was talking about?'

'He says not. He said that on his shift he picked up American transmissions, somewhere on the continent, probably Germany, where there's a breakneck attempt being made to produce a drug similar to Estofort. Apparently the Russians had got somewhere with this thing, but were only producing tiny quantities because of some aberration among their missile people. It looks rather as if there's some kind of conference going on in the East sector of Berlin; but whatever it is, reception is back to normal on all wavelengths.'

Richard snapped, 'Can't we get hold of what's-his-name, the engineer?'

Melhuish sat down before the radio, gracing his hands devoutly, then washing them anxiously together. 'He went into Exeter to try and find a more powerful transmitter. He hopes to make radio contact with Germany over this latest development and says that with this low-power equipment we wouldn't stand a chance of getting heard unless they were really listening out for us on a known frequency.'

Richard said, 'Well, I'd say this new interference was deliberate jamming.'

'That's what I think.'

'Christ. Don't tell the others. Morale is bad enough as it is. June is terribly worried about Diana. She seems listless and completely lost without Alec.'

Not for the first time, this put Melhuish in the tricky position of knowing both sides of the same coin; and at times the temptation to break the tension by flipping it over was almost unbearable. Had he not spent nearly his whole working life in so humbled a position that the constant bickerings at the Hat Rack had trained him for tact and silence, he would probably have replied frankly; in which case the uneasy atmosphere here at the cadre would have exploded into uproar.

Instead, Melhuish stuck to the main issue. His rubbery lips assumed an oddly-angled, helpless sort of smile. 'You do realize what this could mean?'

Richard said curtly, 'I should. I've just been talking to Stan. An advance party is clearing Exeter Airport.' Richard ran an anxious hand through his hair. 'I'll take over radio watch. I'll listen-out on VHF for aircraft, too . . . Bugger! Where's Stan gone now? I wanted to ask him the frequencies. What's he doing, out there? – Keeping some mysterious tryst with that aeroplane of his?'

Melhuish felt in his pocket for a bit of paper. 'He gave me a list of frequencies. It's here.'

* * *

Stan's tryst was not all that mysterious.

Shaven perfectly, as usual, so that the sharp distinction between sideburn and pink skin might have been marked there with a setsquare, he was at that moment marking two precision crosses and a central bulls-eye on the inside far wall of the barn where he'd once again stowed the aircraft after this latest flight. But now he'd completed the modifications to his little machine.

Chalk marks carefully ruled on the ground, so that the triangle formed by joining them up exactly fitted the touch-point of the aeroplane's three wheels, bore a particular relationship with the chalk marks on the wall.

Manhandling the little machine so that the wheels sat exactly on the marks, he then climbed into the cabin.

Here there were some discreet alterations.

In place of the seat normally fixed to the right of his own, he had mounted a modern radar set, swiped from RAF Hanningforth, along with new instruments mounted on the panel.

Hanningforth had turned out a vast disappointment. Stan had hoped to filch an aircraft far more suitable for the purpose he had in mind. He had stared at the disarray of smashed-up machines; then resolutely salvaged what he needed to modify his own.

So in the centre of the control wheel there was now a red button, and before him, mounted suitably on the windscreen, two 'X' verniers through which he squinted at the bulls-eye.

He pressed the red button.

There was an earsplitting explosion, as one round from each machine-gun, mounted beneath the wings on both port and starboard side, zinged across the barn and drilled themselves through the far wall, where the crosses were marked.

Stan did not smile in satisfaction. He just reapplied the safety switch, near the throttle lever, climbed out, and examined the accuracy of the penetration. One bullet hole was out by an inch. So he spent another half hour making fine adjustments, then returned to the hotel for the evening meal.

* * *

It was Diana who came to Melhuish.

It was late but there was still a light showing through the crack in the door. Outside, the regular throb of the new generator had just taken over from the old. In the lounge the doctors were at work analysing brainprints taken of the victims. These had been obtained by installing E.E.G. equipment in the stripped down bus and touring the streets. The doctors had hated doing it. It was a particularly callous operation because afterwards they'd simply left the victims to writhe where they were. The encephylograms showed no organic deviation whatsoever.

Feeling hesitant and somehow admonished, Diana knocked softly on the office door. Melhuish's kindly voice said, 'Come in.' She shut the door behind her.

'I owe you an apology,' she said. 'You expressed a view to protect me and my family, and I just walked away.'

Melhuish, perversely humbled by Diana's humility, felt confused. 'Perhaps I was wrong to say it.'

'No. I'm sure you weren't wrong – to say it. But I would be wrong to comply. June and I share a room. We know each other's habits exactly. If I changed mine now, she'd know at once. That would end a friendship neither of us can afford to lose.'

'Of course. You're right. I understand.'

Diana made no move. Melhuish looked up at her and thought for a second, What a woman. Beautiful, poised, inspiring. How would I have fared, if . . . ?

He suppressed the thought at once and felt ashamed and disloyal. He was Melhuish. And how would Edna have fared, if?

Diana said, 'I know you've been worried about me. I know you wanted to help me. Yet I've been running away from you, because you're the one who understands.'

Melhuish said, 'I think it would have been an intrusion, Mrs Keeling.'

'Far from it. You know about my husband and I've noticed how . . . forebearing you've been with me over my moods. This is hardly the time for eternal triangles and you've been consistently kind. How you've had the patience for it I just don't know . . . ' She was thinking of the burden presented by Edna, but could hardly refer to this. Melhuish looked away a second, knowing well enough what was on her mind. She went on, 'Think of the numbers. You have five children; I have three; June Trent only has her baby, who takes half a capsule to everyone else's one.'

Melhuish said quietly, 'That fact is never off my mind, Mrs Keeling.'

'I can understand how June feels. If she loses Baby Caroline, she loses everything. Do you realize what I'm saying?'

Melhuish sat perfectly still. 'What *are* you saying?'

'If Alec can't get back in time with fresh supplies, we may ultimately have to draw lots; one father; one mother; to act as foster parents for one child from each family. And you have the most to lose.'

'Do I?' He knew she didn't understand just what he meant by that.

'I've shocked you,' said Diana.

'No.' Melhuish gazed at the long list of personnel. It was pinned to the wall. Next to it was the original establishment at the time the three families had arrived. The difference in length between the two lists was frightening. 'I've been wondering myself, along those lines. The point is, you can't reduce human beings to arithmetic. I don't think human nature works quite like that. Or that the outcome would really be any answer. For one thing, if survival depends on the everlasting taking of this drug, it can't matter. If we're all going to be victims, it's only a matter of time. It will be merciful release, in a sense, for those who are sacrificed first. We have guns, Mrs Keeling. We don't need to be driven to using them on each other. If need be, we use them ourselves.'

She said shakily, 'Now that you've said it, it sounds so fearfully – '

' – Real? It may not be. I'm putting the worst case, because you expected it of me. Let's make no bones, Mrs Keeling. You are depressed and upset by your husband's, er, misconduct.'

She said firmly, 'I understand it.'

'You're an intelligent woman. Nevertheless, it affects the way you think. It eats at your natural optimism. Young Stephen is aware – '

' – Don't, I know, I know. But you can't play-act with Stephen. I tried it. It just makes him worse. He runs away and sobs, then tries to play – sort of in slow motion – with the other children, feeling as if the bottom is dropping out of his world in every way at the same time . . . But June and I – already I can tell, in her eyes, that she's thinking the same sort of thoughts as me. Wondering . . . '

'Have you hinted at this to her husband?'

'In a way, Richard is more frightened of June's growing resentment than I am. He's not good at coping with her in some moods and – you must have noticed this – he escapes into his various duties more and more. Nothing can be so tense for him than to sit there with her, avoiding the subject like the plague, yet watching her lovingly feed the baby at the same time.'

Melhuish said, 'Like the plague . . . Yes, it must be hell on earth for you all.'

'You don't include yourself?'

'Not quite in the same way. I've had to come to terms with a great many things, Mrs Keeling, in my long life.' Wild horses wouldn't have dragged him into actually mentioning Edna, but that was what he meant. Instead he said, 'I love my children – please believe that – but something inside me gave up, a long time ago, a certain kind of hope. I've never got it back and despite your husband's faith in me I've been perverse enough to prevent myself getting it back.'

'But why?'

'Too many disappointments, I suppose.' He said, with a certain tragic intimateness, 'I expect very, very little, you know.'

Diana looked at him sharply. She said, 'Yes, I do know,' –

but something in the way he'd expressed himself greatly disturbed her. It sounded like some kind of decision.

But before she could take him up on it he'd changed the subject and went on, 'Mrs Keeling, if you will allow me to say so, I mean about your husband . . . ?'

'Please do.'

'I don't quite know how to put this, except to say that our whole world has changed; and sometimes I squirm at the idea of resuming the sort of things I used to have to put up with – you know what I mean? – need I explain that?'

Diana looked away guiltily. She knew that her own kind of snobbery was the sort that had perpetuated Melhuish's phobia about the Grades. 'I know exactly.'

'Quite . . . Well, just suppose we do pull through all this and survive intact. It could very well be. And if it happens I doubt whether we'll ever go back to "conventional" life . . . the life we knew. It'll be a different sort of world. And, to be utterly frank, I can't see anything to stop Alec Keeling having . . . well . . . two wives. Certainly, nothing will ever stop him loving you. That's why it causes him so much pain to "cheat" you. What neither of you realize is that he is not cheating.'

'I'm afraid I don't quite understand what you mean.'

'I mean that he has done the work of far more than one man.' Melhuish gestured around him. 'All this, the organizing that led to it, the forethought he showed when he first talked about it with me that terrible day at the Institute. He is more than one man.'

She said incredulously, 'You mean, therefore he is entitled to more than one woman?'

'Could he have managed it with just one? Oh, please don't think this personal. I'm talking about the physical factors, the geography of the matter. He made a safe refuge for you and the children. He then had to go to where probably unbearable grief would afflict him. He couldn't take you with him for that, could he?'

Diana said tautly, 'Chance entered into this, Mr Melhuish. That bitch fell into his lap for the sake of her own survival.'

'I admit,' said Melhuish, 'that I felt the same way about her – at first. But, to be honest, I felt you understood it much better than I did. If I may say so, you're a rather conventional person. You were faced with the conflict of what you should think and what you really thought. I watched you going through it. Mrs Keeling, he won't drop this girl Tanya, any more than he'll drop you. How could he? Think what they must have shared.'

'I'd rather not.'

He smiled at her sudden tartness. 'But speaking honestly, would you have had him go back to Staines alone? . . . '

Stephen was lying motionless on his back with his eyes wide open – exactly as Diana had the night of Alec's departure.

When he saw that mummy was feeling better, in some way you couldn't put your finger on, but anyway she was, he came to life, telling her all about his talk with James about Mr Nuttall's air attack.

Diana was taken aback. Shushing him to a whisper, she stooped down close and looked at him hard. 'How did you two know?'

'Oh, we always listen outside the radio shack. We take it in turns, you see.'

'Yes, I do see.'

'You know what the history books say?'

'No, darling. What do they say?'

'Sometimes, to destroy the enemy, you outwit him. That's why the Charge of the Light Brigade was all wrong. If we have to get in that bus and run away, well, it won't really be running. Will it? If this Mr Nuttall attacks, and finds there's no one here to attack, and nothing to help him go on, we'll be winning. At school we learned how Rommel's, um, communications were stretched, right across the desert, because the British seemed to run away. Then there was El Alamein. See what I mean?'

Diana felt emotional at Stephen's obvious recovery but was careful not to show it. 'Whichever we do, dear, stay and fight it out, or conduct – what do they call it? – a tactical withdrawal; if you feel like that, we'll beat him.'

Stephen smiled. 'Anyway, I think we're stronger than Mr Nuttall, really.'

Diana whispered conspiratorially, 'In that case he might even defeat himself. But we'll give him plenty of help. Don't tell anyone else, will you? We'll keep this a secret . . . just you and James and me.'

'Mummy, you're all right now, aren't you?'

'Of course I am!'

And Stephen hugged her.

* * *

'Sunspots be damned!' Alec kicked the set savagely and wrenched the car door open. 'Come on!'

'Where to?'

'Where do you think? If Nuttall is jamming us, what do you suppose is on his mind?' He led off at a furious pace toward the liasion office. 'I picked up France, Belgium, Rome, just a few minutes ago. A bit of luck and Stoddart himself might have called us any moment. Now, no one can.'

Tanya said grittily, 'It must have been Stoddart who tipped off Nuttall anyway. Otherwise how could Nuttall know the frequencies? Fat, overstuffed business slobs in *Who's Who* . . . They play it both ways. Otherwise how do they make all that money?'

Alec said more soberly, 'Or else in using the phones he inadvertently gave us away. In which case he must be in trouble too.'

Tanya said, 'Balls. Why should he need to give anyone else our wavelengths?'

'Because his man from Brunel was trying to fix up a relay station . . . But never mind the finer points. Let's get loading!'

During the last forty-eight hours, Tanya had been tending the lemmings up in Lab Number Four. She had grown to love them, these comic little creatures. But some of them had been sick and almost starving. The thermostatically-controlled atmosphere had been awry since Melhuish had turned off the master switch on that Wednesday. It was hot and airless in the lab, and the weaker ones were in bad shape, curled up miserably in dark corners and whimpering. Alec had restored the climatic conditions through the use of the emergency generator. Tanya had done the rest till the animals were scuttling cheerfully around the lab and barking playfully.

In there, a thorough search revealed a few of the missing pages of Crossley's notes. They seemed insignificant though. Neither his final conclusions – if he'd reached any – nor any sort of guidelines on the basic chemistry of Estofort were mentioned.

There was a bit on sunspots. Caustically, Crossley had scrawled, 'Graves of the Un. of Chicago clutches at coincidence as if anything from a shooting star to a poltergeist is proof positive of his balmy theories. Now – if you please!' – he co-relates changes in the Earth's magnetic field with migratory phenomena!'

'What's that supposed to mean?' Tanya had asked.

Alec dipped into his long-lost physics education, then replied very thoughtfully, 'The principlal cause of changes in the magnetic field is solar activity.'

'I still don't get it.'

He'd slapped the log book shut and stared out of the window toward the evening glow. 'Sunspots,' he'd said . . .

Tanya was saying now, 'All right. Suppose Stoddart is genuine. How can we leave here until the supplies of Estofort we were promised are brought here?'

'All we can do is to try and get hold of the emergency dump we buried at the Exeter garage, and hope that Stoddart catches on about this jamming.' He counted the remaining crates still stored in the back office. Using the Ford's roof-rack, they could easily be carried in one car. 'It's a typical piece of tactical blundering on Nuttall's part to jam us anyway – it just gives away his plans. Stoddart will be on to it. With luck, if he reaches Glasgow, he'll divert supplies straight to Jaybury.'

'How?'

Alec started heaving the boxes into a stack by the door. 'Before he left here he dropped me a hint, though I didn't dig it at the time. He said, "There's more than one way into the Clyde." '

'Boats!'

'What's to stop him sending them right down the coast and docking them in Exeter?'

Tanya felt doubtful about this but didn't say so. Instictively she felt that to suddenly organize a navy while in convoy by road was a tall order, and Stoddart would have plenty to think about if he were still attempting an attack on Nuttall's former position.

Alec wasn't listening. 'We'll do proper load-sheets. I'm going to treat the Vauxhall as an armoured car. That means we'll be fully prepared, ready for attack. And since I can handle a machine-gun a bit better than you, I'll have to be a tank commander.'

'With all the drugs concentrated in my car? – Aren't you rather putting all your eggs in one basket?'

'Yes.' He smiled. 'Literally.'

She said, 'By the way, I feel sick!'

'You are sure? . . . I mean isn't the timing pretty fine?'

She said flatly, 'My period was due on Thursday and my insides work like clockwork.'

'Your cycle could have been upset by what you've been through.'

She shook her head. 'No. I don't know how. But I know – Junior is on the way.'

Alec said, 'It's wrong of me, and it makes things . . . complicated. But Tanya, I'm glad.'

She looked at him softly. 'If you weren't, I don't believe I'd have the courage left to make the journey.'

* * *

At last, Stoddart was able to get the convoy diverted off the motorway. Three successive sliproads had proved jammed solid. The army captain was quite sure that to attempt a cross-country break for the hills, where UHF interception would once again be a technical possibility, would be sheer lunacy. 'Sorry, Sir Ralph. That's an order . . . however nominally in charge you may think I am.'

The Brunel man took off a pair of headphones he'd had clamped to his ears. 'But – '

Impatiently, the captain rapped, 'But what?' He didn't like experts.

'But now that radio is working normally, the cadre link is being jammed.'

'Then can't you call them?'

Patiently, the expert tried to explain that would be hoisting an aerial by its own petard.

'Doesn't alter a thing,' said the captain. 'Unless you want to get us all killed, we take the roads. The next sliproad is less than half a mile. Even in this appalling jam-up we should make it in less than an hour . . . '

But taking the convoy along the winding roads of the Pennines made it very conspicuous from the air. Realizing this, the captain ordered the main body of his patrol to stay under cover of a forested valley, while Stoddart took the telecoms jeep and continued unescorted.

He cursed the good sense and caution of the army captain the moment the jeep had climbed into exposed, open country. An inquisitive-looking reconnaissance aircraft, still carrying R.A.F. markings, had clearly been tracking the convoy for some time. Only the deafening traffic noises on the motorway had obliterated its engine beat.

The pilot waited until Stoddart was on the moor, then landed in an easy field nearby. With a supporting back-up of two armed guards, he set about capturing the board room menace to Nuttall's operations.

A lifetime of company experience had given Stoddart an unholy degree of understanding when it came to dealing with underlings who showed varying degrees of Nuttallness in their make-up. He understood the hokum-nazism of the Nuttall regime with a degree of accuracy which was downright unfair.

Obedient to the guns trained on him from three sides, he rose, rather arthritically as commanded, and stepped out of his vehicle on to the open moor. The Brunel man had to do likewise.

The spokesman for Nuttall – evidently the pilot of the plane – tried to feign a sort of military rasp in his voice that left Stoddart visibly unimpressed.

Stoddart allowed the man to finish blustering and then he spoke. 'I have fired more men like you,' he said, without raising his voice, 'than your celebrated Mr Nuttall has on his entire books. The reason I fired them was because they were basically weak; and where the weakness shows, my friends, is an extraordinary ability to change sides at a moment's notice. In your case I commend it. At least you must have the intelligence to see what Nuttall is really heading for.'

The pilot tried to interrupt. Stoddart raised a hand loosely and allowed two of his chins to wobble in slight impatience. 'As you know so well, the only currency that buys anything at present is Estofort; and despite the fact that you are clearly no gentleman, you and I are going to make a gentleman's agreement. Even Mr Nuttall, with his very limited knowledge of industry, would be able to assure you that I have never broken one yet.'

This time there was no interruption.

'Mr Nuttall is, by reputation, prone to the kind of conduct which Estofort can do absolutely nothing to check. You probably know this already. But I happen to know personally because both he and I are in electronics, though – I like to think – at somewhat different levels. The fascinating part of Mr Nuttall's character is that though he is really the most panic-stricken ass imaginable, it never shows until it's far too late. For instance, you and I both know that he has sold off vast quantities of Estofort. I was one of his customers.

'But whereas he made no effort to ensure a steady supply, I did. And whereas he isn't going to last more than another few days, I can last for months. There is by now a trawler, under the command of Her Majesty's Government, which at this moment is loading very large stocks of Estofort in the Clyde.'

This was sheer bluff; but Stoddart had dealt with enough queasy-minded shareholders in his time, over the financing of daring projects, to fool the feeble little aviator who now cringed before him. 'Were you about to say something?'

'But . . . that's what Nuttall planned to do.'

'He's a little late for that. However, as I don't wish to be further molested by you, as I happen to want to use this UHF link up here, I will, with unprecedented reluctance, give you a chance of survival . . . hardly through choice, merely through necessity. I am taking you prisoner – rather than the other way about, my friend – and I give you my personal guarantee that you three will receive the same issue as all my men – provided you surrender your aeroplane now and hand me your guns.

'One more point. You will be subjected to questioning. In your answers you will tell the truth. For instance, I shall want to know how much of my previous transmission to London, via these UHF links, was intercepted or recorded. And since I know, in part, what has been said by Mr Nuttall's gangsters over the same links, you would be well advised to tell the truth, since you don't know where the gaps in my own knowledge exist.

'Now, decide. Who do you think is going to last the longest? – Nuttall, or me?'

There was a long silence. Then the pilot stepped forward with a question. 'If you succeed in establishing law and order, I assume that there will be arrests?'

'You assume correctly, I assure you.'

'Can you guarantee us immunity?'

Stoddart smiled a grim little smile. 'Weak little men always ask the same question. I doubt it, but we'll see . . . '

Having thus got the crew of the aeroplane to hand over their guns, Stoddart now proceeded to turn bluff into reality.

The Brunel man nodded when the link was through to what remained of the government in London, and Stoddart gave instructions concerning the transportation, by coaster, of drugs warehoused in the Clyde. The shipment was to go direct to Exeter.

After observing, with vindictive amusement, the degree to which the pilot realized he'd been had, Stoddart added a further transmission. 'Tell the French,' he said, 'or the Russians or the Germans or anyone you damn well like, to send an air patrol on the sea lanes on the west coast. They'll find a vessel with no flag and no desire to signal according to the international code.

Tell them to get this vessel in their sights and bomb them to holy blazes. The aircrew won't catch any Virulent Panic from several thousand feet; but they'll be doing humanity a considerable service.'

After making this final call, Stoddart's face looked bloodless from remorse. Calculating the minimum possible speed with which the coaster sponsored through diplomatic channels could chug up north, load up, then preceed via Land's End all the way to Exeter, he knew the chances of the stuff arriving in time were almost nil.

As he climbed back into the jeep along with the prisoners, he prayed also that Nuttall was the miserable failure he judged him to be.

Otherwise, the ship to be bombed might be the one with the priceless cargo.

* * *

Alec checked through the load sheets for the last time and called out to Tanya, 'Spare sparking plugs?'

'Got them.'

'Fan belt, gallon can of engine oil?'

'Okay.'

'Two spare tyres, at correct pressure?'

'Stowed, she said, 'Twenty-six pounds pressure in each.'

Alec disconnected the long aerial which went all the way up to the Hat-Rack tower, and reconnected the radio to the whip antenna of the car itself. All okay. He took a brief look at the little cage containing the two lemmings. They gazed back at him, as if enquiring, what the hell next? 'Just sit tight,' he told them, 'and don't mess up your cage.' They just wiggled their whiskers as if to say, that's our business. You get on with yours.

So he did. For the last time they started the two cars and drove cautiously out into the road.

As before, Alec led in the Vauxhall and Tanya followed in the Ford. By walkie-talkie they kept in touch, even managing occasionally to copy – as it were – their former brand of dialogue, as it had periodically erupted, on the way up, into little touches of verbal love-play. But the jokes were forced and soon dried up. Although Tanya had not seen the river, by proxy she had felt the pangs, and therefore the changes, in Alec. Close to him as she was, with the tiny beginnings of their baby modifying her own mood and bringing it so close to his, she could not pretend that she too hadn't changed.

This did not mean that their spirits were low. Tanya's pregnancy had simply given them a sense of reality and purpose. And there was something else . . . a hidden affinity with those at Dorrington. Nothing as complicated as E.S.P.; merely the knowledge – learned, however briefly from that voice on the radio, before the jamming abruptly curtailed it – that the cadre was still intact, still in existence, waiting for them. Whatever the emitional tangles there was the love within the herd. And two halves of a community, split by distance and radio blackout, were to be united.

And as they drove on, and found the going possible, their spirits rose. The clutter and the death and the gutted buildings where unquenched fires had caught and spread unchecked from block to block – the wrecks in the road and the litter of broken toys and signs of desperate attempts at flight . . . these were part of history. They affected you like an old newsreel; you reacted and felt, but you accepted the tragedy, and being human and normal you used your reactions to stimulate a determination to replace chaos with order.

It was she who yearned for sex on the journey and oddly her vivid demands on the walkie-talkie coincided with the timing chosen by the lemmings in Alec's car. They'd got precisely the same idea and at the same moment.

So they stopped, near Basingstoke, there on the by-pass; and so far as physical release was concerned neither had felt hungrier at any time. They had braked the cars and dashed into each other's arms and loved, naked, in the dying sun.

Tanya lay, panting, on the grass near the road and indicated a deserted truck-drivers' pull-in. It was about fifty yards off and she longed – of all things – for chocolate.

'But you don't like chocolate.'

'I do now. And I want some. Now.'

'I'll get it if you promise to get dressed. Oh, and incidentally, there's something I've always wanted to ask you.'

'Ask away.'

'Who bought you all that disgraceful underwear?'

Tanya's smile was feline. She'd deliberately gone out of her way to stitch and repair the lingerie of before, instead of making use of the less erotic garb grabbed from the Staines department store. 'So at last,' she said, '*you're* jealous, too! I thought you liked me in it, kinky bastard.'

'That's not the point.' He picked up a miniscule garment which, technically speaking, comprised a pair of pants. 'Real silk, and extremely French.'

'Why,' she asked, 'are the British always so jealous of the French?'

Alec said tenderly, 'I'm glad it was a Frenchman.'

'Why?'

'You know why.'

She put on the pants. 'Yes. It's perverse but I understand it. You'd hate to be jealous of someone who might now be a victim. I can reassure you, darling. I'm certain that my benefactor is very much alive.'

'But not nearly as lucky as me,' said Alec. They kissed, and she repeated an urgent and peculiar demand for chocolate; and it wasn't until he was covering the distance to the café that he realized what was happening. At least, he thought, it isn't pickles . . .

It was as he was choosing suitably succulant-looking slabs out of the glass cabinet that he heard the sound of a motor.

The moment he did so, he dropped the armful of sickly chocolate bars and dashed out on to the road.

Immediately overhead was a helicopter and even as he emerged from the door of the café Alec saw Tanya leap up, only half dressed, and grab the Thompson from the other car. She had managed to train it on the helicopter and, in one long burst, scored a hit.

It was Alec's voice that rose to a scream as he saw what was going to happen now.

'Run for cover! The trees! the *trees*!'

She couldn't hear him.

For three seconds the helicopter remained aloft. Pieces of it disintegrated mid-air and fell apart.

Then it seemed to slither sideways, first one way, then the other, as the rotor blades bent upward like a broken umbrella.

Alec was running, shouting, unbelieving; but he could see Tanya was motionless in a state of mesmerized indecision. Where would the stricken helicopter fall?

For a split second she must have seen Alec running towards her, for she screamed something back he also couldn't hear. Throwing up her arms as if in a gesture of fatalism she ran to the wrong car – her own. The fuselage plunged like broken Meccano and pulverized the Ford. Tanya was dismembered instantaneously in the eruption of ignited fuel, then limb by severed limb her bodily remnants were fused into an amorphous pulp, till the combined wreckage exploded. The blast propelled the Vauxhall twenty yards along the road, smashing all the windows.

Death was instantaneous – unbelievable yet following through from a hideous logic. The hell from which she'd been snatched at Exeter had caught her up – unprotected and alone.

Alone! Alec had left her there. Inside her, the tiny beginnings of their baby. Gone.

The irresponsibility which – as she had said – went with his zest for survival had killed the mate who had willed him to survive.

The conflagration spread across the road and set light to the dry branches of trees.

There was nothing left for him to do but to drive the Vauxhall well clear before that, too, went up in flames.

He wished that he felt the urge to die there with her; but the conflict in him was now complete; there were others to save, his living children and his living wife. And though stripped of the means of saving them he could not fight the instinct to go on. For the Estofort had gone. All that was left was the small reserve they'd buried at the Exeter garage and the tiny bottle of the drug he had in his pocket.

Drawing safely clear of the fire, he braked and pulled into the side of the road. He was without religion and yet he had to find some prayer. None of the mumblings learned by rote at school, nor with his parents in the parish church, nor even at his marriage with Diana, could express for him anything but hollowness. Their emphasis on sin outraged him because it was through such sin that Tanya had taken him in her arms, on his return from Staines Bridge, and cooled his head with calm caresses, and enabled him to gather courage enough to go back and observe the human sludge in the river, not as a sickening spectacle that could drive a man mad with revulsion, but as the simple outcome of a truth; seeing them as families, with lusts like his own, conflicts like his own, and souls which were distinct from their festering, insect-ravaged bodies.

His sanity was saved by the memory of her insistence, at whatever cost, to *feel.* He knew, as he stared at the white hot inferno down the road, that if he tried not to – now of all times – he would not only have killed her physically through negligence but would have demolished all that she had given.

Existentially she would then cease to live inside his soul. And there would lie the final treachery.

So this must be his prayer: to go on feeling, whatever the pain, and never harden himself against it, however blinding the tears, or guilty his heart. 'Tanya,' he said huskily, 'you died through my negligence. You forgave it; but you *knew*.'

Then, climbing back into the Vauxhall and restarting the engine, he glanced back at the cage containing the lemmings.

They, at least, were alive. He still had company.

FIFTEEN

Alec might never have noticed it. If Tanya had been alive, if the two of them had still been tearing along in convoy, continually replenishing each other over the walkie-talkie, trying to talk hope when there was so little hope, then the insignificant detail of one tiny change might have eluded them both.

The violent death of Tanya made the difference. Something had to occur which would make up for it. It was impossible for Alec to accept that she had been sacrificed for nothing; and her own philosophy had not invoked the indolent gods of self pity, and therefore had not imbued in Alec that sense of utter futility which would have blinded him. Quite the reverse. Rage against the perpetrators of the attempted smash and grab on their supplies and which had ended thus only heightened his perception.

It happened while he was passing the military camp. At first, Alec only noticed the ghost-white outlines of buildings lining the road behind the wire. The creepy spectacle of a headquarters that had come to a deadly standstill and yet looked so changed from its normal state in the glimmer of the dying sun, did not so much reconjure the spectacle of the chaotic M.I. Room or the blood-bathed duty officer on the floor of the Officer's Mess. He thought of the place, rather, as the crucial landmark in his time with Tanya. It was here that some inner instinct of hers had told her she was pregnant, showing itself in a small domestic act. Her transition from seductress to woman had occurred in this incongruous setting.

Alec glanced to the right as he passed the entrance to the guardroom.

What he saw caused his foot to slam the footbrake hard on the floorboards. The car slewed to a stop with a tortured squeal of tyres.

The boom barrier was not lowered – as they had left it – but raised!

Alec stiffly climbed out of the car and crossed the road. The unmistakable glare of a pressure-lamp was visible through the guardroom window. As Alec got nearer, he heard the characteristic hissing of the lamp.

His first thoughts were that a group of Nuttall's men had taken over and he was ready with a gun – a service revolver he had taken from this very camp. Moving silently, close to the wall, he made his way cautiously to the window, then glanced inside.

Two of the soldiers, recognizably those who had laid in bizarre configuration of military precision on the floor, were now drinking cocoa at the table. They were filthy in appearance; their growth of beard and soiled uniforms would have been a disgrace to any regiment. Moreover, they were clearly frightened, unable to grasp what had happened, unable to raise any response on the phone, which lay with its receiver off on the guard commander's desk.

Through the window, Alec heard them talk.

One of them said, 'Corporal Cresswell is dead.'

'I know.'

'He must have starved there.'

'What day is it, Relton?'

'How do I know?'

'You didn't find the duty officer?'

'I found him, all right!' Relton sipped some more cocoa. 'He was shot.'

'Over in the Mess?'

'In the kitchen quarters.'

'Shot? By himself? Like the others?'

'I'm not so sure. I don't think so. He'd been dragged in there by someone. A horrible great patch of dried blood was all over the floor in the Mess itself. Then there was a long streak of it leading from there through to the kitchen.'

'Did you look anywhere else?'

Relton shuddered. 'Not on your bleeding life, I've seen enough. If you want to know, you can bloody well go and look . . . '

Alec had also seen enough. Nor was he in the mood to engage two very frightened soldiers in polite conversation. Edging back along the side of the hut, he made his way back through the barrier and out to his car.

He drove on, thoughtfully and slowly. There was much to think about.

Soldiers are fit men. They are not allowed to become soft-bellied and feeble; but are trained in self-reliance and the ability to carry on when wounded as soon as the first shock of injury passed. Consequently, long before most others who had survived the suicide, the dehydration, the compulsion to take to the river and seas or annihilate themselves and each other through some frenetic instinct to decimate the population, wouldn't such men logically be the first to recover, if spontaneous recovery were in fact the final outcome?

A sudden fury pounded at Alec's temples. For if this were so, the helicopter attack, which almost certainly had amounted to an attempt to steal Estofort from a convoy of two, a convoy all too easy to identify in an otherwise inert world, had been futile and unnecessary and redundant. Tanya need never have died . . .

Suppose the peak had now passed? – Suppose human society, having reached manageable numbers, had automatically stabilized?

The cadre! Would they know? How *could* they know? Kept alive by regular doses of Estofort, they had endured and survived the danger period. With the swelling of the numbers there – from Richard's defence force to God knows how many strays they'd taken in by now – they must be down to the last ebb of the drug. Would they then assume that, having reached the end of the line, there was nothing left for them to do but face the end? Or worse, take their own lives and each other's, rather than wait to go mad?

Alec turned on the radio, found the jamming louder than ever. The increase in volume of that shattering noise could only mean one thing: Nuttall's gang was nearer – possibly even airborne! – with only one object in mind . . . to attack the cadre for its Estofort supplies! For how could Nuttall know either? At several thousand feet you do not observe the awakening of your fellow men on the ground!

Alec slammed the gears into third and raced up the next hill. He had to get to the Dorrington and prevent the final irony.

Thoughts raced through his mind. What had been in the missing pages of the notes? – and those which, still unread, had fluttered from his grip as he had gazed upon those heaped bodies in the river? Did the ultimate clue lie with the lemmings themselves, which, on reaching stable numbers after the stampede, became calm once more? 'In humans,' Crossley had written, 'terror would eliminate the majority of the species because it would eliminate specialization, where each person plays a distinct role to maintain the equilibrium of society. If and when Virulent Panic strikes, intellect will break down and instinct take over, and the instinct, when society is willfully and terrible consent, society psychotically will decimate itself, will precede the actual case (of overcrowding to saturation point) by the degree to which the brain, once panicked, may see hysterically into an imagined future. All at once, the future has arrived. There *is* no space, there *is* no food, there *is* no money, nor air to breathe, nor water to drink. So, by mutual and terrible consent, society psychotically with decimate itself, in order to make room once again . . . '

In order to make room once again! Could anything be more logical? Could anything else explain an epidemic that consisted of no disease?

Alec hurtled for the next roundabout, only to screech in the nick of time to a standstill.

This time, there was no way past it.

A vast area ahead had been on fire, gutting the buildings and reducing the road to an undulating lava of tarmac which had now become huge, solid blisters. Across the highway, a mass of tottering debris had spilled from ignited buildings and poured impacted ingots of molten metal on to the ground.

Even as he looked, Alec saw a husk of a building, high overhead, slithering away from itself, floor by floor, as if its structure, reduced to dust, couldn't even support the eggshell outline of what remained. Instead of crashing with the thump of solid masonry is showered to the ground in a chalk-like crumble of dust. Evidently it had taken only the vibration of the car engine to start the avalanche; and each building seemed to stimulate the next. Acrid clouds of powdered ash threatened to choke the engine.

Somehow Alec managed to turn the car, straining the suspension to shearing-point in an effort to double back to the roundabout before his retreat was cut-off as well.

Tyres protested, stinking of burning rubber; but he made it to the junction, then took the minor road south that would link him to the main road from Stockbridge. From there he hoped to wend his way back to the Amesbury by-pass.

Without incident he reached the T-junction and there felt a bit luckier. Had he joined the A30 a few hundred yards further south, he would have been totally cut off.

For down to his left, one of those giant car transporters had tried to pass under a low bridge. Carrying seven new cars on two decks, the lorry itself had jammed the arch and scattered bricks until cab and driver were buried. Half the cars – those on the top rack – had shot over the top of the bridge and landed like discarded toys in a heap beyond.

Lined along the hedges were agonized cows, deprived of relief from their souring milk. Their unnatural utterances of pain were comment enough on the situation though there was no evidence here of panic. Presumably the accident at the bridge had occurred early on, sealing-off the route from all but the few who knew the backroads. During the outsurge from London there would not have been any purpose in cutting across; by Thursday Alec and Tanya had found the main road clear where later the fire had blocked it.

Four miles farther on he heard the pealing of church bells.

Momentarily he thought this must be hallucination . . . he'd
had shored themselves up and drawn their own conclusions.
V.P. but from exhaustion and strain and grief.

But surely? Wasn't this the proof of what he'd just been thinking? – Wasn't this confirmation of what he'd just seen in the guardroom? Here were more victims awakening, trying to tell others via the only means of communication left – the most ancient of a christian society – that life had begun again!

The prospect filled him with sudden hope which was transmitted to his foot on the floorboards. Racing past a sign, broken off at the end so that it read *Bishops St Vin* – (Vin what?) he raced for the village ahead . . . only to slam on the brakes in bewilderment.

A hundred yards ahead was a road-block. Where he had now stopped was a temporary signboard which did little to reassure him. It said:

> Bishops St Vincent
>
> Isolation Area. All vehicles will halt at the road-block for medical examination and quarantine.
>
> Any Virus carriers will be detained until released at the discretion of the medical officer.

These were not re-enlivened victims! They were people who had somehow escaped the epidemic! Cut off, evidently, by the smashed bridge to the east, the villagers, ignorant of hard facts, had shored themselves up and drawn their own conclusions.

Alec couldn't go back. If he did, he could only take the route whereby he'd arrived, taking him back to the blocked main road at the roundabout.

He couldn't go forward – unless somehow he could persuade the 'medical officer' (who was he? – local G.P.?) that there was no virus, that 'medical examination' was meaningless, and that in any case there was evidence that spontaneous recovery was imminent and no further precautions were necessary.

Quarantine . . . How long was that? And what would happen to those at the cadre who not only were under threat of imminent attack but were desperate for a drug they didn't even need?

There was only one thing Alec could do: bluff it out, play their game, omit facts about lemmings which would merely make them think he himself was a madman and then somehow make a break for it.

Slowly, he drove the car forward.

Near the road-block a group of men had appeared. They looked odd from this distance; then drawing closer, Alec realized: every one of them wore surgical masks. Presiding over them, complete down to a white coat and a dangling stethoscope, was a doctor. On seeing Alec's car approach, he at once called out to someone in a doorway of a pub. In place of the inn-sign was an impressive red cross. Above it flew the naval flag denoting Quarantine. In Bishops St Vincent they mixed their metaphors with relish.

Abruptly, the church bells stopped. Out of the pub stepped the vicar, with two women dressed as nurses. They waited till Alec had stopped the car at the barrier, then the doctor came to the car window and said, 'Put this on, please.' He handed a fresh face mask through the window.

'But – '

The doctor's smile reassured. 'Just a precaution. Do as you're told. Please?'

Alec shrugged, put the thing on his face.

'Would you step out of the car and come into the examination room?'

Alec said, 'I'm afraid I haven't got time. Perhaps you'd just ask your men to clear this barrier so I can get through.'

The padre stepped forward. 'The doctor,' he said, 'is concerned for you, as well as others. You may possibly spread this schizo-meningitis to another area. It's essential we take these precautions for your sake, as well as everyone else's.'

'Whose diagnosis is that?'

The doctor said, 'We had to give it a name. Naturally a new virus mutant with new characteristics has to be called something.' He seemed quite proud of his freshly coined word.

Alec said, 'Are you people protected in some way?'

The doctor said patiently, 'Do please cooperate.'

' – Have you seen a case of this . . . schizo-meningitis?'

The doctor, a thin, youngish man with a narrow face and an anaemic-looking skin, said, 'We have detailed information about the symptoms.'

'Then you must know that I can't possibly be suffering from it.'

'You may be a carrier.' The doctor's little smile returned. 'There *are* people who carry this disease. We know it's not their fault but obviously they must be isolated.'

Alec marvelled. They'd got one tiny piece of knowledge right, and apparently made the rest up like a fairy story. He persisted, 'I asked you if you've seen an actual case?'

By now, a little huddle of people, all with masks on, had appeared in the streets, as if Alec were some kind of freak from outer space.

The doctor didn't stoop to the indignity of replying to Alec's question.

The padre said, 'We have two other people here who may be carriers. They are undergoing tests.'

The doctor said patiently, 'Do please cooperate.'

Alec stayed in the car. 'What sort of tests?'

'Would they make any sense to you? Do you have any medical knowledge?'

Alec had to prevent himself replying that the kind of tests being contemplated wouldn't make sense to anyone who knew the most elementary facts. But he couldn't help feeling both sorry for these people and also a grudging admiration. They were calm in a crisis they must have realized was desperate. Despite their pompousness they were trying to help, and in an organized way. Alec said, 'I'm an executive for a drug company.'

'Oh? Which one?'

Without thinking, Alec replied automatically, 'Esto.'

There was a long silence. The padre and the doctor cast each other knowing looks. The doctor's little smile vanished. 'Then I must demand that you undergo examination immediately.' He looked at the guns with distaste. 'I take it,' he said, 'you didn't intend to shoot your way through here?'

Alec snapped, 'I can't shoot my way through closed minds. What you so nattily call schizo-meningitis is – '

The doctor cut in calmly. ' – is what the unfortunate Dr Crossley termed Virulent Panic. I know. I read his stuff in the *Lancet.* I read it aloud, amid some mirth, to some colleagues of mine at the Basingstoke General Hospital.'

'Look, Doctor . . . '

The man shook his head, refusing to listen. Rudely he yanked open the driver's door and waited motionless for Alec to get out. 'We'll talk in my surgery,' he said.

The 'surgery', improvised out of the saloon bar, had the same hybrid effect as the outside of the pub. Part surgery, part command post, complete with a field telephone connected to a road-block at the far end of the village – it reflected a misunderstanding of the problems to a degree that would have been comic had anyone felt like laughing. Various 'tests' had been set up – like blowing mercury up a column – which bore little relation even to a diagnosis as far off the mark as the doctor's. But, as valuable time slipped away, Alec was solemnly put through them all, Blood slides were taken; urine samples shaken up into solutions for cultivating; blood pressure solemnly recorded, and all the plodding routine followed down to examination of Ear, Nose and Throat.

Gazing into Alec's gullet with his little lamp shining and a mirror clamped to his forehead the doctor did a sort of running commentary on his deductions. 'No doubt you know Dr Blessing's letter in the *British Medical Journal.* No? No. The "Ah", again "Ah-h-h". Thank you. Perhaps you read Dr Blessing's letter on the *British Medical Journal.* No? No. The first point he made was that it was unwise to study dangerous micro-organisms at – what's that place called? . . .' The doctor removed a swab from Alec's throat just long enough to get the answer.

'The Hat-Rack.'

'Yes.' Back went the swab. 'Dangers of cross-fertilization and so on were quite disregarded. People engaged on micro-organism research were rubbing shoulders indiscriminately with neurology specialists, psychiatrists and – for all I know – investigators into the properties of Christmas puddings. An accident was inevitable. It so happens Dr Blessing knew a colleague of mine at Basingstoke. He told him a leak might well occur. Now look at the consequences!' He at last removed the swab from Alec's throat. 'Have you come straight from the Institute?'

'I went back there from Exeter – after seeing Dr Blessing stuffing his car full of Estofort and trying to get out – '

' – Estofort? Dr Blessing taking Estofort? – the neurotics' dream? . . . I simply don't believe it. Drugs like that dull the wits of people, you know; even Crossley, who developed it. I trust you're not an addict, by the way?'

'Do I look like a drug addict?'

'No. But then, nor did Crossley. Personally, I think it must have been an overdose of that stuff that led him to whatever carelessness caused this outbreak. We never used it down here – Dunlop Committee or no Dunlop Committee – and in my view it should never have been released. Why did you go back to Staines?'

'To study Dr Crossley's notes.'

'I hope you kept well clear of the laboratories?'

'The notes were in Crossley's house.'

'May I see them?'

'Why? – when you obviously disregard everything Crossley believed?'

'Because I might just as well know what kind of superstition is being exploited.'

'I lost them.'

'You *lost* them! . . . Am I expected to believe that?'

Alec lashed out. 'As you clearly believe what you've made up your mind to believe, I doubt whether any assurances from me will get through. But what you mustn't do is to stop *me* getting through. I have to get to Exeter on urgent business and you haven't the right to stop me. I've submitted to your tests. You'll find them as negative as everyone else has who assumed this virus theory.'

'What are those two animals doing in your car?'

'They're pets.'

'And you're trying to tell me they didn't come from Dr Crossley's lab?' The doctor said quietly, 'They're lemmings, aren't they?'

'Yes.' Alec had no compunction in telling a few more lies. 'They belonged to Dr Blessing. Even Blessing thought it worth checking on Crossley's work. He kept those animals down in Exeter. I brought them along for company. I assure you they're quite harmless.'

'Harmless . . . and irrelevant. Well, you'll have to hang on here a couple of days until we've got the test results. We'll keep you as comfortable as we can. The padre wants to speak to you. Kindly wait here.'

There was a long delay before the padre appeared and Alec could well imagine why, just as he could guess at the content of the discussion that was no doubt holding things up.

He went to the window. From here you could see the village street. People were going about their business quite normally; only the surgical masks intruded on the rustic scene. Alec was trying to work out how to make a break for it. Great interest had been taken in his car and no doubt the men on guard had removed the ignition keys. Then, with sudden fury, Alec saw them removing the radio equipment. The jamming had been as loud and persistent as ever when last he'd tried. But from closer range he'd hoped to override it. Now there was no chance, even of that . . . unless he could persuade the padre to change the doctor's mind. On the face of it, hopes of that were slim. There was something so smug about attitudes in Bishops St Vincent – as if the very fact of their being spared through lack of contact was an act of God which rendered them the chosen race.

As he watched the systematic inspection of his car, from which the guns were now being removed, Alec thought of Tanya, wondered momentarily what she would have thought about this self-righteous group. Her words would have blistered the smooth, under-oxygenated complexion of that doctor but her presence would have further outraged the moralities of the padre. Alec managed even to smile at the likely result. Tanya was dead; but in him she was very much alive.

The padre was one of those cricketing vicars who believed that catching a fast ball in the slips was in itself a cure-all for evil thoughts. He was terse, businesslike, and fit. 'Don't goad the doctor,' he said briskly, 'it's unfair. He has an unpleasant job to do – no one wants to hold you here. For one thing, we don't like Nuttall men and we'd rather have you out of it.'

So that was it! Apart from all the mumbo-jumbo about viruses and schizo-meningitis, they were now convinced that they were in the presence of Unholy influences. No wonder the church bells had stopped so abruptly.

'You really think I'm in Nuttall's pay?'

'One of the last radio messages our local policeman picked up was that Nuttall intended to move west. That's why we rang the church bells – as a warning to this small community here that there might be an invasion.' A fleeting smile indicated the padre's sense of relief that it turned out only to be an invasion of one. 'We needn't have troubled. But your radio – and your weapons – have been impounded. We don't want any more of your friends.'

'So that's why you're really holding me? – You think I'm part of Nuttall's gang?'

'You've been driving a car bristling with machine-guns. On the back seat we found a woman's bra . . . Nuttall, as you know, has an entire harem. No doubt you had a few privileges yourself.'

It was the grief in Alec which gave vent to the cruel anger of his reply. 'Padre, you people have sealed yourselves up without a thought to people beyond this village. If you weren't bloated with arrogance and stupefied with ignorance you would – did you but know it – be quite incapable of lending a hand elsewhere. Those respiratory masks are about as useless against this epidemic as a bicycle pump. Only you're not to know that. So to justify your own attempts at exclusive self-protection you have to assume anyone else who happens to show up to be a gangster. Your doctor – perhaps with the best intentions in the world – has invented a theory which only seems sensible to him because he hasn't had contact with the disease. Anyone can do that – your local greengrocer could assert with equal justification that the whole thing was spread by Brussels sprouts. No doubt you think your prayers have been answered – if your prayers were offered for the survival of your villagers regardless of the fate of everyone beyond. But I've seen death and suffering and destruction on a scale which you can't afford to consider. For all I know you've managed to make yourself believe that everyone except the human contents of Bishops St Vincent are victims of the wrath of God. It suits you. The owner of that bra has just been slaughtered by one of Nuttall's men. The woman concerned was carrying my baby. The baby was presumably damned along with the woman because it was adulterously conceived. But the facts of life beyond your barriers are a shade harsher than you have the desire to believe or the opportunity to know. Now let me out of this ridiculous place. Give me back my radio – and the weapons I so badly need to protect my own community – and send up a few prayers for the dying.'

Having said all this, Alec immediately regretted it. He had only to look in the padre's eyes to see the injustice and following so close upon Tanya's death it now seemed like an act of treachery against the concept of love itself to hit out with nothing but hate and contempt.

The padre stood perfectly still for a few seconds, then, very slowly and methodically, he removed his surgical mask. Without flinching, without self-justification, without feeling the need to explain for whom all his prayers had really been offered, the padre said in his crisp, mid-wicket voice, 'Where is Nuttall going to strike?'

'If I'm right, Jaybury. A small place outside Exeter.'

'You are suffering from terrible grief. Can I help? – however different our creeds?'

Alec indicated the mask, which now lay on the examination couch. 'You just did. There's nothing else you can do, except what you're already doing here.'

'What happens if I do go outside these barriers? – mask or no mask?'

'Nothing. The epidemic is over.'

The padre nodded. 'And what do I tell the doctor?'

'That he's up the proverbial gum tree.'

The padre said, 'You will forgive me if I put it somewhat differently?'

'I should put it like this, padre; the disease – or whatever you call it – was an emotional, instinctive matter. In your terms perhaps a spiritual one. You were right to isolate your people. It's all you could do. All I ask is that you let me through.'

'It won't be easy. There is the attitude of the whole community to consider. Contrary to some of what you've just said, they feel it their duty to stop the spreading of this affliction. They believe in the doctor's theory and neither you nor I can disprove it.'

Gently, Alec said, 'I'm running out of time. The people at Jaybury were protected somewhat . . . differently from your parishioners. *They* are the ones under threat from Nuttall. Your own flock have nothing to fear.'

'What about the two other intruders we have under observation here?'

'Let them go. I can assure you they can never have been contacts. Otherwise – despite all the doctor's precautions – this whole village would have been derelict by now.'

The padre folded his arms . . . awaiting patiently at mid-wicket for the bowlers to cross over. 'Just one more question:

How many other communities, like Bishops St Vincent, have you come across or known about?'

'None.'

*   *   *

No delay, in this entire affair, was more of a problem than the ego of the local doctor. While Alec paced anxiously, he could hear the mutterings going on in the next room. From time to time, people from the outside – surgical masks still firmly in place – knocked on the adjacent door and came up with some new revelation about the contents of his car. Frequently voices were raised in anger, or fear. Often the crowd outside were angry, as if on the verge of some primitive instinct for lynching. Their whole creed had been upset and they felt the padre to have been too easily won over, a traitor to their cause.

Alec tried to calm himself by attempting to sympathize. These were villagers, not scientists with personal knowledge of the main protagonists in the initial conflict: Blessing and Crossley. They could not evaluate; they could only react. Like all others to whom survival was still a meaningful word, they had their wives and their children and their futures in mind. They had been indoctrinated by the doctor's propaganda. If, suddenly, he was so wrong then what was there left that they could believe?

Twice, the doctor, tense and white with his own personal conflict, came in to ask Alec questions. The first visit was simply to repeat his question: was Alec taking Estofort?

Alec denied it. You can't take everything away from a cornered man in one go. The padre, who stood in the doorway as the question was asked, nodded almost imperceptibly at Alec's answer.

In the interval between the doctor's two interregations the people responsible for guarding Alec's car seemed to be thrown into a state of oscillation. One minute they were reloading the gear, the next they were taking it all out again. A stuffy individual with a moustache showing through his mask was officiously dangling Alec's ignition keys, as if his was to be the final word about Alec's departure or not.

At last the affronted doctor made his final appearance. He looked as if he'd been soundly beaten at the cricket match. 'I take it,' he said, 'that your business in Exeter is as the padre says? – involving the interests of others?'

'You may take it,' said Alec, 'that it is not business involving the illegal activities of Nuttall. Does that cover the point?'

'If we let you go, will you accept my conditions?'

'What are they?'

'That you swear under oath to take a note from me to Dr Blessing; and that until you have been further examined by him you make no contact whatsoever with any human being.'

Alec replied coldly. 'That would be difficult. Dr Blessing died in the fire at the Exeter factory.'

The doctor started on about this being 'a great loss to humanity' but Alec made no comment, simply explained, 'The only operational group down there is a handful of experts from the Sindham Hospital. They're at our Jaybury place.'

'I see,' said the doctor grimly. 'Followers and disciples of the Immortal Crossley.'

'They're open-minded, doctor. They started out, when Casualty was still functioning, carrying out the same sort of tests as you.'

'Well, take a note to them.'

'Will do. Can I leave?'

'That depends on the squire.'

The squire was evidently the one with the moustache.

Alec tried to keep the offensiveness out of his voice. 'On what basis does the local squire make medical decisions?'

The docor said shortly, 'He's in charge here,' and left the room again.

Alec had been delayed pointlessly for two hours. Finally the squire himself entered the room. He still wore the mask. Through it he said, with commendable brevity, 'You may leave. And good riddance.' Alec was handed his keys as if being released on parole from jail.

The mood of the villagers as Alec drove through was oddly divided. Some had their masks on, some off; and clearly there was about to be a major conflict of leadership, in the lone parish of Bishops St Vincent.

SIXTEEN

Richard came running out of the radio shack. 'Aircraft. I can hear them talking on VHF. Where's Stan?'

Melhuish seemed oddly unresponsive. 'He's helping over by the bus.'

'Well, dig him out of there.'

Melhuish just stood, as if dazed.

Richard felt like shaking him. 'For God's sake, man! It's what we thought – an air attack!'

The plan for the cadre was a desperate one. Richard and Melhuish would stay behind with a nucleus of armed guards while the women and children would leave with the scientists in the bus, escorted by the rest of the miniscule defence force in two army vehicles loaded with emergency supplies.

The bolt-hole was to be the lighthouse at Lizard Point.

This choice arose from three factors: the emplacement would be easy to defend, with guns at the ready high up in the tower; there were no landing fields nearby; and according to Stan, who had flown low over the isthmus, every road bar one down to Lizard Point was choked. The remaining road would be blown up once the rearguard, commanded by Richard and backed up by the police patrol car, had finally quit the Dorrington cadre and joined the others in Cornwall.

What had to be very exact was the timing. For if the bus left too soon it would certainly be spotted from the air . . . nothing else on the ground was moving. So the idea was to wait until the Nuttall force had landed at Exeter Airport – eight miles to the east – then send the bus off at breakneck speed.

But there had been continuous, tetchy argument about the whole idea. Underlying this irritation was the simple truth that supplies of Estofort were now so low that such a survival attempt would be hollow indeed. But no one would admit it. Although the count was a secret kept between Melhuish and

Diana, it was inevitably obvious that supplies were critically low from the way in which Alec's arrival was so anxiously awaited. Stan had been sent out twice in the aeroplane to do a low sweep over the main roads. Of course he couldn't know that Alec had been forced to make a detour.

Till now, the cadre had been at least superficially calm. All that had gone. Everything was happening at once. Stan came running back from the bus, on which research gear, in use within the lounge up to the very last moment, was now to be loaded carefully but with all speed. He joined Richard in the radio shack, listened to the VHF and said that in his estimation the approaching aircraft were still at the very limits of VHF range. According to altitude, this could be anything up to a hundred miles.

To Melhuish, who was puzzled about something much more fundamental than the estimated distance of the invading force, everyone seemed to be rushing about for the sake of doing so. Diana, watching him, wondered why he looked so detached. But he seemed to be making himself deliberately unapproachable, and anyway the children were getting in everybody's way and had to be controlled. She chased them back into the garden.

June, hearing the commotion, came running out of her room, with Baby Caroline in her arms, and hovered outside the radio shack. She didn't voice the question, and for once Richard hadn't got time to break the news to her in that gentle way she was used to, the way which implied that it wasn't really happening, but you and Caroline ought to get some rest, why don't you lie down in your room for a while, I'll be over in a few minutes, we'll have a cup of tea and relax . . . No, all that had gone by the board, and anyway her tension, mounting every hour as the Estofort inexorably dropped lower and lower in the bottle, was so hard to cope with and so liable to stimulate a flare-up into impotent rage, ostensibly about the state of the sheets or the rattling of the windows that even Richard couldn't cope with her. He was sorry, and he loved her, and all that. But.

Melhuish saw Richard come panting up to Diana, heard the conversation distinctly. 'Diana, what the hell's up with Melhuish? He's got definite duties in this and yet he's like a man in a dream!'

Diana said, 'Give him time. He's had so much weight to bear – and now this. He'll be okay in a minute.'

Richard, in his haste, answered in the curiously mixed

metaphor of his two separate images. 'He's got it all hanging out but he'd better snap-to and pull himself together. I'll be in the radio shack.' He dashed back inside.

And still Melhuish stood there. He kept looking at his watch and, for some weird reason – weird at least to June as she watched – kept glancing at his own reflection in the driving mirror of the bus which had now been centred on to the hotel car park.

The peculiarity disturbed her. Normally it was Melhuish who restored calm. Now he was so absorbed with himself that in the end it was Stan, habitually so tight-lipped, who gathered the cadre together and quietly addressed them on the lawn.

'Listen. Shortly it will be dark. In my judgement the aircraft are still a clear twenty minutes from the airport and they will have to make an approach in bad light, one at a time. There is – as far as I could see from the air – only an improvised flare-path and the whole operation, including the time it will take them to embus for the roads, will take them ninety minutes from now at the very least before they can possibly arrive here and make an attack.'

He had succeeded in bringing about an attentive silence. Only Edna's children, who hadn't really taken in anything, continued to interrupt with uncouth squeals and ill-timed games of touch.

Stan continued, 'By then, our bus will be able to move under cover of darkness. Your driver – ' Stan produced the man as if he almost expected a round of applause on his behalf, ' – your driver knows the roads so well he won't need lights. There is no immediate action to take and my advice to everyone is to sit tight and stay calm.'

So they dispersed; and an unnatural lull followed. An evening meal had been laid by Print Dress. Few people ate. Most of them concentrated on the packing while the children, irritable because they didn't understand entirely what was happening, fought sporadically in the garden, where a low sun cast long shadows, like portentous pointers of threatening sundials. Inexorably they marked the passage of elapsed time.

* * *

Melhuish had kept silent about his own personal discovery on two main counts. For though it was now fourteen hours since he'd last taken a capsule, with no ill-effects showing at all, he thought there were two possible reasons to account for his own apparent immunity from V.P. so far. One was that he had been on the drug far longer than anyone else. The other was that he might be a freak exception. He was older than the others and – even if he had to confess it to himself – virtually undisturbed by sexual urges. He had observed that it was the young and the virile who craved chemical restoration the most and who went crazy the quickest. To suggest, until he was sure, that for some reason V.P. had played itself out would have been an unacceptable risk.

He was, Melhuish-wise, in fact merely dithering, whatever his reasons. For however brave his voluntary withdrawal from the drug, the wall-scraping Melhuish of the Hat-Rack was re-emerging through one simple cause: if there was the faintest possibility of things ever going back to normal the Grades would once again take over, if only in his own mind.

. . . Which was why, even though he could sense what was now imminent, he still couldn't bring himself to act. For to do so would have been taking a risk; and at Grade Three you do not take risks. He knew what June was going to do. Yet he couldn't bring himself to intervene.

By all accounts, the omission was a small one, compared with the magnitude of the issues at stake. And yet, for Melhuish, it was fundamental. The one thing he cared about above all others was human dignity, which was precisely what June was about to lose.

Bowed at those hang-dog shoulders, Melhuish walked shambling off to Edna's quarters, just as Diana had to cross the lawn to break up a fight between James and Stephen. This done, Diana gazed thoughtfully after the retreating figure of Melhuish, still wondering. She shrugged it off and joined the anxious group outside the radio shack, with Stephen clinging just behind.

June, on returning to the bedroom, watched, glazed in the eyes, from the window. Move by move, everyone in the garden was becoming obsorbed in different aspects of the crisis. Jennifer, who had been playing on the improvised swing, only to be displaced forcibly by James, stood alone on the grass planning a tantrum. Then she decided against it and ran off to play with one of Edna's children, a backward little girl called Dolores, but to Jennifer merely a playmate.

June glanced across at Diana's chest of drawers. It was unguarded, unobserved and – at last – irresistible.

Actually, June thought herself unfair not so much because she was contemplating stealing a few, only a very few capsules from Diana's supply, but rather that it had to be Diana's small fund of Estofort that should be involved at all.

June was thinking, why the hell should a backward child like Dolores, who hasn't a hope in hell and certainly wouldn't get anywhere in real life – real life, well, she knew what she meant by the phrase – why the hell should Dolores' unhappy prospects for the future be perpetuated? Why should Edna – nothing but a perpetual thorn in good old Melhuish's side – persist in doggedly surviving all this merely to cramp not only her children's style but depress and embarrass nearly everybody in the hotel? It had been Edna who, at a vital moment in the intricate process of analysis in the improvised lab, had rushed in suddenly, knocked over the scientists' table, and pursued one of her gangling boys out into the yard in order to smack his small malnutrition-thinned behind, a rumpless bony extension of thin legs which demonstrated articulately a history of milk starvation woefully unnecessary in a welfare state.

But Edna was a grasping, exemplary archetype of the female who keeps her money in a stocking under the bed. You couldn't have got at *her* savings of Estofort with a hatchet. So it couldn't be her, with her five unkempt kids who were futureless. Baby Caroline *must* have a future. She had a young father and a loving mother and a chance.

So June went up to that drawer she had seen opened so often, once every six hours, and feeling not only a terrible fear of discovery but as gritty self-hatred, always there latent, but now overt and utterly naked to her own consciousness. She unscrewed the bottle and she took six capsules that wouldn't be missed – would they surely? . . . I mean, Alec will be here with some more pills any moment and they could be replaced without anyone knowing and –

'Put them back!'

June felt her whole spine congeal, so that paralysis crept up her arms and down her legs and she could not move.

It was Richard.

'Go on. Put them back.'

'I was only – '

' – You were only thinking of Baby Caroline, is that it?'

'Yes.'

'You were thinking that in a sort of twisted way, she would

benefit? However it was managed, at whatever price to your honesty, to our relationship, and to your own guilt?'

She stared at him for a long time and said, 'Richard, I thought you, of all people – '

' – would understand? Is that it? I do. I understand only too well. I understand that to some degree it's my fault. I've always given in to your terror of reality, until half the time you're capable of doing things you convince yourself aren't really quite real.'

She flared, 'I've done the same back to you! – many times. Remember?'

He said quietly, 'I remember. Let's just thank God it was me who caught you at it, June. And not someone else. I think Diana would have killed you.'

June tried to say, stammering, 'This isn't going to make any difference to our . . . '

'June. We're under attack. I have duties. So do you. One is to play fair by your friends. It was Alec who got us here, and whatever his morals and his lack of understanding of his own wife, he still thought of us – right? And that had the consent of Diana – right? And she, too, loves her children. Don't let's talk about how it affects the picture postcards now. Close that drawer. Go in the garden. And help with the other children. If Baby Caroline cries for a few split seconds, because you're thinking of someone else, she'll gain – believe it or not – in the long run.'

He turned his back and left the room and wondered whether he'd ever want to share a bedroom with June again.

* * *

It was dusk when Stan, who had been sitting motionless by the radio, quietly nodded his head to Richard and said, 'This is it. I'm taking off to intercept.'

'You don't stand a chance in that buggy.' Richard glanced outside. 'And you don't have enough light to get off the ground.'

Stan never blustered. He just stated what was fact. 'I know every inch of that field.'

'Then you'll never spot the invading aircraft. They're hardly likely to show navigation lights.'

Stan collected his maps. 'Radar. I'll get a shot or two in. Change to my frequency now. There's nothing more to learn, from here, about Nuttall's attack.'

'Good luck.'

Stan almost parted with a bow. 'Thank you,' he said.

While Richard gave orders for the initial preparations for embussing, Stan still had to contend with the Major, who fatuously consulted a road map as if to bring his full cartographical knowledge to bear in plotting the position of the approaching Blitzkrieg. This was the next best thing to the Battle of Britain and the Major wasn't going to get left out. Stan accepted the outdated product of the Automobile Association with a grave word of thanks, then scrambled through the woods for the field.

It was actually Stephen, and not Diana, who persisted with the unsolved matter of Melhuish's dilemma. He found it hard to pin Melhuish down, for things were now in a turmoil. Finally he caught Melhuish in the garden, tugged at his sleeve – then guided him like a nephew about to accuse an uncle of keeping secrets. They went to the far corner of the garden, just as Stan's aircraft, banking through a steep turn at the show ring end of the field, roared over the hotel, almost at zero feet, as if to demonstrate that the cadre wasn't dead yet. The rasp of his voice, clearly audible in the garden from the radio shack, advised: 'Hold that bus, Richard, as long as you dare. I can pick at least some of those bastards off.'

Richard said on radio, 'How many in the formation?'

'At least four blips on my radar screen, not sure yet, I'm a bit low. Bandits are about two-zero miles north-east of the airport. I'm climbing to six thousand. I'll be well above them because they'll be in descent for an approach. Don't call me, they may listen out and catch on!'

The sound of his motor faded as he climbed steeply for the east.

Stephen waited for the engine noise to die down, then he said, 'Mummy and you know something.'

Melhuish was surprised on two counts. '*Mummy* knows?'

'I mean,' said Stephen, more experimentally, 'she keeps looking at you as though *you* know something.' The honest, keen young eyes searched the uncle's. 'Something very important. Do you?'

'I admit there's something on my mind.'

'Aren't you sure?'

'Not quite.'

'Hadn't you better be sure pretty soon?'

Melhuish thought, God, what uncanny instinct.

'I mean,' said the boy, 'the way you're watching all this

running about, and people getting into that bus, and the aeroplane and everything. Perhaps what they're doing isn't right. I mean, not any more. See what I mean?'

'Yes, I do.'

'If you haven't told Mummy, don't you think you should? I'll make her absolutely *promise* not to tell anyone else. Honestly. She always does what I tell her in the end.'

'Does she really!'

'Well, *she* doesn't think of it quite like that. It's just something I've noticed. See? If I say something like "Mr Melhuish has got something very important indeed to say to you but you mustn't tell anybody else" and if I say "you must absolutely promise" she'll keep it a secret until you say.' The boy kicked a grass tuft with his foot. 'I mean, suppose it's something you can't make up your mind about? Do you often,' he asked, with great interest and total innocence, 'find it hard to decide things? You sort of crinkle your face, Mr Melhuish, and screw up your eyes and then I think "Mr Melhuish can't make up his mind again." '

Melhuish's smile was not the rubbery kind. The truth was too much for him. It produced a broad grin. 'All right, I'll go and talk to her.'

Mummy's good at making up her mind. That's why,' he went on in exactly the same tone, 'she's decided to put up with Tanya, you see.'

'I see,' said Melhuish, practically transfixed. 'I *see.*'

Man and boy were standing there talking on the lawn when June came into view. Melhuish glanced at her and realized from her expression he was too late. He felt as if it were his own lapse, and not hers, which had led to her disgraced slouch across the lawn toward the radio shack, where Richard was.

But Melhuish hadn't entirely gauged this complex woman. He didn't know, for instance, that she was capable of so many assorted reactions at once.

June was back in her dream world. Shaken and grim after being discovered by Richard at Diana's precious drug supply, she resumed her own private world of make-believe and, ignoring the irreconcilable conflicts contained in her own reasoning, chose to believe every thought contained therein. She believed that Baby Caroline would grow up to go to a better school than she'd been to herself, that cocktail parties would resume, carpets would be stained, awkward authors would continue to revile suburban life. And as far as Richard was concerned, she thought his attitude pretty unforgiving. At the appropriate time, she would remind him of a few pretty suspect acts of his own. By this means she knew she would restore the balance.

'Listen!' said Stephen.

Melhuish stood quite still, there on the lawn, and strained his ears.

Far in the distance, still very faint, was the combined beat of heavy aircraft engines.

Melhuish smiled conspiratorially at Stephen, and promised to speak to Diana at once.

He was just about to cross the grass when with a screech of brakes a very dirty and weather-beaten estate car skidded to a halt on the gravel. From the garden, Stephen couldn't see who it was in the car, but he heard a door slam and someone running, and then he watched Melhuish's face which for once he couldn't read, for Melhuish had himself in that moment very much in control, and for once he'd guessed what Stephen hadn't. So he put out an arm gently and restrained the boy and said, 'Let's just wait a few moments and think this out, shall we?'

SEVENTEEN

Nuttall's private empire achieved one unique distinction: it disintegrated midair.

The cause was simple though unusual: Nuttall was faced with a choice of two alternative things to panic about. As they were in diametrical conflict no neurotic could hope for a better reason for coming apart.

On the one hand, he had run out of Estofort, except for what he carried on the plane, and the small reserve dug up by his hoods at the Exeter garage.

On the other hand, he had a growing suspicion that something or other had changed . . . He wasn't good at analysing detail. But it seemed distinctly odd that shortly after taking off from Ringway Manchester he noticed a group of people frantically waving improvised flags at him from a derelict area on the ground, where before there had been just this groping conglomerate of human refuse, sprawling in its own dung.

There in the North, where the pattern of the illness had been perceptibly different from the West, slower to spread and – evidently – quicker to disperse, cars were moving where cars had not moved before. From the air it was apparent that the suburbs of Manchester were showing signs of life – sparse, tortured but unmistakable. From his window aloft, Nuttall actually saw a woman scrubbing her front doorsteps. He glanced furtively at the others travelling with him in the plane. Had they noticed?

Since the solidarity of the regime depended solely on withholding of Estofort from those who disobeyed, there remained no reason for Nuttall's minions to serve him if the drug turned out now to be so much chewing gum.

If, on the other hand, the alternative case applied, he and his followers were about to become babbling lunatics at 25,000 feet. Even Nuttall's capacity for logic enabled him to appreciate that there was no room to manœuvre – even in an aeroplane –

between the devil and the deep blue sea.

Not holding with any old-fashioned ideas about leading his men into attack, he travelled in the rearmost aircraft. Among his command staff were the choice specimens from the harem. They were of little use. Toward the end of his orgiastic phase, the intricacies of which he had virtually got from an instruction book, he had needed such a complexity of muddled perversion, in order to aspire to orgasm at all, that finally no combination of concubines, whatever their sex, could apply the erotic mustard plaster that might revive his ill-humoured prick from its sulky indifference. As one of the girls put it, 'Oh Jimmy, you've gone all flipperty-flopperty!'

That, at least, he could have explained to his own satisfaction, if not hers. Sex had overworked his hormones. Humiliation was not, therefore, the problem. Much more serious was the outcome of this coital black-out: he was forced to think. With the comic strips removed, he had to face the newsprint.

No longer slouched in his characteristically arrogant pose, he sat on the edge of his seat with the safety strap done up nice and tight. He was well on the way to bursting the buckle when a new thought suddenly struck him.

He couldn't trust the advance party! They were traitors, every one of them!

He was certain of it now; and indeed he wasn't at all sure he could trust his own aircrew. They flew him, to be sure, but they were openly contemptuous, planning, for all he knew, a revolution in what remained of the palace.

It was this frantic notion of ultimate paranoia that caused him suddenly to unhitch the seat belt and lurch forward to the flight deck. In a voice the captain hardly recognized he croaked, 'Leave the formation. Circle Exeter until I give you further instructions.'

'But . . . ' The Captain tried to sound reasonable. 'But if we do that, the crews that have already landed will be without orders.'

'Then we'll give them their orders by radio.'

The Captain tried not to sound as if he were speaking to a backward child. 'We have enough fuel aboard to stay airborne for forty minutes at the most. To make a safe landing we must have fifteen of those minutes in reserve.' In case Nuttall couldn't do subtraction he explained, 'That means we have to land in twenty-five minutes, you see.'

Nuttall did see. But hysteria took precedence over such

inconvenient arithmetic. 'Never mind your damn reserve. Break formation. I don't trust what's going on and I want to take a look for myself before we land.' Nuttall tried to focus his eyes on the tail-plane of the aircraft in front. But the dials of the instruments on the panel kept hypnotizing him. The fuel gauges . . . he understood them, all right. Twenty-five minutes. hardly enough time in which to reconcile the impossible conflict.

'What,' asked the Captain, insolently swapping a look with the co-pilot, 'are your instructions?'

'I *said!* Break formation!'

'Very well.' The Captain banked sharply. The fin of the leading aircraft swung suddenly out of view. Exeter had miraculously appeared sideways on, through the left hand window. 'I'll maintain two thousand feet and stay in pattern until we are forced by the fuel position to make the descent. Okay?'

It was anything but okay. To Nuttall the Captain was an arch enemy in league with the emptying tanks. It was a supernatural plot between man and machine. But the Captain thought differently. Mouthing softly to himself, he muttered, 'And where do we go from here?'

The question didn't demand an answer, but Stan had one ready.

Cruising just above and behind the maverick that had suddenly slewed out of formation, he eased forward on the control and clicked back the safety switch for the firing button.

Those at the cadre would have been frightened by his expression. The pink face was that of a fanatic. The quiet, rather secretive and highly composed friend of oganized society had made the transition from Jekyll into Hyde. The target was in his sights. It represented nothing else; merely the obvious complement of the machine-guns at his disposal.

For a lonely man, the deal between gun and bulls-eye was enough in itself.

* * *

They stood, Diana and Alec, several feet apart. Profoundly though Diana craved to relieve some of that deeply aching pain that showed in his eyes – eyes so different from those she had grown used to as his wife – and the warping; crevacing muscles that stretched his facial skin, thinned the mouth, deepened the hollows of the cheekbones till the muscles that stretched them must themselves have become sore, she had heard his first words and knew that comfort from her could only come much later. She felt the agony of a wife who could do nothing for a husband whom, on sight, she rediscovered in one jolt and yet from whom she was fundamentally estranged.

Diana managed, 'I won't try and take the responsibilty of her death from you.'

'You couldn't anyway.'

'I know. But it's what you shared, the horrors you fought together, Alec. We'll be strangers for a long time. I accept that.'

'Diana, at least hate me. For God's sake, give me that to bite on.'

She shook her head. 'You don't need it. You think you do now; but you're the one who used to chide me for conventional reactions. You're trying to fall back on something standard and accepted. For you, after what you must have seen and coped with, it would be play-acting.'

'What do I need?'

'For the moment? – friendship . . . distant friendship, that doesn't play too hard on your exhausted emotions. My shoulder isn't any use for crying on.' It was costing her a lot to say this, but she went on, 'It won't feel like Tanya's, and you must have cried on hers – I can see it in your eyes. Now you want to cry for her. You loved her, which means among other things that she mothered you, just as you must have fathered her.'

'What about Stephen? Have I disillusioned him? Will it twist him forever?'

'No.'

'You sound so sure.'

'When you see him you'll understand. Don't expect him to run to you and hug you, Alec. Things have been fearful here too, in their way.'

There was silence. Diana, so alone, swatted at an insect, and missed. There had been no flies to speak of at the Dorrington, till now. Print Dress, finicky about everything from Harpic in the loo to furniture polish on the dining table, had stuck throughout to what she called her Standards. And why not? . . . Diana whammed the fly again. This time she got it.

Alec watched the futile little act. It was so like Diana, so unlike Tanya.

Diana, having squashed the thing, glanced at Alec and realized what he was thinking. She knew there was nothing between them to discuss. 'Alec, will you speak to Melhuish? He told me it's urgent.'

'I can't face anybody.'

'Then speak to Stephen.'

'I'm not ready. If he sees me looking like this, he'll just want to cry.'

'That won't do him any harm. He probably wants to.'

'Give me time.'

'Alec, you *must* speak to Melhuish!' Diana was quivering, now. Alec watched her, realized it was something that mattered to the cadre.

'All right.' Alec slackly lifted an arm. 'No, stay in here. If it's that important we'll discuss it together.'

She was grateful, just for that.

Melhuish, on seeing him, wondered how he could even stand. But he said, with factual calm, 'This Estofort. I haven't taken any for nearly twice the endurance period.'

'Any particular reason?'

'A private experiment.'

'Well, as you see, it worked. You're a brave man. I did know. But I wouldn't have tried it that way.'

Melhuish just said, 'I had the least to lose.'

Alec didn't presume to comment, on this. 'But you *are* right, Melhuish. It's over. The epidemic is over.' Alec heard a new sound in the distance. He didn't recognize it for a moment.

Melhuish said, 'Air-raid sirens.'

'Yours?'

'No.'

'Then there must be others alive . . . They're waking from it.'

Diana said, 'Can't you see you've won?'

He stared at her blankly, 'Won?'

Diana jerked her eyes away, watched through the window. Outside, Print Dress was agitatedly setting about Alec's stolen Vauxhall with an aerosol insect spray. Diana asked, 'What are those animals in that cage?'

'Lemmings.'

Melhuish cleared his throat. 'Stan has just radioed. He's up there in a converted aeroplane.'

'Converted?'

'I mean, he's fitted his plane out with guns. He's identified what he thinks must be Nuttall's plane. He's about to pick it off. We should be safe from attack.'

Alec said with sudden curtness. 'Tell him to break off.'

'But – '

'Immediately, Melhuish! Before it's too late. Run to the radio shed and command Stan to break off the attack.'

Melhuish stood for a second, quite incredulous. Then doubled away across the lawn.

Diana stared at Alec. 'But why? For God's sake, are you just going to let them turn a hotel full of children into a battle-ground? Aren't we even allowed to protect our children and ourselves?'

For a moment he didn't speak. She couldn't understand his silence.

'Alec! What was this place *for?* Answer me!'

'A refuge for the living.' He seemed entirely detached. 'Not a fortress to shoot from, and kill.'

'So you're going to let them do it, these madmen? Overrun us and take lives. And we're not allowed to fight them off before they get here?'

In a calm, remote voice he said, 'It isn't necessary.'

'You're taking one hell of a chance!'

He woke at last to her. 'Don't you realize? It's staring you in the face! The moment Nuttall's henchmen know what Melhuish knows, he's finished. Can't you see that? Do we have to shoot down aeroplanes full of people when there's some other way?'

'But if he lands before his helpers know – '

'He won't. We'll radio his aircrew. And who knows? – Are people like Nuttall's pilots, or his girlfriends, so contemptible, just wanting to live?'

Diana took a long draw from a cigarette. She couldn't look at him. In a low voice she said, 'What you must have seen!' She wanted to say something more intimate, at whatever cost to her pride. She turned to speak.

– And Melhuish came rushing back into the room. 'He won't answer, Stan won't answer, I think he means to – '

The explosion in the sky cracked down and shook the windows. Brilliant light silhouetted the trees beyond the garden, a series of flashes like summer lightning. Then just the faint note of Stan's pretty little aeroplane, humming contentedly overhead.

There was a long silence between the three of them.

Then Alec said, 'That plane of Stan's was hired to rescue life.'

Diana said, 'You surely don't blame him?' She was angered now. 'You don't blame the man who rebuilt it as a pitiful little fighter, then went up there single-handed, to protect your own children?'

Alec thought for a long time. Melhuish looked down at those cracked old shoes. Diana's eyes didn't flinch as she held Alec's.

Alec said, 'No. He knew there was no need for that attack. I still don't blame him. I just see what sort of a world we're going back to. Why did I think it would change?'

Melhuish left the room unnoticed, closed the door very quietly, walked in a sidling sort of a way back to the lounge. In there, one of the scientists was fiddling with one of the microscopes. It had been left unpacked in the scramble.

The man was focusing the instrument and looking mildly interested. Then he called out to a colleague. 'Hey, take a look at this!'

'What?'

This house-fly is a bit of an oddball.'

The other man looked briefly. 'It's a horsefly.'

'Nope. Look at the wings.'

The colleague squinted through the instrument again. 'It's neither.'

'Recognize it?'

'No, where did it come from?'

The scientist gestured toward an ashtray. In it were a few discarded capsules of Estofort. There were several dead flies lying in it. 'I picked it off there.'

'Why?'

The scientist put on a Lord Hunt voice. 'Because It Was There.'

His colleague cracked, 'Well, at least we've found a new use for those pills. Fly repellent.'

'Some of your jokes aren't funny.'

'Well, why not? . . . ' He focused the microscope. 'Poor old Blessing always said Estofort had some unknown property. Now we know! Where have they sprung from, anyway? – not our beautiful home from home, surely? The Major's wife would be outraged.'

Through the window, the scientist glanced at Print Dress. She had just finished with the aerosol, and was slamming the car doors. 'Probably from Keeling's car.' He lost interest in the alien-looking insect, feeling suddenly very tired. 'It's a new one on me,' he said abstractedly. 'Some foreign job. I'm afraid it's not quite my subject.' Another one buzzed him and bit him. 'They bite too. Ugh!'

'You'll get over it.'

'The fly won't,' said the scientist. 'It's dead.'

'Poor thing. Let's go and have a drink. A fly that has lost its sting needs an alcoholic requiem.'

* * *

Diana had listened, without interrupting, as Alec forecast a society relapsing into what had existed before.

Now, at last persuading Alec to rest on the bed, she spoke across the room from the window. She'd been watching something outside. She said, 'I think you've forgotten one thing.' She gazed motionless at a hovering little figure in the dimly-lighted garden. 'Here's your future, Alec.'

The door opened tentatively. 'Hello, Dad.'

'Hello Stephen.'

'Dad, you seem very tired.'

'I am a bit.'

Innocently Stephen asked, 'Where's Tanya?'

And suddenly Alec remembered his prayer by the roadside. Recalled those vital words of hers, saw now that if any sort of life could be lived by him again, without permanent deadness and this universal sense of loss, not only of Tanya, but all those he had seen on the way, then he must live by that prayer.

Slowly, as Stephen watched, and as Diana gently, diffidently approached him, he began to shake until, melted by a silent river of tears, he lay back crying on the bed.

He held out a hand, limply, for Stephen. Diana did not intrude. Then the convulsive sobs began to tear at his body, till his face began to soften, line by line, muscle by muscle, and the inhuman eyes, so distant and afraid, were able to see, through the mist of tears, that his wife was there, waiting.

DUNE

by Frank Herbert

DUNE is the finest, most widely acclaimed science fiction novel of this century. Huge in scope, towering in concept, it is a work which will live in the reader's imagination for the rest of his life.

'DUNE seems to me unique among science fiction novels in the depth of its characterisation and the extraordinary detail of the world it creates. I know nothing comparable to it except THE LORD OF THE RINGS.'
—*Arthur C. Clarke*

'Certainly one of the landmarks of modern science fiction . . . an amazing feat of creation.' **—Analog**

NEW ENGLISH LIBRARY

T011 682	ESCAPE ON VENUS	*Edgar Rice Burroughs*	40p
T013 537	WIZARD OF VENUS	*Edgar Rice Burroughs*	30p
T009 696	GLORY ROAD	*Robert Heinlein*	40p
T010 856	THE DAY AFTER TOMORROW	*Robert Heinlein*	30p
T016 900	STRANGER IN A STRANGE LAND	*Robert Heinlein*	75p
T011 844	DUNE	*Frank Herbert*	75p
T012 298	DUNE MESSIAH	*Frank Herbert*	40p
T015 211	THE GREEN BRAIN	*Frank Herbert*	30p

War

T013 367	DEVIL'S GUARD	*Robert Elford*	50p
T013 324	THE GOOD SHEPHERD	*C. S. Forester*	35p
T011 755	TRAWLERS GO TO WAR	*Lund & Ludlam*	40p
T015 505	THE LAST VOYAGE OF GRAF SPEE	*Michael Powell*	30p
T015 661	JACKALS OF THE REICH	*Ronald Seth*	30p
T012 263	FLEET WITHOUT A FRIEND	*John Vader*	30p

Western

T016 994	No. 1 EDGE – THE LONER	*George G. Gilman*	30p
T016 986	No. 2 EDGE – TEN THOUSAND DOLLARS AMERICAN	*George G. Gilman*	30p
T017 613	No. 3 EDGE – APACHE DEATH	*George G. Gilman*	30p
T017 001	No. 4 EDGE – KILLER'S BREED	*George G. Gilman*	30p
T016 536	No. 5 EDGE – BLOOD ON SILVER	*George G. Gilman*	30p
T017 621	No. 6 EDGE – THE BLUE, THE GREY AND THE RED	*George G. Gilman*	30p
T014 479	No. 7 EDGE – CALIFORNIA KILLING	*George G. Gilman*	30p
T015 254	No. 8 EDGE – SEVEN OUT OF HELL	*George G. Gilman*	30p
T015 475	No. 9 EDGE – BLOODY SUMMER	*George G. Gilman*	30p
T015 769	No. 10 EDGE – VENGEANCE IS BLACK	*George G. Gilman*	30p

General

T011 763	SEX MANNERS FOR MEN	*Robert Chartham*	30p
W002 531	SEX MANNERS FOR ADVANCED LOVERS	*Robert Chartham*	25p
W002 835	SEX AND THE OVER FORTIES	*Robert Chartham*	30p
T010 732	THE SENSUOUS COUPLE	*Dr. 'C'*	25p

Mad

S004 708	VIVA MAD!	30p
S004 676	MAD'S DON MARTIN COMES ON STRONG	30p
S004 816	MAD'S DAVE BERG LOOKS AT SICK WORLD	30p
S005 078	MADVERTISING	30p
S004 987	MAD SNAPPY ANSWERS TO STUPID QUESTIONS	30p

NEL P.O. BOX 11, FALMOUTH, TR10 9EN, CORNWALL

Please send cheque or postal order. Allow 10p to cover postage and packing on one book plus 4p for each additional book.

Name ....

Address..

....

Title ....

(SEPTEMBER)